THE
PILGRIMAGE

THE
PILGRIMAGE

Ann B. Ross

MACMILLAN PUBLISHING COMPANY

New York

Macmillan Publishing Company
866 Third Avenue, New York, N.Y. 10022
Collier Macmillan Canada, Inc.

Library of Congress Cataloging-in-Publication Data
Ross, Ann B.
The pilgrimage.
I. Title.
PS3568.084198P5   1987   813'.54   86-23897
ISBN 0-02-605140-0

This novel is a work of fiction. Any references to historical events, to real people,
living or dead, or to real locales are intended only to give the fiction
a setting in historical reality. Other names, characters, places, and incidents
either are the product of the author's imagination
or are used fictitiously, and their resemblance, if any,
to real-life counterparts is entirely coincidental.

10 9 8 7 6 5 4 3 2 1

Printed in the United States of America

An Account of our Travels & Travails on the Roade to Oregon (by way of the Overland Trail) in the company of Mister George Donner & Family (& of their many courtesies to us); of the Many Friendships Pledged & Continued (& how they affected our Lives); of our Excursion into Absaroka & how we got out of it; Culminating with the Doleful Tale of Waiilatpu, & with the Manner in which Jessie found her calling in a Mission Field of her own Making,

BEING

THE NARRATIVE

OF

EMMA LOUISE HEATH

WITH

EXCERPTS FROM THE PRIVATE JOURNAL

OF

JESSIE ELIZABETH HEATH

THE
PILGRIMAGE

Now, get yourself fixed, Emma Jane, and quit squirming around. If you want to hear this, you've got to sit still and listen. Lord knows you've pestered me enough about it, but I expect it's time you heard it, anyway—how we got here and why, and who helped or hindered us.

Seems like everybody's looking back on those days now, telling what they know, or think they know. First one and then another taking pen in hand to tell the real and true historical story, and half of them not even in the Territory at the time. Bunch of know-it-alls, if you ask me. Even the Reverend Mr. Spaulding's not immune to it. I'll tell you this, Emma Jane, pen and paper in the wrong hands can change history and don't you forget it. Now I'm not saying anything against the Reverend, but you'd think Mrs. Spaulding would put a stop to it. When you put something down on paper, it just gives every Tom, Dick, and Harry a chance to say you're wrong. You won't catch me doing it, I can tell you that. Keep your own counsel, I always say.

And that's another thing. I learned a whole lot that year I'm telling you about, but it wasn't always what I was supposed to learn. But being out on the trail, and living with Indians and then with missionaries, who could help it? Not that there was that much difference between the last two named, what with all the quarreling, fussing, backstabbing, and getting even that went on with every last one of them. Made no difference whether they were in God's missionary army or in the devil's own host of heathen. Well, they all paid for it one way or another, so far be it from me to pass judgment. But there were some, Emma

Jane, just a few here and there, who were as fine and decent as you'll ever find, and I include some of the red heathen in that too. Course some of that kind got taken up in payment along with the others, which I didn't understand then and still don't to this day.

And here's something else. I don't want you sitting there thinking how much better things are now than they were then. Not all of it's better by a long shot. Most everybody who took to the trail back then was running away from something. Sometimes it was from the law or from poor farmland or from starving families. Some said there were too many people back in the States, and not enough opportunities, or enough room to move around in. So what did they do? They came out here and set about building up the very same thing they'd run away from. Stores and shops and sawmills and ships coming and going all over the world. And I can't tell you how many came with a zeal for missionizing. Sent by the Lord, they were. Or thought they were. Where are they now, I ask you? Every last one of them, just about, is looking to turn a dollar, and most are doing it too. You'd think Oregon would be another Paradise by now, since every other emigrant that came started out as a missionary of one stripe or another. It's a fact that they've got enough churches in and around Oregon City to Christianize China, Chile, and Peru if they'd put their minds to it. But they can't even civilize their own flock. Had to hire themselves a peace officer, of all things. Well, I'll tell you this, Sheriff Matthew McHenry Stone better not come around here looking for trouble or he'll get more than he bargained for.

You needn't smile at me, Emma Jane, he's just trying to pry around in my business, and that's the only reason he turns up on our doorstep every living day. No other reason in the world. Just doing his duty, he says. Well, his duty's with the riffraff in town, which we've got the Lord's plenty of, and not out here pestering me. Why, every time I turn around, here he comes on that fancy horse of his, making out like he just happened to be in the vicinity. I've told him I don't have time to fool with him, interrupting my work and meddling in my business. Hardheaded, is what he is.

But what man isn't? They get one notion in their heads and wouldn't turn it loose for love nor money. And part of what I'm going to tell you is about that very thing—how men-folks're liable to hold on to just one thing even when it's drag-ging them and their wives and everybody around them down to death and destruction. They're like mules, Emma Jane, and you've got to be strong to put up with them, notwithstanding what the Bible says about submissive wives, of which I've heard enough to last me a lifetime and then some. I'll tell you the truth, I can't see any edification in a woman becoming a fool just to follow a fool. I'm speaking in general now, Emma Jane, not having any particular case in mind. But you remember what I say—a woman's got to stand on her own two feet and use the brains the Lord gave her. Especially out here in Oregon.

Well, enough of that. Right here's your mama's journal, the very one she kept on that long trip we made back in '46. That was before you were born, and when I was a girl not much older than you.

I wish she'd been more faithful in setting it down, but there you are. That's all she got around to doing. See, it's in her own handwriting. Didn't she write a fine hand, though?

No, I didn't keep a journal. Probably should have, but that was the last thing on my mind back then. Too much to see and do, and too much happening for me to worry about keeping a record. That's why your mama's is no longer than it is. She used to get on to me about it, though. Said I ought to keep a reminder in writing and practice my penmanship while I was at it. But I told her that the Bible came down against it, saying that there's no end to the making of books and too much study is a weariness of the flesh. She couldn't think of anything to counter that, so she let it be.

But I don't need a piece of paper to remind me, because it's still as fresh in my mind as if it happened yesterday, and will be to my dying day. Sometimes I dream about that year, and it's just like I was back there living it all over again. And that's the way I'm going to tell it, so you'll know what it was like when Oregon was no more than a wilderness, and so you'll know why we left Missouri to come out here bent on Christianizing the Indians, and how we made a fair mess of it in the doing. Back then your mama was the prettiest girl west of the Rocky Mountains, and made a fair run to being the prettiest east of them too. She purely turned your papa's head, and that's a fact. And worried me half to death almost all the time. Seems like about all I did during that year was worry about what my sister was going to do next.

Anyway, there I was all wrapped up in a blanket, lying under one of Mr. George Donner's wagons in the spring of '46 . . .

I

Get thee out of thy country . . . and from thy
father's house, unto a land that I will show thee.
—*Genesis 12:1*

The reason I was lying on the ground under a white-topped
wagon instead of in the bed I was born in, and wearing
Hiram's greasy britches instead of my usual calico, and worrying
about Missouri River snakes crawling in under my blanket, was
because Papa died last fall and Jessie took it hard enough to get
religion.

Back in Caleb's Corner, where we came from not three
days before, Pastor Clemmons was always saying that it sometimes takes a brush with the Grim Reaper to get hardheaded
people right with the Lord. For myself, I don't think Papa's
untimely demise ought to have been the cause of me and Jessie
taking to the heathen mission field, yet there we were on our
way to Oregon to rescue the perishing Flathead Indians, and I
wasn't a bit happy about it. But once my sister gets something
in her head, you might as well tag along and keep her out of
trouble, which was what I was trying to do.

The way it came about was like this. Papa and Jessie and
me were all that was left of his three matrimonial states. Sickness,
unforeseen accidents, and general decline had just about wiped
out the Heath family, but we were farming our acreage and
putting food on the table without too much worry about the
winter months, and I guess I thought, if I thought about it at
all, that things would go on that way forever. The only thing
that nagged at Papa and me, at least as long as I can remember,
was what was going to happen to Jessie. I know Papa pondered
it in his heart, even though he never talked about it to her or
to me. I watched him watching her, never letting her go anywhere by herself, not even to church meetings, which are the

worst places for trouble and devilment, if you want my opinion. Papa was a smart man, though hard, and he knew the nature of Original Sin, having been involved in some of it himself. He was never taken in by all those gentlemen and otherwise who sought his company, listened to his advice on crops and livestock, and all the while keeping their hungry eyes on my sister.

And she was something to look at too. When you live with somebody all your life, you don't generally notice what they look like, but Jessie was different. As the Holy Scriptures say about Rachel, who Jacob loved enough to put up with her weak-eyed sister so as to get the one he wanted, Jessie was both beautiful and well-favored. But the difference between her and Rachel was that Rachel knew that Jacob was taken with her, what with the seven years of hard labor he put in, while Jessie never did understand what she did to menfolks. She went about her doings heedless of what was happening to all and sundry around her. So after Papa died it was left to me to take his place, even though I'm younger than Jessie and, at the time I'm telling about, had not got my monthlies.

As I was saying, it was religion that had us camping on the edge of Independence, Missouri, along with about a thousand others who had their own reasons for being there. Everybody knows that religion has addled a lot of brains, and Jessie's was among them. The problem with it is that some folks get struck with just one calling and they put everything else right out of their minds. They read one thing in Holy Writ, or more likely hear one thing a preacher has to say, and think that's all the Lord ever expressed Himself on. Like Mrs. Ridley back home, who thinks if somebody is Temperance, it makes no difference what else he is. As for me, though, I think King David went about it the right way because he was a farmer of sorts, a singer of songs, a dancer of some note, a poet better even than Lord Byron, a soldier and leader of men, a crowned king, and besides handling all that, he never lost his touch with the ladies. He didn't just clamp down on one thing, he tried it all, including the matter in the Fifth and Sixth Commandments, which I don't recommend even though he got away with both.

So there I was, looking up at the bottom of one of Mr.

George Donner's wagons, and I'll have to say that so far Jessie
had been right. She kept saying that the Lord has His eye on
the sparrows, and that on the way down to them He takes us
in too. Since I don't have the assurance that every preacher I've
ever heard, which is a lot, says we ought to have, I plan to stay
close to her so I'll be included in His gaze. Jessie said she was
following a call from the Lord to the mission field, and I was
following her because I didn't know what else to do.

Through the wheel spokes I could see campfires still burning and people who ought to have been asleep still moving
around talking about California and Oregon. Everybody had
his mind set on one place or the other, and they spent their time
arguing over which one was the best to be going to. Even if I
hadn't received a personal call from the Lord, which was the
case with most all the emigrants there, my education wasn't
suffering a lick. Already I'd found out, just by listening, that
Oregon was about overrun with missionaries of all persuasions,
and that the Hudson's Bay Company was taking over all the
best land for the Britishers. On top of that, California was owned
by Mexicans who didn't appreciate it or work it like Americans
knew how to do. That's what Mr. George Donner told his wife,
Tamsen, that very day, and when he said it he patted the side
of his supply wagon that held the goods he aimed to get rich
with in California just like he already had in Illinois.

I'd of felt better about the whole expedition if Jessie and
me had something to sell or trade when we got there, but all
we had with us was Jessie's message to the savages of Oregon.
Since that very same message had been widely known in Missouri for some years with no decline that I could see in the
outward manifestations of greed, envy, lying, stealing, killing,
backbiting and -sliding, and general, all-around mayhem, I wasn't
too hopeful of its success in Oregon.

As I was saying, though, when Papa died I figured Jessie
would marry since I was too young for it even in Caleb's Corner.
We needed a farmhand bad, and marrying one was all you
could do if you didn't have the cash money for hiring. Lord
knows Jessie had every opportunity to take her pick; they swarmed
around her doing the winter chores that Papa had left undone,

stacking firewood, filling the cellar, and trying to outdo each other so as to win her favors. But all that changed when the Presbyterian Church decided to send the Reverend MacCarson Perkle around the Missouri circuits and he showed up in Caleb's Corner at the Holy Light Meetinghouse right before the spring thaw. Right from that I knew he wasn't too levelheaded; he should've waited for the ice to melt. But a man on the Lord's business, as he put it, couldn't wait for propitious weather; he had to plant early and reap late. That must have been the reason he was preaching instead of farming, because he never would've made a crop that way. We trudged through frozen mud to get to the meetinghouse because Jessie felt the same way about the Lord's business.

Now, I've seen my share of preachers, but the Reverend Perkle took the cake. He was tall with a lean and stretched look to him, like Cassius in that play, I expect. His face was like a new-furrowed field, and his eyes were filled with godly intent. He had big, hairy hands that swooped through the air when he got going on his sermon. His black, swallow-tailed coat flipped around behind him as he strode back and forth behind the railing. And when his deep, booming voice took off on the merits of heaven and the demerits of the place below, I can testify that he had Pastor Clemmons and Elder Bolton beat by a country mile.

But to tell the truth, the Reverend Perkle hadn't come to get Caleb's Corner straightened out, which made him the first preacher I'd ever heard who congratulated us on the condition of our souls. He was worried, instead, about the heathen savages, and he told us we were the only ones who could save them from eternal and infernal torment.

I'd been watching something interesting crawl up Mrs. Harris's shoulder and didn't have my mind too much on what the Reverend was saying until he started talking about our red brethren in the Oregon Territory. He got my full attention then, for it was a different tack from what most preachers take. He really got warmed up talking about how they ate raw meat and didn't have any plows or decent houses, and how they didn't know beans about how to work their farms, or how to plant and lay by their crops. All the men looked downright smug when he was talking about that, because they knew how to do those things. But then he got onto something that really took my interest, along with everybody else's. He started talking about how the Indian squaws needed Jesus worse than anybody on God's earth. He said they were so ignorant that they kept having these deformed babies, which is why one whole tribe was called the Flatheads and why another one was called the Split Noses. And he said that half the time those squaws didn't wear a stitch; buck naked as they were born, I believe were his very words, and when they did wear something it only came to their knees because they didn't know what decent Christian attire was.

This seemed to shock the womenfolk worse than no clothes at all. When he began to go into detail about how the savages were running headlong into all manner of sin and wickedness, the men leaned forward in their seats and it wouldn't have surprised me if every last one of them hadn't volunteered for the mission field that very night. It was a most animating sermon and a humdinger of a meeting, I can tell you that, because the Reverend left off just at the most interesting part, saying it wasn't fit for the ears of decent Christian women.

I waited outside in the cold while Jessie stayed to shake Reverend Perkle's hand and to tell him how inspiring his sermon was, a habit she'd taken up ever since she went forward the morning we sang "Jesus Is Tenderly Calling." I had a feeling she was inviting him to supper sometime that week, as all the other church ladies would be doing, too, and none would be refused, for seminarians are taught better than that. I wanted to hear more about the heathen savages, but I was worried about what we would feed him. A preacher's supper almost always calls for a chicken, and our flock couldn't stand many losses. Not that they were laying that many eggs, but where there's a hen there's hope.

Jessie finally came out and we started for home. I wanted to talk about the Indian squaws and their peculiar habits, trying to picture in my mind what a naked bunch of them would look like. I couldn't get Jessie to talk about it, though. She kept humming about gathering in the sheaves and I finally gave up the effort. I did find out that the Reverend was coming to supper the next night, which didn't surprise me.

The next morning she had me up early cleaning and mopping just to get ready for him. I've always wondered if preachers' houses are as clean as the ones they visit, though it's not likely, for if they were, they'd cut down on the visiting and stay home more. I also got the job of catching a hen and wringing its neck, which I mortally despise. Jessie is always telling me I ought to do everything I do to the glory of God, but for the life of me I can't see where a chicken flopping around with a broken neck that I've inflicted on it does much for God's glory. But she believed all the Scripture she knew, and lived it, too, as far as I could see.

She stewed the hen all day, and along about suppertime she dropped in some dumplings and I felt a lot better about the glory business.

The Reverend Perkle came riding up to our door on a mule that looked so worked down that I began to worry about the state of the Presbyterian Church in general. Maybe it had been a bad year for tithes and offerings, or maybe all the collections were going to the mission field like the Reverend wanted. He walked right in to our front room and commenced to tell Jessie how brave she was for taking on the care and upkeep of a farm as well as a child. Then he sat himself down in Papa's place at the head of the table and applied himself liberally to Jessie's chicken and dumplings.

As soon as he'd wiped his plate clean the second time, he started in on a prayer that was as good as many a sermon I've heard. He thanked the Lord for the nourishing, life-giving food; he thanked Him for the rain (which we'd had enough of for my money) and the soil that had helped the crops to make; he thanked Him for shelter from the weather, and for health and for freedom and for President James K. Polk and for the sweet and tender hands that had prepared the meal. He took on about Jessie's hands an uncommonly long time, and I was fidgeting in my chair before he was through.

"Now, Sister Heath, it's time this child was in her bed," he announced in the same breath with "amen."

"Why, not yet, Reverend," Jessie said, sweet as honey, right before I about pitched a fit. "Emma Louise wants to hear about the needs of the Presbyterian Church in the Oregon Territory just like I do."

He scowled at me from under his black, bushy eyebrows and I glared back as bold as I dared. I wasn't about to go to bed while there was a chance for philosophical inquiry into the heathen state and condition. I take every opportunity I can to develop my character and increase my knowledge.

"Train up a child, Sister Heath, like Proverbs twenty-two, six tells us to do, and don't spare the rod while you're adoin' it," he said, as if that wasn't the first Scripture she'd learned to my daily grief. "But about the heathen in the Oregon Territory. Their condition is dreadful, just dreadful, and it behooves us as Christians to take the Lord's message to people in such need. I want to tell you, Sister, them naked squaws and their wickedness just prey on my mind, night and day. I so want to go to them and wrap them in the love of Jesus, but my work is right here on the circuits. We can't all do what we want when we commit our lives to full-time Christian work."

"But what can we do, Reverend?" Jessie asked with an earnest look on her face. "What can Christians like Em and me do to help? We want to, but we don't know how."

"Oh, Sister Heath," he said, leaning across his dirty plate and grabbing her hand. "Go to them. That's what somebody has got to do. Go and, lo, I am with you, the Lord said, Matthew, twenty-eight, nineteen and twenty. Somebody's got to get up out of their easy living and take the message of love and forgiveness to them that're headed straight to hell. Books and letters won't do the job; them pore souls can't read a lick. They ain't never going to learn to work their land and put on their clothes if we Christians don't go and show them how."

"I want to, Reverend," Jessie cried, her face lit up like a campfire. "I want to go and take that message of comfort to those who need it. Tell me how to do it, for I know now that this is what the Lord wants me to do."

She leaned across the table and his big, hairy hand that was holding hers came perilous close to being mashed under her bosom. Papa would've been scandalized, just like I was, and probably would've done something about it.

But before I could take Jessie in hand, the Reverend Perkle jumped out of his chair and plunked himself down on the floor so hard I thought his knees would crack.

"On yore knees, Sister!" he yelled. "Get down on yore knees! The Lord has just sent you a call to the heathen!"

Jessie knelt on the floor beside him, and I got up from my side of the table so I could see better. He pressed her head down on his shoulder and clasped her hands to his breast. His bony frame was quivering all over, and if I hadn't known he was a preacher taken with a fit of glory, I'd of thought the same thing was going on that I caught Elizabeth Harris and Jacob Hollinger doing last summer under the scuppernong vine.

"Praise Him, Sister!" the Reverend Perkle commanded. "Praise Him with yore voice and praise Him with yore soul! It ain't ever' day that the Lord sends a call so true and clear! Oh, Sister, you make preachin' worth all the time and trouble I give to it!"

"Oh, Reverend Perkle," Jessie said in a trembly voice, while she closed her eyes and smiled up in a saintly fashion at his nose. "I do praise God for showing me what needs to be done, and for calling me to the heathen, and for sending you among us with this urgent message. Thank you for all you've done for me."

"Sister, I ain't done enough for you," he said, looking at her like he'd looked at his chicken and dumplings. "There's a lot more to do before you'll be ready to tackle them heathen. I'm agoin' to put off my other meetings and prepare you in the Scriptures so you'll be fit for the job ahead."

His lanky body was shaking so hard by then that Jessie was practically holding him up. I was getting tired of being shut out of everything, and besides, I wanted to talk to Jessie about this call to the heathen. I figured where she went I'd have to go, too, and I hadn't gotten word one from the Lord about visiting the Oregon Territory.

So I just broke right in and told Jessie I had to go to the outhouse and was afraid to go by myself. The Reverend Perkle gave me a hard, mean look, but Jessie hopped up and said that earthly matters had to be tended to as well as spiritual and for me to wait a minute.

He had to hold on to the table to get up off his knees and his bones creaked like a garden gate while he was doing it. He pulled himself upright, tugged his waistcoat down, and brushed off his knees like I hadn't swept the floor just that morning.

"Now, Sister Heath," he said, and then he stopped and frowned with a troubled look. "There's another matter that's got to be taken care of afore you go off to the mission field. And this is a serious thing that can't just be jumped into without a lot of thinkin' and prayin'. I'll tell you right now that a help meet that's got the same calling has got to be found for you."

"There's no need for that, Reverend, though I thank you for thinking of it," Jessie told him sweetly. "I'm trusting the Lord to look after Em and me."

"That ain't the point, Sister." He waved away what I thought would've been the prime reason for being a missionary in the first place. "The American Board of Commissioners for Foreign Missions ain't agoin' to commission you in the unwedded state. That's a fact you got to face. But you don't need to worry about it; if there's nobody around here waitin' in the wings, so to speak, the Board will assign you to one of the unmarrieds on their list who's just waitin' for a wife afore goin' himself."

Jessie looked stricken for a minute, but she pulled herself together and let him have it. "I never heard of such a thing," she said. "The Scriptures don't say a word about having to be married, as far as I can see. And look at Lydia and Martha and Mary. Not a one of them had a husband, and they did the Lord's work just fine. In fact, I recall that it says it's better not to marry at all."

"That may be," the Reverend said in his stern, teaching voice. "But it also says that it's better to marry than to burn, First Corinthians, seven, nine, and the Board of Commissioners don't aim to send out workers who're likely to catch on fire in all that Oregon wickedness. Now, Sister, this ain't a matter to argue about; it's done been settled. The Board knows a thing or two that you don't, and you might as well submit yourself to it, Ephesians, five, twenty-two. My counsel is for you to write a letter informing the Board that you're waitin' their pleasure in both the matrimonial and missional assignments. I'll take it myself to St. Louis, where it'll bring rejoicin' to some fine Christian man who is at this very minute praying for a help meet for him. You don't want to be stiff-necked about this, Sister Heath; the Lord intends to take care of every need we have, and that's why the Board won't hardly let anybody, male or female, go out from civilization by theirselves. Remember that the Scriptures say that the marriage bed is undefiled and that fornication has to be shunned and abstained from, Hebrews thirteen, four and First Thessalonians, four, three."

Well, when he said that word right there in our front room without turning a hair, I looked for lightning to strike every one of us. I cut my eyes over to Jessie, for she'd taken a switch to me one time for saying it before I knew it wasn't polite or genteel to mention fornicating activities out loud, and there was no telling how she'd take it now. She didn't mind hearing it in a sermon, for you can hardly avoid it if your text is from the Epistles or the Old Testament, but she didn't like it bandied about in everyday use. She had this high color on her face and she looked like she was having all she could do to abstain from reproof and correction, even if he was a preacher and all.

But she took a deep breath and told him she would lay it all before the Lord and seek His guidance. Then she got him on his way and me in bed without listening to another word on the subject no matter how hard I tried. I think she was probably in a hurry to check out the Reverend's Scripture verses for herself. He'd spouted a few she'd never heard of, and ever since she'd become assured of her salvation, barring any intentional backsliding, she couldn't stand to have somebody know something from the Holy Word that she didn't, including me.

2

If we tarry till the morning light, some mischief will come upon us. . . .
—2 Kings 7:9

I had every intention of watching through the night and helping Jessie pray about this matter of missionizing, as well as about matrimony from a distance, but I dozed off while she was still sitting by the fire. I didn't know it then, but the Reverend Perkle wasn't the first to put the idea in her head of forsaking the world and doing good works in far-flung places. She told me later that it had come to her sudden and almost full-blown at the same time she'd gotten right with the Lord after she saw what happened to Papa. At the time she hadn't known just which group of worldwide heathens the Lord wanted her to go to, but that night she spent sitting by the fire opened her heart once and for all to the needs of the Oregon sort.

I woke up once or twice during the night and saw her holding her head in her hands, and once she was down on her knees. If I had known what trouble she was having trying to rightly discern the word of truth, I'd of gotten up and helped her. The fact of the matter is, it didn't come to me until after we got there just what torment Jessie went through to accept the call to the mission field. To turn your back on the rules of church boards and ministers of the Gospel, who could quote Scripture at the drop of a hat, was a hard thing for anybody to do, but Jessie only had that one night of troubling over it. After that she never looked back nor asked another soul what to do, though it might've helped sometimes if she had. It seemed to me that we should've had all kinds of permissions, sanctions, farewell send-offs, and such before we up and took off from home on denominational business, to say nothing of the Lord's business.

But that wasn't Jessie's way. When she took something on she didn't fool around with store clerks. She always went right to the top, to the owner, so to speak. She said all she needed to know was in God's Word, which she could read as good as anybody, and when it said get up and go, she got up and went.

The next thing I knew she was shaking me awake and telling me to make haste.

"What's the matter, Jessie?" I asked. "It's still dark outside, and no time to be getting up."

"Past time, Em," she said, spreading a quilt on the floor. She began pulling things out of the cupboard and stacking them on the quilt. "I've wasted too much time already. I know now what I have to do and where I have to go to do it. Come on, now, we've got to get ready before daylight."

I jumped out of bed and hurried to stand in front of the fire. She had bread already baking, and coffee was bubbling in a pot.

"What are we getting ready for?" I asked. "Is somebody sick or dying?"

She stopped her packing and looked at me. "Yes, Em," she said, all serious and softlike. "Somebody—lots of somebodies—are sick and dying, and I've got to go to them. And furthermore," she said, as if I was going to dispute her, "it's going to take more than a Reverend Perkle and a Board of Commissioners, none of whom has seen fit to go themselves, to stop me."

I wasn't about to stop her, having tried it a few times to no avail, but I didn't know but one lady who was in sudden danger of giving birth and said as much, which got me one of her sharp looks. Then her face changed and she stopped what she was doing.

"Come here, Em," she said, sitting down and pulling me next to her. "The thing that's bothered me all night was not the fitness nor the rightness of the call I've received. It was what to do about you. But I have peace about that now, for I know we have to stay together."

I swallowed hard, since I'd never thought there was any doubt about us always staying together. That's what families did, it seemed to me, unless somebody died or was too mean to live with like Mrs. Etheridge's mother-in-law.

"What are we going to do, Jessie?"

"Why, Emma, I told you the Lord has called me to Oregon, and that's where we're going. We're heading out for Oregon tonight."

My heart gave a thud somewhere under my ribs, and something tingled across my shoulders and down my arms.

"Tonight? Right now? Without telling anybody?"

"We've got to do it this way," she said, looking a little bothered and not quite so sure of herself. "Think about what would happen if we announced it all over. Every deacon and elder, to say nothing of Pastor Clemmons, would come up with every reason in the world why we shouldn't go. Why, I do believe they'd try to prevent us from it, don't you?"

"They probably would," I said, thinking as fast as I could, for to tell the truth I didn't know but what that wouldn't be for the best. "Jessie, are you sure we ought to just strike out by ourselves? Seems to me that somebody ought to take up a collection for us, or give us some official papers, or tell us how to get there, or give us some lessons in how to save the heathen, or something. And what about matrimony, like the Reverend said you had to do?"

"Now don't you worry about that," she said, getting up and taking the bread pan off the coals. "We've got the best Leader and Teacher there is, and all we have to do is follow wherever He leads. As to matrimony, well, if the Lord is in the habit of issuing calls to unwedded women, and He certainly is in my case, then I expect He knows what He's doing. Far be it from me to say He doesn't. I've prayed about it, Em, and I don't find it in my heart to let somebody else match me up with a stranger, even if he is a fellow Christian and a missionary like I aim to be.

"Besides, I'm not going to have any trouble containing myself, regardless of the amount of wickedness in Oregon, and he can just do the same thing himself. If he's a real Christian gentleman with a true call, he won't have a speck of trouble. And another thing, it surprises me at the lack of faith that Board is showing forth. The idea!" And she slammed the pan on the table and turned the bread out like she had a personal grievance against it.

Well, I'm not one to worry something to death, and it was a settled fact that I wasn't going to let her go off by herself, especially since she was bound and determined not to take guidance from those who were supposed to give it. So, even though I hadn't received a call to Oregon, my duty was clear and plain, and I didn't intend to shirk it. I turned toward the fireplace to let my front side warm up for a while and thought about the sudden turn everything had taken.

This time yesterday I didn't have a care in the world, except when I thought about Papa, and now here I was all roiled up with missions and matrimony, and nobody there to help me but Jessie, who needed help worse than I did but didn't know it. I took one thing at a time and thought over leaving home first. And the more I thought about it, the better I liked it. Not one person I'd ever read about had sat around and waited for adventures to happen to them; they all got up and went out to look for them. Childe Harold, for instance, who loathed to dwell in his native land, and Abraham, too, for that matter. I decided right then that if Jessie was set on this particular course, which she was, I wasn't going to be a hindrance to her.

Then I turned to thinking on that poor soul in St. Louis who was waiting for the Lord to send him Jessie. What would happen to him? If she didn't show up, would the Board make him stay home? And if that was the case, what would happen to those heathen Indians he was predestined to save? I quit thinking about it then, because I'd gone as far as I could go in that direction without getting mixed up in theological disputes in my own mind. I know such things occupy the minds of lots of people, for I've heard them discussed around the stove in Mr. Edwards's store. Since they'd never come to a satisfactory conclusion, I figured I wouldn't either in the little time I had, especially since Jessie was busy packing and wouldn't discuss it.

I'd better say right here that I was still smarting because she had made all her plans without saying a word to me, and because she had even thought about going without me.

So I said, "Jessie, the Reverend Perkle's going to have you up before the elders or take a hickory switch to you if you don't get yourself married."

She turned around and smiled at me. "Why do you think I'm hurrying to leave? I want us on the road before he knows we're gone. Once we get there, it'll be too much trouble to call us back."

That put a different light on everything. Once I'd seen the Reverend up close at our table and saying words right to our face that shouldn't be said except in a sermonial context even if they are in Holy Writ, he hadn't struck me as worthy of all the honor due a man of the cloth. I figured if he was against something, I'd probably be for it, and if Jessie was going to outright defy him, I wanted to be around to watch her do it. So in spite of some misgivings about the whole project, I plunged in to help with my whole heart and soul.

We did our share of scurrying around for the rest of the night. Jessie stirred up the fire and put on more bread while we got our belongings together. She made me put on a pair of long johns and two pairs of stockings on top of that. We rolled an extra pair of underclothing and a good dress apiece in our blankets. I found an old tarpaulin and wrapped that around the blankets; then I had to unroll it again and put in my ma's gold locket that had a lock of her hair in it. My ma and Jessie's ma were not one and the same, even though our papa was. That's probably why we neither look nor act alike, and why she had the looks and I had the common sense, which Papa said I was going to need in full measure to watch out for her and to make up for certain deficiencies I was born with and couldn't help.

Jessie kept trying to fit the family Bible in with everything else, but I told her Red could only be expected to carry about two tons and the Bible would make us overweight. Besides, if she needed to know any verses, she only had to ask me and I'd fill her in. She gave me one of the looks she saves just for me and told me to slice the bacon and pack it with the bread and to keep my comments to myself.

She took a lantern down to the cellar to get a poke of dried apples, and by this time we'd about cleaned ourselves out of food except what was running around on foot.

"All right, now, Em," Jessie said, surveying our packed possessions. "Have we forgotten anything?"

"Well," I said, still feeling the sting of being left out of her plans, "I guess it depends on what it takes to travel the road to Oregon. Seeing as how I've never made the trip, and seeing as how all the planning has been done without me, I can't rightly say."

"Now, Em," she said, tiredly, "don't go getting your back up. Help me think."

I began to feel sorry for her about then, what with her being hit with a true call and a proposal by somebody who was filling in for an unknown prospective husband all in one night. So I put my mind to the problem and tried to think out what we were going to run up against and what we would need to meet whatever it happened to be.

"Papa's gun," I said, thinking hard. "Dr. Allbright's physic. Cash money, Jessie, if we have any, and what about the cow?"

"I'm going to let the cow out when we leave and she'll wander over to the Ellisons' place by milking time. And as for Papa's gun and Dr. Allbright's physic, I can see you still don't understand that we'll be doing the Lord's work. We won't need guns and medicines with Him looking out for us."

You can see from that how far away from practical matters Jessie's mind was and how much my common sense was going to be called on time and time again. First off, if the Lord had a mind to watch out for people doing His work and keep Indians and stomachaches away from them, why, that didn't include me, since I didn't have a call. And second off, the Lord, according to the Reverend Perkle, hadn't as yet got acquainted with the Flathead, Cayuse, and Oglala families, and might not have notified them that we had special protection.

"I guess I don't understand, Jessie," I said. "But it stands to reason that we'll need the gun for hunting, as I don't suppose they've got general stores out in the Indian Territory as yet. And you know what happens whenever I eat green apples, and I'm planning on eating a bait of them this spring."

"Maybe you're right about the physic," she said. "Put that in, but neither of us knows how to prime a gun, much less shoot one. It'll just be dead weight and a sign that we don't trust the Lord to protect us. It stays here. Now, as to money, I had planned on selling as much as we could, but we don't have time for that now. But we do have some, due to Papa's foresight and good management."

She pulled a rock out of the side of the fireplace and brought out a leather pouch. She opened it and drew out some bank notes and two gold twenty-dollar pieces.

"Jingies!" I breathed. "Where did we get that?"

"It's Papa's life savings," she said. "I can't think of a better use for it, nor one he would take more pleasure in, than for us to use it in the Lord's work."

I could have disputed her on that, recollecting Papa's views on money and a number of other things, but I restrained myself and felt better for it.

"How much do we have?" I asked, feeling rich as King Solomon just looking at it.

"Enough, I hope, to get us outfitted in Independence."

"Is that where we're going to deliver the heathen?"

"Em, I declare, you act so ignorant sometimes. Independence, Missouri is only the first stop. The road to Oregon starts there."

"Well, how do you expect me to know everything when you don't tell me anything?" My feelings were hurt, but at the same time I could feel the excitement growing. Independence, Missouri! It sounded like the best place in the world to start an adventure to the Oregon Territory. If I'd had the job of naming a town, I couldn't have named it any better than Independence, Missouri, for it had the ring of shackles and chores being cast aside in favor of liberty and freedom for all, like I learned in school.

Jessie took off her dress and began to sew the bank notes into the seams of the bodice. She cut up a sheet and then quickly stitched it on to make a lining to go over the money. With all the extra padding, I had my doubts as to how she was going to get herself back into it.

"And after we get to Independence, how far is it to the Oregon Territory?" I asked, watching her button everything together.

"Oh, I don't know. About a hundred miles, I guess."

I soon discovered that she was as far off on distance as she was on a lot of other things. But what I didn't know then didn't hurt me until later.

"Here, Em, take off your frock. I'm going to sew some of this money in it, so if something happens to one of us, the other won't be left destitute."

I thought that was a sensible plan, but my stomach didn't feel so good at the thought of something happening to Jessie and leaving me alone, even with a frock full of legal tender.

It was about an hour before sunrise when we finally pulled the door shut and climbed up on old Red, Jessie in Papa's creaky saddle and me holding on behind. The moon was hanging low in the sky by that time and the wind had dropped, letting the cold air slide down into the valley like a heavy thing looking for a place to hide.

"Hold tight, Em," Jessie said as she clicked her tongue at Red. "We're on our way, just like Abraham, to a new land that the Lord is going to show us."

"How are we like Abraham?" I asked, with my suspicions on the rise.

"You know how the Lord called him out of the land of Ur and sent him to the Canaan Mission Field. And he did just what he was told to do. Took his family and went right out on the trail to save the heathen Canaanites."

Now I know that I don't have Jessie's looks in any way, shape, nor form, but I wasn't behind the door when brains were handed out. I'd been reading as long as I could remember, and I count myself well grounded in logic, rhetoric, and natural law as well. So I know my Bible; I know it because a copy of Mr. William Shakespeare's complete plays and sonnets, Lord Byron's *Childe Harold*, and the Bible have been in our family since before I was born and I've grown up with them all. I don't need to mention Dr. Peter C. Gunn's *Domestic Medicine or The Poor Man's Friend in the House of Affliction, Pain, and Sickness*, because

Jessie wouldn't let me read that. Jessie, now, had been reading the Bible only since she got religion, which is to say not as long as I have, so when she started talking about Abraham being sent out to save the souls of the heathen Canaanites, I knew I had her.

"You say we're going to do the same thing in Oregon that Abraham did in Canaan?" I asked, hoping to catch her in a theological trap, which is pretty easy to do to most anybody.

"That's exactly what we're going to do," she answered, with as much assurance as a messenger straight from the Throne of Grace. "What Abraham did is what the mission field is all about."

"Well, let's get cracking," I said. "We're gonna need two or three shooting pieces, about a hundred bags of powder and shot, and, let me see, maybe a dozen sharp knives. We can get them all at Independence, I expect, so I don't see any problem there. Can you think of anything else we'll need for inflicting bodily harm, Jessie? How about your sewing scissors, or a hatpin or two?"

"What are you talking about?" She craned her head to look back at me.

"Why, I'm trying to think up all the things we'll have to have to do to the Oregonites what Abraham did to the Canaanites."

"We're not going to need those things, and I don't know where you got such a notion. All that reading, I expect. You have to keep your thoughts pure, Emma Louise."

I let that go by and said, "It's like this, Jessie. Before you start acting on what Abraham did, you'd better find out what he did. The Lord told him to go to the land of Canaan and kill every last one of the heathen—men, women, and little children too. And I figure we'd better get ourselves ready for a similar massacre in Oregon."

I could feel her drawing up straight and taking a deep breath, so I huddled down closer to her and hid my face against her back.

After a few minutes she said, "I knew that all along, but what you don't know is that you can't take everything in the

Bible as the literal truth." She stopped a minute and thought about what she'd just said.

"Well, it's all true, of course," she went on, "but some things have to be looked at harder than others and you have to put a spiritual meaning on them sometimes. You understand what I'm saying; the real truth might be underneath what you think is the truth. You have to keep looking out for it and reading between the lines and praying for understanding. Now take that part about trees clapping their hands. What that really signifies is joy in the hearts of Christians; it doesn't mean that trees have hands like we do."

I turned that over in my mind and decided she was getting information from somewhere that hadn't made itself available to me. Then it struck me with full force that that was what she'd been telling me all along.

After a long spell of thinking and silently suffering Red's bony backside and ragged trot, I brought up the other thing that was troubling me.

"Jessie, what about what Reverend Perkle said about marrying? It might be a good idea to look over whoever they pick out for you. I think we're going to need somebody to show us the way, at the very least. We don't even know how to get there."

"That doesn't worry me a bit," she said as if she meant it, and I knew she did because she's not as given to worry as I am. "Now, I know we're supposed to submit to those in authority over us, but, Em, I can't disobey the Lord. And I know this is what I must do, and He sends a sickness in my heart at the very thought of marrying for the sake of convenience and safety, or for the sake of somebody to read road signs, which either one of us can do for ourselves. If He'd wanted things convenient and safe, He would've kept me home and put me in mind to marry the Widower Harkness, who's got everything any woman but me would want. No, Em, I've got to trust my own heart, for the Lord is leading and I'm not going to do something He hasn't made His intentions clear on. Clear to me, that is."

"Reckon why the Board thought up such a thing?" I was picturing in my mind this wide slab of lumber with a few elderly gentlemen sitting around it, thumbing through a Bible and making up rules. "I know the Reverend mentioned a certain matter, which I won't repeat, but I didn't know preachers and missionaries could be afflicted with it, and I didn't know marrying would cure it if they did get into it."

"Oh, Em," she sighed, "I don't know and it's not fit to talk about, but it's probably because they've had some bad people . . . well, I don't expect they've had them in the mission field, but they have to prevent things, you see. Look at it this way. I know that all the disciples and apostles and patriarchs were men, and I know a lot of people take that to mean that the Lord only speaks directly to Christian men."

"That's exactly what Pastor Clemmons said when he was preaching on orderliness in the meetings. He said if the womenfolks wanted to know anything, they were to hold their peace and ask their husbands and fathers when they got home."

"Yes," she said, and I could feel her sitting up stiff and straight in the saddle. "And what did he expect those of us who have suffered loss of fathers by death to do? Just go ignorant? I'll tell you, Em, I was reading just the other day where the Lord commanded Mary the Magdelene to go tell the disciples about Him rising from the dead. Now that goes to show that ladies can receive messages and instructions from the Lord just as good as anybody can. Because if He'd wanted to, He could've sent Peter or Paul or John the Baptist or even Daniel instead of her."

Jessie got her Old and New Testaments mixed together every now and then, but she'd given me a lot to think about, and I started doing it to take my mind off how lonesome it was getting to be out there by ourselves.

3

Let the wicked fall into their own nets, whilst
I escape.
—*Psalms 141:10*

We didn't talk much after that for the cold seemed to settle
around us and dig under our clothes with a vengeance.
I huddled against Jessie's back, glad for the warmth she offered.
Red plodded on, only turning his head every now and again,
as if to see if we meant for him to go so far from home.

"Jessie, I'm about to freeze to death," I said. "Aren't we
close to Independence yet?"

"It's still a long way off, Em," she answered, her voice muffled
in the folds of her shawl. "Are your feet cold?"

"I don't know. I can't feel them."

"Well, wiggle your toes and get the blood circulating. It
can't stay this cold for many more days. After all, it is April."

"I wish somebody would tell the weather what month it
is," I complained. "This cold is going to kill everything, including me."

"As soon as we get a little further on, we'll stop and stretch
ourselves. We'll eat something too. That should warm us up.
Besides, it'll get warmer up in the day."

She kicked Red into a trot, and with the bouncing I took
from his hindquarters, I began to warm up. As the sun climbed
higher in the sky the day began to warm and my disposition
improved as I took notice of our new surroundings. I had been
to Jefferson City once with Papa, but other than that this was
the first time I'd taken an extended trip away from home. There
wasn't much to see. It looked about the same as the countryside
around Caleb's Corner. For a while we were on the same road
that would take us to Jefferson City. There weren't many people
out that time of day, since most folks were close to home and

a good hot fire, which is where I would've liked to've been. Every now and then, though, we'd hear the creak of a wagon and the clop of horses' hooves off ahead of us and Jessie would pull Red off into the bushes until the road was clear again. I still thought she was worried about meeting some of our neighbors and didn't want to have to tell them what we were doing with all our worldly possessions on the back of a mule. Later I noticed that even when we were too far from home to meet anyone we knew, she still pulled off the road.

"Jessie?" I asked after one such maneuver, "why do you keep doing that? Nobody around here cares whether we go to Oregon or not, and they don't care if you marry or stay an old maid."

"There's a lot you have to learn about human nature, Em," she said. "I don't want to scare you, but it's not too safe for two females to be traveling around the countryside by themselves."

I digested that for a minute, then asked, "You mean they'd rob us?"

"That, too," she answered. "But also there's some awfully mean people in this world and you have to be on guard every minute. Not that the Lord won't look after us, but it behooves us not to tempt Him."

I considered some of the things those awfully mean people could do to us if they took a mind to. Then it came to me what she was talking about and a great hollow fear opened up inside of me. I'm pretty familiar with what goes on between men and women, and I know some ladies don't mind it at all. At least that's what I learned from Elizabeth Harris and Jacob Hollinger under the scuppernong vine last summer. Elizabeth had been moaning and taking on so, that I thought Jake was killing her. I'd dashed right in under the vine and told him to leave her alone and what did he mean picking on somebody half his size. Well, I hope to tell you I've never seen anybody so mad in my life as Elizabeth was. She let me know right quick that I had jumped in on something that wasn't my business and that I'd better clear out fast so Jake could carry on to her satisfaction. So I didn't think Jessie had that in mind, but I also remembered the vile and salacious looks that some men had given her, and

I figured there had to be something else that men could do to
ladies that they didn't like. I felt a little sick when I tried to
think what it might be, but all I could come up with was that
I didn't want whatever it was to happen to Jessie.

To get my mind off of it, I changed the subject.

"Whereabouts in Oregon are we going? Or is it big enough
to have a choice?"

"Oh, it's big, all right," she said. "I've been reading the
Pathfinder's book and he tells all about it. He says the Rocky
Mountains are majestic and that the land is richer and greener
than anything we can imagine, just made for farmers and settlers."

"And what about the Indians? Does he say anything about
them?"

"He says they're not a problem—you just have to be firm
with them. And you know, Em, they're pleading for an opportunity to know our Lord. A few years ago two or three of
them came to the States asking us to send them missionaries so
they could learn the right way to live."

"Will we be the first ones to go and have to live out there
all by ourselves?"

"Mercy, no," she laughed. "Dr. Marcus Whitman and the
Reverend Henry Spaulding have been there for I don't know
how long. Some ten years or so, I think. they have two mission
stations and are teaching the Indians how to farm and read and
write, and how to worship too."

"Which one will we go to?"

"Whichever one that needs us the most, I reckon."

"But what will I do, Jessie? They're not expecting either
one of us, but they'll take you in since you have a call. What's
going to happen if they don't want me?"

"They'll want you, don't worry about that. You are my
family, just like the wives of Dr. Whitman and Mr. Spaulding
are their families. They might even have children your age, so
there'll be plenty for you to do."

She pulled Red to a stop in the middle of the road and I
looked over her shoulder to see what was going on.

"What's the matter?" I asked.

"Nothing. Here's the the fork that'll take us to Independence," she said. "This is where we really start our journey. Are you ready, Em? Ready for the trip to Oregon, because for us, it really begins here."

I looked at the path that branched off from the road, and the wooden marker that pointed the way to Independence, and felt a great excitement welling up inside of me.

"I'm ready, Jessie," I said. "Let's go give them heathen what-for."

"What a way to put it," she laughed. "But you're right! Let's go give them what-for!"

She kicked Red in the side and he plunged down the path and we were truly on our way.

The day finally warmed up enough for us to shed our coats, and by that time I was so sore from straddling Red's bony back that I stuffed mine under me for a cushion.

We stopped late in the afternooon and none too soon for me. We were both so stiff, we could hardly stand when we slid off. Red heaved a blubbering sigh of relief that said everything I was feeling too. We took the packs off his back, and I led him to the stream we'd picked to camp by. The spot was some little way from the trail and thick with bushes. I knew Jessie had chosen it on purpose, for she had passed up several places that had seemed fine to me.

All I wanted to do was lay down under a tree and take a nap, but she had me gathering twigs and branches for firewood before I could even get comfortable. When I had a fire going and the kettle filled with water, she let me rest while we waited for the hot coals that would warm our supper.

If I had known then how many campfires were going to come after this first one and how many loads of wood and other interesting fuel I was going to have to bring in, I might have pcked up right then and headed back to Caleb's Corner. I might even have walked over to the Ellisons' and told Tom, the oldest son, to come and marry Jessie, for she was all his. But I didn't know, and maybe it's a good thing, for I'd have missed a lot of excitement between campfires.

Jessie fried slices of bacon over the fire while I turned the cornbread to heat it through. Then she cut the bread and fried it lightly in the hot grease. With strong coffee to wash it all down, I hadn't had a finer meal since the last dinner on the grounds at the Holy Light Meetinghouse. I finished up with a wrinkled apple from the poke, and was more than ready for bed.

We laid our blankets on each side of the fire, and after a trip to the bushes for the natural necessities, we wrapped ourselves up and lay looking at the embers of our fire. As it grew quiet I could hear rustling in the bushes around us, and something fluttered in the tree above my head.

"Jessie?" I whispered. "You asleep?"

"Just about. What's the matter?"

"Oh, nothing. It's just hard to get to sleep with all this noise going on."

She laughed under her breath and said, "Don't let it worry you. Red is tied up right over there, and as long as he's quiet, we don't have a thing to worry about. If he hears anything wrong, he'll let us know. Now try to get to sleep. We've got a long day tomorrow."

I rested easier after that, for she was right. There's nothing better at being a watchdog than a mule or a horse. They'll let you know if anything out of the way is going on, and won't bark at the moon, either.

I didn't think I'd ever get to sleep. I was so tired and sore, feeling every place where Red's bones had gouged into my backside, and stiff from my neck to my feet. Yet I must have dozed off, for when I heard Red stomping in the underbrush and grumbling deep in his throat, I came awake and saw that the fire was almost gone. I could feel my heart thudding in my chest, like when you wake up from a scary dream and it's so real that you're afraid it's really happening, and, in fact, something had just happened right before you woke up. I think I must have heard a strange noise in my sleep, something more than a dream, for as soon as my eyes flew open I knew something was still wrong.

"Jessie?"

"Sh-h-h."

"What is it?"

"Be quiet, Em. Pretend to be asleep until we see what it is."

That was the end of my hope that I'd dreamt it. I knew Jessie wouldn't be having the same one I was having. She'd heard something too. I lay back down and swiveled my eyes all around, but I could only see the outlines of the trees, with bright little stars twinkling through the branches. The clumps of bushes around us were just blobs of black, but Red was still restless. I can tell you I didn't like it one bit. I didn't know what manner of beast or wild thing was in the bushes. I couldn't hear anything, but I could feel something out there that hadn't been there when we went to bed.

After a while I could make out shadows moving in the trees on the other side of our fire, and I wished I could stir up the coals so we could see better. If a wild beast was there, our only hope was to build up a blaze, yet Jessie had told me to stay still.

Then I saw two dark forms slide out of the shadows. They stood close together for a minute, then moved apart. I thought I'd pure-tee die of fright then and there.

"Up outta them blankets!" a deep voice called, and I heard the snick of a hammer being drawn back on a shooting piece.

"Yeah, git outta them blankets," echoed a high, whiny voice.

I looked over at Jessie and saw her slowly throw back the cover and stand up. I did the same, and we stood looking at what manner of beasts had come creeping out of the woods. The low fire didn't give out enough light to let us see them clearly, but it gave enough to let them see the game they had flushed.

"It's females, Homer! Wimmenfolk! D'ye see 'em? Hurrah, Homer! It's a brace of females!" The little one with the whiny voice looked as if he'd never seen a female before. He began to jump up and down like he'd won first prize at the county fair.

"Shet yore mouth, Hiram. I got eyes. I kin see what we got, so jest settle down an' lemme think." The deep voice came from the big shadow on the right.

"What ye got to think about? Huh, Homer, huh? What ye got to think about?" The little one was giggling and jumping up and down to beat the band.

"I said shet yore mouth and lemme think!" the big one bellowed.

"Ain't nothin' to think about," the little one said in a higher whine and getting mad about it too. "Ye done tole me, Homer, and ye know ye did. This here's my turn. That's whut you said, this here's my turn now. Yessir, hit's my turn this time."

So far, neither Jessie nor I had said a word. We stood there waiting to see what was going to happen next. It crossed my mind to be thankful we had slept in our clothes. I didn't care to be seen in my flannel gown.

The two men walked closer to us and, in the dim glow of the fire, I could make out what they looked like. And they didn't look too good. The big one was almost fat, with a heavy belly that drooped down over his belt. He had a heavy, long beard that shadowed his face under a floppy-brimmed hat. The thing I noticed the most, though, was the long gun he had pointed right at Jessie. The other one was tiny compared to the first one. In fact, he hardly looked much bigger than me. I knew he was older than me, because even though he had a thin sound to his voice, you could tell it wasn't a little boy's voice. There was a heavy smell hanging around both of them. I got a whiff of woodsmoke and whiskey, but the worst was the sharp, sour odor of winter underwear that had missed last summer's washing.

"Mister, I don't know what you're doing with that gun pointed at us, but I'd recommend you put it away before our papa gets back," Jessie said, as calm as if she were telling the gospel truth.

"Listen at her, Homer," the little one giggled. "Jest listen at her. Ain't she pretty? Remember now, this 'un's mine first."

"I hear her and will you shet up?" The big one sounded like he'd like to take a swat at his friend, but that long barrel didn't swerve an inch.

"Ain't no need to be tellin' no fairy tales, missy," he said to Jessie. "We ain't been watching this here camp for nigh on to a hour to be taken in by anythang you say. Thar ain't no pappy nor anybody else gonna come along and interrupt this little meetin'. Ain't that right?"

"Tha's right, Homer," the little one said, dancing around. "Kin I now? Huh, Homer, kin I now?"

"All right, go ahead, but be lively about it. My turn's next. We'll save the runt for later."

I had this sick feeling way down inside, and even though I've been sick over a lot of things, like eating too many green apples and seeing my papa in his coffin, this was the first time I'd had this peculiar kind of sickness.

Before I knew what was happening the little man unbuckled his belt and began to slide his britches down around his feet. I couldn't believe my eyes. That scrawny little hillbilly didn't have on a lick of underclothes. I've always been told that only people of the lowest order went without underclothes, even if nobody knew it. So, if I hadn't known before this, that very deficiency would've marked him good.

Just as he was hopping up and down on one foot trying to pull one britches leg over his boot, Jessie stooped down to the fire.

"What ye think ye're doing thar?" The big one swung the gun toward Jessie's head.

"Why, I was just poking up the fire so we can see you gentlemen better," Jessie said as sweet as pie. And then she said something that shocked me to my feet. Here's what she said with a great big smile on her face: "And so *you* can see us better. Wouldn't that be nice?"

A wide smile split the hairy beard around his mouth and he said, "Missy, I thank you got a good idear thar."

"Goddamn it!" the little one squealed. "He'p me with this dang thang, Homer. I can't git my britches off!"

"I swear, Hiram, why didn't ye take yore boots off first?" The other one came back at him, but he didn't offer to help.

Hiram hopped around in a circle trying to pull his breeches over his boots, swearing a blue streak as he went. By this time Jessie had the fire in a blaze, and before I knew what she was planning she'd grabbed a good-sized stick with a flame on the end and, quick as a flash, stuck it right in the face of the one with the gun.

I have never in my life seen such a sight and hope never to again. His beard must've been dry as a cornfield that hadn't seen rain all summer and on into the fall. Besides that, it had all kinds of dried food tangled up in it, for when it blazed up I could smell the bacon sizzling.

He let out a bellow that could've been heard back in Caleb's Corner and dropped the gun as he reached for his face.

"My eyes!" he yelled. "My eyes is burnin'!"

Hiram was so shocked that he jerked his britches leg and pulled his foot out from under him. He fell with a thump, and by the time he recovered himself, he was looking down the barrel of the gun.

Jessie had it pointed at him, while old Homer was streaking through the bushes on his way to the creek, screaming and blubbering as he went. We watched his hair flame like a torch until he stumbled into the water and put his whole head underneath.

"Walk right down to the creek with your friend," Jessie said, prodding Hiram with the gun.

"Yessum, jes' lemme git my britches on, ma'am," he said, being more polite than I thought he had it in him to be.

"No need for that," Jessie said. "Just get on down there the way you are."

"But, ma'am, I, uh, don't have but half my clothes on," he said, like we hadn't noticed.

"You can walk or you can crawl, makes no nevermind to me, but get yourself down to the creek."

He scrambled up, holding the loose britches leg against his privates, and walked to the edge of the creek with his head bowed down in mortal shame.

"Pull your friend out of the water," Jessie ordered.

I'll tell you that was a sight to be seen. I wish we'd had a better light, but what we could see made an awful interesting picture. Homer's beard was gone and so was his hair. I don't believe his own mama would've recognized him. He was still blubbering and crying, and I think Jessie really put the fear of the Lord in him with a stick of firewood.

"Now, what'd you have to go and do that for, huh, ma'am?" Hiram whined when he got a good look at Homer. "We didn't mean no harm. What'd you have to go and hurt ole Homer fer?"

"My eyes is gone," Homer moaned. "I can't see! My eyes is gone!"

"Your eyes are gone so you can no longer look upon evil," Jessie told him, and I expect she was right. "Now," she snapped, "you were so anxious to take your clothes off, let me see how fast you can get them off now."

I whipped my head toward her and my mouth fell open.

"Uh, Jessie," I said quietly, "if it's all the same to you, I've seen all of these two I've a mind to see."

"Never mind that, Em," she said, not taking her eyes from the two of them. She had the gun trained on them like they were the meanest varmints in the country, which was probably the truth. "You've got two choices. Either get those clothes off right now or get them filled with holes. Take your choice. The Lord will not stay my hand from striking down evil."

I'd never heard Jessie sound so determined and so sure of herself, and I was glad to be on her and the Lord's side. The two men began peeling off their clothes, but they were none too happy about it.

"Put them right here on the bank," she told them. And she stood there watching until every scrap was off of them. I declare if I hadn't been afraid they'd try some deceitful trick, I would've turned my head in mortification. But I felt I owed Jessie my vigilance and, in the process, I took the opportunity to add to my previously defective understanding of the male anatomical arrangement with studious attention to detail. It was a sight, and no mistake about it.

4

Take his garment that is surety for a stranger.
—*Proverbs 20:16*

"We'll need some rawhide, Em. Go get some out of the packs," Jessie told me.

I ran back and untied the loop from Red's saddle and carried it back to her. She then told me to wet it good in the creek.

"Now, you two lay down on the ground right over here," she ordered.

Hiram and Homer looked into the end of that unwavering gun barrel and, meek as lambs, walked out of the water and laid down on the cold ground. Both of them were covering their private parts with their hands and they looked like two scolded dogs with their tails between their legs. They acted like they expected to be kicked, but they were in for worse than that.

She motioned them with the gun to lie down away from each other, and made them put their heads toward one tree and their feet toward another one. Then she instructed me, in the same cold manner, to tie their hands and feet to the trees. Rawhide has the property of tightening up as it dries and Jessie knew it. We tied them so that they were stretched between two trees in a stark state of nature. It was a case of *naturalia anteponantur non naturalibus*, like last year's schoolmaster had said that Cicero recommended, though he probably didn't have this in mind when he said it.

Only then did Jessie begin to let down her guard. She threw the gun as far as she could down the creek. Then she gathered the clothes of the smaller man and walked back to our campsite without a backward glance. She had settled their hash and was done with them.

36

"Their horses, Jessie," I reminded her. "They have to have some horses tied up around here somewhere. Want me to go find them?"

"No, we don't need their horses, and they sure won't need them for a while."

"But we do need them," I pleaded. "We could each have a horse to ride and we could use Red for the packs. Come on, Jessie, let me go find them."

"Emma Louise," she said, glaring at me. "Are you suggesting that we steal those horses?"

"Wel-l-l, not exactly steal them, but anyway think what they were planning to do to us. I don't think borrowing their horses comes anywhere near what they were going to do."

"Thou shalt not steal," she said, "regardless of what man may do unto you. Now forget about the horses."

She began to roll up our blankets and pack the cooking utensils. I helped halfheartedly, for I was still sulking over missing out on decent horseflesh to ride. I muttered under my breath about how she'd feel different if she was the one bouncing up and down on Red's bones without anything between her backside and his.

"Get a move on, Em," she said. "We're leaving this evil place even though it's still the middle of the night. I'll never get any sleep knowing those two are so near."

"I don't think they'll be bothering us after the Christian treatment you just gave them," I said, still longing for their horses. "You really know how to jerk a man up out of sin, I'll give you that."

Then I started laughing. I laughed until I couldn't get my breath. Soon Jessie was laughing with me, and I suppose it came from the relief of getting out of an awfully tight spot, which we had done all by ourselves. It was like a good omen for the rest of the journey.

"What came over you, Jessie?" I asked, between fits of giggles. "How did you ever learn to set a man on fire and handle a gun like that?"

"Oh, Em," she said, smiling in the firelight. "You don't have to be taught a thing like that. I just did it without thinking. The Lord helps those who help themselves, you know."

Now, I've heard that all my life, and once I'd taken it upon myself to look through the entire Bible to find chapter and verse, but it's nowhere to be found. But you ask your average run-of-the-mill-Bible-believing Christian and he'll swear up, down, and crossways that there is such a verse. But there's not; yet even so I guess if it gives comfort to those who feel the need for it, it maybe ought to be there.

We saddled Red and he, having some sense, didn't like it at all. He knew it wasn't daylight and he wasn't used to working overtime. We persuaded him that it wasn't healthy where we were and, after throwing dirt on the fire, we headed out again on the road to Independence.

The moon was still high so we had enough light to pick our way along. We soon came to a wider road and made better time. We rode through the darkest part of the night after the moon went down. And finally, when a gray light began to outline the trees, Jessie told me to start looking for a place to camp.

"We'll need a stream," she said, "and we'll follow it a good piece away from the road. What we ought to do is travel at night and sleep during the day, don't you think?"

At that point I would've agreed to anything she came up with. I was so tired that I had been dozing against her back, and I didn't think I'd ever be able to sit or walk in a proper manner again. Jessie at last turned off the road onto a trail in the underbrush. I heard the rippling of water over stones and knew she'd found what she wanted.

When we dismounted our knees nearly buckled under us. I'd hate to have to count up the number of hours we'd been stretched over that mule's back out of the last twenty-four, but it would amount to a considerable number.

We quickly made camp and, without any thought of breakfast, rolled up in our blankets and went to sleep.

I don't know how long we slept, but nothing disturbed us, and the sun was throwing long shadows when we finally woke up.

"I'm starved, Jessie. How 'bout you?"

"I am too. If you'll find us some firewood, I'll cook us a meal that'll make up for all the ones we've missed."

And she did just that. She fried meat, then potatoes in the same grease, which made them taste wonderful good. Then she sliced dried apples in the pan and sprinkled sugar over them, and I'm here to say that it was handsome eating. We ended up with a cup of hot, black coffee with enough sugar in it to make a spoon stand alone.

"How far out of Independence are we now, Jessie?" I asked, leaning back against a tree to take my ease.

"Not too far, I wouldn't think," she answered. "I heard several wagons pass off and on during the day, so a town must be nearby. Maybe only one more day of travel, if that much.

"Take these pans to the creek, Em, and wash them. I have something I need to do."

She went over to the packs and brought out the filthy clothes we'd taken off Hiram and, holding them at arm's length, walked down to the water.

"What are you going to do with those smelly things?" I asked while I scoured the pans.

She smiled a secret smile and said, "It's a surprise for you."

I generally like surprises, but I wasn't sure I was going to like anything connected with what we'd left tied to a tree.

As soon as she scrubbed the britches, shirt, and even the floppy hat, she spread them over a laurel bush to dry. Then she took his boots and, glancing at me in a measuring sort of way, she dunked them in the water and, bless me, if she didn't scrub them inside and out with lye soap just like she'd done the clothes.

I begged her to tell me what she was going to do with them, but she just smiled and said I'd find out as soon as they were dry. I had some suspicions of what she had in mind, but couldn't figure out her reasons.

We ate again when dark fell, and because Hiram's clothes weren't yet dry, Jessie decided to wait out the night before striking out again. I didn't much like sitting by a campfire in the dark after our last unpleasant experience, but she said we'd take turns sleeping to forestall any surprises. She let me have the first watch, since Red was still awake to keep me company.

Neither of us slept too well, though. Maybe because we'd gotten our fill of it during the day. By the time the sun began to lighten the landscape, we were both more than ready to be on the move.

Jessie took the clothes off the bush and felt them to see if they were dry enough for her secret plans.

"All right, Em, you've heard about a wolf in sheep's clothing?" she asked with a smile. "Well, we're going to turn that around and put a sheep in wolf's clothing."

"Huh?"

"That's right," she said, more than a little pleased with herself. "We're going to pretend that you're my brother, and when you get these on, nobody'll know the difference."

I stood there looking at her, trying to decide if I liked the idea. I've not yet met a boy I'd trade places with, yet there are certain advantages they have over the female members of the race. One being that no older sister or busybody neighbor-lady will tell you to behave yourself and learn some manners. The more I thought about it, the better I liked it. I just couldn't come up with Jessie's reason for it. After all, she'd been the prime one to remind me of how ladies are supposed to conduct themselves, and that didn't include running around in a pair of britches.

"Suits me right down the line, Jessie," I finally answered. "But will you tell me why? It goes against everything you've tried to learn me."

"Teach you, Em," she corrected, unable to help herself. "And the reason is, I think we'll be safer from just such as happened last night if one of us appears to be a male. Strange people think twice about males of all ages, and two females together are just asking for trouble. It would really be a whole lot better if I could be the boy, but these clothes won't fit me. They're too small, and the other one's clothes would swallow us both.

"And the main thing, Em," she went on, "I want you to be safe. A change in your appearance will protect you from harm."

My guileless sister was beginning to show a previously undetected aptitude for fraud and deceit. I considered her with new respect. Fact of the matter is, I should have thought of it myself, for only the past week I'd been reading about two gentlewomen from Duke Frederick's court who took refuge in masculine garb from similar perils.

"We're not the first ones to try such a trick. Listen to this, Jessie." And I began to spout forth in my best declaiming manner, " 'Alas, what danger will it be for us, Maids as we are, to travel forth so far! Beauty provoketh thieves sooner than gold.' "

"I declare, Em, where do you pick up such things?" she asked, without expecting an answer.

Hiram's clothes had been handmade by somebody, but for the life of me I couldn't picture some loving mother stitching up anything for him. In fact, I'd be willing to wager he didn't even have a mother. My money was on a steaming cow heap somewhere. Be that as it may, his britches had seen a lot of wear, but they'd hold together for our purpose. They sure needed a flatiron taken to them, but the last thing we'd have thought to pack was a flatiron. If I had to choose the thing I least wanted to do for the rest of my life, it would be the job of ironing. Once you've had to heat up an iron in a bed of coals, and then wrench your back out trying to pick it up without burning yourself, and then push it back and forth over rough-dried clothes, you've had enough of it to last awhile. I don't like it worth a lick.

I pulled Hiram's britches on and buttoned up the front, feeling a little funny about what the area had once covered. The legs were too long, but a couple of turns fixed that. Jessie cut a length of rope to run through the belt loops, and when it was tied they didn't look half bad. At least I thought they'd stay up.

The homespun shirt was rough against my back, but it wasn't a bad fit. I'd seen worse. Then I tried the boots. They were too long, but we wadded up some scraps torn from my petticoat and stuck them in the toes so my feet wouldn't slide around, and then they fit just fine. Well, the toes turned up a little, particularly after the washing Jessie had given them, but nine out of ten boys I knew wore hand-me-down boots anyway and they all looked like the ones I had on. I didn't think I would stand out in a crowd.

The hat was something else again. It had been big on Hiram, flopping down around his face and hiding enough of his physiognomy for him to be presentable in public. From the way it had fit him, I think he may have borrowed it from its rightful owner. I tried stuffing my braids up under it to make it fit better, but that didn't work too well. They kept sliding out the back. I just jammed the hat on my head and let it come down over my face like Hiram had done.

"Em," Jessie said softly, with a sorrowful look on her face, "I'm not going to tell you to do this, for it breaks my heart to even think of it. From the front, no one would think twice about how you look. But, honey, from the back, with your braids hanging down, everyone will know you're a girl dressed up in boy's clothing. And that'll cause even worse problems for us."

I knew what she was talking about. I would have to cut my hair. I thought about all the pulling and snarling and combing I had to endure every day of my life, and I couldn't see why she was so near to crying.

"Gimme the knife," I said. "Let's cut these worrisome things off and good riddance."

"But, Em, your beautiful hair!"

That stopped me for a minute. No one had ever told me I had beautiful hair and I hated to part with something that somebody thought well of. I didn't hesitate too long, though. All I had to do was think of that empty sickness inside of me when Hiram and Homer jumped us and I began to saw away at one of my braids.

"Here, let me do it," Jessie said. There were tears in her eyes, but she cut both off as evenly as she could, leaving me with a fringe that came to the collar of the shirt, about the length most men wore their hair in between bowl cuttings.

"Oh, Em," Jessie wailed. "The Holy Scriptures tell us that a woman's hair is her crowning glory. What have I let you do?"

I turned my head back and forth, twisting it around and moving it up and down. I couldn't believe how much those braids had weighed on my head. I'd been so used to them that I'd had no idea of the burden I'd had on my brains.

"Don't cry, Jessie," I said. "Just think how much freedom my brains have now. I'll be able to think just that much quicker without all that weight pulling my head out of kilter. I like it. Don't cry."

"I'll make this up to you someday," she said, between laughing and wiping away tears.

"Don't worry about it, it'll grow back. But I just might keep it cut off. I really think I'll get along better this way."

She put her arms around me and hugged me tight. She didn't often do that, and even if I had regretted cutting my hair, I would've changed my mind right then and there.

"Let's get on the move," she said, turning toward our packs.

"Just one more thing, Jessie," I said. "We need to have an understanding before we go any further."

"What about?"

"If I'm going to look like a boy, and act like a boy, so as to give us protection from the likes of those two last night, then you're going to have to treat me like a boy."

"Just what is it you have in mind?" she asked, giving me a slanty-eyed look.

"Well, you can't be telling me to go wash my hands, or set the table, or comb my hair, or sit ladylike, or any number of other things that would make folks think something was wrong with me."

"Now, Em . . ."

"Wait, hear me out," I interrupted. "If you think about it, you'll see I'm right. We're not going to fool anybody if you're forever after me to do female work and conduct myself in a female manner. If you hand somebody that looks like me a piece of embroidery, folks wouldn't know what to make of it. It seems to me that we're either going to have to carry this through all the way or just not do it at all."

"Well, I see what you mean," she said. "But I just had in mind to keep this up until we get with some Christian folks on the Oregon Trail."

"Now that's where you'll have to think again, Jessie," I

told her. "There's lots of lewd and dissolute folks who call themselves Christians, and you know it as well as I do. What we need to do is keep our guard up until we know exactly who we'll be traveling with. And I intend to act as rough and tough as I know how. I learned a lot of manly behavior from watching Papa, and I think we'd better just pretend that I'm your little brother who hasn't had much training in civilized ways. I think the best thing for us to do is pretend you don't have a tight rein over me and that you're always worried over what I might do if I get riled or something."

"I don't know, Em. It doesn't sound right somehow."

"Jessie, don't the Scriptures say for us to put on the whole armor of God so we can withstand the wiles of the devil? That's all we're doing. We're going out where the wiles of the devil are in full force, and I say that we need everything we can get to pull the wool over his eyes, so to speak."

"Maybe you're right," she finally said. "I'll try, Em. I'll do my best to think of you as my little brother."

"Your scary little brother."

"All right, then," she laughed, "my uncontrollable, scary little brother."

I laughed with her, and if I had been looking forward to our trip to Oregon before this, it was now doubled. I could do everything and anything I wanted to do. Never before had I realized how different being a boy was from being a girl. Not many people get to live through that kind of change. No more sitting down and checking where my skirt tail was; no more making sure my knees were clamped together; no more watching how far I leaned over so my drawers wouldn't show. From that minute on I determined to get all the good out of my assumed gender that I could and enjoy every minute of it before Jessie made me change back.

"One more thing, though," Jessie said, looking over her shoulder at me. "Let's don't carry this too far. Remember that the Lord made switches to grow on trees."

That girl always knew how to take the pleasure out of a person's good times, and she was an expert at doing it too.

5

The stranger did not lodge in the street, but I
opened my doors to the traveler.
—*Job 31:32*

We sallied forth the next morning before the sun was no
more than a promise. In fact, it hardly got going all day
long. Sometime in the night the clouds had moved in and a
steady, drizzling rain had begun with a slow persistence that
foreboded no quick relief. We were a miserable two people who
huddled together on Red's back and he wasn't feeling much
better about the prospect of being out in it all day. Red had
never liked bad weather, including rainy weather, cold weather,
and hot weather. In fact, I'm not sure he really liked any kind
of weather. He was what you might call a home body or, rather,
a barn body. He liked his own dry stall with a trough full of
corn and a week full of Sabbaths.

He'd learned by this time not to give Jessie any sass, though.
When she switched him up he went. Like me, and I don't need
to mention Hiram and Homer, he'd learned not to be a hindrance to somebody on the Lord's business. We plodded on
through the misty rain, feeling large drops splattering on our
heads from the overhanging trees.

Pretty soon we began to meet more people, some on horseback and some in farm wagons, all headed in the same direction
as we were. Most of them hardly gave us the time of day, though
a few farmers kept their eyes on us a little longer than I liked.
A good many had their whole families with them, boys and
girls and grandmothers clinging to what looked like all their
household plunder. Others were rattling along in empty wagons,
going in for supplies or the latest news. This Independence town
really drew the commerce, which meant it was something more

than Jefferson City, the only city I was used to, seeing that I had been there once.

We approached the town with some trepidation, for the streets teemed with every manner of beast and type of human-kind. But everybody was intent on their own purposes and took little notice of two more bedraggled specimens. I figured Jessie was safe as long as she stayed wrapped up in her shawl and the rain kept her that way. To be on the safe side, I made sure that Papa's leather-handled knife was hanging well in sight from my belt. I pulled Hiram's floppy hat down over my eyes so I could look up out from under the brim with what I hoped was a baleful gaze. I wanted everybody to know that this was a customer they couldn't fool around with.

As we entered Independence I forgot my evil-looking in-tentions and began to feel the excitement of all the hubbub. I had never seen anything like it in my life. Before we even reached the center of town, the street, which had broadened considerably, was fairly packed with people, wagons, horses, mules, and herds of cattle all going and coming with the most barbarous and excessive racket this side of the Tower of Babel. The road was muddy and slippery from the rain, and as wheels began to mire and horses' hooves began to cake with mud, tempers got shorter. Jessie pulled Red to the side of the track, seeking out the grassy edges. At one point we had to pull all the way over to let three wagons go by as they tried to get ahead of each other. Jessie took the enforced hiatus to commence laying down the law to me.

"Listen now, Em, and hear me good. If anybody asks what we're doing, tell them our family is camped outside of town and we're in to buy supplies. Don't let anybody know that we're on our own. And another thing. Remember who you are, so nobody will guess, or even suspicion, that you're a girl."

"I'll remember, Jessie. Our family is camped outside of town. They sent us in for supplies. And I'm not a girl. It won't be hard because I don't aim to talk to anybody around here. But I meant to ask you—what about my name? Don't you think we ought to change it to something a little more in keeping with my outward appearance?"

"Em is perfectly all right. It can stand for Emmett just as well as for Emma."

"Well, I was thinking more in the line of Tex or the Missouri Kid, or something like that."

"For goodness sakes, Em, be sensible," she said. "We're going to have a hard enough time as it is without trying to remember what to call you."

By this time we were able to get back into the stream of traffic, and even Red perked up his ears at all the agitation around us. The closer we got to what seemed to be the center of the mayhem, the more people there were and the louder they got.

I have never heard such swearing and immoderate language in my life, and Papa hadn't been a slouch at it. Those benighted mules, horses, and oxen were raked over every coal in the book, even though it wasn't their fault that the streets were muddy and the rain was cold and wet. But to hear the drovers, you'd have thought the animal kingdom was the cause of Adam's fall, and Eve's as well.

By the time we were fairly in the middle of everything, we could hardly move for all the turbulent multitudes. I saw a gentleman dash from one side of the street to the other right under the forelegs of a rearing team. How he escaped with his life, I'll never know, but he didn't escape without being damned to hell and back by the driver of the team.

"Don't listen to this, Em," Jessie said, much distressed by the language on all sides.

"No'm," I assured her, "I won't." But since I wasn't stone deaf, I couldn't help but learn a thing or two.

About that time my eyes about popped out of my head. Strolling down the wooden sidewalk were two of the drunkest Indians I'd ever seen. That's not saying much, since as far as I know I'd never seen any drunk Indians. They were leaning into each other, and if one had slipped, the other would surely have gone down with him. They both had these ragged blankets around their shoulders that, gaping open, revealed not one stitch of clothing on their torsos. Rain was streaming down their faces, making the paint run into interesting patterns. As a matter of fact, at first I thought they were bleeding from the way the red paint in their hair was running down their faces. Right behind them came the fanciest and most decorative spectacle Independence had yet offered for my delectation.

"What in the Sam Hill is that?"

"Hush, Em, and don't stare. I think he must be a Mexican, or maybe a Texan."

"Jingies!" Not counting the two Indians in front of him, he was the first foreigner I'd ever seen.

He strolled past us as we sat waiting for a drover to untangle his team. The foreigner was singing a song in some tongue I couldn't understand, and I knew in my heart that it had to be Mexican. He wore britches of a tighter fit than modesty required, and they were slashed open up to his knees. The edges had bells on them that tinkled with every step he took. Even his wide-brimmed hat had little bells on it, and they swayed and jingled as he swung along the sidewalk. He wore high-heeled boots that sported the biggest and sharpest spurs in the Western world. I turned my head almost all the way around to watch him amble down the walk and turn into what a sign said was the Dry & Dusty Saloon.

There were so many sights to be seen on the streets of Independence that I would've liked to have found a dry spot under a tree somewhere and watched all the folks and events passing by. It would've spurted my education far ahead of anybody's in Caleb's Corner.

Jessie suddenly jerked Red even farther off the road as we heard a commotion behind us. I looked around to see a long, heavy wagon careening down the road, pulled by all of eight teams of mules. The dirtiest human that probably ever lived was standing up in the wagon, holding all the reins in one hand. With the other he was cracking and popping a bullwhip that was long enough to reach the lead team. And he wasn't sparing the rod, either.

"HOO-eee, yip-yip, git up thar!" he bellowed. "Make way fer the roughest, toughest, meanest team and drover what ever headed fer Taos! Outta the way fer the best!"

Horses and buggies scattered before him, and one rider

got dumped in the mud when his horse shied in fright. I thought I'd heard descriptive language before, but not like I heard then. There was this one lady who was standing on the walk waiting for a chance to cross the street. She had on a shiny green dress that either had been made for some other lady or else she had put on considerable heft since she'd purchased it. She carried a ruffled green and yellow parasol to shelter her curls from the weather, and just as the wagon flew past her it splattered mud on her skirts, which just had to be her Sunday best. Well, the things that lady said made her number one in my book for a specialized knowledge of the Holy Scriptures. If she'd rearranged some of those words, she would've made an A-number-one Sabbath school teacher. I mean, she knew about the Whore of Babylon and Balaam's ass and that stuff that Lot's daughters did when he got drunk after his wife turned into a pillar of salt. She also had a nodding acquaintance with the sins of Sodom and Gomorrah.

"We've got to get out of this wicked place," Jessie gasped, as amazed as I was at the lady's command of Scripture. You don't often find somebody so well versed and so willing to demonstrate it on the public wayfare.

"What exactly was it that Lot's daughters did, Jessie? Have you got that far yet?"

"Don't ask me any questions now," she said, giving Red a kick and turning him out of the mainstream of Independence.

The side street wasn't much better, although there was less moving commerce in the road. There were plenty of people on the sides, though. This part of town didn't have wooden walkways, so there were clumps of men standing under the trees talking with a lot of hand waving and shoulder shrugging. A little farther on I could see a blacksmith's shop with a crowd of horses and mules tied up around it. There was a sign hanging overhead announcing Robert Weston's Smithy. The mules in the pen next to it milled around, squealing and rushing from one side to the other. The odor of singed mule hair rose from the open door of the shop, and everywhere we could hear the sound of men calling on the Lord, though I do believe they did so without any real expectation of an answer.

By this time the misty rain had not only made the streets slippery, but the ruts deeper, and one fine gentleman stepped off the edge of the street and mired up to the top of his boots. I would've laughed if he hadn't looked so serious about it.

As Jessie urged Red on, disregarding the heavy clumps of mud sticking to his hooves, we heard what I immediately took to be gunshots from the street we had just left. I could feel Jessie tighten up as I clung to her with a harder grip. This business of leaving home was getting to be perilous.

"Lordamercy, Jessie, let's get outta here."

"I'm trying my best, but this mule is as stubborn as . . . as a mule and won't do anything I say. Kick him, Em, we've just got to get somewhere decent."

I think she was about to cry, she was so mad and scared, and I wasn't in much better shape, for Red had taken that very minute to spraddle his hind legs and relieve himself, and neither hell nor high water could budge him while he was doing it.

About that time a great, tall Indian with a feather drooping down the back of his head came high-stepping down the road toward us. He had a shiny medal strung from a ribbon around his neck, a little apron that barely covered what was important, and two huge clumps of mud on each foot. He walked right toward us, his eyes on something far in the distance, and his feet making sucking noises as he lifted each one out of the mud. He made for us without even seeing us, and Red didn't like it at all. What with that rank Indian in front of him, and not being finished with the business behind him, and Jessie switching him with the reins, and me trying to kick him, it's no wonder he was in a quandary. He was dancing and shifting around, and if I hadn't known he was too lazy to run or rear, I'd of been afraid of both. Jessie didn't know it, though, and she was fuming.

"Stop! Stop it, you mule you! Get up, there! Help me, Em. Make him stop and get up!" Jessie was about to cry, like she always does when somebody won't do what she wants. I'm not talking about sulky crying; she cries because she's mad as thunder. And I couldn't do a thing to help, seeing that I had all I could do to keep from falling off.

"Need some help?" I caught a glimpse of a tall man in a woolen poncho standing just beyond Red's gyrations. He had his arms folded across his chest, looking like he'd just as soon watch the show as stop it.

"Don't just stand there like you're feebleminded! Stop this . . . this mule!" Jessie was about to lose her religion, and just as Red whirled again his hind feet slipped out from under him. As he tried to gain a purchase with his front feet, he began to slowly sit down.

I started sliding down his hindquarters, pulling Jessie with me. The man moved right up beside us, put one hand on Jessie's midsection to steady her, and took hold of Red's halter with the other. I slid on off into the mud while Red stopped his prancing around and stood there like he'd never done a wrong thing in his life.

Jessie didn't like unexpected favors from strangers, and she didn't know whether to thank him or stay mad at Red. She decided to jump on me.

"Get back up here, Em! Look at you, covered with mud! I thank you, sir, but if you'll kindly take your hands off me and my mule, we'll be going." She stiffened herself up and tried to look like she hadn't been scared to death a minute before.

"I'll be more than happy to accompany you to wherever you're headed, in case you have any more trouble," the man said, being none too hasty to withdraw one of his hands. "Can't be too careful with these spirited animals, you know." The white lines by the sides of his eyes didn't change, and I couldn't tell if he was laughing at us or not.

I grabbed the back of the saddle to pull myself back on, getting in the process a most surprising boost from him. I couldn't do a thing about such familiarity without giving myself away, so I pretended not to notice.

"We don't need any more help, thank you, and we have to be going," Jessie said, looking as dignified as a lady can astride a mule.

The stranger noticed it, too, because he up and called attention to the very matter that was real close to Jessie's feelings.

"May I say, ma'am," he said, like he was offering a gentleman's compliment, "that I'm glad to see one lady with neither pride nor vanity. If you'd been riding sidesaddle, like most young ladies without any sense, you would've landed in the mud before I could catch you."

Well, that just mortified Jessie, because she knew it wasn't ladylike to ride astride and only did it because it was the only way we had to travel. Her face got red and she pulled up so straight she almost lifted herself out of the saddle.

She sniffed in that haughty way she had and said, "How fortunate for us that you were here, Mr. . . . ."

"Garrett," he said, and that made her even madder, because she wasn't asking his name. She was just catching her breath.

"Let's go, Em," she said, like I had anything to do with it. "Get up, mule."

I looked back as Red finally started moving. Mr. Garrett tilted up his hat with one finger and stood watching us for as long as I could see him. I'd noticed right off that he was a different kind of man than I'd ever come up against before. For one thing, he wore outlandish garb of a kind that I'd never seen, but later came to know as the usual mountain attire. But there was something else about him that made him stand out from the crowd, and made the crowd stand out from him and give him plenty of room. It was like there was a space around him that nobody could get into unless he said they could. I think it was his eyes that did it, because they hooked on to you in such a way that you were so taken up with looking, and being looked at, that you couldn't even put your mind on what color they were. He had a way of looking down in you, even when you knew his mind was on something else. So even if he hadn't put his hand on a most unlikely place in helping me get back on Red, he would've caught my attention. Mr. Garrett gave me a strange feeling right off, but by the time we'd passed the smithy the crowds had closed in behind us and I couldn't see him anymore.

All of a sudden Jessie pulled Red to a stop, and I looked over her shoulder to see the same dignified Indian coming toward us again. I wasn't afraid, because he still wasn't looking where he was going and it wasn't us he was after.

"We'll wait right here," Jessie said, "and let that moronic Indian get by before he scares this mule again."

"Reckon who he is?" I asked.

A voice beside us answered me in refined and reassuring tones. "That's old Running Bull. Don't let him frighten you, he's perfectly harmless."

I looked down and saw a man I speculated to be about in the fifth decade of his life. He had on a suit of clothes I'd wager had been purchased in a bigger town than Independence, for it had a flowered waistcoat with a gold chain stretched across the middle. His hair and whiskers were neatly trimmed, and there was a certain air about his manner and dress that proclaimed him a prosperous gentleman. Like everybody else on the street, though, his boots and the bottom of his trousers were caked with mud.

He took off his hat and said, "Pardon me for intruding upon your conversation. I take it that you are new to Independence and perhaps, as I was, a little overcome with the great range of humanity one encounters in a place like this. Permit me to introduce myself. I am George Donner, Esquire, from Illinois, even now preparing myself and my family to undertake travel on the Overland route to the West."

"How do you do, Mr. Donner," Jessie said, accepting his courtesy with some of her own, which she hadn't done for Mr. Garrett. "I am Miss Jessie Elizabeth Heath of Caleb's Corner, Missouri, and this is my . . . my brother, Emmett Heath."

"My pleasure, Miss Heath," he returned pleasantly, and even though I can usually spot somebody who's after Jessie even before they know it themselves, I didn't get that feeling from him. "Are you just visiting here in this fair city or would you, too, perhaps be preparing to move across the Plains?"

"We are headed for Oregon, Mr. Donner, to be missionaries for the Lord," Jessie answered, with every bit of the advice she'd been so careful to give me completely gone from her head.

I kicked her on the off side and chimed in, "Our folks are camped outside of town. They're waiting for us to get back with supplies. Besides, Papa told us not to strike up with any strangers, Jessie, so let's get a move on."

Even though I was inclined to trust this Mr. Donner, who seemed both courteous and amiable, I figured it better to be safe than sorry later on.

"Missionaries!" Mr. Donner exclaimed with respect. "Well, now, I must hear more about this. Pull your mule over here and light a spell under this tree out of the rain."

And I declare if Jessie didn't do just that. She tied Red to the tree and stood there in front of Mr. Donner and did everything she'd told me not to do.

"Mr. Donner, we are in the hands of the Lord and we're waiting for Him to show us the best way to get to Oregon," she said while I fumed at her lack of sense.

"Come on, Jessie," I urged. "Papa's gonna be mad as fire if we don't get back soon."

She went on talking to Mr. Donner as if I hadn't said a word, and before I knew it she'd even told him that we didn't have a papa and that we were away from home all by ourselves. I thought Mr. Donner looked a little taken aback when he realized what we were up to without any official backing or anything, but he said he admired courage wherever he found it, which wasn't that often.

"Miss Jessie," he said, and from that you can tell how far along the conversation had come from "ma'am" to "Miss Heath" to now "Miss Jessie." "Mrs. Donner and myself have five children with us, all daughters. We had hoped to hire a young woman to help with them before leaving Illinois, but at the last minute she was unable to come. If it suits you and your brother, why don't you come out to our camp at Indian Creek, at your convenience, of course, and meet Mrs. Donner. If it's agreeable to you, it might be that we could come to terms in a mutual agreement to the satisfaction of both parties. Mrs. Donner needs help and you need companions for the trip. Would you consider such an arrangement?"

"Mr. Donner," Jessie smiled with that peculiar glow of hers, "I think you and Mrs. Donner are the answer to our prayers. My brother and I would be happy to travel with you and your family, depending, of course, upon Mrs. Donner's acceptance of me."

Mr. Donner smiled back and good-naturedly answered, "I've never been called an answer to prayer before, Miss Jessie, but if I can be of service to either you or the Lord, then I'm more than happy to do so. Whenever you're ready just follow this very street out of town, past the courthouse, and you'll find Indian Creek some eight miles out. There are a good many wagons already camped there, but anyone can direct you to my camp. I'll tell Mrs. Donner to expect you."

He bowed to Jessie, shook my hand, which I tried to accept as if I'd done it a hundred times before, and he left looking well satisfied with business done.

"Jessie," I said, about half mad, "you have sure got us in a peck of trouble. What if this Mr. Donner is not who he seems to be? You told me to be careful what I told people about us, and here you just gave him our life histories without knowing anything more about him than his name, which we only have his own word about, even then."

"Now, Em," she said, "we must be open to the leading of the Holy Spirit, and I know that Mr. Donner was sent to this particular spot at this particular time to help us get to Oregon."

Now, I wasn't about to argue with her or with whoever was leading her. She called it the Holy Spirit, but I was inclined to lay it to hardheadedness. The only thing I knew to do was tag along after her and hope for the best. And the best would be if I didn't have to ride double on Red all the way to Oregon.

"See, Em," she said, with that saintly look on her face, "if you have faith, the Lord will provide for all your needs."

"Well, the needs I have right now include a dry place to sleep and something hot to eat," I muttered under my breath, but bless pat if she wasn't standing under that dripping tree giving thanks for having her prayers answered by God and Mr. Donner.

When she finished we scrambled back up on Red. He gave a tremendous sigh, as if he was being put upon beyond endurance. As we made our way through the crowd I caught sight of Mr. Garrett leaning against the side of a building, watching us from under his hat. I wondered why he was so taken with us, but then I remembered and pulled Jessie's shawl back up over her head and gave Red an extra kick.

6

God setteth the solitary in families. . . .
—*Psalms 68:6*

On our way out of town we passed what must have been the biggest house in the state of Missouri, and as we got close enough for me to read the sign hanging from the porch, I could see that it was Colonel Noland's Tavern and Inn for Gentlemen, Accommodations for 400 Guests. Colonel Noland was doing a thriving business, for gentlemen of all sizes, shapes, and stages of dress were going in and out. Jessie took offense and kicked Red into a shuffling trot.

The people on the walks and in the streets were enough to keep me entertained for some time to come and I would liked to have lingered awhile. When I mentioned that we were passing up a golden opportunity to further my education in Rhetorical Eloquence and the Humanities, Jessie snorted in a most unladylike fashion.

Several hard-looking cases took note of us. They followed us with squinty eyes, and I realized that we were probably the only two young ladies in the whole state out riding by ourselves. It was a good thing there wasn't two skirts draped across Red's back, for we'd have truly caught attention. I stopped clinging to Jessie and tried to look manly and brave, but it put a strain on me.

There were so many stores, shops, taverns, smithies, and saloons that they crowded on top of each other, and every one of them was mightily prospering from the looks of things. One of the busiest places of all was a long, low log cabin that proclaimed itself the Jackson County Courthouse. The only empty spot as far as the eye could see was a vacant lot right next door

to it. There were no horses or mules corralled in it or tied to
any of the trees. No one took a shortcut through it; it just
seemed that everybody on their way to some business or another
made every effort to pass it by. I thought it was strange that an
empty place would be going unused in a town that looked to
need every inch of space it could get.

Fortunately for my curiosity, Jessie pulled Red out of the
way of a herd of horses being driven down the middle of
the street. Betwixt the "Hi-yi's" and the "Git on thar's" of the
drovers, I took the opportunity to lean down and ask another
of those dark-skinned, bell-trimmed Mexicans what the town
of Independence had planned for that empty lot.

"No hablo Englais, muchacho," he said around the shuck-
rolled cigarillo in his mouth. The smoke curled up in his eyes,
but he didn't blink as he spoke to me and stared at Jessie.

"Stop talking to strangers," Jessie snapped, which put my
dander up after the conversation she'd just had with a stranger.
Of course I'll have to admit I didn't have the spiritual guidance
in picking out which strangers to talk to like she had.

"Wanna know about that thar empty lot, littl'un?" a voice
asked from behind the Mexican.

I looked over at a leathery man whose long beard grew
down his shirt almost to his homespun trousers. His hands were
big and gnarled, and his face was weathered in the way only a
farmer's can get.

"Yessir, I sure would," I said, paying no mind to the nudge
Jessie gave me.

"Wal, that thar is the center of the earth and of the starry
universe as well, and we have it on the word of the prophet,
Joseph Smith hisself. Seems like that's whar they're gonna build
a temple, so this whole state of Missoura is appointed and con-
secrated for the gathering of the Saints. What ye think of that,
littl'un?"

"So this is the spot where the Mormonites are going to
build their temple. We heard about that back home."

"Wal, now, us Missourians have had a word or two to say
about them plans. Old Joseph Smith ain't around to make no

more prophecies, seeing as how he met his end in the Clay County Jailhouse. 'Fore he passed on, I heard tell he hung the wrath of God over all of Jackson County."

"Where 'bouts is Jackson County?" I asked, not wanting to be too close to the wrath of God, what with all I'd heard about it.

"Why, this here's it," he said, with a cackle. "Can't you see God's wrath all around ye?"

Jessie got us going again since the road had cleared somewhat and we moved away from my friendly informant. I mulled over what he'd said, but couldn't figure out whether he'd been funning me or not.

The crowds thinned out as we left the town proper, but there was still a lot of going and coming, and we never had the way to ourselves. Once when I looked back I thought I saw Mr. Garrett threading his horse between wagons. I couldn't be sure it was him, but I got the feeling that we were being followed for unknown reasons. I figured I'd better not tell Jessie or she'd take a bullwhip to him. She'd already said that neither man nor beast was going to keep her from her calling. Still, I'd of given a penny to know if he intended to make mischief for us, even though I wasn't too worried after the way we'd handled Hiram and Homer.

We got to the Indian Creek Campgrounds a little before sundown, and there must have been a few thousand campfires, all sending up streams of smoke and some of the best-smelling supper aromas it had been my pleasure to inhale.

"How in the world are we going to find the Donner camp amongst all these people?" I asked Jessie, for there were wagons upon wagons in every direction.

The wagons were big, top-heavy, covered contraptions that Lieutenant Frémont in his book called Conestogas. Some had red-dyed tops made from Osnaburg cloth; some were blue, more were white, but all were dirty and streaked with rain. Women screeched and yelled at their children, hitting out at them as they ran by. Horses milled around, dogs yapped, oxen lowed, and cows bawled. I thought to myself that no self-respecting Indian could bring himself to attack such a motley crew and felt a whole lot better about the dangers of the trail. At least as far as our red brethren were concerned.

"Mr. Donner said everybody would know where he's camped. It's pretty plain, Em, that he's a person of importance, which is no more than I expected the Lord to lead us to."

I rolled my eyes back in my head but made no answer. Mr. Donner was well-known, though, for the first lady we asked pointed out the general direction for us.

"Set down a spell," she urged, her tired face lit up with hospitality. "Whar ye folks from? Us, now, me and my ole man, and the youn'uns is from Illinoy. I got some stew here and only too happy to oblige ye with some supper. I declare, ye're a pretty little thang. Git on down off that mule and set with us awhile."

"Thank you, kindly, ma'am," Jessie said. "But the Donners are expecting us and we have to be getting on."

"Wal, ye're welcome anytime, ye hear?" she called after us. And she stood there watching us as we left. She had the same lonesome look on her face that the women in Caleb's Corner had. They all liked to have company and would just beg you to stay and eat and talk until it was hard to get away from them.

I saw her lean over and swat the backside of a child as he ran past her, like it was time he needed it. Then she turned back to her cook fire.

We rode through the camped wagons and it was almost as good as reading newsprint. Painted on the wagon covers were such interesting comments as "California or Nothing," "Never Say Die," and "Bring 'Em On." Some had a more poetic ring to them. One proclaimed "The Whole or None" and another cautioned "Patience and Perseverance." "Oregon or Bust My Gut" expressed one emigrant's stoutness of heart. All in all, it was a most stimulating view of the company we'd be traveling with.

Jessie stopped again to ask the way to the Donner campsite from a halfway clean-looking family, but the men and boys sidled up too close for my liking. They pointed toward the creek and we continued on.

As we rode into an area that had a more settled and

prosperous look to it, we saw tents pitched by the side of the wagons. I found out later that some of these people had been camped for almost two months waiting for the spring rains to stop and for the grass to start growing out on the prairie so the cattle wouldn't starve.

Down near the stream, under the trees that edged it, we found the Donner family. One look at their camp told me that maybe Jessie was right in saying that the Lord would provide for us. Their camp was far and away the neatest and cleanest of any we had passed on our way. I hoped we'd see Mr. Donner but he was nowhere in sight. I had the feeling that we'd arrived from town before him, and that meant that his lady wouldn't know us from Adam, or Eve as the case might be.

"Are you looking for someone?" asked a woman sitting on a rocking chair under a large tent. "Perhaps I can help you."

She was a most pleasant-looking woman, with a round, smiling face and a short, chubby body. Her eyes sparkled and she looked as if she took a lot of interest in anything and anybody that came her way. She gave me the feeling of wanting to drag my tired, wet, aching bones down from Red's back and crawl into her lap. It's funny how some people can affect you like that, but I'd not met many of them, so I didn't have too much trouble fighting down the impulse.

"We're looking for the Donner campsite, ma'am," Jessie said.

"Why, bless my soul, you've found it!" the lady said, putting down her sewing and walking out in the drizzle toward us. "I'm Tamsen Donner, Mrs. George Donner, that is. What can I do for you?" She smiled like our arrival was the nicest thing that had happened to her all day, and I found out later that that was the way she always was.

Jessie told her about meeting Mr. Donner in town and how he'd offered her a job, seeming somewhat abashed that we'd gotten there before he'd had time to tell his wife what he'd hired for her.

"Thank the Lord!" Mrs. Donner cried. "I surely do need help, what with five girls to mind. Get down off that mule, now. I know you're tired and hungry and soaked to the skin. Come on by the fire and dry off."

Those were welcome words to me, but so far nobody had said anything to me or about me. I just hoped that Mr. Donner understood that where Jessie went, I went too. So I tagged over by the fire and accepted a bowl of thick soup just like I belonged there. I figured if I kept quiet enough, nobody would bother with me.

"And what is your name, young man?" Mrs. Donner turned her smiling face to me just as I took a big mouthful of bread.

"This is my little—" Jessie started.

"My name is Em," I cut in. "Short for Emmett."

I didn't want to take any chances that Jessie would let the cat out of the bag. These folks were mighty kind, and they certainly looked decent enough. But you can't be too careful until you see how the wind blows.

"Yes, my brother, Emmett," Jessie said, giving me a skeptical look. I hoped she wasn't running the Commandments over in her mind, because there was one there that would cover this particular situation.

"I hope you'll be pleased with my work, Mrs. Donner," she went on. "I've had lots of experience looking after children, and teaching too. I only hope that something can be found for Em to do, so we can pay our own way to Oregon."

"Oh, so you're going to Oregon?" Mrs. Donner asked. "Well, now I hope you understand that we're going to California, but there will be many who will be turning off to Oregon. We'll all travel together for a good bit of the way, and if you'd like to stay with us till then, I'm sure we can find a nice family for you to go on with. And I'm sure Mr. Donner can find something for this little man to do." She smiled at me and I squirmed a little.

"Not going to Oregon?" Jessie seemed surprised that the Lord would so mishandle her plans. "But I thought the whole train was going there."

"No, no, my dear, but don't you worry. We'll look out for you and see that you have someone pleasant to travel on with.

I'm delighted to have you even for part of the trip, but wouldn't you consider going on to California with us?"

"Oh, no, ma'am," Jessie said. "I've had a call to the mission field in Oregon and I must follow the Lord's leading."

Tamsen Donner shook her head with a small sigh. "Well, my dear, you are very young to devote your life to the rigors of the mission field. I hope your calling is a true one."

"I know it is," Jessie said with that don't-tell-me-any-different tone. "Why, just look at the doors God has opened already. Em and I are here at Independence for the first time in our lives, and He has led us to you. And I know He will continue to hold us in the palm of His hand."

Jessie had a lot of faith, and so far, as she'd pointed out, the Lord hadn't let us down too bad. Mr. Donner rode up about that time on one of the finest horses this side of Virginia.

"Well, well," he said heartily, as he tied the horse to the end of the wagon. "So you found us! Mrs. Donner, do they meet with your approval?"

"Indeed they do!" I was glad to hear her say.

They made a handsome married couple, though it was clear that Mr. Donner had a wife some years younger than himself. I found out later that she wasn't his first one. He must have been all of Papa's age and she looked pretty near to Jessie's, but plump people age well, so I expect she was somewhat older than that. I'll have to say that Mr. Donner made a more corpulent figure than Papa ever had, but then Papa had been a hard-scrabble farmer, and Mr. Donner looked as if he'd never seen the back end of a mule.

"Now, about this young fellow," Mr. Donner said, turning to me. "What can you do to earn your passage west?"

"Oh, Em can do just about anything," Jessie said quickly. "He can help with the children, take them for walks, and just about anything."

I gave her a disgusted look, but before I could say anything Mr. Donner started laughing.

"Now that wouldn't do at all," he said. "A lad doesn't need to be tied down to women's work. I'll tell you what. I need a good hand to help my men with the livestock and horses.

But I especially need someone I can count on to take messages and run errands around the camp for me. We're going to be one of the biggest trains to ever leave Missouri, some three hundred wagons, it looks like. To keep that many people in touch with what's going on is going to be a big job. Think you can handle that, sir?"

"Yessir," I said, hardly able to believe my good fortune.

"I take it you can ride?" he asked.

"I can ride anything on four feet," I said, not daring to look at Jessie. She knew I'd never ridden anything on four feet except Red, but I figured if I could ride him, anything else would be a snap.

"Fine," Mr. Donner said. "We'll get you saddled up tomorrow, and from then on you'll be the official camp messenger. How's that?"

I grinned at him, for I could think of nothing finer for my particular talents. And all that I've just told about was the reason I came to be lying under a wagon on the edge of the Great Western Desert getting ready to take the Gospel to the heathen, who needed it worse than we did. I was beginning to think that the Lord God of Israel really was preparing a path unto our feet, like Jessie was always saying, for so far He had brought us unscathed through fearsome trials and hooked us up to some decent folk who could help me look out for Jessie. And if that Mr. Garrett really was on our trail, why I figured he'd back off once he found out we belonged somewheres.

7

I said in my haste, All men are liars.
—*Psalms 116:11*

It's a peculiar thing about families. I've taken the time to study a number of them and it wasn't too long ago that I discovered that our family wasn't like most of the ones I saw. For one thing, I never missed my mother until I met Mrs. Donner. I didn't even remember my mother until I met Mrs. Donner. There was something about that lady's wide lap and ample bosom that kept me thinking about how it would feel to curl up next to her. She even tried to hug me close every now and then, but I remembered I was a boy and not supposed to like it. That wasn't too hard to do, seeing as how I was unaccustomed to having hands laid on me, except on the occasions when I'd been slow to fill the woodbox or to draw water from the well.

Jessie used to hold me in her lap while she rocked by the fire, but it never seemed to work out. Oh, she had an ample bosom, all right, like mothers are supposed to have, but her lap was nothing to write home about. Too narrow and bony for real comfortable resting, and besides, I soon got too big to feel right about it. Papa wasn't the kind of man who would let on how he felt except when he was mad, and there was no mistaking his feelings then. I missed him, too, and somehow missing him got all mixed up with somebody else, just like missing my mama got mixed up with Mrs. Donner.

The Donners were people of the first quality, even the five daughters, and it was hard not to wish that I had been born one of them and really belonged to all of them. It even crossed my mind that maybe something had happened when I'd come along so that the Donners had had to give me away. I kept thinking how glad they would be if they found out I was their long-lost baby girl, all grown up now and smart enough to make them proud. But then I'd start worrying about how to fit Jessie into the picture and, since it didn't seem likely that they would've given away two baby girls, I gave it up.

Anyway, maybe it was better the way it was. If I'd been born one of them, I might've been like the Donner girls, and they didn't share my ideas of what makes life interesting and worth the living. They were more polite and dainty in their doings than I ever had it in me to be. Which is only natural, seeing as how they had never had to worry about crop failures, drought, hard winters, headstrong sisters, dead fathers, or what they were going to eat next. The fact is, they were as docile and easy to get along with as a pack of hounds fed too many table scraps.

They were as much alike as five peas in a pod. And except for their ages—the oldest one being about my age, give or take a year or two—you could hardly tell one from the other. I tried to get Lizzy to walk around the camp with me to see what was going on, but she acted like I'd brought up something indecent, so I left her to the embroidery hoop after that. None of them had much get-up-and-go. They hung around their mama, getting their hair combed and plaited, or pressing wildflowers in a book, or some other such domestic activity. For myself, I'd rather watch a rousing game of euchre any day than spend my time making French knots and chain stitches.

Speaking of euchre, Mr. Donner didn't mind taking a hand now and again, but he wasn't much of a sporting man. He did it more to be sociable than to win anything, which goes against the aim of the game, to my way of thinking. And he was sociable. The fact is, I never saw him mad too often, considering the fact that when we finally got on the trail he had more than enough aggravation. People liked him because he was friendly and remembered to ask about their wives and sick babies. They looked up to him, too, rightly figuring that anybody who was as prosperous as he was had to be pretty smart. I've found, as a rule, that most folks put a lot of stock in those who have a hefty share of this world's goods. But you'll notice that they're the very ones who'll shout "Amen" when a preacher starts talking about how hard it is for a rich man to get through the gates of heaven.

Once folks got away from stores and farms and banks, though, their thinking changed. Out on the trail, men who could turn a dollar in any trade just wasn't worth a hill of beans when everybody was burnt out from the sun, the dust, and the alkali, and when mountain fever took hold of their babies, and when Indians were totting up our livestock.

It was then that I discovered that the amount of this world's goods a man had wasn't worth anything if there was no water and no food and no safety to buy. Folks began, then, to admire and respect men they wouldn't have looked twice at on the streets of Independence.

Which brings me to somebody that I would've noticed anywhere in the world and he didn't have two coppers to rub together.

The way I met him was after I'd wandered along the creek looking for a place far enough away from the camp to let my britches down in private. I had just come out of a canebrake when I just about tripped over what I thought was a crusty old log sticking out of a clump of bushes.

I put my foot on it and considered giving it a kick to see the dusty powder fly out. Just as I pushed at it, it moved by itself and a rumbling snarl came out of the thicket. I jumped like I'd been stung and my first thought was that I'd stumbled onto a grizzly.

"What in tarnation air astandin' on my laig?" The bushes parted and I found myself looking eye-to-eye at the most interesting specimen of humanity it had been my fortune to run into up to that point.

His black, greasy hair hung down around his face and a red scar zigzagged its way across his left eye, making the eyelid droop like he was winking at me. The lower part of his face was covered with a growth of beard that stood in need of lye soap and water. What part of his face I could see was even browner than mine, and after discarding the thought of a grizzly, I considered the possibility that he was an Indian of some kind. But then I saw the gray eyes, one looking straight at me, and the other half glinting from under the sagging lid. They both looked red and puffy, as if they'd put in more than their usual share of work the night before.

My suspicions were confirmed when he suddenly opened his mouth and yawned so wide his jaws creaked. I got a gust of stale whiskey from his breath that was so strong I had to stagger back against a sapling for support.

"Wal, young'un, cat got yore tongue?" he asked, smearing his hand across his face.

"Nossir," I said, standing out of breathing range.

"Name's Mego Cobb, formerly of Virginny, latterly of the Rocky Mountains," he said, friendly as a neighbor. He stood then, lumbering up out of the thicket and stretching himself with another yawn, which scorched the leaves off two willows leaning over the creek.

He was tall, with a lean, wiry kind of frame that looked able to do most any kind of work he wanted it to do. He had on a red calico shirt that was laced with rawhide to hold it together in front, and around his midsection he had a bright multicolored sash that seemed to be a stashing place for all sorts of curiosities. I could see the carved hilt of a knife, the handle of a pistol, the revolving sort, I believe, and something else that had a heathenish look to it.

Excepting a few quality gentlemen, no one in our company was noted for sartorial elegance, but this apparition was in a class of his own—sui generis was what Colonel Russell later called him and almost got his throat cut for it. His buckskin britches were black and shiny with grease, tight-fitting on the limbs, but loose and baggy in the seat. Down the seam of each leg ran a straggly fringe of rawhide strips, some shorter than others and some missing all together. And on his feet he wore what could've only been real, honest-to-God Indian moccasins.

All in all, and taking into consideration the effluvia of grease, woodsmoke, tobacco, and old whiskey that floated around him like a cloud, he offered the most exciting possibilities for my continuing education in human nature I'd yet seen.

"What's yorn?" he asked, squatting on his heels to look closer at me.

"Huh?" I asked like a dunce. My mind was racing so fast to take in every bit of him that I couldn't free it enough to get a firm hold on what he was saying.

"Somethin' ailin' ye, chile?" he asked, looking concerned. "Somethin' ole Mego kin he'p ye with?"

"Nossir," I said, trying for a better impression than I'd made up to then and saying the first thing to enter my head. "It's just that I've never seen a pair of real Indian moccasins before."

"Wal, ye like 'em, do ye now?" he said, like he was pleased I'd noticed something he liked too. "I'll tell ye, these hyar moccasins war handmade by the sweetest little woman a man ever took to his blanket. Yessir, thar ain't no squaw like a Snake squaw. Shoshoni, she war, an' pretty as a pitcher, an' handy around a lodge. Real handy, that 'un war. This chile war too sorry to see her go, but she got a hankerin' atter her own folks an' when two lodgepolin's wouldn't keep her home, I jes' give up an' let her go. But these hyar moccasins keeps me in mind of her, fer she war good at sech like."

I didn't know at the time that Mego Cobb was considered by most to be a man of few words. "Taciturn" was what Mr. Donner called him, but not in his hearing. But with me he started talking almost from the minute we met and kept it up as long as I knew him. I never met a man who had so much to say, and although a grain of salt was required every now and then, not one bit of it was ever wasted on me.

"Air ye one o' them emigraters?" he asked.

"Yessir, my sister and me are hired on to Mr. George Donner."

"Wal, split my hide fer Californy!"

"Nossir, we're going to Oregon. Leastways, I hope we are, but it looks like we're hooked up with a bunch of amateurs in the emigrating business. Have you ever been that far west?"

"I tellee now, this chile have sot traps fer beaver all over them Shinin' Mountains, acussin' ever' Injun atween the Heely an' Bayou Salade. An' ain't I seed some sights!"

"What about the Indians, Mr. Mego," I asked, "do you think we'll have trouble with them?"

"Naw," he said, shaking his head and feeling for his pipe fixings. "Ye jes' have to know what goes on in them varmints' headpieces, which I'm hyar to tellee, ain't much 'sides thievin' hosses and beggin' foofaraw, with a leetle sculp-takin' throwed in when they jump ye onexpected like."

"Scalp-taking?" I repeated, swallowing hard and clamping my hat tighter on my head.

"Aw, thar ain't nothin' fer ye to be afeerd of. Jes' keep yore eyes skinned an' yore ears picked an' yore Green River to the ready. Lookee hyar now," he said, drawing out a wickedly sharp knife from his sash.

"This hyar's a genuwine Green River knife an' by grannies if it ain't seed some doin's. Why, I recollect the time I were in Montaner atrappin' the Marias, which ye'll acknowledge war Blackfoot country. Them's devils, too, an' ain't no mistakin' em fer nothing else. Wal, thar I was, santerin' 'long a canyon mindin' my own business, when Bug's Boys come ascreechin' right onter me. I'll acknowledge I felt streaked, an' cold sweat broke out all over me fer they war aimin' to make meat of this chile. Thar warn't no way out of that canyon, fer when I turned to make tracks backard, hyar come another troupe of 'em, yellin' an' screechin' an' shakin' their lances, an', I swan, if I didn't say to myself, 'Wal, ole Mego,' sez I, 'ye're agoin' under this time, fer they got ye hemmed in tighter an' a redbug in a itchin' place.'"

"How'd you get out?"

"Wal, it jes' galled me to pitcher my hair ahangin' in some Blackfoot lodge, an' I says hit's time fer this beaver to be movin' fer yon buttes. So, I pulled this hyar sculp-taker, fer I didn't have time to prime my rifle atter the first shot 'cause they war on me. One swipe with my Green River give me breathin' room, so this chile taken a deep breath an' made one jump clean outta my moccasins, landin' atop the canyon an' arunnin' like a gutshot buffler war araisin' my shirt with his horns! 'Hyar's fer high timber!' yells I, to the tune of Comanche take the hindmost."

"And you got away from them?"

"Sartain I did!" he declared. "I clum a mountain with only my bare hands and bare feet. I sot up thar an' watched them buzzards make medicine, fer they ain't never seed the likes of this chile afore. Then they went off with my mule an' counted theirselves lucky fer it too."

"What do they look like, Mr. Mego?" I asked, wanting to get as much information as I could before the time came to use it. "Are they really red-skinned?"

"Naw, they ain't no redder than you nor me. They're jes' kindy brownlike. Folks is knowed fer givin' addlepated names to whut they don't know nuthin' about. Why, I ain't never seed a Nez Percé with ary hole in his nose neither, an' ever' Flathead Injun I seed had a head round as a bilyard ball. An' I tellee somethin' else, I ain't never seed a Blackfoot with feet any dirtier than the rest of him. Seed a lot of Blackfeet without no noses, howsomever. Squaws, them war, without a nose on their face. They's bad about cuttin' off noses on squaws. They don't like loose women and wouldn't put up with it atall. Didn't stop them squaws, though. Guess they figgured oncet the nose war gone they mought as well warm a blanket as not.

"Now I ponder on it, young'un," he continued, peering straight at me. "Whar'd ye git that brown skin and them black eyes?"

"My papa said my ma was a Creek, or close to one."

"Wal, he ort to knowed," he said. He sat down then, crossing his legs in front of him with a power of creaks and groans and mutters of "rheumatiz."

"Puts me in mind of the time I war trappin' up beyon' Jackson Hole in the winter of '35. That war a bad 'un. Cold, I ain't never seed the like. Wal, my hoss had done up an' let the Crows run off with him an' I war ahightailin' it to camp whar Ole Gabe Bridger an' Tom Fitzpatrick war cached awaitin' fer me. I come to this hyar creek what war plum froze over, or so's I thought. An' I sez, 'Mego, hyar's two hours saved by crossin' on the ice.' So, off I goes, an', by grannies, if that ice warn't thinner than I thought, fer next I knowed, I war in the water, acoughin' an' asputterin' an' the ice ajabbin' at my Adam's apple. An' I says, 'Mego, this time yore a goner, sartain!' 'Bout that time I heerd this awful crashin' an' commotion in the bushes on the bank an' hyar come this great roan hoss with a leetle Injun boy on his back, arunnin' fit to kill. He rared back his head an' taken a leap over that creek, headin' fer high country. 'Wal,' says I, 'hyar's onexpected beaver!' An' I reached up an' ketched hold of his tail as he jumped over me. Outta that ice come I like mules in a stampede! Now, I'll acknowledge I war weaker 'an a goat on short rations an' I figgured a leetle run would loosen up my laigs, so I jes' clamped down harder on that hoss's tail an' he run me up and down them mountains fer three whole days."

"Didn't you get tired?" I asked, beginning to wonder if Mr. Cobb was familiar with the Ninth Commandment.

"Tard! This chile war plum wore down to a nubbin," he said, as solemn as a preacher. "I'd a dropped off two days afore if I could've let go, but, I'll be fly-blown if my hands hadn't afroze onto that tail an' warn't nothin' I could do but keep arunnin'. Attar a while, when I couldn't run no more, I taken my knife and disrelocated that tail so's I could drop by the wayside. I swan, it war so cold, it took I and my pards the whole winter to melt them hoss hairs offa my hands. But, I tellee this, Injun boys no higher 'an a hoppergrass has always been good medicine fer this chile. Ole Mego needs a *compañero* hyar in these civilized doin's."

He grinned then, showing tobacco-stained teeth, and I smiled back at my new *compañero*.

"Feelin' wolfish?" he asked.

"Sir?"

"Peckish, then?"

"Huh?"

"Hongry!" he yelled up close to my ear. "Air ye hongry?"

"Oh, yessir, I could eat."

"Wal, let's go find some meat, fer I could eat a buffler turnin' green, though I ain't likely to find sech eatin' round hyar."

He put his hand on my shoulder as we walked toward the camp. I was wondering what Jessie would do when she heard that the Flathead Indians weren't any more deformed than the rest of the heathen. She was likely to be real tore up over it.

"Now, don't ye go afrettin' over bein' a mite deef," Mego said, patting me on the back. "Ole Mego'll watch out fer ye."

ᶑ

Ye blind guides, who strain at a gnat, and swallow a camel.
—*Matthew 23:24*

We headed back toward the camp brushing through the
reeds and hanging branches of the willows that grew by
the creek. I was drenched by the rain still dripping from the
leaves, even though the clouds had begun to move away. Mego
Cobb moved like a pointer dog nosing in on a covey of birds,
each foot carefully and deliberately put right down where he
wanted it to go. At the same time he covered the ground so
fast that I had to take three strides to his one.

When we got back to camp I could tell that something
was going on. Men stood around in groups, some talking earnestly while others listened, or, here and there as we passed, a
man would talk to one group for a minute, offering his hand
to be shaken, then he'd move on to another group.

Most of the men were silent, looking around as if they
hadn't a thought in their heads, studying the clouds and nodding.
Yet I could tell by the way some of them worked the tobacco
in their mouths and by the deliberate way they expectorated
that they were thinking hard and seriously on some matter.

The womenfolk weren't bothered at all. Fires burned in
front of every tent and beside every wagon, for suppers have to
be cooked come hell or high water, for which expression Jessie
would've tanned my hide. But it's the truth. Whenever there's
any kind of trouble, sickness or death or money matters, I've
noticed that the ladies solve it by stoking up a fire and putting
on beans and cornbread. I've seen it time and again. "Eat, and
you'll feel better" or "You've got to put something in your
stomach" or "You have to keep up your strength," they'll say.
I sometimes wonder if grown women haven't gotten their brains

and their stomachs mixed up and think that a bowl of stew is a good substitute for a few minutes of reasonable cogitation.

While the women cooked and the children chased each other over wagon tongues, the men gathered and talked and argued and speechified. The smoke from more than a hundred fires hung heavy in the still air, seeming to threaten more rain, which we certainly didn't need.

As we walked toward the Donner camp in like agreement as to the most likely place for a bite to eat, I learned the subject under discussion.

"Wal," one man said as we passed by, "I ain't votin' fer no Missouri Puke."

"We have to have a man everybody'll look up to, one that can command," somebody else pleaded.

"It's every man for himself, I say."

"No, no, Brother, when we get to Indian Territory, we have to show our strength."

"Did you hear about them Mormonites?" one man asked another. "They're arming ten thousand men to avenge the massacre of Joseph Smith. And they got five brass pieces with 'em too."

"Ye don't say!"

"That ain't nothing. I heerd at Colonel Noland's Tavern that they's British agents amongst the Kansa, stirrin' 'em up to kill ever' emigrant that tries fer Oregon. They aim to keep the whole territory fer themselves."

"Them English has got to be stopped. Oregon belongs to the States just as much as to them. And I say, oncet we get it filled up with settlers, it'll all be ours."

"Wal, we beat that crew twicet already, boys. We kin do it agin if we have to. Soon as President Polk settles on the line, we kin make it stick. And ye kin put money on it."

"The Mexicans're getting riled up too. They don't want any more emigrants coming in to California."

"General Scott will settle their hash, friend. There's already an army gathering in Texas aiming to push on to the Pacific."

A voice of oratorical authority boomed from the back of a wagon at a cluster of farmers below him. "It's the destiny of this great nation of the United States of America to possess the land from sea to sea. Nobody can stop us, neither Mormon nor British nor Spaniard nor Indian. President Polk, with God to lead him, will see that we have it. And, gentlemen, we're in the forefront of a great emigrating movement that's going to open up the West!" He received a smattering of applause and a few "Hear, hear's."

"I say hit's up to the guv'ment to help us. What we need is sojers to go along with us till we get to Californy."

I could hear the same arguments, conclusions, and fears from every group we passed. It sounded like the whole country was taking up arms to fight enemies from without and from within.

"Ye shore kin get a eddication, jes' santerin' along, can't ye, young'un?" Mego said with a smile.

"Does any of it worry you, Mr. Mego? It sounds like the whole of England and Mexico, with the Mormonites and the Indians thrown in for good measure, are going to be after this one train of emigrants."

"Naw," he said, brushing a fly away from his beard. "Don't worry yoreself none. Long as I got Bloomin' Betsy, the rifle I took offa Suckaree Sam, and a possible bag full of Galena pills, thar ain't a Mex nor a Britisher that'll come near ye. As fer Brigham Young, he's got his hands full feedin' the bellies of all them wives to be aworryin' over this hyar cavyard."

I felt better after hearing that, for I'd already decided that Mego Cobb knew more of what lay beyond the Missouri River than all the men in our camp put together. It seemed that each family had a copy of either Lieutenant Frémont's *Report on the Expedition to the Rocky Mountains* or Mr. Lansford W. Hastings' *Emigrants' Guide to Oregon and California*, which they read from at the drop of a hat and trusted as if the words were Holy Writ. They traced the pages with thick, gnarled fingers and repeated what they'd learned to their neighbors just like they'd gotten the message straight from the Pathfinder himself.

Now, even though I'm a great believer in what can be learned from books, it seemed to me that in a case like this,

firsthand experience would count for a lot more than what
somebody had written in a book that he wanted to sell. I've
even heard preachers say that you can't get to heaven with a
wet finger. In other words, as Pastor Clemmons used to say,
turning the pages of a book won't do you much good if you
don't use a little common sense along with it.

And walking right along beside me was a thirty-third-
degree mountain man who had been to California and Oregon,
who knew the Indians on the personal side, who could find his
way in the dark, and not one person asked his opinion. Fact is,
they acted like he wasn't even around. It was a pure waste of
human talent, if you ask me.

When we got to the Donner wagons we found another
group of men discussing the same subject, which I had now
learned was the election of a captain for the train. That was
why there had been several men going from group to group,
shaking hands and holding forth in that modest, yet earnest
way in which some politicians offer themselves, like they were
lambs, willing to lay aside their own concerns and go to the
altar for the public good.

Politics has always been a matter of curiosity to me. Papa
had taken me in to Jefferson City before he took sick, which
was in the spring of '45. We'd heard several speakers on the
courthouse steps talking, or, rather, bellowing, their heads off
about the virtues of James A. Polk, the Democratic nominee
and Senator Henry Clay, the Whiggish one. From the way the
orators had to strain to make their points, faces red and sweating,
and chests heaving to get enough breath for declaiming, I wouldn't
of given two cents for any of the candidates. It seems to me
that if a man is worth electing President, the people doing the
electioneering oughtn't to have to work so hard to prove it.

It turned out that James A. Polk won the election and
mostly because there were men all over the Republic just like
the ones in our train. None of them liked the idea of two other
countries standing between us and the Pacific Ocean. And, besides that, Mr. Polk had God on his side, because a lot of sermons
were preached on Deuteronomy 31: 6, 7, and 8, which told us

Americans just what to do. It's a source of wonderment to me how the Scriptures can almost always help out when you want something bad enough.

The fact of the matter is that the election of a wagon-train captain was just as monumental as the election of a President. He was supposed to be in complete charge of everything and have the final say-so in all decisions, keeping in mind the welfare of every member of the company. Any man who could get the cooperation of that many Democrats, Whigs, Freethinkers, and Baptists would have to have some saintly qualities mixed in with a goodly amount of righteous anger to whip them all into line. But we didn't have another Moses among us.

Mrs. Donner welcomed Mego Cobb to her cooking fire just as warmly as she had taken in Jessie and me. We sat under a tent flap and ate the stew she dished up, listening to the men talking over the election.

Mr. Jacob Donner, Mr. George's uncle, had walked over, and it seemed to me that the two of them were doing more listening than talking. Mr. George Reed, a quiet man, was there, and so was Mr. Patrick Breen, who kept interrupting the one doing the talking.

The talkative one said, "We need a man who has experience in leading others. Experience is what counts." Colonel William H. Russell was a man who could talk about himself without once mentioning his own name. He cut a fine figure, with his broad-brimmed panama and pointed beard.

Colonel Russell was a powerful and wonderfully expressive speaker, and I could tell he had a lot of experience in political matters. He orated at the two Mr. Donners, Mr. Reed, and Mr. Breen like they were a whole crowd of people. It didn't seem to matter to him how few or how many listeners he had. The fact is, he took to speechifying like it was an ailment he'd been born with and couldn't get rid of. He had my vote if I had one to give, which I didn't.

Mego Cobb ate his stew, stabbing chunks of meat with his knife until it was down to the liquid, which he then drained like it was coffee in a cup. He seemed to take no notice of the conversations going on around us. He leaned back, picking his teeth with a straw, and looked about ready for a snooze.

"Now, you all know that I was appointed a colonel of the U.S. Army by Henry Clay himself, and I don't mind saying I'm proud of the honor, for besides being the most powerful man in Washington, the senator is a bosom friend of mine," Colonel Russell declared, as everybody around him nodded in agreement.

"Not that there aren't others here with more abilities than I possess," he went on. "Any of you gentlemen could do the job more than adequately. However, it seems to me that you'll have your hands full with your own families and might prefer to leave the care and guidance of the train in other hands. Now, I only have my good lady to look after, and even though her health is none too good, I can honestly say that I will give my full attention to the needs of others."

Colonel Russell went on in that vein for a while, then after shaking hands and complimenting Mrs. Donner on the strength of her coffee, he moved on to spread the word of his availability to the rest of the men. I watched him pick his way along the muddy lane between the wagons, lifting his hat to the ladies as he passed by.

Mr. George Donner shook hands with his uncle and Mr. Reed and Mr. Breen, then he came to the fire, where Mrs. Donner presented him to Mego Cobb. I'll say this for Mr. Donner; he pulled up a stool, took a cup of coffee from his wife, and commenced to visit with Mego as if there wasn't a lick of difference between the two of them. He questioned Mego carefully about his experiences on the trail and in the Rocky Mountains; he asked about the Indian situation, and discussed how long it would take to get to Fort Laramie, which would be the first place we would resupply the train.

"Mr. Cobb," Mr. Donner said, after listening for a while, "it seems to me that we could use a man of your abilities and knowledge. Would you consider lending us the benefit of your experience as we travel? The offer is, of course, subject to approval by the captain, whoever he might be."

Mego lifted his hat and scratched his head. "I'll have to

cogitate on that, friend. Don't know as I keer to take on so many talkified city folk. Mought be this chile kin put his oar in now and agin, howsomever."

Mr. Donner smiled at this sideways agreement and shook Mego's hand. Hiring Mego Cobb was about the smartest thing Mr. Donner did, but at the very time he needed his advice the most, he didn't take it.

That night after supper all the men gathered on the bank of the creek to hold the election. All, that is, except Mego Cobb, who stretched out on the ground under a tree some ways away from the crowd. I found a spot of moss beside him, which kept my britches about as dry as a mud puddle would've done.

Mego took his pipe and a twist of tobacco out of his possible bag and began to fix a smoke. We could see the shadows of the men in the light of the flares around the speaker's podium, which was somebody's trunk. We listened to one speaker after another offer himself as a leader of the people and as a fitting receptacle of the public trust.

After arguing, testifying, orating, cursing, praying for the Lord's guidance, and finally voting, they settled on Colonel Russell, the bosom friend of Henry Clay.

"That'un will mean trouble," Mego said from around his pipe.

"I know Colonel Russell doesn't know beans about Oregon or California, seeing as how he's never been to either place, but I don't know that anybody else could do any better," I said.

"Ye hit that nail square on the head," he agreed. "But I got me a feelin' about this hyar cavyard of emigraters. And this chile don't ever disrelocate his feelin's. Saved this ole sculp many a time. Yessir, thar's too many cooks awantin' to stir the stew. Don't like it atall, neither."

I wondered if I'd missed anything during the election, but the arguments and disagreements seemed common enough to me. Folks in Missouri conducted their business in the same contentious manner, whether it was of a political, commercial, or doctrinal nature. Since Mego was from Virignia, he probably had never seen the way we did things.

I heard Jessie calling me to come to bed, so I said my good-

byes to Mego. He told me not to let the bedbugs bite so I wouldn't
have to scratch all day tomorrow. I scuffed along toward the
Donner wagons, soaking up stray ends of talk and arguments
as I went. I purely hated to go to bed when just about everybody
else was still up and doing.

I rounded the back of one of Mr. Donner's big wagons on
the way to the tent Jessie shared with three of the little Donner
girls. It still felt strange not to scrooch up to her back on a chilly
night, but being stuck in a temporary opposite gender, I had to
sleep in a bedroll under a wagon nearby. It wouldn't do for me
to crawl in with the ladies, but I always let Jessie know I was
going to bed so she wouldn't worry about me or come looking
for me with fire in her eyes.

A sudden small glow of light on the edge of the campsite
pulled me up short. It faded out almost as soon as I saw it, so
I stayed real still to see what was coming next. Another warm
glow lit up the tilt of a familiar hat, and I knew it was that
Mr. Garrett from Independence smoking a Mexican cigarillo
over in the dark. My heart thudded for a minute or two while
I decided if I was scared enough to raise a racket and flush him
out to explain himself. Then it came to me that if he was up
to no good, he sure wouldn't be announcing his presence like
he was doing. I had half a mind to go over there and ask him
what he wanted, but then I remembered how he'd put his hand
on a particular part of me, which he'd taken for male anatomy,
and I felt so funny that I couldn't do it. So I looked around to
see if I could tell what had drawn him to this place, and there
against the tent wall was Jessie's form outlined and backlit by
a lantern.

"Confound it all," I said to myself, "I should've known."

A Journal of Westward Travel

BY

Jessie Elizabeth Heath

May, 14, 1846: This bodes to be one of our last nights at Indian Creek & more rain threatens. Already the spring has been wetter than usual and, if they needed further assurance, the farmers among us take the rainy planting season as a Sign that the westward path they have chosen is the right one.

For myself, there have been other signs, which have descended from the Power that is over us all. Our fortuitous encounter with Mr. Geo. Donner on the streets of Independence, the warmth of our reception by Mrs. D, and the security of traveling with a large train assure me that the path we have taken is watched over by those Eyes that travel to & fro over the earth seeking those whom He can help.

I am ever mindful of his Care, for in all ways He makes his Presence known. On our journey from home we were accosted by two Servants of Satan, with hearts filled with evil, yet I had no fear, for I knew that the Lord God would not have called us to serve among the heathen in Oregon only to stop us not twenty miles from whence we started. Indeed, he thrust a Rod and a Staff into my hands to comfort me.

I pray daily for contriteness of heart and humility of spirit, even as I pray for his continued Guidance and Protection. I pray also that he will ever make us mindful of his Bounty toward us, & that Emma Louise will learn some sense. She has taken up with a ruffian of the lowest order, one that looks and speaks like the Heathen that I am convinced he is. This association can only serve her ill, for Mr. Cobb has no refinement of mind nor grace of deportment. Her lessons suffer greatly from neglect, for she constantly seeks his company, seeming to prefer his ill usage of the English language to the study of the *McGuffey Reader, the Fifth Eclectic Primer*. It is to my sorrow that I do not seem to have the time to supervise her studies. If only she had the agreeable nature of the Donner daughters, who spend their days in the pursuit of knowledge. Lizzy reads to her sisters from the pilgrimage of *Childe Harold*, of which Emma Louise says our pilgrimage is of greater interest. The Donner girls botanize with zeal, pressing flowers and leaves between pages, of which Emma Louise says they could better spend the time learning their medicinal virtues. The girls work some time each day on their Samplers, of which what Emma Louise says would not bear repeating. She is a source of constant anxiety to me, for I fear that the ill-mannered company she keeps will serve to harden her in the ways of the world and, as she is headstrong by nature, she doesn't need more help in that direction. I fear also that I erred in suggesting she don Male Attire & present herself in such a guise, for it has only served to make her less amenable to my guidance. But O, she is all that is left of our dear family, & a great comfort to me withal. I must not desist without being fair to Mr. Cobb. He does seem to watch out for her & enjoy her company. I asked him yesterday if he minded having her around and he said, "No more'n I mind boudins from fat cow," or some such outlandish remark, which did not enlighten me at all.

May 16: I must not fail to mention the Diversity of peoples that are represented in our party, for this journal is to serve as a lifelong memento of our westward trek. Mr. D says we are undoubtedly the largest and best-equipped train to strike out from Independence since the first wagons crossed the Rocky Mountains in 1843. We total some three hundred wagons & are like a small town on wheels with almost all professions & trades represented. There is Dr. Bryant for our medical needs, both Mr. Donners, uncle and nephew, represent the grocery and dry-goods trade, and Mr. Reed, the manufacture of furniture. Most of our party are farmers, but craftsmen and mechanics like blacksmiths, wheelwrights, tanners, and gunsmiths are among us. The professions of the Law, Journalism, Eduation, & the Ministry of the Gospel are represented as well.

Most are God-fearing men who have sold all they own for the opportunity of opening a new country before the English take it over. There is great suspicion of the Hudson's Bay Company, for it has already laid claim to some of the best land in Oregon, making many emigrants the more anxious to get there. The women among us, wives, mothers, even grandmothers, speak with longing of homesteads and families left behind, yet not one has murmured against their men in this matter. I can only wish that they had the call to the Heathen as I have, for then they could go forward without a backward glance.

Emma Louise & I are leaving only a few graves on a Missouri hillside, so there is nothing and no one to hold us from the pursuit of our call. I think often of Papa & of how his strength and knowledge would aid us. I dreamt of him last night.

May 18: God has bestowed many blessings upon us, & as a further Sign of his Favor he has sent one of his own amongst us. This morning The Reverend Thomas Green joined our company. He is what might be called the general administrator of the Whitman Mission in Waiilatpu, Oregon. His duties consist of the spiritual leadership to the station members as well as to the Cayuse Indians, whom he is also instructing in the benefits of farming and the discipline of an ordered & humble life. He is also responsible for reporting to the American Board of Commissioners on the progress of the mission, and it is from the fulfillment of this last-named duty that he now returns.

He tells me that the primary thrust of the Mission is to the Cayuse Indians & not to the Flat Head tribe at all. I wonder if I have failed to heed a Sign from the Lord & thus have taken a wrong turn somewhere. But I fear it is too late & shall go forward with the knowledge that He will direct me to the place He has prepared for me.

May 19: Spent the day preparing for the morrow, the day our journey begins. There is great excitement among us, for truly we seek a land promised to us. Much evidence of dissension among us. Colonel Russell, our able leader, has been in constant demand to settle arguments between those who feel ill-used. It is clear that not everyone can be first in line and that our leaders have settled the matter most democratically. We will travel in rotation. That is, the lead wagon will drop back to the end of the train each day & the furthermost wagon will progress up until the head is reached. It seems most fair to me, but there are some who will always put themselves first, regardless of the injustice to others. There is much dissatisfaction. Yet I carry the Light of the glorious Gospel to those in Outer Darkness, & nothing shall divert my steps.

The Reverend Green has decreed a prayer and praise meeting at first light on the morrow, in order to start our westward journey with the blessing of God. I commend our souls into the Care of him who is able to guide and protect us, & pray that I will not be unworthy of the Holy Mission to which I am called.

9

Ye shall not afflict any widow or fatherless child.
—*Exodus 22:22*

Lordamercy, what a mess. Our first day out of Independence and we made all of six miles toward Oregon, or Paradise as some called it. I'd always wondered why it took Moses forty years to get the Israelites to the Promised Land and now I knew. If he had to put up with the contentiousness and the argumentation and downright vile tempers that were displayed among us, it's a wonder he made as good a time as he did.

What happened was this. First off, the men had drawn lots the night before to determine each wagon's place in the line, but the luck of the draw didn't suit the losers. So, before half the teams were hitched, Mr. Abernathy declared he was a suck-egg dog if he was going to travel amid such confusion and he turned back. The next thing that happened was that the Reverend Thomas H. Green, who'd just joined us and who acted like he knew more than anybody else, insisted on having a prayer meeting before the train pulled out and wouldn't be swayed on the matter. This created a stir that delayed us till late in the morning, for all the ladies and a few of the men wanted some praying done over them, but a lot of others wanted to get an early start. What was so bad about it was that half the mule teams and ox spans had been bought practically unseen and entirely unbroken. So there was Brother Green exhorting us to kneel and pray, and the ladies trying to get the wagons packed, and the men cursing and swearing and damning to hell every ox, mule, and crooked trader between the Missouri and the Ohio.

When we finally began to move out the last wagons in line got mired to the hubs in mud churned up by the first ones.

Then the ones in front had to stop and pull them out. All told, forty years to get to Oregon didn't seem unreasonable, since we put six miles behind us on the first day and had only seventeen some-odd hundred more stretching out in front.

But we got across the Missouri River and headed down the old Santa Fe Trail, which was somewhat of a surprise to me. I wasn't too knowledgeable on geography, but I wondered if we weren't going a little out of the way.

Mr. Donner assigned a little gray horse named Polly for my use and she was just as anxious as I was to be on the move. I saw ole Red rambling around amongst the other loose stock and he looked close to being frisky. I guess it was the first springtime of his life that didn't come attached to a plow.

I spent some time the first day riding up and down the length of the train keeping Mr. Donner informed of any trouble, which kept Polly and me right busy. There were always loose packs tumbling out of wagons, or wheels rolling off, or some other delay-causing accident. Polly gave out before I did, for three hundred or so wagons strung out a mile long and a mile wide made for several lengthy jaunts. We finally settled down to plod alongside Mego on his rangy bay.

"Pore doin's," he announced, turning around to survey our company. "Reckon if this bunch makes it to Fort Laramie, hit'll stupify this chile. Never seed so many know-it-alls and jes' plain cussedness in my borned days, an' I've seed Blackfeet what beat all till I run into this hyar conglomeration."

"Come again?"

"Plum foolishness," he muttered through his beard. "Why, lad, ever' man jack of 'em has a rifle primed fer Mormonites! Gonna blow somebody to smithereens if they ain't keerful."

"I thought it was Indians they're worried about."

"Pshaw," he said, squirting tobacco juice between his horse's ears to land three feet in front of us. "Don't have to worry none about Injuns till we git to the Platte an' likely not then."

"But Mr. Reed said the Kansa and the Pawnee would be on us as soon as we cross the Big Blue."

"Thievin' beggars is all they is." He dismissed them with another well-aimed squirt. "They ain't dangers onless ye turn yore back on 'em. Don't fret none about them kind. Most dangers thang now is a store clerk with a primed rifle in his hands and a onwarranted scare on him. Makes this hyar ole back feel sorta nekkid-like. An' 'sides that, hit makes ever' man thank he knows whut's best fer ever'body else when he's got a gun in his hands. This chile don't like it none atall."

I mulled this gloomy utterance over and then said, "Well, sir, if you don't mind me asking, why is it that you're traveling with us?"

"Hit's like this, littl'un," he told me as he hooked a long leg over the saddle horn. "Thar's a brace of orphans what mought need a leetle extry keer. Know what the Good Book has to say 'bout orphans an' sech?"

I grinned at him, for I knew it had plenty to say on the subject, and it was gratifying to know that a man of Mr. Cobb's qualifications took the matter seriously. Then I decided that if that was the reason he was traveling with us, I might as well enlist him to help me look after Jessie. There was no use in taking on a task single-handed if you didn't have to, so I plunged in.

"Mr. Cobb?"

"Mego, lad. I ain't answered to no Mr. fer nigh on to thirty year."

I grinned and repeated it after him to get used to manly doings. "There was a certain Mr. Garrett that Jessie and me met up with right beside a mudhole back in Independence, and I was wondering if you happen to know him?"

"Know him! Haw!" Mego laughed. "If we're atalkin' 'bout the same Garrett, he don't be from Independence. He be from beyan the Rocky Mountains. Tall feller? Kinder slow-talking, an' smokin' them leetle thin ceegars?"

"That's him."

"Wal, now," he cackled, "this chile'll have to keep his eyeballs peeled more keerful. Didn't know that worthless feller war atrappin' these parts."

"Worthless?"

"Jes' a manner of speakin', lad. J. C. Garrett ain't none too broke to the plow, but he'll do. Yessir, he'll do in a pinch."

Colonel Russell rode up and interrupted us before I could find out any more or tell Mego of my suspicions. But I put what I'd learned in my pipe and smoked it. In a manner of speaking, that is.

Thirty-four miles, three days, and half a dozen creek crossings later, we came to Lone Tree Station, which, unbeknownst to me, would be the last tree worth the name till we crossed the Rocky Mountains. The station was nothing more than a campsite around one elm tree sticking up out of the plains like a last warning of what we were leaving behind. The old Santa Fe Trail veered off to the left, and some thoughtful soul had stuck a wooden stake in the ground pointing the way to Oregon. We were well on our way.

But not without problems. By that time the train had split asunder because of a disagreement between two men whose peaceable natures had become so agitated that they'd drawn knives on each other. I never learned the exact cause of the argument, though I heard several versions of it. Mrs. Donner seemed to think one of them, and him a married man, had looked too long at the other's young wife, but Mr. Donner said it was caused by one letting the other's milk cow wander off when he was on guard duty. Mego just said, "Some is made fer the mountains, an' some ain't."

However it started, it ended with the train splitting apart. Colonel Jessy Q. Thornton was elected captain of the split-off group, which seemed a demotion in rank to me, but Mr. Reed said he'd been nominated a colonel only because he used such elegant language. Colonel Russell remained the captain of the group we were with, but not without persuasion. When we were camped at the Big Blue crossing, somebody accused him of misfeasance and malfeasance in office, and Colonel Russell's feelings got hurt so bad he resigned. Then the men had to calm a few tempers and reelect him all over again.

Colonel Thornton pulled all the Oregon wagons into a separate train, which gave me and Jessie a jolt, thinking they might go on without us. Mr. Donner told us that the two trains would travel no more than a day's ride apart and that we would all meet up again at Fort Laramie. He assured us he wouldn't let us get stranded without a way to fulfill Jessie's mission to the Oregon heathens. He then took the opportunity to suggest that there was an untold number of heathen in California that Jessie could turn her hands to if we cared to go on with them, but Jessie had her heart set on the particular strain living in Oregon. To show you how uncommonly stubborn she was, not even the Reverend Mr. Green, who was associated with the Whitman station and on his way back there after a visit to St. Louis, could turn her against Oregon. Not that he tried to, mind, but if he was any example of the missionaries already there, I'd have lit out in the opposite direction if it was up to me. Which it wasn't. I took Mr. Donner's side and put in my two cents in favor of California. Jessie said the Lord Jehovah had shown her where her clear calling lay and she wasn't of a mind to listen to Satan trying to tempt her in another direction. I think Mr. Donner was somewhat surprised to find himself placed in the devil's camp, but he took it with good grace.

Somewhere in all the upheaval and delay, Mr. Gordon decided we were too slow to suit him, so he and thirteen other wagons struck out ahead. After we crossed the Big Blue several wagons stayed behind with Mr. Hall to hunt stray cattle. At least that's what Mrs. Donner told us they were doing. I hadn't thought anything about it till she came out with that, and then I was interested because nobody had taken the trouble to explain when other wagons had turned off or back or gone on ahead. So it was a curiosity to me when the Hall family caught up with us and, instead of milk cows, they'd found brand-new twin boy babies.

Mr. Hall wandered by our camp a few days later, and on being asked about Mrs. Hall's health, he announced with a big smile that she was miraculously restored to her former temper. He said it was a matter for rejoicing, too, because being in the family way didn't suit her too well, particularly since she'd had two of them to drop.

There were any number of ladies in the increasing way when we started out, which made me wonder how they got that way so far from home. I knew how cows and horses got in that condition, but it didn't seem a likely method for human people since the ladies I knew wouldn't stand for it. And those that had stood for it didn't much like it. Take the time Mrs. Thomson, whose days were almost accomplished, came over one nooning and had a cup of tea with Mrs. Donner. She prattled on about her unhealthy state all unawares of Mrs. Donner's shushing motions and head-noddings toward her daughters and me.

"I declare," Mrs. Thomson said, smacking her lips after a long draught of tea, "a woman married and in a certain condition has a hard time of it. The internals make themselves known all the time. What with headaches, gas, heartburn, cramp, and various other symptoms, it's a wonder any woman would ever want to marry at all."

So I knew you had to be a married lady to get that way, and that it changed your form to a considerable degree in the process. I asked Jessie about it once, and she said that I'd know all I needed to know when I got married because my husband would tell me. I guess that meant that menfolks knew a lot more than I'd heretofore given them credit for, and being taken, now, for a member of the opposite gender, I stood a good chance of finding out what it was all about without having to marry to do it.

Not long after that we passed a slab of wood marking the grave of one Mary Ellis, who died May 7, 1845, aged two months. I hoped Mrs. Hall hadn't seen it, for I have no doubt it would've caused her to worry over her own babies. She was of a practical turn of mind, though, for when I asked her what she planned to name her twins, she said she'd studied on it for a long time, since twins ran in her family. Her favorite paired names in all the world, she said, were Oren and Goren, but she wasn't about to settle them on the babies until she saw whether or not the Lord was going to let them live long enough to get full use of them.

Old Lady Keyes passed on one night, which was a mortal shame, for she was bound for Oregon to meet her son, who had been there for two years. Mrs. Keyes had been feeble and failing for some time, but she wouldn't let her family leave her behind in Illinois. She'd said, "I'd rather be on my way to meet

something than left behind to wait for it." Well, she met something, all right, but she was doing what she wanted to do
beforehand, so I don't expect she had many regrets.

Things began to settle down somewhat as we got used to
prairie travel. Tempers were still quick to flare up, and there
was always somebody who had a grievance. But after the train
divided the men seemed able to handle them a little better. Also,
everybody was tired, a condition that generally has a calming
effect on choleric natures.

One evening we were on the receiving end of one almighty
thunderstorm when the lightning seemed bound and determined to turn somebody into a blue flame, and then the skies
just flat dried up. One day after another stretched white and
hot before us, and a cloud of dust hung over the wagons like
the pillar of cloud that led the Israelites. The prairie rolled on
to the horizon in a never-ending roll of knobs and knolls and
hills, each one covered with grass and stifling with dust. We
forded streams with banks so steep that rear wheels had to be
chained to keep the wagons from falling headlong on the teams.

When the Kansa was crossed we saw our first Indians, and
a mangier bunch I never hope to see again. Mr. Donner assured
us they were civilized, but that's what I thought I was and we
didn't have anything in common. They were Kansa Indians,
who had tried to make a living raising cattle and hogs at the
Methodist Mission not far off the trail. They hadn't been too
successful at it, for they'd turned their hands to a new line of
work. Namely, begging.

Four bucks rode right up from behind a low hill and
stopped the train. You could tell they'd had experience in that
sort of thing, for they went straight up to our captain. Their
entire heads were shaved except for a strip of hair running from
front to back like a clipped horse's mane. They had a few
straggly feathers stuck in what hair was left, and I declare if I
didn't see a mess of vermin scrambling for a foothold on the
head of the nearest one.

I'd have laughed if I'd seen that on the head of somebody
at school, but I didn't laugh when I saw it on a savage. And
that's what they were, make no mistake about it. Why, they

hardly had a stitch of clothes on, though several layers of dirt made up for some of the deficiencies. They had lots of paint on, too, stripes and zigzags and dots and what-all. Mego told me later that the red circles painted around their eyes made their eyesight especially sharp. Their eyesight must have been terrible poor if they needed help in spotting our long caravan.

"You help Kansa," their spokesman said to Colonel Russell, as if we'd come with that purpose in mind. "Much hungry."

"Get out of here, you mangy polecat!" Mr. Keesburg yelled. "Don't let 'em stand you down, Russell. We don't have to give them a thing."

There was a murmur of agreement among the men around Mr. Keesburg, and one of them reached in a wagon for his rifle.

"Hold on, fellers," Mego said calmly. He urged his horse slowly through the men and moseyed up beside Colonel Russell and conveniently between the Indians and the crowd.

"No reason not to be neighborly, air there?" he asked, staring hard at Colonel Russell.

"None whatsoever," Colonel Russell agreed, looking relieved to have a little help in the situation.

"Coffee?" Mego asked the Indians.

"No coffee," the leader said, with something less than his previous assurance after taking Mego in from head to foot. "Take wohaws. Take goddams."

"No mules. No oxen," Mego said firmly. "Kansa want coffee, tobac?"

"No coffee, no tobac. Take whiskey, take guns. Kansa want whiskey, want guns." The leader shook his rusty musket in Mego's face.

"We're not giving away our whiskey!" somebody shouted from the crowd.

Mego turned his head toward them and looked each man straight in the eye.

"Nobody's givin' away a thang," he said. "A trade is atakin' place. We'uns be atravelin' on Kansa land an' they know it. All we're tryin' to settle is what it's gonna cost us to do it. Any hoss what wants to make the deal can come on up hyar an' do it, an' this chile'll retire."

There was silence while the men looked down at their feet or gazed off at the prairie. None of them would meet his eye and take up the challenge.

"Colonel," Mego said, and I realized that from the first word he'd spoken he'd never raised his voice nor changed the slow cadence of his words. "I recommend a leetle coffee, tobaccy, and a few pounds of flour be floated out 'bout now, so's our friends hyar can see we're honest traders."

It didn't take long for the honest traders, who a few minutes before had been ready to skin a couple of Indians, to display their goods. Mego allowed the Indians to see only what he was willing to give them and not the fifty-pound bags it had come from. He had to ransack his possible sack for a string of blue beads, though, for each Indian wanted something to carry back with him. They wheeled their ponies and left jabbering and poking at each other's loot, seeming to think they'd made the best of the trade.

"Colonel, it 'pears to me that hit's time to lay down some trail law," Mego said.

"Why, we have our compact drawn up," he answered, surprised that anything else might be needed.

"Compacts ain't worth a hoot in hell iffen they ain't fol-lered," Mego declared. "From now on, ye can't afford to allow any stragglers, fer hit's the ones alone what'll git jumped. Injuns won't start nuthin' less the odds is in their favor, so when one wagon stops, ever'body else better stop too. Ye got to keep guards on the cattle at night an' ye got to make camp better'n ye been doin'. Mought as well git in practice, fer the Kansa ain't gen'ly this brash."

"You don't think they plan to attack us, do you?" Colonel Russell asked in a bewildered sort of way. Indian troubles weren't supposed to happen this early on the trail, according to Mr. Hastings' *Emigrant's Guide*.

"Naw." Mego spit out a mouthful of tobacco juice and looked slowly around the horizon. "Not that passel. But their bold ways tell this chile that they has a reason behind 'em. They knowed somethin' we don't. An' I'd wager my last twist of 'baccy that what they knowed is Sioux."

"Sioux?" The word was repeated from mouth to mouth, and it got more filled with dire and dread each time it was said.

"Why, Mr. Cobb," Mr. James Reed said impatiently, "if those Indians who just left are samples of what we'll meet in the future, I don't think we have anything to fear. They certainly weren't my idea of noble warriors. Just a bunch of half-starved, vermin-ridden, poorly-armed beggars, for my money."

"So they be, Mr. Reed," Mego agreed. "But ye got to learn to read a sign an' I jes' read it. An' one more thang," he said as he turned away, "ye ain't met any Sioux yet."

I tagged along after Mego as he kneed his horse through the muttering crowd. I'd just made up my mind that if the Lord had in mind for me to meet up with any Sioux, I was going to do it from one pace behind Mego Cobb.

10

*They wandered in the wilderness in a solitary
way; they found no city to dwell in.*
—Psalms 107:4

Colonel Russell took Mego's warning about posting guards at night and none too soon, for as soon as we crossed the Red Vermilion we were in Shawnee country. The guards began to report strange doings in the night and every morning one or two of our horses had disappeared. Coupled with the mournful howling of wolves during the night hours, nobody slept in peace.

Tempers were even shorter, and I thought to myself that if we had to cross another piddling little creek that grew steeper and deeper as the wagons got farther into it, I was going to figure that Somebody had it in for us. You'd think with Jessie and me on one of His own missions that the going would be easy and that we'd get a lot of outside help.

But no, after wagon wheels were repaired and horses and mules chased every tarnal morning, the One in charge of such matters sent another gift. The skies clouded over with the worst thunderstorm I've ever lived through. The rain hit us like a solid wall, falling straight down without any warning sprinkles. Hail the size of hen eggs was part of the package, along with lightning that was keen as a knife.

After the first sheet of rain, which lasted almost an hour, a steady downpour continued the rest of the day, and Mr. Higgins said he'd never seen clouds with such an incontinence of water. Mrs. Brawner, who was from South Carolina, held a parasol over her cook fire for two hours so she could fix a hot meal for her children. I asked Mrs. Donner how an old lady like that could have such young children, but Mrs. Donner just said she wasn't as old as she looked.

We crossed Thirty-Two Mile Creek three times, for the

straighter route was easier for us, and the creek looped and curled like a snake in our path. Finally we topped a sandy hill and there was the Platte River stretching out before us. As far as the eye could see, rolling sand hills tumbled away from its banks. The Platte Valley held not a single tree, except for a few stunted willows and cottonwoods on islands out in the middle of the river.

Rivulets flowed down the hills to join the broad Platte, and here and there I could see water standing in pools on the banks.

"That's whar the buffler come to waller," Mego told me, pointing to one of the pools. "We ort to see some of 'em pretty soon now. Be a sight fer sore eyes."

"So this is the Platte," I said, considerably disappointed, for Mr. Donner had said the night before that we would follow it for three hundred miles, and it was nothing like the rivers I knew back home.

"Yessir, this hyar's the Platte, what the Injuns call the Flat River, fer that's what she is. A mile wide and a inch deep and not fit fer man nor beast. Now don't ye go adrinkin' from it, neither. Hit's mighty nigh full of animalcules."

"Animalcules?"

"Leetle wiggly thangs," he answered. "Hit's all right iffen ye're nigh on to perishin', but otherwise I'll caution ye not to drink it."

The Right Reverend Mr. Green kept on making his piety known to one and all, fomenting strife and confusion everywhere he went. He wasn't happy with Colonel Russell's leadership, so for a few days of blessed peace he joined the other train, which was traveling some miles behind us. He rejoined us after Colonel Thornton refused his demand to refrain from travel on the Sabbath. I think the Oregon emigrants were vexed that they were behind us anyway and were afraid we'd reach the Promised Land before they would. They didn't take kindly to the Reverend's suggestion of any more delay.

He met with equal success when he told Colonel Russell that people who traveled on the Sabbath were on the road to hell.

"I can believe that, Reverend," the Colonel told him, "for with all we've had to put up with in the way of falling weather, broken axles, thieving Indians, and dissatisfied people, I'd say we've been on the road to hell ever since we left Independence."

All in all, though, I thought things were going fairly well, excepting a few minor adjustments I had to make to the rigors of prairie travel. I had the most fretful time trying to arrange a little privacy for the natural necessities, for when I'd wander off behind a knoll by myself, I had to be forever on the watch for rattlesnakes, Indians, or some of the boys who desired company and conversation any time they let their britches down. Even Mego asked me if I wanted company one time, and it startled me so bad I lost my place. The ladies were just as bad off. They had to accustom themselves to outdoor privies fashioned with sheets, which they took turns holding up around the one who was occupied.

We began to see more evidence of buffalo, and Mego couldn't stop talking about them. He said they provided everything a person could ever need for full and satisfactory living and he'd been away from them too long. According to him, you could use the hide for robes and coverings of all kinds, the sinews for lacings, the bones for making medicine and marking trails, the bladders for water bags, and, of course, the meat for every nutriment required by the living human body.

"A daily mess of buffler meat, fat cow bein' the preferred sort," Mego told me, "keeps a body runnin' nigh to top speed. Why, littl'un, a mountain man never suffers from civilized ailments. Ye won't never hear tell of toothaches, bellyaches, nor headaches. 'Less o' course there be a arrow through one of them parts. The only thangs a mountain man suffers from, barring outside influences from bows and muskets, is rheumatiz from wadin' the rivers lookin' fer beaver plews and the venereals from co-habitatin' with loose squaws."

We got our first taste of it early in June after Mego took some of the men on a chase. He said it wasn't quite fat enough for feasting since it was early in the year, but it "purely put light bread an' beans to shame." I took to it right away, but Jessie got a little squeamish from it at first.

The buffalo gave us something else, though, that was just as needful as its meat. Without a stick of firewood on that wide prairie, we needed buffalo droppings for cook fires. Some of the ladies didn't want to use it, saying it would adversely affect the flavor of their cooking. But it was either that or raw dough, so they learned to get used to it. Before they did, though, the gathering of said fuel occasioned official discussion among the men. They thought the women should be spared contact with such lowly functions of wild beasts because it might upset some sensitive soul. Further arguments sprang up about the least offensive name for what was just buffalo manure, plain and clear. Several suggestions along the lines of prairie fuel and California chips were proffered. The name I liked best was dung cakes suggested by one wit, who was silenced by the other men, who took the protection of their womenfolk from unsavory matters more seriously. We finally settled on cowchips, because that's what everybody was already calling them. It naturally fell to my lot to be one of the gatherers every morning and evening and, let me tell you, it was nothing like the gathering of manna. The most peculiar sight of all, though, was little Mrs. Jackson holding a parasol over head while picking up cowchips in white gloves.

We soon got into the routine of rising before dawn, hitching the teams, drinking scalding coffee over a fire, rounding up cattle and children, and then moving over the never-ending rolling knolls. Nooning provided a rest, but just barely. There was no shade except what could be found under a wagon, and even then I found it prudent to rake around with a long stick in case a rattler had settled there before me. Mego told me if I would lay a horsehair lariat in an oval on the ground, I could rest inside it with no fear of snakes, for they have a natural dislike of horsehair. I tried it and it worked, for I was never bothered by the fearsome creatures.

We followed the banks of the South Platte and crossed it at the only fordable place, which was several miles from the junction of the North tributary. On its western side we hit the worst traveling conditions yet encountered, for the land became harder and dryer and noticeably steeper. Akaline dust lay over us the likes of which I'd never seen, and we all walked around layered with white masks. We were hard put to even breathe, for particles of dust floated weightless in the air. We chewed grit regardless of whatever else we were trying to eat. Eyes were red and inflamed, and Mr. Jacob Donner remembered that goggles sold for thirty-seven and a half cents in Independence. He said he was willing to lay out fifty dollars for a pair, but nobody took him up on it.

Right soon before we reached Ash Hollow I was riding Polly out to the side of the train away from the dust churned up by the wagons. Mego was somewhere up ahead, and I'd just made up my mind to go find him when I saw something way off that looked like a tree moving along with us. I knew that couldn't be right, for there wasn't a tree in that whole country, much less a moving one. As I watched, the tree turned into something that looked more like a house, and I knew I was being visited by a mirage that had afflicted any number of us. Still and all, there was something out there, so I galloped up to Mego and pointed it out to him.

"I seed him a while back and yestiddy too," he said. "Ye'd thank that feller'd come on in and set with white folks fer a change."

"You're not worried about him trailing along beside us?"

"Worrit? Naw, hit don't worry this chile none. That thar's Garrett, an' when he gits ready he'll move on in. 'Course I wouldn't blame him none iffen he don't want no truck with this hyar cavyard. I'm 'bout to git gutshot over hit my own self."

"That's Mr. Garrett?" I turned to look again, but my eyes weren't that good. "What's he doing out there? Why's he tagging along with us?"

"Hit do beat all, don't it? I'll prolly santer out thar come nightfall an' put it to him."

"Can I go too?" I asked, thinking to face Mr. Garrett down and find out why he was following us.

"Naw, better not this time. Garrett mought be on some business I don't know nuthin' about. Ye don't wanna mess with a feller when he's got business on his mind."

I rolled that over in my own mind and asked, "You think it might have to do with somebody in this train?"

"Lemme study on that'un fer a spell. Yep," he said after a minute, "I 'spect it do. Garrett ain't knowed fer slow travelin', an' if he's langerin' along with us, then he's got some reason fer it. But I'm poleaxed if I know what it is."

We finally reached Ash Hollow, an oft-used campsite in the triangle formed by the South Platte and the North. As campsites go, it had a lot to be desired, but in that godforsaken land there was no better choice. Reverend Green seemed opposed to using it, telling Colonel Russell that there was little to recommend it and one site was as good as the next and we ought to move on.

Our captain, who was a man of dyed-in-the-wool habits if nothing else, would have nothing but a traditional campsite.

"Reverend Green," he said, with a dry expectoration, "we've been pushing these animals for days, and man and beast are tired. If this campsite has been fit for trains before us, then it's fit for us as well."

With shoulders drooping, the Colonel turned his back and walked away. That was sign enough of the bone-tiredness and loss of courtesy evident among us all, for Colonel Russell was head and shoulders above the rest when it came to politeness.

So we put down at Ash Hollow. It had been the plan to stay in camp for several days every two weeks to give the men time to repair wagons and replenish the meat supply. The ladies planned to rest and wash clothes, which seemed something of a contradiction to me. We hadn't exactly kept to that schedule, since there'd been so many delays for other reasons, but we were going to lay over at Ash Hollow. And it's a good thing we planned it that way, for an epidemic of rushing bowels swept through the train and compelled us to stay awhile. Dr. Bryant was kept on the move even worse than his patients, and there was such a run on his supply of calomel that he liked to've run out. Jessie longed for more of Dr. Sappington's celebrated fever and ague pills, for it held a money-back guarantee if it didn't cure asthma, corns, canker sores, and other scorbutic diseases, as well as dysentery.

The Reverend Green commenced to visit the beds of the sick and the anguished. Prayer came first with him, and he couldn't understand why griping bowels wouldn't wait for him to wind up with an amen. He kept urging us to move from the pestilential spot, but many were in no condition to move.

"The Reverend Dr. Green sure wants us to get away from here," I remarked to Mego as we rested under a wagon.

"Nary a doubt about that," he said, breaking off a twist of tobacco. "And hit's purely a wonder to this chile how he's took up doctorin' an' preachin' an' prayin' on his own say-so, fer he ain't none of them thangs. Dr. Whitman hyard him on as a mechanic carpenter, but looks like he warn't satisfied with that."

"He's not a doctor nor a preacher?" I dropped the weed I was chewing on.

"Naw, neither one. But the puny soul mought have a conscience, atter all." Mego cut loose with a long splat of tobacco juice.

"How's that?" I pulled my hat over my eyes and laid back in the shade.

"Why, hit were right hyar at Ash Holler that he met up with the Sioux."

I sat up to let the chill run all the way down my back.

"Yep, he come through hyar on his way back to the States back in '37 with two, three Injun boys, chiefs' sons they war from the Nez Percé up around the Clearwater. They was sot on by the Sioux, who had bad hearts fer everybody that summer. Perticular fer a small cavyard like Green had. He'd been told he war a damn fool fer trying it without extry men, but he war sot fer it an' nobody could budge him. They was alayin' fer 'em and they come asplashin' acrosst the Platte afixin' to lift hair off ever' man jack of 'em. But, Green, now, he knelt hisself in prayer an' then declared that the Lord wanted no part of a Injun fight. So with a little palaver, the chiefs' sons war aturned over to the Sioux and Green headed on to the States, scot-free."

"What happened to the chiefs' sons?"

"Why, I reckon their hair be afixed to a lodgepole som'ers, or mebbe aflappin' on a Sioux pony."

"You mean they got scalped?"

"Shore as beaver rises to castoreum."

"Didn't Reverend, I mean Mr. Green know what would happen?"

"He knowed it." And Mego clamped his teeth together like he had Mr. Green's neck between them.

After a while he said, "Joe Meek and Black Harris almost done him in fer it too. Green was on his way back to Oregon atter that shindig, an' the boys caught up with him som'ers beyan the Wind Rivers. They come to lift hair fer sartain, but Green, having somehows acquired a wife, hid amongst her personal b'longin's an' they couldn't fetch him out."

I tried to picture Mr. Green, as sober-looking and dignified as he was, covered over with petticoats and bodices and bloomers, but it was hard to bring to mind.

"Come to thank on it," Mego said, "J. C. Garrett had a hand in that too. As I recollect, he war aplannin' to strip his hide with a lashin'. He war plum crazy fer a lynchin' of some kind, and vowed he'd git Green if he ever showed hisself by his lonesome. But then, they's lots of boys in the mountains that thanks he's overdue fer killing."

My stomach took a slow turn and growled an accompaniment to the movement. I had set out from Caleb's Corner with adventure on my mind and responsibility on my back, in the person of Jessie, and here I was with rampaging Indians behind every knoll, bowel-wrenching dysentery draining us out, a pretended minister of the Gosepl fit for killing, and a crazy man watching Jessie in the dark. It was enough to make you want to bawl if you were the bawling kind. Which I wasn't. At least, not often.

II

Ask a sign of the Lord, thy God; ask it either
in the depth, or in the height above.
—*Isaiah 7:11*

It was while dysenteric ailments kept us on at Ash Hollow that
something downright scary happened. At least it purely alarmed
me, who knew the agent and cause of it.

Jessie was kept busy with the Donner girls, for the sickness
had struck there as well. Between her and Mrs. Donner, who
was also feeling poorly, bedclothes got washed, children tended,
and the sick nursed and fed. Jessie complained only once in my
hearing, worrying that she had too little time for studying,
praying, and journal-keeping. It was on one of her many treks
to the riverbank for water that she caught the eye of a recent
convert to active religion, courtesy of Mr. Green.

Mr. Green, which was what I called him after learning of
his self-bestowal of the titles of Doctor and Reverend, had begun
to proselytize anybody who'd sit still for it. His whole reason
for making the trip to St. Louis had been to round up more
ministerial help for the Oregon mission stations, and he hadn't
had any success at it. It looked like he was going back to Dr.
Whitman and Mr. Spaulding empty-handed and he couldn't
stand it. He commenced talking up the missionary virtues and
benefits to anybody who'd listen. You'd think he would've been
happy to find Jessie and me already committed, but that wasn't
the case. He was looking for strong backs and skilled hands
that could build and plow and handle the Lord's livestock.

The only success he had was with Mr. Freedom Kessler,
a big, slow man from Pennsylvania who turned out to be like
a dog with a bone. Mr. Kessler couldn't handle but one thing
at a time, but whatever that one thing was, he wouldn't turn
it loose till it was concluded to his satisfaction. From what I

could see, he was one of those people who never changed their minds once they were set, and never verged from a path once their feet were planted, regardless of any new information or change in the circumstances.

With his mop of straw-colored hair and his slow-blinking pale eyes, Mr. Kessler lumbered around behind Mr. Green, determined to follow him all the way to Oregon like he said he would. They spent an inordinate amount of time sitting in the shade while Mr. Green instructed him on his duties, both spiritual and practical. I watched them now and again, since there was little else to do as we waited for the dysentery to run its course.

Whenever I was around them I heard Mr. Green preparing Mr. Kessler to take on his own load of work. Mr. Green kept saying how he'd been called to preach and to doctor, and he didn't have time for menial tasks, and that Mr. Kessler, with his robust frame, had been called to take up the slack. Mr. Kessler would nod and agree, not saying much, but latching onto every word that proceeded out of his instructor's mouth. He never argued and never questioned; he just did whatever Mr. Green told him to do. The two of them suited each other right down the line, for Mr. Green liked to tell people what to do and Mr. Kessler liked to be told. And as far as I could see, fairly needed to be.

I had settled under a stunted cottonwood one afternoon, intending to await the arms of Morpheus, when the two of them hunkered down not too far away. I listened to Mr. Green drone on about Christian duties without paying too much attention, until he said something that startled me full awake.

"Now, Mr. Kessler, our stations are located far from the Willamette settlements. Dr. Whitman's at Waiilatpu and Mr. Spaulding's way up at Lapwai, and we're surrounded for miles around by nothing but wilderness. If we're to have any of the blessings of civilization, we have to bring them in ourselves. What I mean is, don't look to find anything that you don't already have when you get there. Now, the Lord don't intend for man to live alone, so my advice to you is to take the bull by the horns and find a helpmeet right here in one of these trains. I'm telling you, Brother, a single man amongst savages is a pure temptation to the devil, and you don't want to start off on the wrong foot if you can help it."

Mr. Kessler mulled this over for a while, nodding his head to show that he was thinking.

"You're saying I need me a wife," he finally came out with.

"That's right," Mr. Green said. "Mrs. Whitman and Mrs. Spaulding paved the way, being the first white ladies to cross the Rockies, and my own dear wife wasn't too far behind them. But except for the tag end of emigrants that hang around for a few months before moving on to the Willamette, there ain't no field for you to choose from there. I say your best bet is to look over this stock of emigrants right here, make your choice, and by the time you get to Oregon you'll be set for the Lord's work, having outmaneuvered Satan before he gets ahold of you. Me and Mrs. Green honeymooned on the trail, and so did the Eells and the Walkers and the Smiths, though I don't recommend the close quarters we shared in doing it."

"I've done some studyin' on takin' a wife," Mr. Kessler said in his slow way, "but I never thought on it like it was a commandment. You think we ought to pray about it, Pastor Green?"

"That's what I been doing." Mr. Green sounded a little testy. He was a wiry, active man that could hardly brook delays, unless it was on a Sabbath. When he gave out the word he wanted it acted on right then.

"Now listen, Mr. Kessler," he said, pointing his finger at him. "There's an unmarried gentlewoman traveling with the Donners who gives out that she's been called to the mission field. She's headed for the Whitman place without so much as checking in at the Mission Board. You can tell right there that she's had no true call. You know and I know that the Scriptures teach that God deals with the man, and the man with the woman, and the woman with the blessed issue. It's a hierarchical arrangement, see, so that everything is done decently and in order. Now, it seems to me, that even though this Miss Heath has been deceived in thinking she has a call to mission work, she could have a call to be the support and solace of a man in the Lord's pathway."

Well, wouldn't you know that Jessie took that very time to walk down to the river to draw water. I saw Mr. Green point her out, and Mr. Kessler sat there and made all the connections. That night after supper he showed up, hat in hand, at our fire and announced to Mr. Donner that he'd come to walk out with Miss Jessie.

I was surprised that Miss Jessie agreed to go, but I guess she needed a respite from tending the sick, and he took her in right from the start by saying he was a new missionary. Besides, she didn't know what was in his mind like I did. I followed as they strolled around the camp and listened as Jessie shared her testimony with him. He didn't say much, just took everything in while looking more and more pleased with himself as he realized what, according to Mr. Green, the Lord had in store for him.

He followed Jessie around all the next day, either with his feet or his eyes, all unbeknownst to her. In her way she was just as set and determined as he was, but their paths went in different directions. She didn't have a notion of his intentions, thinking of him as a fellow laborer in the Lord's vineyard, although "a tad slow in the mental department," as she told me.

One night after another stroll with him she flounced back to our camp with a full head of steam. I took one look at her and knew he'd declared himself.

"Let's go for a walk," she said to me, grabbing my arm and marching me out of earshot of the others.

"What's going on, Jessie?"

"I'll tell you what's going on," she fumed. "That Mr. Kessler has just announced that we are to be married. Have you ever heard of such a thing? I don't know where he got such a notion, for I'm sure I didn't give it to him, and I can't imagine the Lord did either or He'd have given it to me as well. Em, that man said it was my duty—my Christian duty—to marry him and give him solace! He said that was the only reason I was here and the only reason I was even born—that the Lord has brought us together right here for that very purpose! What do you think of that?"

"I think I've never heard Mr. Kessler talk that much."

"Well, it took him long enough," she said. "In fact, it took him so long that I was slow in getting his meaning. You just better know I set him straight after that, though. The idea of telling me my duty! He's no minister of the Gospel to be telling me what to do!"

Nobody told Jessie what to do once she'd staked her way, and I figured Mr. Kessler had learned so to his sorrow. But I figured wrong.

The next morning he took leave of the man who'd hired him back in St. Louis and, before Jessie had a chance to forestall it, got himself hired on to drive one of Mr. Donner's wagons. After that he was under Jessie's feet all the time, and she didn't like it a bit. Mr. Donner would've unhired him when he found out the problem, but Mr. Kessler wasn't a nuisance to anybody but Jessie and me, and I think Mr. Donner found some humor in the situation.

Everybody soon got used to seeing Mr. Kessler at the campfire with his big pale eyes trained on Jessie all the time. I tried once to tell him he was barking up the wrong tree, but he just looked through me and said he was only carrying out the Lord's orders and all he had to do was be patient.

He didn't really bother Jessie as far as courting ways go; she just couldn't get rid of him. She tried explaining nice and slow that she wasn't up to marrying him, and he nodded like he understood. Soon as she finished, thinking she'd done a good job of it, he said, "We ought to have the words said over us afore we leave Ash Hollow."

Jessie had never run up against anybody as stubborn as she was, and she flat didn't know what to do with him.

"Maybe he's right, Jessie," I told her, trying to sound serious about it. "Maybe that's what the Lord wants you to do. Have you thought about that?"

"Emma Louise," she said with her hands on her hips. "I don't want to hear such a thing from you. I can put you back in a frock just as quick as I put you in those britches. Then we'll see how you like being followed around and pestered every minute of the day by somebody you can't stand!"

That shut me up right smartly. I had to go off by myself and think about some man wanting to marry me, in or out of the Lord's will. I just hadn't thought much about it before, knowing of course that almost every lady took a husband sooner or later so she could have a household of her own. Nobody seemed to want to spend all their lives with their own mama and papa, and folks always thought it was a shame when it worked out that way. But I didn't have a mama or papa to forsake as the Bible tells us to do, so I hadn't thought much about marrying. Now, Jessie had up and told me that I might someday be on the receiving end of unwelcome attentions and, not only that, all I had to do was put my frock back on to start receiving them. It didn't seem likely, though I knew there were some married ladies among us who weren't many years older than me, and some of them didn't have half of Jessie's looks or shape any more than I had. At that time I was lean and flat and just about straight up and down from my shoulders to my feet, and the difference between her and me was just about too much to think about bridging. Yet almost all the ladies seem to've grown at some time in their lives, because they sure weren't born with full bodices. The question was, when did it start and what brought it on? All Jessie would tell me was that a blossoming time came to every girl, but I wanted to know if it came on gradual like or did you just bloom out overnight? I didn't want that to happen to me and catch me unprepared for it. What would I do with ladies' blossoms in Hiram's clothing? I needed to know those things so I could take steps.

Now, the reason this weighed on my mind is that it looked like something was beginning to bloom and I didn't know what to do about it. I'd taken to studying some of the young ladies, like Lizzie Donner, to see if they were having the same problem as I was. It was hard to tell with her, though, because she wore pinafores over her frock that forestalled any kind of scientific scrutiny.

Boys don't have this problem of being born one way and

then veering off track into a new silhouette when they get about grown. I hoped it would hold off on me till we got settled somewhere. It was hard enough to keep remembering how somebody in male attire was supposed to behave without having to worry myself with how somebody in a blossoming state deports herself.

It came to me not long afterwards that ladies didn't blossom all on their lonesome. Gentlemen callers must have had something to do with it, though I couldn't figure out how they did it. I remembered what had happened to Lovisa May Morgan back home. She was of an age somewhere between me and Jessie, and just as skinny as a rail. I mean there wasn't hardly anything to her, and her bodice was as flat as a flitter. Well, she got herself married to Wendell Harkness at the Holy Light Meetinghouse, and I didn't see her for nigh onto a year afterwards. She showed up then at the Summer Revival, and I didn't hardly know her, she had changed so much. It was a wonder how she had blossomed, and all the ladies were whispering about the joys of marriage or, at least, the joys of that particular marriage.

But now I didn't think it was marriage that had brought on Lovisa May's transformation. Jessie wasn't married, and look at her. I thought it had something to do with your own mind, what you thought about, and what you felt. And that's probably why everybody's so determined to keep their thoughts on pure and holy things.

But my mind had been burdened with troubling thoughts lately, and a lot of them had to do with that Mr. Garrett. I didn't know what it was about him, but there had been something in his eyes and in the way he was following us that disturbed something in me that I hadn't even known was there. And what I wanted to know was, did he know he was doing it? Because if he did, then he knew that I was not any more of an Emmett than Jessie was. To be on the safe side, I thought I'd better not ever let him look at me real close up. He might see something there that would tell him about the mighty stirrings going on inside. Then if I could get a grip on the stirrings themselves, especially when I went to bed every night, I figured

I could carry off my disguise before I commenced to blossom enough to notice. I wasn't ready for such doings and didn't think I would be any time soon.

I'll have to say that Jessie's words tumbled around in my mind for some little time, and I began to wonder if she knew something about me that I didn't know. Even so, I determined to stay in male attire for the rest of my life if need be, because I wasn't about to leave her and take up with somebody else, in spite of any fleshly longings that might come my way.

Things came to a head the night before we pulled out of Ash Hollow. Everybody was repacking the wagons to get an early start the next morning, and Mr. Kessler tagged along beside Jessie trying to do her work and his too.

"Leave it be, Mr. Kessler," she told him as he tried to take a crate of dishes from her. "I don't need any help."

"A man's supposed to relieve his wife," he said, holding on to the crate.

"I am not your wife and I don't intend to be. Do you understand that?"

"I only know what the Lord God tells us to do," he explained to her with the world's patience. "His instructions are plain as day, and I know my duty. You better listen to the Lord, Miss Jessie, it won't do for you to be wayward."

Jessie pushed the crate at him and stormed off by herself. She went down by the river and I followed to be sure she was all right out there in the dark. She stopped under a tree, and just as I started to say something to her she knelt down and commenced praying out loud.

"Lord," she said, to get His attention, "I've put up with about all I can stand. You know that I only want to do what is pleasing to You and, even though it tears me up to say it, if it's Your will that I take Mr. Kessler as my wedded husband then I'll do it. But I ask you, Lord, to show me clear and certain that that's what You want me to do. I ask for a sign, dear Lord, and if You will send me one, I promise to obey it."

She sat down then and leaned back against the tree, waiting, I expect, for a sign to present itself. I was a little worried about the course of things, because my sister wasn't used to bending her will to somebody else, and here she'd just promised to do that very thing even if it did go against the grain. I knew if the Lord sent anything she could take for a sign, she'd up and marry Mr. Kessler even if it turned her stomach, which shows what dire straits religion can get you into. I began to put in a little praying myself so that no signs would be forthcoming. Mr. Kessler wasn't my idea of a husband for Jessie and I didn't want her to tie herself up for life with somebody she didn't even like. Besides, I didn't like him either.

Then Jessie started crying and I started getting scared. I thought she might've gotten a sign I hadn't noticed, and crying was her way of acknowledging the same.

"Lord," I whispered, "if You've sent one, won't You take it back, for You can see how miserable Jessie is about it."

I saw her wipe her face with her skirt tail, then she whipped herself back into praying position.

"And Heavenly Father," she said, strong and clear, "if it's not Your will that I marry Mr. Kessler, I ask that You make it known to him in a way he can't mistake. Send him a sign, Lord, if this is not Your will, and I will abide by whatever You decide to do."

She got up, brushed off her clothes, and walked back to the camp, like she'd left all her burdens by the riverside. She even smiled in a distant sort of way at Mr. Kessler when he stumbled in his haste to make room for her by the fire. She had put her troubles in Somebody else's hands, and didn't intend to take them up again.

The next morning was when it happened. The whole camp was scurrying around to get back on the trail and, as was usual, noise and confusion reigned over all. A bunch of the men had gone to round up the livestock that were grazing on the prairie; others were packing wagons and hitching oxen while womenfolk were collecting the last wash off the bushes.

In the midst of the commotion Mr. Hall came galloping up to Mr. Donner, looking like he'd seen a ghost.

"Mr. George! Mr. George! Lord have mercy, Brother," he gasped, reining in beside him.

"What is it? Indians?" Mr. Donner was already reaching for his musket.

"No, it's Mr. Kessler, your hired man. He's dead, Brother, he's dead!"

We all stopped and Jessie dropped a load of fresh-washed clothes.

"Dead!" Mr. Donner said as if he couldn't believe it. "What happened out there? Tell me what happened!"

Mr. Hall dismounted and wiped his face, trying to catch his breath. His hands were shaking and he allowed he could use a spot of brandy.

When he got it he said, "I ain't never seen nothing like it. Nossir, never in my life. We were out there after the stock, and we'd just got 'em bunched up and ready to drive, when this little cloud come up. Not much a one, most of the sky was still blue. And it didn't even rain, just one clap and he was gone!"

"Gone?" Mr. Donner looked like he wanted to shake him. "You mean he just vanished?"

"No, he didn't just vanish. Struck by lightning, Brother, that's what I'm tellin' you. One flash and one clap, and when it was over Mr. Kessler was lyin' on the ground dead as a doornail!"

Jessie walked around in a daze while they were bringing Mr. Kessler in. She looked stunned and a little scared as she helped get the Donner wagons packed. When everybody was ready to go we took time out to bury Mr. Kessler in a spot not too far from Jessie's praying tree.

After the words were said and a marker put up, Jessie and me walked back to the wagons together.

"Em," she said, putting her arm around my shoulder, "don't ever ask the Lord for a sign if you don't think you can stand one."

And I didn't intend to.

12

We put Ash Hollow behind us, having had our fill of its overflowing anthills and odoriferous sagebrush, as well as its dysentery and bolts out of the blue. It went against me to find myself in agreement with Mr. Green, but it was a pestilential spot, though not as godforsaken as it looked since Mr. Kessler had had a visitation. We left his fresh grave among those of cholera victims from earlier trains, and were heartily glad to be on our way again.

Jessie didn't have much to say to anybody, going around with a scared look on her face, which Mrs. Donner put down to travel fatigue. I knew better, but was afraid to bring it up. Instead, I rode Polly fairly close to her wagon in case she had a mind to talk it over, but she never did. I'll have to say that my interest had been redirected away from the landscape and the excitements of the trail to center in on my sister. I'd heard a lot of talk about prayers being answered, but I'd never seen such visible evidence of it before. I began to watch her closer than ever, for it was plain that the Lord listened to what she had to say, and I didn't know what she might ask Him to do next. It came to me that I might be getting a previously un-suspected hand in looking out for her, but I wasn't in touch with Him like Jessie was, and I didn't know but what the two of them might cook up something else when I wasn't around. I didn't want her to get in trouble with the law, such as it was on the trail. The compact the men had made and agreed on back at Indian Creek had a clear provision for folks found guilty of fomenting strife and taking life. If they found out she'd had a part in Mr. Kessler's demise, there's no telling what they'd do to her.

Mr. Green didn't help matters. He rode up beside her wagon to, as he said, offer his commiserations on her loss.

"I've had no personal loss, Reverend Green," she told him, still honoring him as a shepherd of the flock in spite of what I'd told her. "We all grieve Mr. Kessler's passing, but we know he's in a better land than we are."

"That's an admirable testimony, Sister Heath," Mr. Green returned, " 'specially for somebody who's lost her betrothed. Put all in the Lord's hands, I always say, without a lot of whining and complaining, and He'll see you through."

"He was not my betrothed and I'll thank you not to refer to it again." Jessie was about to get her dander up even though she took him for a true ordained minister of the Gospel.

He looked sharp at her and cut loose with a storm of reproof. "Sister Heath, if you plan on going to our mission field, which I might as well tell you is of the utmost irregularity, you're going to have to learn some submission to authority. It's unbecoming of a young woman, alone and unwedded, to be so headstrong and outspoken. You may find yourself unwanted and unwelcome in our Christian community." He jabbed his horse with his heel and rode off like he'd fixed her good.

She sat there on the wagon seat looking white-faced and stricken, and I couldn't tell whether she was just mad at him or scared by his threats. I rode up by her and said I needed to find a private knoll to go behind and did she want to go with me. She climbed down and got behind me on Polly, and we loped away from the train out of eye- and earshot.

We got far enough away to do our business, then continued on afterward at a walk, keeping pace with the train.

"What are we going to do, Jessie, if Mr. Green is right and the missionaries won't let you mission with them when we get there?"

"I don't know, Em," she said. "I just never thought that a person with a true call would be turned away like that. Once we get to Oregon, there's no way to get back home, for everybody's traveling west and not east. I don't know what we'll do, and it just fires me up to have a human man stand in the way of me and my call, which doesn't have anything to do with him. It doesn't seem right, and I've a mind to put Mr. Green before the Lord in prayer. It's the only thing I know to do."

"Don't do that, Jessie," I said with some urgency. "There's two things you ought to think about before taking such a step."

"What's that?"

"One is, Mr. Green's no preacher and no doctor, like I told you. He's just a hired hand, and can't speak for Dr. Whitman and Mr. Spaulding. If he stirs up as much strife and discord among them as he does us, then he might be the one turned away and not you."

"Well, that's possible, I'll admit. But what if you're wrong and we get there and they won't let us stay? I know the Lord will provide, Em, but it scares me to go against clear warnings. The Lord may be speaking through Mr. Green, although you'd think He'd let me know direct. But," she said, with a catch in her voice, "He doesn't always do like we expect."

"That's another thing," I said, striking while the iron was hot. "It bothers me like it does you to think that Mr. Green is the Lord's appointed messenger, but the Oregon door may be shut, and this is His way of telling us. Now, the Donners have been begging us to go on to California with them and, Jessie, we may never have such a good setup again. They want us, and we like them, and I say that we don't know when we're well-off if we cut loose from them. Why, we wouldn't have another worry in the world if we throw in with them for good."

She didn't answer for a while and I let her think it through. The fact is, I had taken to the Donners and didn't want to part from them. I'd never been around people as generous and easygoing as they were. It didn't seem likely that the Oregon missionaries would measure up to them, since nobody else ever had, which certainly included Mr. Green.

"I've been thinking about that too," she finally said. "It seems such a sensible and easy thing to do, but, Em, the Lord doesn't call us to what is sensible and easy. It's the hard road He wants us on, the one that looks foolish to the world. Every time I'm about to give in to California, I get this awful lonesome feeling, like I'm forsaking my Lord. We'll just have to rely on Him. If He wants us in Oregon, and it seems plain that He does, then He'll prepare a place for us."

I was mighty disappointed, but I wasn't about to argue about it. I intended doing everything in my power to keep her from laying me before the Lord.

On our way back to the train I let her have the saddle while I hung on behind. Just as we topped the last dusty rise before catching up with our wagon, I caught a glimpse of that same rider way out beyond us. I let Jessie climb back on the wagon without saying anything to her about him, but I decided to find out right then what he was doing and what he wanted and whether it was us he wanted it from.

I went looking for Mego to tell him that, business or no, I was going to mess with Mr. Garrett. Back at Ash Hollow I'd asked Mego if he'd sauntered out to him like he'd said he was going to do, but I hadn't got much out of him. He'd taken a coughing fit and went to hawking and spitting so bad he could hardly talk. All he would say was that I didn't need to worry, that Garrett had a couple of things on his mind, and neither one of them ought to bother me or him. Curiosity and plain suspiciousness about poleaxed me, as he would say, for I didn't figure Mr. Garrett would let on to Mego about his uncommon interest in my sister. And another thing, I'd got so used to Mr. Garrett showing up in unexpected places that I'd taken to watching and listening for every little shadow and rustle. It was interfering with my peace of mind and my rest.

Anyway, I went looking for Mego, only half aware of Courthouse Rock looming over the craggy countryside to the south of us. That blamed rock had been the occasion of near fisticuffs between Mr. Brawner and Mr. Kingsley when they disputed which county courthouse back home it looked like the most. I'd had my fill of natural curiosities by that time and took no notice of it.

Mego was nowhere to be found. He'd either gone on ahead to scout the ford at Laramie Creek or was out looking for game. So there was nothing for it but to strike out by myself and look

Mr. Garrett in the face. I knew it would be hard to get close
to a trail-wise man if he didn't want me to, but I could at least
show him how it felt to have somebody dogging his every step.

It was dangerous to ride out too far alone and we'd been
warned against it. Still, Mr. Garrett was fairly close in and
Colonel Thornton's Oregon group was only a few miles behind
us. I could see their dust and knew I had time to flush him
before getting worried about being left on the prairie by myself.
My plan was to circle out between the two trains and see if I
could find him.

It worked better than I'd hoped or wanted. Polly threaded
her way around and between the rises on the crumbling landscape, both of us stifled with heat and dust.

We topped a knoll and there, sitting his horse loose and
easy, was Mr. Garrett waiting on us. At least that was the uneasy
feeling I had, that he'd been watching Polly and me ever since
we'd left the train and was just waiting to see how good we'd
be at locating him. It gave me the jitters.

It wasn't that I was afraid of him. Exactly. I don't know
what I was of him, and wasn't any better informed afterward.

But I put myself in mind of Jessie's welfare, and determined
within myself to see it through. I walked Polly right up in front
of him and stopped.

He was busy rolling a corn-shuck cigarillo and only gave
me a quick glance as I waited for him to say something.

He didn't, so I said, "Mr. Garrett, are you following us?"

He took his time answering, for he had to lick his makings
and put it in his mouth and scrutinize the countryside before
turning his full attention to me.

"Do you think I am?"

I didn't know what to make of that, so I swallowed hard
and did some looking around myself.

"Well, it sure looks like you are, and if you're aiming to
make trouble for me and my sister, you better know that we've
got friends in high places."

He struck a match on his boot and took his time lighting
his smoke. "No trouble from me," he said, with the smoke

curling up. Then he looked straight in my eyes and said, "Unless you want some."

It startled me so bad that I just sat there locked in his gaze. A feeling I'd never had before begin to spread around inside of me, and I finally had to look aside.

"Well," I said, "well, I'm not looking for trouble. But if you keep on following us, I'm going to have to tell my sister."

It took a while, but he begin to smile a little. "And what would happen then?"

"Why, mister," I said, for I was a believer in Jessie by this time, "my sister would take you to the Lord in prayer and you wouldn't stand a snowball's chance in hell after that."

He raised his eyebrows a little, but didn't look as worried as he should have. "I better think on that some," he said, leaning on the saddle horn and putting a finger against his mouth in thought.

"I wouldn't think too long if I was you," I warned him. "You can ask anybody here and they'll tell you what happened to somebody else that bothered her."

He cut his eyes at me again and said, "You tell me."

I was starting to feel light-headed every time he looked at me, and I had trouble standing my ground. I wanted to ride off somewhere by myself and think about the funny feelings churning around inside, but I also wanted to stay and wait for him to look at me again.

I took a deep breath and plunged in to tell him about Jessie. "It's like this, Mr. Garrett. My sister is going to be a missionary in Oregon and the Lord has put a hedge around her so nobody can bother her. There was one who wouldn't listen to neither advice nor warnings, and kept pestering her till she finally had to pray about it. The next day lightning struck him stone dead." I shivered a little because I still hadn't gotten over the suddenness of it. "I'm telling you for your own good, Mr. Garrett, don't mess with her."

He looked at his smoke a long time and then blew the ashes off. "I appreciate the warning," he said. "But she wouldn't do that to a friend of yours, would she?"

"Friend of mine?"

He nodded and said, "We are friends, aren't we? You and me?"

I didn't take likings and dislikings as quick as Jessie did, but this was different and outside my field of experience.

"Well," I said, "I guess we are or could be, except you're going to have to stop watching me and Jessie from afar. It makes us nervous."

"I won't have to do that anymore," he said like he was pretty happy about it. "Now that we're friends, I can get up closer to both of you."

My eyes almost crossed with the effort of keeping my face from showing what his words had done to my heart. It started swelling and beating and carrying on till I was sure he could hear it. But all he said was, "Better get on back now, before they leave you."

He touched his fingers to his hat, so I turned Polly around and left. I looked back once, and he was still sitting there watching us. I hadn't found out a whole lot about him, but I'd discovered something new about myself, and that unsettled me considerably.

What I'd discovered was how somebody else could do something deep down inside of you. Well, of course I knew that other people could hurt your feelings or make you feel glad or ashamed, as the case may be, but nobody had ever made me feel the way Mr. Garrett had. And he hadn't done anything but say a few words and look at me. Jessie had told me after the Hiram and Homer escapade that nobody was ever supposed to touch me until my wedded husband did. "Keep yourself clean and pure, Emma," she'd said, "so as to present yourself as a worthy vessel to your husband."

I knew that was Bible talk, but it came to take on new meaning after I met Mr. Garrett, because every time he looked directly at me I felt like something was filling up and then emptying out somewhere in the bottom of my stomach. And the suffusion and defusion that rose and fell in my face and other parts of me was more than I could handle. I just couldn't help myself. It was like something was going on inside my flesh and bones that brought about a weakness of the mind. I was ashamed of it, too, for I remembered Mrs. Emmons and Mrs. Harris back home talking about a certain girl being blinded by love and having her head turned and filled with foolishness. I knew now what they'd meant, because I do believe that Mr. Garrett had turned mine completely, and if the name of what he'd done was love, then it had caught up with me before I was ready for it.

I asked Jessie later on what it meant to love somebody, and she said it meant being closer to that person and knowing him better than anybody else in the world. I guess that included knowing the carnal part as well, which the Bible didn't think too much of, but it interested me considerably.

13

But now it is come upon thee, and thou faintest;
it toucheth thee, and thou art troubled.
—*Job 4:5*

Tracking Mr. Garrett down hadn't done me a whole lot of good. I still didn't know what he was really up to, and he stayed on my mind to such an extent that I was having trouble thinking of much else. I kept having these unfamiliar stirrings that made me want to lay down somewhere by myself and think up another reason to ride out and see him. I wanted him to look at me again, and then I didn't want him to, because if he ever looked hard enough he'd surely see the real Emma Louise and not Emmett at all, and then where would we be? I figured he knew just about everything, and he'd never be able to miss what he was doing to my inner workings if he looked hard enough. My best bet was to stay as far away from him as I could, but I kept thinking about him and feeling drawn to him and wanting, and not wanting, him to know that I was Emma. It got so bad that Jessie asked me if I was sick, and upon being told no, she made me take a dose of calomel on the grounds that it couldn't hurt me.

It just added to my vexation, because then she took it in her head that the monthlies were about to come upon me. I didn't want to hear about such things right then, since it got all mixed up with Mr. Garrett and what I would do if my body took such a notion while I was still attired in Hiram's garments. But Jessie wasn't about to meddle too much with what was supposed to be my husband's job to teach me, so she just said that if they came, they came, and that it was a condition that was part and parcel of being a woman, and that I wasn't to worry myself about them until I had to. She said I'd have plenty of time to study on them, what with all the collecting and

120

washing of rags that went along with the whole condition. I declare there's more to being a female woman than I'd previously thought. It purely suited me to take time out to be Emmett for as long as Jessie would let me. But it was hard staying that way. When I looked at Mr. Garrett or thought of Mr. Garrett, it felt like a spurt of blossoming came on me from out of nowhere.

I even took to tying Polly to the back of the wagon and riding inside with Jessie when the little Donners were down for naps.

"Was it really true what you told me the other day, Jessie?" I asked as we swayed together in the wagon.

"I expect it was since I don't usually tell stories. What was it I said?"

"You said, or halfway said," I corrected myself, "that if I put my frock back on, I'd generate some attentions."

"You certainly would. Especially since you've got everybody around here fooled. Even Mr. Cobb, who I thought would've guessed by now, seeing you spend so much time with him."

I steered her away from that line, because Jessie wasn't convinced that Mego had been brought up right. She had to close her eyes every time he took out his knife for supper.

"That's not what I'm talking about," I said. "I'm talking about another kind of attention." It mortified me to have to spell it out for her, but she had her mind on higher things.

She looked at me for a minute and then smiled. "Why, Em. Are you thinking about taking up with somebody?"

"No, I am not. Don't start on me, Jessie. I just want to know how much damage a frock is liable to do once I get back in one. And besides," I told her, "there's nobody around here I could take to, frock or no."

"I thought that middle Jackson boy might've caught your eye," she said.

"I'm not talking about Jake Jackson or anybody else, especially him. I'm talking about frocks, Jessie. Frocks!" I was about to get put out with that little smile she kept giving me.

"All right. I'll stop teasing you," she said, "but it's not just frocks by themselves, Em. They're just the, well, I guess they're the outward signifiers of the difference between men and ladies.

And men are just born liking different things." She stopped and thought about what she'd just said. Then she said, "What I mean is, gentlemen like what's different from them. And that's why frocks catch their eye."

Well, I'd of never figured that out if I'd studied on it a lifetime. I had to rearrange some of my previous thinking to get it settled in.

"I think it's about time for you to get out of those trousers, anyway," she went on. "This whole deceitful business worries me to death, and it's not something a missionary ought to encourage."

"That's just what I was coming to, Jessie," I said, thinking fast. "I was thinking how the Lord must've put it in our minds, because just think of all the added attentions we'd of had if I'd been in a frock all this time. Remember Homer and Hiram, and what almost happened when they saw the difference between us and them."

She shuddered and said, "I remember, and that's why, in spite of the Donners' kindness, it's probably better for you to stay as you are. We'll be leaving them in a few days, and there's no telling what kind of people we'll have to travel with. Unless, of course, you want to be Emma again, and if you do, we'll manage."

"I don't, Jessie. I really don't. I was just asking for when the time comes. So I'll know what to expect."

That funny little smile came back and she said, "You know that the Lord has a husband already picked out for you, don't you?"

"Who?"

"Well, I don't know. I just know He does. He knows everything."

"Oh, me," I moaned. "I hope it's somebody I like, because if it's not, I may have to go against the Lord Jehovah and get myself in awful trouble."

"Em," Jessie said with a warning look.

"Well, would you have somebody you didn't like?"

"If I knew it was the Lord's will, I would," she said, and

I knew she meant it, even though she didn't sound especially joyful about it.

It was the day after our talk that we topped a rise and looked across Laramie Creek at the fort we'd been aiming for all this time. It sat on a broad, flat meadow in the triangle made by the Laramie and the Platte. The scene fairly took my breath away, for the plain around it swarmed with Indians and lodges and horses and traders. There must have been upwards of a thousand lodges pitched there, though Mego said it was about half that number, but since it was Sioux, then that accounted for the double commotion.

Our wagons strung out along the edge of the lodges and we headed downriver to set up camp where the noise level was tolerable and where we could graze our stock. I could hardly wait to get back to the fort and get my fill of the greatest spectacle I'd ever seen, and that included Independence, Missouri. Everybody else was anxious, too, for the fort was the first trading post we'd come to in six hundred and forty-two miles, according to Mr. Bryant's reckoning. The men rushed to unhitch the teams, giving them swats on the rump to send them to water. Nobody paid any mind to guarding them, thinking, I guess, that we'd come up on a center of civilization and not just an outpost in the wilderness. The womenfolk drug out rough-dried finery and dressed up to visit the wives of the traders. Some of them were right put out to discover later on that every lady at the fort was an Indian of some stripe. "And wearing silk dresses too," Mrs. Conners sniffed as she tied an apron over her good muslin and slammed a lid on a pot.

"Now, don't you go wandering through that Indian camp by yourself," Jessie warned me. Then she laughed like a little girl. " 'Cause I want to go with you."

I was eager to get in the midst of what looked to be about three county fairs and a revival rolled up together. Nothing would do, though, but I had to wait for Jessie while she changed her attire, brushed out her hair, and put it back up again.

And not only that, I had to wait for Mego to eat. He said he couldn't bring himself to go amongst that ruckus without something on his stomach, and I wasn't to go without him. He never had paid much attention to the way of the sun or to the regulated mealtimes that my system, and everybody else's, was on. I'd seen him sleep all day in camp and be awake all night with nothing to do but smoke his pipe and sing Injun, as he called it, which could be pretty eerie till you got used to it. Back on the trail, he'd oftentimes wake up hours before sunrise, ride out by himself for game, and then camp miles up the trail to feast on whatever he'd caught, and be sitting there, fat and sassy, waiting for us to catch up to him. When I asked him why he didn't eat and sleep when normal folks did, he said mountain time was different and so were mountain folks.

"Why, I recollect the time," he told me, "when ole Gabe Bridger war aleadin' a passel of preachers an' sech like to kindy scout out the country fer a mission place and they was cotched by the snows. They had to winter over close to Bayou Salade, an' ole Gabe never could git used to civilized doin's. He war nigh on to bein' a Injun his own self in them days, an' he didn't see no use fer change, but I'm hyar to tellee, he 'bout drove them folks shiny-eyed. He'd rise up from his blankets 'bout two o'clock of the A.M. an' clatter roun' fixin' vittles, an' when he'd et enough, he'd take this hyar pie plate an' play a tune on it with his Green River. He'd commence to sing 'Hi-yi-yi-yi, Hi-yo, Hi-hi-yo,' Injun style, to keep in practice, ye onderstand. An' them pore folks never could git their full sleep fer they wasn't sot on the same clock as the Blanket Chief, which war what the Injuns called him.

"So's, one of 'em come up with this ongenious idear to keep Gabe quiet when he felt a need to git up afore sunrise. He taken on to learn him to read. Did a good job of it, too, fer Gabe could read any book handed to him atter that, an' pick right up on them words like he was born to it. An' that's how the Rocky Mountain College come about, all from the way he et."

I didn't much believe him, but couldn't refute him, as I'd seen stranger things come about from lesser matters.

About the time Jessie jumped down from the wagon, all combed and polished, Mego put out his fire, wiped his knife clean, and asked if we wanted an armed escort before taking on the Sioux Nation.

"We would indeed, Mr. Cobb," Jessie said, and took his arm like she was starting a promenade and a do-si-do. Mego walked gingerly beside her, with his arm cocked out to his side for her to hold on to.

"Hitch it up thar, littl'un," he said to me. "Me an' Miss Jessie aim on takin' a leetle air an' callin' in at the fort."

As we walked through our camp he greeted each lady with a tip of his hat and acted, all around, like Jessie had turned his grizzled head.

We had to walk through the Sioux encampment to get to the fort and it was an education in itself. I'd never seen such a sight nor heard such a racket. There were Indians on ponies, Indians in lodges, Indians singing, dancing, sleeping, cooking, gambling, and gamboling. The braves didn't pay us much mind, though some of them spoke in an outlandish tongue to Mego and one or two eyed Jessie. The squaws were something else, though. We picked up a string of them as they crooned over Jessie, fingering her dress and her hair and touching her skin.

"They don't mean no harm, Miss Jessie," Mego told her. "They're asayin' ye're a purty leetle thang, but they misdoubt ye could do much work."

"I don't mind, Mr. Cobb, they seem very nice. I do wish I had some tracts to give them, though."

"They can't read, Jessie," I said, and she looked a little put out at the reminder, but we'd gotten to the fort by that time, so it didn't matter.

Fort Laramie was built like two square boxes, one set inside the other. There was only one way to get in, and that led us into a wide hallway between a set of thick doors in the adobe walls of each square. The hall was lined with storerooms where the clerks traded with the Indians. Mego told us that when the Indians started working up their medicine and getting too big for their britches, the traders closed and locked the inner doors so the Indians couldn't get inside. Today, though, both doors were open, and we went through into a quadrangle that was filled with people from our train and the Oregon train, along with Indians and trappers and traders of all sorts. It looked and sounded like a free-for-all that hadn't quite come to blows but was on the verge of it. The problem was that the emigrants had come in expecting to pay St. Louis and Independence prices and found instead scandalously unparalleled markups, which was what I heard Mr. Reed call them.

We wandered through the crowd looking at buffalo robes and Indian beadwork, examining the fineness of flour, and scrutinizing bolts of cloth. Mego stopped to slap the backs of old pards and I looked around while Jessie smoothed out a length of gingham. Just as she stretched it out between her nose and hand to measure the first yard, she stopped and held it there like a face veil.

I looked over at what had caught her attention, and there, leaning against a wall with his hat tilted over his face, was Mr. Garrett. He might've been asleep except, when Jessie saw him, he straightened up and came right over to us. I got that same feeling I had back on the prairie, the one where everything shifts over a peg, leaving you more troubled with what's going on inside than outside. I don't know how he managed to do that, but I think Jessie felt it, too, for she just stood there looking up at him over a stretch of blue and white gingham.

"Miss Jessie," he said, lifting his hat, "I believe we met in Independence."

If Jessie had the same feeling I had, she shook it off, for she came back at him right smartly. "Met, yes. But not introduced," she said, stung by his use of her given name.

"Allow me, then, Miss Heath," he said, with what looked to me to be a great deal more nicety than the occasion required. "J. C. Garrett, at your service."

"Pleased, I'm sure," Jessie said in a way that didn't sound it. But since she'd demanded courtesy of him, there was nothing for it but to offer her hand as well. He took it and held it and turned it over and looked at it, and bless me if he didn't lean over then and plant a kiss right on it.

Jessie snatched it back like he'd burned it. And that was where Mr. Garrett made his mistake and canceled out all the goodwill he had started building up. Jessie liked courteous doings, but she didn't take to flat-out familiarity. And in her book, hand-kissing was more familiar than she could stand.

She drew herself up and dressed him down. "Mr. Garrett, you have a shameful habit of touching ladies in ways that go beyond the bounds of common decency. No doubt that comes from inadequate training and the keeping of wicked company somewhere along the line, and cannot be laid entirely to your account. But a gentleman does not engage in unwelcome and unexpected conversation and social intercourse with ladies—especially with missionary ladies, which I'm one of."

"Maybe you'd give me a lesson on the proper kind of intercourse for missionary ladies," he said, and cut his eyes over at me with a wink that curled my insides.

Before Jessie could digest that, Mr. Garrett went real still and looked beyond us in a way that made me turn and look along with him. It was Mr. Green who'd caught his eye. He was across the way haranguing a trader for un-Christian profit gouging, a state of affairs that the trader apologized for, and he offered to hike his prices up to a Christian level if Mr. Green would indicate how much higher he ought to go. Mr. Green didn't think the sally was too funny, even though a number of folks did.

"I'll take that lesson later," Mr. Garrett said. He settled his hat on his head and threaded his way through the crowd toward Mr. Green.

I saw when Mr. Green spotted him, and I saw him turn white around the gills. He lost interest in profit margins and made a beeline for the doors. Mr. Garrett didn't hurry, but he didn't linger either as he left the fort right behind him.

"Reckon what that's about?" I asked Jessie.

"It's about bad manners and poor raising," she said, surprising me, until I realized she hadn't made the connection between Mr. Garrett and Mr. Green. "Let it be an example to avoid, Em."

We got back to our campsite tired but pleased with the

excursion to what Mego said was the Washington City of the West. Fort Laramie didn't strike me as a metropolitan hub, but it sure beat the wasteland we'd just crossed. We settled down for a few days to rest, wash, repack, and repair.

It came to me in a day or so that I hadn't seen Mr. Green making his rounds of the camp and stirring up his usual amount of discord. I kept an eye out for him then, and finally saw him sitting with three ladies, who were listening as he explained the finer points of dispensationalism. I took note of his hat, which remained on his head even though he was in the presence of ladies and engaged in the exposition of Scripture. That was not Mr. Green's usual practice, so I strolled by fairly close and cut my eyes in his direction to see what ailed him. The edge of a bandage showed underneath his hat, sparking my curiosity even more. I made it my business to get behind him and saw that the bandage went all the way around his head. Then I went to find Mego.

"What happened to Mr. Green?" I asked when I found him stretched out in the shade. "He's got his head bandaged."

"Air he still abreathin'?" he asked from under his hat.

"Not only breathing, but preaching. What happened to him?"

"I 'spect Garrett fin'lly took a Green River to his noggin."

"Good Lord!" I said before I could help myself. "You mean he scalped him?"

"I misdoubt that," Mego said with a jaw-creaking yawn. "Not if he's still apreachin'. More'n likely he jes' nicked him round in the gen'al way an' bloodified him some. So's to give him the idear, like."

Well, I had to sit down and get my breath back after that. "Does this sort of thing go on very much out in Oregon?" I finally asked, wondering again about what we were getting into.

"Naw, not hardly atall," Mego answered, scratching himself in a lazy sort of way. "They gen'lly go fer the whole shebang, an' cut an' slash the whole thang off. Hit's easier, ye see, 'cause ye don't have to be so keerful with yore cuttin'.

But Garrett now, he's a keerful man, an' a Christian to boot."

I leaned back against the tree, thinking I'd have to take this up with Jessie. Either Mego and Mr. Garrett had been misinformed on what made up a Christian, or she had.

14

Only by pride cometh contention, but with the
well-advised is wisdom.
—*Proverbs 13:10*

Mr. Green didn't make any more visits to the fort. He stayed
close to his own tent; in fact, he came out in the open only
when he could gather two or three of the womenfolk to be in
the midst of. He gave out that he was suffering the consequences
of being in the proximity of a hornet-stung mule, garnering
thereby a certain amount of female sympathy and covered dishes
for his pains. The whole affair had made him edgy and anxious
to get the train moving again, since for him Fort Laramie had
become as pestilential a spot as Ash Hollow.

And he wasn't the only one to begin thinking of moving
on. For a while everybody in the train had been in a holiday
spirit, congratulating ourselves on getting this far in a fairly
sound state of body and mind. But the last lap of the journey,
rumored to be the worst traveling of all, lay ahead of us and
we began to turn our minds to it. It was the chief topic around
the campfires and in the daily gatherings of the men, especially
among the California-bound.

The Oregon emigrants didn't have any decisions to make,
other than when to pack up and move on. There was only one
route to Oregon and all they had to do was get on it. It was
the ones who were set for California who argued and harangued
and studied and planned, for there was more than one way to
get there. The tried and true way was to stay on the route to
Oregon up to Fort Hall and then split off onto the California
trail. The problem with that, though, was that it was some four
hundred miles farther than a straight and direct route over the
Wasatch and Sierra ranges.

"Instead of going northwest to Fort Hall and then turning

south," Mr. Connors said, drawing a map in the dirt to picture his meaning, "I say 'twould be better to go southwest to Fort Bridger, then set our noses straight west and foller 'em to California. It's a nigher way and we ought to take it, and not be dawdling on a roundabout route."

"I ain't inclined to make four hundred extry miles if I don't have to," somebody else put in.

That seemed sensible to me, too, especially since Mr. Lansford Hastings, the friend of emigrants and the writer of books, had put out that there was an easier trail on his Cutoff, and that he'd traveled it and marked it and recommended it. But Mr. Hastings wasn't there to lead them himself, so there were some who didn't want to be the first to strike out on an unknown way.

Others, including both Mr. Donners, Mr. Reed, and Mr. Bryant, could think of nothing but saving all those extra miles. Even Mr. Jim Clyman, an old friend of Mego's who showed up one day, couldn't unpersuade them. He said he'd just come off of Hastings' Cutoff and it was the nearest place to hell he'd ever been.

"Ye can't git yer wagons acrosst the Wasatch," he said, "an' the Great Salt Desert is worse'n I kin tell ye. Don't take it. I been thar an' I'm tellin' ye, ye can't make it."

Mego nodded and put in his two cents worth. "This chile crosst it with Jedidiah Smith back in '27, an' come outta that fearful barren place more dead 'an alive. We'uns et hosses an' ants to do that good. Hit ain't no way fer waggins an' wimmenfolk."

Some listened and took the advice. They would stay on the familiar trail up by Fort Hall. Others, including the Misters Jacob and George Donner, got it in their minds that Mr. Clyman and Mego were lying, though they couldn't figure out why. I heard Mr. Jacob say that they probably had a stake in the Fort Hall trade and that was why they wanted the emigrants to go that way. And he didn't blame them, he said, it was only good business practice and the kind of thing he'd engaged in himself. So the Donners and a few others set themselves for the Cutoff, aiming to be in California ahead of the rest. So the camp began to rearrange itself into smaller groups of wagons, depending on which route had been decided on. A delegation of the Sioux, in an act of neighborliness, came by and advised us not to split up too much. They said their hearts tended to turn bad when they saw a few wagons off by themselves.

I didn't pay much attention to the whys and wherefores of the various routes. There was only one road to Oregon, and Jessie intended for us to be on it come hell or high water.

"I'm done with 'em," Mego told me from around his pipe-stem. "Ye can't tell some folks nuthin' an' ye mought as well let 'em be. Pore doin's' is what this hoss has to say. Now if you an' Miss Jessie was aheadin' fer Californy, I'd hawg-tie ye an' carry ye on the old trail. But I ain't up to manhandlin' so many dang fools."

We were sitting together on the bank of the Laramie away from the bustle of the camp and all the argumentation that went on from morning till night. It was a warm, lazy afternoon tending toward evening, and I didn't want to be put to work, which I would've been if Jessie spotted me. With all the talk of splitting up and reaching destinations and settling in a new land, I was feeling like we didn't have too many more days of what I'd come to get used to. I'd taken to trail life, and sometimes thought I'd like to be on the move forever. Still and all, there were lots of nights when I got real lonesome for a bed of my own and a place of my own. Papa used to say we were farmers born and bred, and couldn't ever take to anything that didn't include our own fields around us. We didn't have that on the trail, and didn't look to ever get it, what with Jessie's heart set on being a missionary and not ever owning anything you could walk on and plant.

I was about to nod off when Mr. Garrett suddenly showed up right beside me. I've always blamed the state of my stature on the scare he gave me, in spite of his warm hand on my shoulder.

"Ye ain't lost yore touch," Mego told him. "I only heerd ye the last twenty foot or so."

"That's room enough for hair-lifting," Mr. Garrett admitted.

"Set a spell," Mego invited. "This hyar littl'un is a Oregon emigrater an' a pard o' mine."

"We've met," Mr. Garrett said, flicking his eyes toward me and starting up that warmish feeling I got every time he was in the vicinity.

"Air ye through with Thomas Green? Or air we'uns in fer more entertainment?"

"Through for now. Unless he asks for more."

"That ain't hardly likely. How's yer other medicine agoin'?"

"It could go either way," Mr. Garrett answered, taking out his makings. I watched his hands as he made his smoke, and thought about the things they had done to Mr. Green. I began to feel more than a little squeamish, but I couldn't stop watching them.

"The trouble is," Mr. Garrett went on, "there's nobody to deal with, unless it's this one here."

They both looked at me, and Mego started laughing while Mr. Garrett smiled a little around his eyes. I didn't know what I had to do with anything concerning his medicine, but they were acting like I did.

"I'd say about six horses and some tobacco, wouldn't you?" Mr. Garrett asked.

"Better throw in a jug or two o' pepper whiskey fer that 'un," Mego said. "Ye got to offer a fair price agoin' in, er this hyar littl'un'll take his business som'ers else." Then Mego got real serious and said to me, "Ye want this chile to make the deal fer ye? I know the goin' price fer Shoshoni an' Nez Percé an' Crow an' all of 'em, an' I won't let him rook ye none."

"What are we talking about?"

"Why, we'uns air atalkin' 'bout Miss Jessie. Garrett here is amakin' ye a offer, but I thank if ye play yer cyards right, ye kin up him considerable. Miss Jessie ort to brang a pretty penny, an' by gum if ye won't be sot fer life when the deal's made."

"Sell Jessie?"

"Yep. Hit's the done thang in these parts, an' ye don't want to go agin the grain of normal doin's. Set yore price an', aye grannies, we'll make him pay it!"

"Well, by gum, my sister's not for sale! What's the matter with you, Mr. Garrett, that you have to buy a wife?"

"Oh, I'm not thinking about a wife," Mr. Garrett said. "It's getting on toward winter, and I have to think about keeping my blankets warm."

"I'd think it'd be cheaper to build a fire," I shot back, about tired of the joke.

Mego slapped his leg and said, "Don't that beat all! Build a far, Garrett! That's all ye need fer warmin' blankets! That littl'un don't take nuthin' offa nobody, do he?"

They settled down after that and talked about how bad the trapping was and how they missed the rendezvous and one thing and another. I only half listened, caught up with watching Mr. Garrett and wondering what he'd do if he saw me in a frock. Would he offer a bride price for me if he knew I could be a bride? Even as I thought it I knew that all the silk dresses in Fort Laramie wouldn't draw that kind of attention from him. For one thing, he was a lot older than me, and older than Jessie, too, but at least she was in shooting range and I wasn't. It's strange how you can know all the facts, and figure out in your mind what's likely and what's not, and at the same time keep on thinking about what you know couldn't happen in a month of Sundays. Well, the Bible says even old men could dream dreams, and I figured I could too.

"Let's go find your sister," Mr. Garrett said to me, and then to Mego, "Does that suit you?"

"Hit shore do. This chile wishes somebody'd light a far under 'em an' git 'em movin'. Float yer stick an' see whichaways hit goes."

I'd missed something of a serious nature while engaged in reverie, but didn't have time to ask what it was as Mr. Garrett was already headed for the Donner camp. I caught up with him and we walked over to where Jessie was sitting in Mrs. Donner's rocking chair brushing out her hair. It fell all around her shoulders, and looked so pretty that I was proud all over again that she was my sister. I wanted to point it out to Mr. Garrett, but he'd already noticed.

"Miss Jessie," he said, removing his hat, and holding it like a gentleman, "I'd like a word with you and your brother, if you'll walk with us awhile."

"This is a most inconvenient time, Mr. Garrett. As you can see," Jessie said, trying to pin up her hair in a hurry, but having little success. She didn't like people to see her in a state of dishevelment.

"I think it's important, Jessie, so you better come on," I told her, and she did.

We walked away from the camp, so we could talk without half the train listening in, and ended up strolling along the bank of the creek.

We'd gone some little ways when Jessie stopped and said, "Are you going to speak, Mr. Garrett, or do you plan on walking us all the way back to Independence?"

He smiled almost to himself, like he didn't want her to know he was about to laugh. But then he turned serious, and when I heard what he had to say I did too.

"Miss Jessie, some of us who know these parts are getting worried about this train. You'll be caught in the snows if you don't get moving."

"Well, I don't have any say about such things," Jessie flung at him. "Besides, this is July and winter's a long way off."

"Not that long in the mountains. Even if you started to-night, you'd likely run into snow up in the Blues. And the longer you wait, the worse it's going to be."

"Then tell somebody, Mr. Garrett! What do you expect Em and me to do? Pack up and go by ourselves?"

"First, we've already told everybody and they won't listen. And second, I could take you and Em, along with Mego Cobb, on ahead, but it's too dangerous with the Sioux and the Crow in their present state of mind. We've decided it's better for you to stay with the train."

"That's what we're planning to do, anyway," she said, sounding like she'd just remembered that long-suffering is one of the fruits of the Spirit. "Is that all you wanted to tell us? Because if it is, I need to get back."

"No, listen to me, now. If you don't get to Fort Hall till late August, stay and winter there. Don't let anybody talk you into trying to beat the snows. Let the fools go on without you. Mego'll stay with you, and I'll be there come spring. We'll get you on to Waiilatpu early next year, if you're still determined to go. We'll do it either by ourselves or with the first emigrants that come through, depending on what the Indians are up to then."

"Are you telling us not to go to Oregon until next year?"

"I'm saying if it takes this crew till September to get to Fort Hall, you stay there. I'm contracted to drive some horses from here to St. Louis or I'd hang around and see that you do it."

That was the wrong thing to say to Jessie and she let him know it.

"Mr. Garrett, I know you mean well and think you're doing the right thing, but I take orders only from the Lord. He's sending me to Oregon, and I don't have a mind to wait around for the weather to suit you."

Mr. Garrett just stood there looking at her with a little smile on his face.

"Well," she demanded, "do you think you know more than the Lord Jehovah?"

"I know the country and I know the weather," he said, and then turned to me. "Em, if Mego tells you to winter at Fort Hall, will you do it?"

I looked from him to Jessie and tried to figure out what I'd do if Jessie didn't want to stay. I'd never gone against her before, seeing it as my duty to follow along and keep her out of trouble. But now I might have to take the chance that she'd just leave me if I dug in against her. To look at it another way though, it was high time I started having a say in what we did.

"If Mego said stay," I said, "I'd stay. They know what they're talking about, Jessie, and the Lord uses some terrible strange messengers sometimes, as you well know. Mr. Garrett may be one of them. Besides, you wouldn't leave me by myself, would you?"

I thought she was going to cry, which she usually did when she didn't get her way.

"Well," she fumed, "the three of you have it all planned

and, Em, you know very well I wouldn't leave you, in spite of being provoked to death. And as far as the Lord's messengers go, I know He works in strange ways, but this beats all, and I'm not convinced of it!"

She flounced herself off, but then stopped and looked back at us.

"I'll stay in Fort Hall, Mr. Garrett, if I'm forced to." And she glared at me. "But I don't like it and I don't think it'll be necessary. I'm going to lay this before the Lord and let Him straighten it out."

We watched her leave, and I took a deep breath and said, "We've done it now, Mr. Garrett. When Jessie and the Lord get together, somebody'd better watch out."

"Maybe so," he said, still watching the place where she'd been. "But I don't think the Lord wants her to freeze to death any more than we do. It'd be a shameful waste and that's a fact. You stick to your guns and do what I tell you. Some people have to be taken care of whether they want it or not."

Now, that was exactly the way I felt about Jessie, and it did me good to find an active partner in the enterprise.

"What about this praying business?" I asked him. "If she cuts loose against us, there's no telling what'll happen."

"She's not going to pray for something that'll get her in trouble."

"You don't know her like I do," I said.

"No, but I intend to." He looked at me right sharp then and said, "You wouldn't mind, would you?"

I shook my head, knowing that if he was after Jessie, which I'd figured all along, then that was the best I could hope for, taking all the facts into consideration. I felt good about it in one way, for that meant he'd stay around. But in another way I felt like I'd lost something I'd never even had a chance to have and probably never would. There couldn't ever be but one Mr. Garrett.

"Mr. Garrett?" I remembered something that a brother might be expected to ask. "I hope your intentions are more honorable than they've appeared to be up to now."

He laughed a little and said, "As honorable as they have to be."

That wasn't much of an answer, but it didn't worry me too much. I knew how Jessie felt about good manners and social intercourse and other such matters of honor, and he wouldn't get far if he commenced any dishonorable business with her. Besides, I could always throw in with her and the Lord and clean his plow good if it looked like he needed it.

15

Come, my beloved, let us go forth into the field.
—*Song of Solomon 7:11*

We kept on lingering at Fort Lamarie, even though folks talked about how winter was out there somewhere and how it came earlier in the mountains than in Ohio or Virginia. But the days were long and hot and soporific, and it was easier to talk than to move. There was always another axle that ought to be fixed, or somebody would decide it would be better not to fool with wagons at all and he'd swap his whole outfit for a string of mules. Then everything would have to be unloaded and repacked, accompanied, as Mr. Reed said, by a surplus of swearing. People were also trying to sell things they didn't want anymore, things like chests and dressers and trunks that had seemed vital back East but had become worrisome now that the mountains were so near.

It was strange how, along with dividing up into smaller traveling groups, people's feelings had divided up too. Most were happy and lighthearted, not at all daunted by the prospect of the travail before us. But there were some, like Mrs. Donner, who suffered from a morbidness of the spirit that couldn't be explained. She told Jessie that crying for no reason had never afflicted her before, but now she was about overcome with it. Mego said that the mountains did that to some people. But we weren't hardly in the mountains yet, so it didn't seem to bode well for Mrs. Donner that mountain sickness had reached out for her while she was still on the plains.

I heard her tell Mr. George that they had many unneeded articles in their wagons and she'd be glad to be shut of them if he wanted to lighten the load. He just laughed at her worries and said there was no call to leave anything behind since the road they were taking was broad and level and would accommodate the heaviest of wagons.

Our group of twenty wagons joined some of the Oregon-bound with plans to travel together up through South Pass to where the Hastings' Cutoff began. Mr. Donner made arrangements for Jessie and me to go on from there with Colonel and Mrs. Thornton. As Mrs. Nancy Thornton was ailing most of the time, Jessie would do the cooking and the tending to domestic needs. Since her duties would be increased, I told her I'd take on the water-drawing for her, and she told me she'd already thought of that.

We left the fort early on a July morning and camped some twelve miles beyond it that night. I was sad to be leaving Mr. Garrett behind and feared that I might take to sudden crying like Mrs. Donner because of it. Jessie wasn't one of the joyous souls, either, in spite of the fact that we were on the last leg of our journey.

When we camped late in the afternoon that first day, she drew me apart from the others, saying we had things to talk about.

"I declare, Em, I don't know what's wrong with me," she said. "I feel such an inner turmoil of the spirit that I have lost my peace of mind entirely. I feel I am out of fellowship with the Lord, and it's all because of that Mr. Garrett."

I didn't want to admit to the same feelings, though I was somewhat surprised to find she had them too.

"How's that, Jessie?"

"He's got me all dispirited and worried about the weather and our slow pace. I didn't think about such things before he came along to put them in my mind. I left all that to the Lord, but now I can't get my mind off him. Off what he said, that is. What if we stay at Fort Hall and he doesn't come back? We could be stranded there forever with my mission work stopped dead in its tracks."

"That's not likely to happen, Jessie," I told her. "Mego would get us on through. But I'm inclined to think that Mr. Garrett will do whatever he says he'll do. You don't need to worry about him not showing up."

"Well, a gentleman's word is his bond, I reckon," she said, "but I fear that Mr. Garrett may not be much of a gentleman."

I had to agree with her on that, for he didn't wear embroidered waistcoats or use eloquent language or do much of anything like the gentlemen I knew. It seemed to me, though, that a gentleman might not be the first requirement in our situation and said as much to her.

"Yes, things do seem to be turned around out here, don't they?" Then she leaned toward me and lowered her voice. "What's he really like, Em?"

"Who?"

"Mr. Garrett, of course. You've been around him. What's he like?"

"Well, I don't know, Jessie. I guess he's like most men, only bigger somehow, or better. Maybe just different in some way."

"That's not telling me anything. I want to know if we can trust him. That's what I'm interested in."

I think she really believed that then, but I recognized the symptoms of something else, having had a dose of it myself.

"I guess he's hard to get to know because he doesn't talk a whole lot," I said. "More of a doer than a talker."

"What else?"

"Let me see. He smokes little Mexican cigars and likes them a lot."

"I declare, Em. Tell me something about his character, not his habits."

"Well, Mego says he's a Christian."

"He is!" She jumped up and brushed off her skirt. "Let's get back. My heart's at ease now. A Christian! I would never have thought it, but we're not supposed to judge. Probably he hasn't had proper instruction, living out here away from a church and all, and that's the reason he looks and acts so much like a heathen."

"That's probably it," I said, thinking about what he'd done to Mr. Green but deciding not to mention it. "And think about this, Jessie. He said he wanted you to give him some lessons."

"So he did." Then she stopped, with a stricken look on

her face. "And I failed him, Em! I let his uncivilized behavior get in the way and didn't recognize a soul that was hungering and thirsting after knowledge."

"You're just beginning missionary work, Jessie, and can't expect to be perfect in it right off. Besides," I told her, "I don't think Mr. Garrett's suffered any permanent damage."

"Oh, I hope not, for we're talking eternal damage, Em, and I don't want it laid to my account that I failed in my duty toward him."

"He'll let you rectify any past failings, more than likely."

"I truly hope so, Em. Oh, I wish I could see him again, even for a little while, so I could redeem myself."

I began to think, after that, that Jessie might ought to be muzzled for her own good. Every time she prayed for something, she got it. And now even her wishes had an unnatural power, for as we were going to our rest that night, Jessie to her tent and I to my pallet under a wagon nearby, Mr. Garrett stepped out of the dark. He gave us both a singular scare and Jessie forgot her former resolution.

"Mr. Garrett, you are the worst man I've ever seen for unexpected behavior! What do you mean coming out of the dark like that? You don't have a lick of sense!"

He laughed and said his horses hadn't yet arrived so he thought he'd pay us a call before we got too far away.

"Well," Jessie said, smoothing back her hair and getting herself together. "I am glad to see you, in spite of everything, for I feel remiss in not giving you the attention you needed back at the fort."

Mr. Garrett's eyebrows went straight up at that, but he handled himself in a modest way. "I'm still in need of it," he said, giving my shoulder a squeeze.

"I know you are, and I intend to meet it this very night. I wish you'd come earlier when there was enough light to read a tract. I have one that lays everything out so well that you couldn't fail to grasp its meaning. We can use a lantern, though. Em, run to my tent and get one, along with the tract in my Testament. That one called *Savagery or Salvation*."

It took me a little while to get a lantern lit and find the

particular tract required. By the time I came back out Mr. Garrett and Jessie were gone. I didn't know what to do. It might be that they no longer wanted a light in the darkness. But on the other hand, Jessie didn't generally change her mind, and she'd be expecting me to show up with what she'd sent me for. So I went looking for them.

I headed out away from the circle of cook fires toward the spring we'd camped by. They couldn't miss hearing or seeing me, for I swung the lantern and made no effort to be quiet as I went through the brush. Even so, I called Jessie as I went.

"Over here, Em," she said from the dark, and I found them standing together beside the spring.

"Here's the lantern and here's the tract," I said. "And I think I'll go on to bed now, since I'm not up to a prayer meeting tonight."

"Wait," she said, "sit down over there while I talk to Mr. Garrett. It won't do for me to be out here alone with him just because he gets nervous with a lot of folks around. I declare, Mr. Garrett, you mountain people certainly have peculiar customs."

"Don't we, though," he agreed.

Then they sat on the ground with their heads close together near the lantern. Jessie opened her tract, and I moved out of the circle of light, feeling torn between doing what she'd told me to do and what I was certain Mr. Garrett wanted me to do. I sat down as far away as I thought decent to please them both and hugged my knees waiting for them to finish so I could go to bed.

I heard Jessie go on and on, reading aloud every word of the tract and explaining it to him as she went.

"Now, Mr. Garrett," she said, "we have a clear choice before us. We can either be a savage or a Christian. There's nothing in between, and you have to be one or the other. There comes a time in every man's life when he has to make that decision, and even if he does nothing, he is actually making a decision for savagery. I think you're at that point right now, don't you?"

"I think I am," he said.

I glanced over and saw him watching her. Even when she
pointed out things in the text, he'd nod and keep his eyes
traveling over her face. To tell the truth, I don't think he was
half listening.

"Now listen to this," she said. "I'm going to read this part
again, for it's important and you should keep it in your heart."

"If you get on to the Whitman mission at Waiilatpu this
year," he said to her, "I'll be there in the spring and see you
then."

"Fine, Mr. Garrett. Listen now."

"No, you listen. I figure you'll have enough of mission
work in the course of a year and be ready for something else
when I get back."

"That's hardly likely," she snapped and stood up, knowing
finally that his mind wasn't on spiritual matters. "I didn't come
out here with you to discuss my personal plans and have you
tell me I'm not cut out for mission work. You're not the first
one to tell me that, and you're not the first one to be wrong,
either. What I do in the course of a year is of no concern to
you, and I'll thank you not to take up any more of my time
pretending to an interest which you clearly don't have."

"Oh, I have an interest, all right," he told her, standing
up straight and close beside her. "The same one you have, if
you'll admit it."

He put a hand to the back of her neck then, and drew her
face toward his. I thought she'd smack him good, but the next
thing I knew he was kissing her and she was letting him, and
may even have been taking an active part in it. Before they were
half through he put his other hand around and below her waist
and pulled her in awful close to his lower limbs, and I felt like
King David did when he said something melted in the midst
of his bowels.

I stayed real still and tried not to look, and had a hard
time doing either one. I know for a fact that Jessie had never
submitted to such wraparound familiarity before, and it was
hard for me to know what I was supposed to do to keep her
out of the trouble she was undoubtedly into now. Always before
she'd wanted none of it, and my duty was clear to take her side

against all comers. But from the looks of things now, she didn't
need or want any help from me.

Mr. Garrett finally lifted his head and, without looking
around, called, "Em?"

"Yessir?"

"You can go on to bed now."

"Yessir."

"Em?" Jessie called.

"Yessum?" I answered, already on my way.

Mr. Garrett kissed her again, so I had to wait to see what
she wanted.

"I'll be along soon," she said.

So I went back to the camp and crawled in my blankets
and tried to quiet the stirrings of my heart. It's a settled fact
that I would've liked to have been on the receiving end in Jessie's
place. But somehow I didn't think I would've liked it as much
as she had. I guess I felt better with Mr. Garrett in the mind
and in the heart than in the living flesh. So to speak. I started
thinking how it would be to have him with us all the time, me
and Jessie and Mr. Garrett, and it made a nice prospect to ponder
on. If that happened, I could quit worrying about Jessie and all
the Hirams and Homers and Mr. Kesslers and let him have the
load. If he settled her in one place for good, I could also stop
worrying that she'd get another sudden call to the Canary Islands
or to some other foreign place that had needy savages. Once
she submitted herself to a wedded husband, I didn't think the
Lord would interfere in a legal contract. I planned out how the
three of us would be together on a farm somewhere, and it
wasn't long till my heart was comforted more than it'd been
since Papa passed, and I went to sleep.

The next morning Jessie was uncommonly quiet and
wouldn't answer any question I put to her. I asked her how
long she'd stayed out in the dark, and had she and Mr. Garrett
come to a meeting of the minds, but she kept saying, "Not now,
Em, I'm busy."

There was nothing to do but leave her alone, and as it
turned out she stayed too busy to talk for some days to come.
And during that time the trail got rougher and steeper as we

toiled up toward South Pass and the Great Divide. To tell the truth, I was too weary to do much talking myself, but I worried about her. Mr. Garrett was gone till spring now and it was in my mind how he was getting farther and farther away from us as he went east and we moved on west. We camped a day or two at Independence Rock for a celebration, and had hard going around Devil's Gate. Then we hit the Sweetwater, the river that was named for the load of sugar dumped in it one time by a bucking mule. We followed it up along a wide plateau and finally across the Divide.

We got to Pacific Springs late in July, though there was some argument as to the exact day it was, since we'd lost track of how long we'd been traveling. It was our last camp with the Donners, and with the separation nigh on us, Mrs. Donner cried all during supper and Jessie couldn't eat at all. It was like some awful dread had infected them both, and even Mr. George's high spirits couldn't cheer them up.

"Come on, Jessie," I said to her. "Let's look this place over."

We walked around the wagons, but, heeding Mego's warnings, didn't stray from sight.

"Sit down here on this wagon tongue," I told her. "Now, Jessie, something is bad wrong with you, and has been ever since you walked out with Mr. Garrett. I thought from the way you two took to each other that maybe you'd gotten a different call from the Lord. I thought maybe we'd found somebody who'd take care of us, and get us out of mission work, which I'm not suited for. I thought all that, but here you are going around sad and downhearted and won't talk to me. And I want to know what's going on."

She started crying then and went on with it an uncommonly long time.

I patted her on the back and said, "Jessie, he's going to come back. He said he would and he will."

She kept on saying no and crying some more, and I was hurting about as much as she was, since I'd never seen her carrying on that way before.

"Oh, Em, you don't know. It was just awful. Awful."

"What was, Jessie? Did Mr. Garrett do something?"

"He most certainly did. He took liberties. Liberties, Em! And that's not even the worse thing."

"Jingies, Jess. What could be worse than that?"

"That I let him and wanted him to. That's what's worse. But see, Em, I thought he knew that when a decent lady does, or lets, well, I mean, permits certain things, that meant an honorable state would ensue."

"I'm not following, Jessie."

"For goodness sake, Em," she said, wiping her face. "I thought, like any decent woman would, that he was making an offer of marriage!"

"And he wasn't?"

"No, he just laughed. Laughed, Em! When I said Mr. Spaulding could marry us and commission us in the Lord's work together, he said that wasn't the way they did things in the mountains and that, besides, he wasn't studying marriage or mission work."

"What in the world was he studying?"

"Oh, Em, you don't understand. He wanted the liberties of matrimony without the responsibilities. He's infected with heathen customs, that's what he is."

I thought about that for a while, trying to straighten out in my mind the different states of what could go on between men and ladies. I knew the marital state. That was the common one and everybody got real happy whenever it was entered into. I also knew the uncommon one, which involved the likes of Hiram and Homer, and that didn't make anybody happy but them, and was to be avoided by ladies even if it meant laying down their very lives. Now here Jessie was telling me about a third state, one where the lady was willing and so was the man, but without any troths being pledged in public services. Maybe that's what the Bible meant when it talked about having carnal knowledge of somebody, which you aren't supposed to have. I know Jessie said she'd pulled back before any damage had been done, but she'd admitted to being tempted while she thought his intentions were honorable. I figured then that she'd been troubled with some of the same mortifications that had been bothering me, but I truly hoped they wouldn't cause her to blossom any more than she'd already done. I gradually shut off my dream of the three of us together somewhere away from the mission field. It was plain that Mr. Garrett had a set of rules different from ours, but maybe it was just as well that we found out about it before he stirred up any more havoc inside Jessie or me. It was a shame, but there it was.

"Well, Jessie," I said, "if that's the way it is, then I guess the Lord still wants you on the mission field. That's what we started out for, and we'll just stay with that. So it's not like we didn't have something waiting for us."

"No, we don't even have that," she said with her face all covered over with her apron. "I'm not fit to be a missionary now. I've entertained impure thoughts in my heart and I fear they've ruined me for the Lord's work."

I ran that over in my mind for a while and came to the conclusion that it didn't make good sense. "If that's the case, then," I said, "it's hardly likely that anybody's fit for it. The Bible says that a man's heart is deceitful above all things and desperately wicked, who can know it? So you're probably not the first one to entertain whatever it was in your heart. And besides, Jessie, it was an honest mistake, for I had the same thoughts as you did."

She snapped her head up and said, "What!"

"Well, anybody would. Matrimony is part and parcel of courting, and that's sure what he was doing."

"Oh."

"And another thing, Jess. If you think you're unfit for missionizing, we could just go on to California with the Donners. How about doing that?"

She shook her head. "No, I'll stay on the path that the Lord set me on, and hope that He'll cleanse my heart in the doing. But it'll be hard, Em. Real hard."

I patted her again and told her that the Lord would probably be dealing with Mr. Garrett, too, but it didn't seem to bring her, or me, much comfort.

A Journal of Westward Travel
and Private Matters
(Property of Jessie Elizabeth Heath)

July 1, 1846: I am resolved to be more faithful to my journal, knowing how easily the mind forgets even those events and personages that would seem indelibly printed on the memory. One such is a certain Mr. Garrett, who made our acquaintance in less than propitious circumstances in the town of Independence. He was again at the Fort when we stopped there. He followed us here & seemed at first open to the leading of the Holy Ghost. It was my first opportunity to lead a soul into the knowledge of our Lord & Saviour, but something went wrong. Satan, who is ever ready to cast us down, surfaced in his breast, thereby causing me great anguish of mind. My sleep has been disturbed by all manner of impieties, the confession of which does not give me that sweet refreshment of spirit for which I long. Emma Louise offers no help, being less & less eager for the work which calls us, & being much enamored of Mr. Garrett. A condition that I find impossible to understand. May the words of my mouth and especially the meditations of my heart be acceptable to you, O my Lord and my Redeemer.

July 3: Camped near Independence Rock, a turtle-back mountain of reddish-gray stone rising some one hundred feet or more above the Sweetwater. We have at last abandoned the Platte, our constant companion for many weeks, and will, God willing, cross the Continental Divide in a few days. We shall then be in Oregon, though still a long way, I fear, from our final destination.

The trail to this point has been worse than even the most pessimistic could have envisaged. Very tedious going in oppressive heat. We left Fort Laramie well rested and eager to complete our journey, but each day has brought an increasingly hostile land for our perusal. I had not thought such barrenness possible. The trail is tortuous, heaped with boulders, cut with gullies and chasms, & the air is entirely without moisture. It is filled with an alkaline dust that parches and burns the skin along with the scorching rays of the sun. None but the most useless and fearsome of creatures survive in this rocky desert. We have always difficulties with the wagons, none having been built to withstand the kind of travel we are now engaged in.

In this land of brazen heat I am truly brought to submission before the Lord. I pray that he will equally bring my thoughts under submission, for I cannot seem to discipline them alone. They wander in the most distressing of paths.

July 4: We continue in camp to celebrate the Declaration of our Independence from Britain, still in sight of Independence Rock. Colonel Thornton, who had the last watch of the night, opened the festivities by firing his rifle and revolving pistol to welcome the coming day. Some of the ladies fashioned Old Glory from scraps of dress material & it was run up on a wagon tongue to rule over the celebration. Patriotic songs were sung, a reading of the Declaration was given, and various orations were delivered to remind us of the liberty which is our right as citizens of the Republic. We dismantled wagon beds to serve as tables & feasted on antelope, sage hens, rabbit, and Sweetwater Mountain cake. I fear that the collation made by some of the ladies proved too strong, for there has been much drunkenness, an agent of friction and rowdiness.

July 6: Still we linger in the shadow of Independence Rock, though I speak metaphorically, for there is no shade in all this miserable land. Dr. Bryant & Colonel Russell, with others, left yesterday on horseback for Oregon. Emma Louise & I wanted to go with them, but the ladies would not hear of our undertaking the journey without the comfort of wagons and the company of other women. So we remain until that time when the Oregon wagons turn toward Fort Hall. Governor Boggs now captains the California train & Mr. Rice Dunbar the Oregon. Many had been unhappy with Colonel Russell, & his extended drunkenness at the Fort did not improve matters. For the drunkard & the glutton shall come to poverty, & drunkards shall not inherit the Kingdom of God.

Before the Oregon troup left, the Reeds, Donners, & Boggses pledged the Bryant & Russell families from the store of fine wines which Mr. Reed has brought with him from Springfield. As I am a member of the teetotal Society, I would not partake. It is sad to see some of our friends leave us, but how well I understand their desire to go on ahead. No one that is left seems to hurry, but I am anxious to see those fields white unto the harvest & turn my hand to them.

July 8: Camped now at a cluster of hot springs with a water temperature of seventy degrees or more. It has been named the Emigrants' Wash Tub, & we have made use of it to launder clothes badly in need of cleaning, having not been touched with soap and water since leaving the Fort.

The country is steeper now, and more broken. It is the same scenery day after day, with nothing at all to recommend it. Mr. Cobb fell to entertaining the Donner company last evening after the evening repast with some of the most unbelievable tales. He swears that they are true. According to him, Independence Rock came about when a Mr. Bridger threw a stone across the Sweetwater. When it landed on the far side it began to grow & ended up the huge mound it now is. He also tells of a glass mountain north of us somewhere. He says that if a hunter will bend the barrel of his gun, it will shoot a curving bullet. In that way, he says, one can sight something through the clear mountain & hit it without walking around it. I hesitate to call Mr. Cobb a prevaricator, but I find such stories difficult to account for in any other way. However, I must admit that this is a wild and strange country & may indeed harbor all kinds of amazing sights.

July 9: The way is so hard and the path so difficult. Lift up mine eyes unto the hills from whence cometh my help. The countryside heaves us higher into air so dry that spokes & hubs are shrinking. Wheels fall off constantly, to the detriment of the goods packed within.

We are beginning to reach toward South Pass & soon will be in Oregon. I had thought this arid land had shown all its inhospitalities, but I was mistaken. We have been plagued with droves of fleas that blacken one's clothing & make even more miserable the lot of our beasts of burden. This land is unspeakably bleak and desolate.

We have been warned to be on the alert to danger from the Indians. As yet God has been kind, for we have not seen any evidence that they know of our presence. I have yet to find that peace of mind that I once possessed before knowing Mr. Garrett. Lord, I trust that You will provide.

July 12: We have crossed South Pass, twenty miles of sagebrush plain, & drank today from Pacific Springs. We are on the soil of Oregon, & I am so tired in body, & feel so low in spirit, that I can as yet detect no traces of Eden.

Pacific Springs covers almost a half acre of alkaline swamp, over the surface of which a tough sod has formed. Even though the ground quaked around us, we could walk over it to fresh water. Unfortunately, it would not bear the weight of cattle, & several fell through & drowned before they could be driven back. It was wretched to hear their pitiful lowing for water, which had to be hand-carried to them.

Many of the travelers are now afflicted with Mountain Fever, often noticed in these high elevations & diagnosed by the presence of headache, vomiting, nervousness, & depression of mind. Perhaps, I, too, have been infected with it, for I have never experienced such fatigue & weakness. Thoughts of Mr. Garrett do not help in dissipating my low spirits. Perhaps I shall never see him again, & that would be all to the better, for he diverts my mind from its proper sphere.

July 15: Did not travel far today, perhaps eight miles, perhaps less. A young man, from the family of Boswell, died today from grievous wounds suffered when a heavily laden wagon he was repairing collapsed & crushed his vital organs. We buried him beside the trail. Today, also, a child of the Massey family fell from a fractious horse, breaking his leg. Dr. Green urged immediate amputation, for the bones were splintered. But the mother, contrary to all advice, held him off with a butcher knife, saying she would not allow her son's leg to be removed. She threatened her husband with the same dire consequences if he persisted in helping the doctor against her wishes. The poor soul looked demented as she bared her teeth at the physician & those who would drag her away from the boy. Dr. Green finally conceded to her wishes, warning her of the imminent danger of gangrene. I cannot say what I would do under similar circumstances, for gangrene is a future concern & death through amputation an immediate one. The mother put the leg in a splint & wrapped it in clean rags, not allowing the doctor even that. The child suffers, but the mother is in constant attendance, warding off sleep lest the men take it upon themselves to administer medical attention & force upon the child that which she so fears.

July 17: We parted this day from our dear friends & my heart is heavy within me. If I were not so convinced of the Lord's leading to Oregon, I should have gone to California with them. We have received the kindest of treatment from the Donners, & it was with sorrow that I bade them farewell. The grief of separation makes the world a forlorn place. Emma Louise & I are now traveling with what is left of the Oregon train, captained by Mr. Kirkendall, & much reduced in size. The only familiar faces now are those of the Thorntons, with whom we travel. Mrs. Thornton lies ill in her wagon most of the time. We are on Sublette's Cutoff, heading northwest for Fort Hall, a British outpost. The Donner group turned southwest & are, I pray, well on their way to Fort Bridger, from whence they shall strike off along the route proposed by Mr. Hastings. Mrs. Donner was much overtaken with grief at our parting & she left us with a heavy heart. I wish them travel mercies.

Each day Mr. Cobb rides farther afield, going off in one direction & returning from another. With our diminished number, it would seem that he would stay closer in, but he looks for Indian signs.

At last the Lord has answered my prayers for release from troubling & disquieting thoughts! I now understand that there are many sent among us in the guise of personable beings who are in reality only stumbling blocks and temptations set before us to tempt us from the path of righteousness. I have turned Mr. Garrett over to the Lord, knowing that He will deal with him in the manner that he deserves.

> *Who that knows the worth of prayer,*
> *But wishes to be often there.*

16

Lord, how are they increased that trouble me!
Many are they that rise up against me.
—*Psalms 3:1*

We parted from the Donners and their traveling companions the next morning amid tears and hugs and promises of seeing each other again when we all got settled. I didn't know how far it was from Oregon to California, but figured it couldn't be as far as we'd already come. If we continued to survive the journey we were on, then maybe someday we could take on California too. Not only did I purely hate to see the Donners go, I was liking the idea of the mission field less and less the closer we got to it.

Probably the reason for it was that we'd come so near to getting out of it in the prospect of Mr. Garrett taking us on. And another reason was that it came to me that the only people I knew who had anything to do with mission work was the Reverend Perkle back in Caleb's Corner and Mr. Green, who'd gone on ahead with a group on horseback. Neither one of them inspired me with any anticipation of getting to know them better or of living in a community of like-minded folks. If all the missionaries were like them, I plain didn't want to go amongst them. I tried to talk to Jessie about it, but she said that missionaries were called from all walks of life, and that even if every one of them was as cranky as Mr. Green, it would only serve us right for entertaining impure thoughts. That didn't seem fair to me, for even though I admitted to a few of those thoughts, I hadn't had the chance to act on them like she had, and didn't think I deserved the punishment she'd mapped out for herself. There was nothing to do, though, but to follow her on to Waiilatpu, a heathen place within the heathen territory of Oregon, and hope we wouldn't have to suffer too much for a lapse or two in our mental activities.

After we left Pacific Springs, Mego began to ride out away from us more and more. I never knew when he'd go or when he'd get back. He seemed to come in only for an hour or so of sleep and a meal every now and again. He let me ride out with him once in a while, but only when the train was in sight and never after dark.

He led us to grassy spots, which were becoming more frequent now that we'd left the desert behind us. When we got to Soda Springs, a veritable oasis, as Colonel Thornton called it, the men voted to rest there for a few days in spite of Mego's cautions against delay.

"Hit's Injun country now an' no mistakin' hit," he told me. "This hyar puny leetle train be like a toy on Christmas morn to 'em. I sware, I wisht we'uns had more far-power than we got. These hyar store clerks don't hardly know one end of a shootin' piece from another'un, an' they don't thank of nothin' but stop an' rest, stop an' rest. An' this hyar valley be the worst place fer it."

I looked around at the tall grass that was restoring our cattle to health, and at the clear, fresh water bubbling in springs and shooting up out of little geysers, and at the timbered hills filled with game that surrounded us, and thought that I'd never seen a place so peaceful and healthy. But Mego didn't like it. He said neither the smell of things nor the looks of them suited him.

"Thar ort to be huntin' parties out an' around. We ort to have a hoss missin' ever mornin' or so, or a tradin' party ort to be pokin' its nose in, but thar ain't nuthin' movin' out thar."

"Seems to me we ought to be thankful for it," I said, helping him unsaddle his horse after one of his reconnoitering sorties.

"Naw, if they ain't apesterin' us in their gen'al manner, hit means theys somethin' ungen'al goin' on. Could be the Sioux has forsook the plains an' moved up in hyar an' skeered ever'-body witless. Or mebbe the Crows is astirrin', which I mortally hope ain't the case. See, lad, this hyar whole country we'uns be goin' through don't belong to no perticklar tribe. They all uses hit fer huntin' an' fer a passageway, like, atween one location or another'n. Hit ort to be ateemin' with Injuns atter game, or Injuns movin' to winter camps, or Injuns on some kinda business. Hit ort not to be so peaceful."

He turned his horse loose to graze, then squatted down beside me. He didn't do much laying around and sleeping anymore, but stayed restless and squinty-eyed, like he was expecting company any minute.

"This whole sittiation puts me in mind of the y'ar when we couldn't find hide nor h'ar of the Blackfeet anywheres. Kept 'spectin' 'em to jump us outta ever' bush an' cranny like they usu'lly did. But 'tweren't none of 'em thar. Hit got so's we all had this awful dreadsome feelin', like somethin' was abearin' down on us we'd never seed afore. An' then we commenced to find 'em, one or two hyar an' thar, an' then whole villages with not a livin' soul in 'em all alayin' hyar, thar, an' yon, dead whar they'd dropped. Nobody left to bury 'em. That were what the smallpox did to the Blackfoot tribe, an' it couldn't a happened to a more desarvin' passel neither. Why, lad, if hit hadn't a been fer the smallpox, thar wouldn't be no emigraters today. Them skunks wouldn't a stood fer it. Mean, I ain't never seed the like of 'em. Can't no other tribe hold a candle to the brand of meanness they had. I tellee, thar was rejoicin' in these hills amongst Injuns an' trappers alike when the smallpox struck them devils down."

"Jessie says there's always some good that comes out of everything."

"I 'spect she's right. Though this chile admits to havin' to look hard fer it in some cases."

"Me, too."

We sat for a while in silence, considering the philosophical direction our discourse had taken. Then I decided it was as good a time as any to bring up the matter of Mr. Garrett.

"Take, for instance," I said, "Mr. Garrett. Seems to me he's a case of bad coming out of good, instead of the other way around. Jessie and me were both mighty taken with him and thought he had good intentions, but he didn't. It was plain shocking, Mego, what he had in mind for Jessie."

Mego cackled a little, then he turned serious and said, "He ain't a bad man nor anywheres near it. He's jes' sot in mountain ways an' can't help hisself. Tell yore sister to tongue-lash him good an', if that don't do the trick, to take a bullwhip to him. He's pert nigh a Injun, which ain't oncommon in these parts. An' I don't reckon thar's much chancet of changin' him neither."

"He said he would come see us next spring," I said, "either at Fort Hall or Waiilatpu, wherever we are. But I don't know now. It may be he's thrown us over, since learning that Jessie's intentions are different from his.

"Besides," I went on, "it's not hardly likely that he'd ever take to missionizing like she wanted him to. Even if they agreed on everything else, which they don't. I don't guess we'll ever see him again."

"I misdoubt that," Mego said as he scraped out his pipe. "I don't 'spect he's through with you'uns. Once he decides he wants somethin', Garrett ain't likely to quit prospectin' that vein sudden like. Why, I recollect the time when he had his heart sot on a leetle Shoshoni gal. Mountain Lamb war her name. An' I tellee this. Wal, I guess I better not tellee. Hit don't do to banter a man's private enjoyments aroun' too much."

"You mean he cohabitated with squaws?"

"Don't take on so, lad. Hit ain't onheerd of atall. Ever' man out hyar has to take his hymeneal pleasure whar he kin git it, an' you'll find the same temptation when you git a ya'r or two on ye."

"Well, I doubt that," I said, without letting on to him why. I was sick at heart to learn that Mr. Garrett had not been able to contain himself, like the Mission Board feared for unwedded men. But then I recalled that Mr. Garrett had probably never heard of the stand that the Board had taken and probably wouldn't have cared if he had. To give him his due, I concluded that their rules didn't apply to him since he wasn't a missionary or a Christian of any ilk I was familiar with. Then I remembered that the apostle Paul, or maybe it was in one of Mr. Shakespeare's plays, but somebody had said that when he was in Rome he became a Roman, and when he was among the Jews he became a Jew. I figured that whoever it was would've become an Indian if he'd ever made his way out here and would've taken up Indian ways as well. Especially since the Indians looked to be the remnants of the Ten Lost Tribes of Israel. The thought made me feel some better, but I didn't think it would help Jessie, so I decided not to explain it to her the way I had done to myself.

But Jessie had done her own explaining somehow, for all of a sudden she'd shed her cloak of gloom and perked back up almost to her old self. She commenced to sing again while doing Mrs. Thornton's chores, and she brought her journal up to date after long neglect, and began to be cheerful about things in general. She looked to have laid Mr. Garrett before the Lord and left him there, for she was acting like she had when she'd done the same to Mr. Kessler.

"Jessie," I said, while I watched her roll out biscuit dough, "you sure have taken a turn for the better. What's happened to the impure thoughts that were troubling you so bad?"

"They're all gone, Em," she said, her face lighting up with the joy of victory. "I was foolish to forget that we worship a God of mercy and forgiveness. I sinned in my heart, but now it's as white as snow. Praise God! I am renewed and refreshed and ready to expend myself in His service."

I watched her cut out biscuits with a glass and considered this turn of events.

"And thoughts of Mr. Garrett don't bother you anymore?"

"Not a whit. He had his chance to get right with the Lord, and now I'm done with him. Shake the dust of the stiff-necked from off your feet, the Scriptures tell us. Also, out of sight, out of mind, I always say. And that's where he is, completely out of my mind!" She was cutting out biscuits like I'd never seen them cut before. Flour was flying around as she kneaded the leftover scraps into balls of dough and pounded them flat again.

"And I'll tell you something else, Em. This whole experience has made me a stronger Christian. I've been tempted and I almost fell, but now I know what to watch out for. Mr. Garrett has a lot to answer for, though, I'll tell you that, and believe me, he will! It's a fearful thing to fall into the hands of an angry God, which he'll learn to his sorrow. Vengeance is mine, saith the Lord, but I declare, Em, I hope I'm around to witness it!"

She was slapping biscuits in a pan as fast as she could, and when she picked up the rolling pin I moved out of the way.

"I'm glad to hear you're no longer troubled with impure thoughts," I said. "I expect they won't bother you anymore."

"You're right about that! My heart is free of them, but woe unto Mr. Garrett, for the day of reckoning draws nigh! I tell you, Em, every time I think of his outrageous conduct, I am consumed with a godly anger. But it has cleansed and purified my heart, and he'll soon get his comeuppance, if I'm not mistaken!"

She started flailing coals around in the fire to make a place for the biscuit pan. Sparks flew about her and coals rolled every which way. I sidled away from the zone of danger and, before leaving, told her I was glad she'd regained her former serenity of mind, to which she said she certainly had, and punctuated it by slamming the pan down on the coals.

I wandered over to one of the springs where the little children were splashing and playing in the water. I sat down and watched them for a while, but since I couldn't partake in public bathing of any kind, I soon grew tired of it. Mego came riding back in, so I went to see if he'd found anything that would explain our lack of Indian visitants.

"Chile," he said to me as soon as he lighted from his saddle, "I want ye to stay in close, ye an' yore sister both. Hit's spooky up in them hills an' somethin's creepy-crawlin' 'long my spiny colyum. I'm agonna git us movin' in the mornin' if I have to lash ever' man in this cavyard. I got me half a mind to take you and Miss Jessie an' light out fer Fort Hall tonight. But I'm amovin' ye tomorry whether the rest of 'em go or not. Be ready to ride afore sunrise, the both of ye."

"You think it's Sioux?"

"Naw, them critters couldn't keep a war party together this long. I'm athinkin' hit be Crows. They's the only ones that kin stupefy ever'body an' clear out the countryside like this'n be. 'Sides, I got me a Crow feelin' in my stommick now, an' hit's about to puke me."

He went off to find Colonel Thornton and Mr. Kirkendall,

who was acting captain now. I ran to tell Jessie that we were leaving the next morning, with or without the train. I figured I'd get some back talk from her about leaving Mrs. Thornton in the lurch, but I trusted Mego's stomach rumblings and intended to have both of us ready to go.

It didn't come to that, though, for after everybody had eaten that night, Mr. Kirkendall came around to tell us we'd break camp in the morning and push on for Fort Hall. I was glad Mego's warnings had taken root with somebody in charge.

I helped Jessie pack up as much of the Thorntons' goods as we could, then we wrapped up in blankets under their wagon. The nights were already noticeably cooler and a powdery blue mist had begun to hang low on the mountains in the early morning hours, which meant that the fall of the year was almost on us.

Sometime before dawn that night a rifle shot jerked us awake. Somebody yelled out in the meadow, and we heard horses and cattle milling and snorting close by the wagon.

"What is it?" Jessie asked, grabbing me so I couldn't run out to get an answer.

"Lemme go, Jess. I have to find Mego."

"No," she said, and clamped down on me hard. "We have to stay together. He knows where we are and he'll find us if he needs to."

That made better sense than running amok, so we crouched together and looked out between the wheel spokes. Men and horses and cattle were dashing around stirring up dust, and we couldn't tell what was going on.

Colonel Thornton jumped from the wagon above us and called out, "What's going on? What is it, somebody?"

"Indians!" somebody yelled back as he ran past, trying to catch a horse. "Half our herd's gone and the guard's dead! Get your gun, man, they're on us!"

I swallowed hard and felt Jessie breathing fast and ragged-like. She held me in a grip of iron and began to pray out loud. Then from out of the dark there came the most unearthly and bloodcurdling screeching that the human mind can imagine. It sounded like the gates of hell had swung open and let every one of its inmates loose to grab and torment us.

17

Fear and a snare are come upon us, desolation
and destruction.
—*Lamentations 3:47*

We stayed crouched under the wagon while the melee around
us increased in volume and furor. Above us we could hear
Mrs. Thornton calling weak and pitifully for Jessie.

"Stay here," Jessie whispered in my ear, though she could
have yelled it and no one else would have heard her. "I'm going
to try to get her down here with us."

Then she was gone, crawling out from under the front
wheels, just when I remembered that Mr. Thornton's given
name was Jessy and that's who his Nancy was calling.

I followed my Jessie to pull her back and looked up in
time to see a mounted Indian jump the wagon tongue just as
Jessie stood up. At the same time Mrs. Thornton leapt from the
wagon and landed between them. She hit the ground on the
run, nightgown and braids streaming out behind her. I caught
a glimpse of bare white limbs as Mrs. Thornton lifted her gown
for running room. The Indian pulled his pony to a screeching
halt and swung his tomahawk high, with the clear intention of
splitting somebody's skull open. He whirled it over his head to
take aim at Jessie, who was too surprised to move. Just as he
gave it the final flip the stone head flew off the handle and
struck his horse in the backside. The animal screamed in pain
and reared up, flailing the air with its front hooves. The Indian
swung the horse around, trying to keep his balance, and then
reached over and rapped Jessie on the head with the handle of
his tomahawk.

Jessie dropped to the ground as the pony spun on its hind
legs again and, with the rider fighting for control, lit out for

parts unknown, with the head of the tomahawk embedded in its flank.

"Oh, Lord, Jessie! Are you dead?" I was feeling her head for bumps or blood.

"No, I am not dead. Quit that, and let's get out of here." She scrambled up and, pulling me along, ducked back under the wagon.

"You're not even hurt?"

"No, he just scared the daylights out of me. Em, we've got to find a safer place than this."

She was right. In the gray mist of dawn the awful screeching, yelling, and cursing was all around us, and horses, riderless and otherwise, were thundering every which way.

"Let's crawl under the wagons until we can get close enough to make a run for the creek. We can hide in the bushes down there until Mego cleans up around here," I said between chattering teeth. The words didn't come out with quite the note of courage I was aiming for, but she nodded in agreement.

She started crawling toward the next wagon, with me right behind her. We were fairly well hidden until we had to run between wagons. The gunfire was still scattered and our defenders were still running around in confusion, while the skin-crawling shrieks split the air in alarming promixity. Horses galloped on both sides of the wagons, and it was too dark to tell who was riding them. Our cattle milled around, bawling and bumping into the wagons as they looked for a leader, which we all could have used.

When we reached the last wagon in the row, Jessie stuck her head out and looked in both directions.

"Now, Em! Let's run for it!"

She gathered up her skirts and took off, with me right behind her. We headed for a patch of shadow behind a supply wagon that was sitting off to itself. Jessie threw herself around it and pulled up short. I ran right into her, and we both looked up into the face of a deformed Indian sitting on a horse, which was what Jessie had run into.

There, in the midst of the most god-awful racket and the

most disorganized battle in the history of the West, sat an Indian holding a pan of biscuits, stuffing his mouth so full that his cheeks bulged out like a chipmunk's. He was cramming more into his mouth when Jessie ran into him, and he looked about as surprised to see us as we were to see him, but he recovered faster.

Holding the pan of biscuits in one hand, he leaned down and scooped Jessie up with the other. As he gave his horse a kick I grabbed Jessie by the lower limbs and held on for dear life.

"Turn her loose!" I yelled.

Jessie was flailing away at him with both fists and the horse was skittering and dragging me around and the Indian was spewing biscuit crumbs all over us.

I know now that that pan of biscuits saved my life, for if he'd been willing to drop it, he'd have hacked me off Jessie with his tomahawk. As it was, the horse finally slung me against a wagon wheel and I lost my grip on her. The Indian slung her across his horse and headed out of the camp.

I picked myself up and ran after them, crying and yelling and scared to death.

"Mego-o-o! Help! Murder!" I screamed and ran and got tangled in the high grass but kept on in the direction they had taken.

My heart was pounding and pure terror for my sister made me forget any other danger. All the other noises were shut out with the echo of my own screams as I ran. I had only one thought, even while screaming bloody murder for Mego, and that was not to let Jessie out of my sight.

A riderless pony cantered right in front of me and, without thinking, I grabbed the trailing rein and gave him a jerk. He stopped and I mounted without benefit of stirrup or block, which shows what fear can do for you.

I wheeled the pony to follow Jessie and saw Mego running toward me.

"Hold on thar!" he yelled. "I'm acomin'!"

I about cried with relief and steadied the pony just as

another horse, with an Indian crouched low on its neck, came galloping between us.

"Look out!" I yelled, and kicked my pony toward him.

Mego turned and raised his Hawken to shoot, but the Indian was on him. I saw the flash of a tomahawk and saw Mego fall to the ground.

The Indian whirled toward me and I screamed again for Mego, until there was no other sound anywhere but that one lost name echoing in my head.

The Indian scooped the reins from my hands and jerked the pony into a full gallop across the meadow into the trees. I hung on for all I was worth, knowing that Jessie was ahead of me and there was nothing but emptiness behind.

My pony raced through the trees, barely keeping up with the other horse as he was pulled along by the Indian. I had glimpses of the countryside as I clung to the mane and heard the pounding of other hooves around us. Except for that sound, and the crash and snap of undergrowth as we streaked through it, everything was silent. There were no more screams nor savage war cries, only a deadly intent to move for high country.

I soon gave up hope that we were being pursued by the men from the wagon train, for other Indians pulled alongside us. Though the pace didn't slack off, I knew we wouldn't be bunched together if a rescue party had been mounted.

They're all dead, I thought, and put my mind to forestalling the same fate for Jessie and me.

We rode all through the day at various speeds to rest the horses, mostly on high ground, avoiding the valleys and open meadows. From the position of the setting sun, I figured our heading was somewhat east of north, though what good that was going to do me, I didn't know.

Finally they stopped and made camp. I was so glad to get off that saddleless pony and ease myself to the earth that I didn't much care what happened next. I sank to the ground, too tired and scared to look around. After a little while of listening to the Indians at their domestic activities, it came to me that maybe they didn't aim to kill me right off. I ventured a look at what was going on, and there was Jessie huddled up by a tree with her skirts wrapped around her feet and her arms clasped tightly around herself.

We didn't speak to each other, for none of the Indians had opened their mouths, being busy with tethering horses and preparing food. About that time another Indian rode in and announced something in a self-satisfied sort of way.

The rest of the Indians just all at once loosened up. They commenced laughing and talking and bragging, it seemed to me, about the day's exploits. It was clear that there was no pursuit for them to worry about and that they had got away scot-free with all the depredations they'd inflicted on us. They got right down to enjoying themselves and relaxing after a hard, but satisfying, day in their line of work.

This awful lonesome feeling welled up inside of me when I thought again of Mego's fate and the fact that nobody was looking for us. But I put my mind to closing it off for the time being and turned to something I might could do something about. Like as not, I told myself, there'd be an old pard of Mego's at Fort Hall who'd like nothing better than to take vengeance out of a few Indian hides on general principles. The thing for us to do was to stay alive until that came about.

The Indians built a fire, which showed how safe they felt, and then settled down to some serious cooking and jabbering. I remembered Mego laughing fit to kill at the emigrants' idea of silent Indians. I watched them carefully, trying to get a bead on what tribe they were, for my ace in the hole was Mego's friendship with the Sioux and the Shoshoni. If these scoundrels were from a tribe who knew him, there might be somebody among them who wouldn't be pleased at what had happened. I could rest easy if that was the case.

It wasn't long before I knew there would be no rest at all. I thanked Providence that I had not been forward enough to test my few Sioux words on this crew, for I soon was convinced that they were Crows, bitter enemies of the Sioux, at least for that summer.

These were tall Indians, much bigger than the Sioux, with muscled torsos and finer features. The one thing that made them stand out, though, and put them in a class to themselves, was their long hair. Mind, I'm not talking about squaws—these were all braves. They all had their hair tied up with some contraption of beads and feathers on the backs of their heads, with long tails of hair streaming down their backs. One of them even had hair that touched the back of his knees, and it flowed and switched around every time he moved.

I cut my eyes over at Jessie, not wanting to move much for fear of calling attention to us. She looked scared, or maybe she was mad. It was hard to tell, for she put a certain, pinched look to her face for use under both circumstances. I tried nodding my head at her to show that things weren't as bad as they looked, but it didn't seem to lift her spirits very much.

Gradually, to my surprise and interest, I found I was following some of the Indians' talk. Not all of it by a long shot, but a word here and there clicked, mainly because they talked with their hands as much as with their mouths and threw in some American every now and then as well.

By this time they were eating the meat they'd roasted on green sticks over the fire. They took it right off the flame and began to gnaw at it without benefit of blowing or cooling it in any way. They weren't particularly careful cooks, for the meat was still red and runny, but they sucked and lapped on it like it was ambrosia from the gods. While they were so occupied I slid over close to Jessie and they didn't seem to mind.

Then one of them jumped up and strode over to us. He carried a stick with a chunk of ash-covered, dripping meat. I could feel Jessie tighten up beside me.

He squatted down in front of us and I took a good, close look at him. He was a fine specimen for an Indian. His face was beardless and clean-featured, and his eyes were clear and friendly-looking. With his deportment, he was fairly close to being handsome, and probably would've been in a silk tie and frock coat.

"Eat!" he said, and dropped the meat into Jessie's lap, where it made a bloody stain.

"Get away from me, you . . . you heathen!" Jessie cringed away from him, and flipped the chunk of meat away from her.

The friendly look went clean away as the Indian pinched up his mouth worse than she ever had. I was afraid he was going to hit her or worse. I could understand his feelings, for not many people like to have their gifts thrown away or their cooking criticized.

"Eat!" I cried, grabbing the meat and stuffing it in my mouth.

He looked at me in surprise and asked, "Eat?"

"Eat," I repeated, and smacked my lips. Then I took a big chance and said, "Damn Sioux," as I pointed off to what I thought was south so he'd know I wasn't calling him a Sioux, damned or otherwise.

He looked even more surprised, and then his face split into a wide, gaping grin, for there was hardly a tooth left in his head.

"Damn Sioux!" he yelled, jumping up and laughing and pointing to me.

The others came over to see what was up and Toothless poked me in the shoulder.

"Damn Sioux!" he prodded.

"Damn Sioux," I repeated, like I was a prize pupil called on to recite.

Well, I never heard such carryings-on in my life. They were twittering, jabbering, smiling, and laughing like I had called up from memory the entire catechism.

"Damn Blackfoot!" I yelled, just to let them know my heart was in the right place, for I knew the Crows thought the Blackfeet were the scum of the earth, and dumb besides.

That set off a whole new uproar, and one of them pulled me to the fire and gave me a buffalo robe to sit on. I was offered another piece of meat and a pipe, which I accepted as a gift hard to refuse under the circumstances.

I looked across the fire and saw Jessie's shocked face. She was mortally offended at my behavior, but I puffed and choked and coughed my way into some valuable friendships.

18

And thy life shall hang in doubt before thee;
and thou shalt fear day and night, and shalt
have no assurance of thy life.
—*Deuteronomy 28:66*

A kick in the small of my back brought me out of the blankets
the next morning before the sun was up. I thought I was about
to meet my Maker, but it was only my gap-toothed friend, Man-
Who-Chews-Bear, rousing everybody for the day's ride.

We were soon on our way, though at a more moderate
pace than before. They chattered and grunted among themselves, occasionally throwing me a "Damn Sioux" and a slap on
the back. I was beginning to feel tolerably at home with them,
but still watchful. They were known to be unpredictable and
subject to sudden acts of savagery on the say-so of the twittering
of a bird or the way the wind happened to blow. I put myself
out to be friendly and courteous, as I've found such doings pay
liberal dividends in the long run.

But Jessie just didn't have the knack for mingling with
common folk. She didn't think she was too good for them, but
she had her mind on her Christian witness so much that she
couldn't unbend enough to take an interest in other people.

I knew she didn't like me getting friendly with the Crows.
If we'd had a chance to talk, it wouldn't have surprised me to
hear her quote the apostle Paul's first letter to the Corinthians,
chapter ten: and verse twenty, which says something about not
having anything to do with devils and such like. But another
of his admonitions is "Come ye out from among them," which
was what I was aiming to do, preferably with all my hair. And
hers too.

In the meanwhile, though, I saw no reason not to be neighborly, even if Jessie would see it as consorting with the enemy.

We were crossing into north country, far from any emigrant trail that I'd ever heard of. Once when we came out from the trees and crossed a meadow, I could see a dusting of snow on the mountains to my left, and later, on a ridge, gusts of wind whipped the Crows' hair around their shoulders. I didn't like the thought of being their guest all winter and feared getting snowed in with them.

We stopped another night, or maybe it was two, but finally the Indians pulled up their horses in the middle of the day. We were on a grassy knoll, protected from the wind by a growth of evergreens that grew up to the foot of a nearby mountain. Everybody dismounted, and with some pushing and shoving, they pulled out dibs and dabs of this and that from their possible bags, and I never saw the likes of what they proceeded to do. That bunch of grown men commenced to paint up their faces worse than any common lady I'd ever heard about. They took great pains to get it on just right, holding pieces of mirror so as to see themselves and admire the results. Some drew red zigzags; some painted yellow dots across their noses, and some put black circles around their eyes. One of them painted the part in his hair red and ended it with a tiny half-moon on his forehead. Chews Bear and another brave, who I later learned was called Thunder-on-the-Mountain, started in with black paint. It was a curiosity to me why, with all the bright colors to pick from, they'd opt for black. And they didn't have the artistic talent to make designs like the others were doing, for they smeared their entire faces with it. I was ashamed for them and wondered why no one helped them do a better job.

But matters took a turn for the worse when Thunder saw Chews Bear copying his color and his method of painting. He didn't like it one bit, and I had no trouble understanding that Thunder wanted him to cease and desist. He got right nasty about it, too, which purely entertained the rest of them. They laughed and snickered and watched with interest, particularly when Thunder got up and walked over to Jessie. I about died of fright when he pulled out a headless tomahawk and tapped her on the head with it. Then I understood that he was proving that he'd counted coup on her before Chews Bear had taken a hand in the case.

"What is it to count coup on a squaw?" Chews Bear sneered. "Are you so proud of such bravery that you must proclaim the fearless deed to our people by painting your face black?"

"No more than you," Thunder came back, glaring at him with his hands on his hips.

"There is a difference between attacking a squaw with a useless tomahawk, which I'll admit surely turned your bowels to water, and bringing in a captive as I have done. I intend to have many fine horses in exchange for her." Chews Bear said this pretty bravely, I thought, in view of Thunder's agitation.

"Nonetheless, shitface, the squaw is mine, for I counted coup first, and I shall trade her for more horses than you can number."

Things were heating up, and their friends weren't helping matters, for they nodded and agreed with each of them, occasionally giving Thunder or Chews Bear a shove to hurry the quarrel into a fight.

"Who are you calling shitface, Woman?" Chews Bear asked.

Oh Lord, I groaned inside myself, hoping Jessie didn't understand what they were saying. And to tell the truth, it was only later, after I heard enough of the Crow tongue to understand it, that I was able to think back to this time and realize what they'd said. And also I heard this same quarrel about a hundred times afterwards, so I'm able to give a good account of the first one, without putting too fine a point on it. But neither Jessie nor me had to understand the exact words to know that she was the source of the quarrel. She looked sick and scared, and I felt a little shaky myself.

The two Indians continued to glare at each other and give each other a shove now and then. Finally one of the spectators announced he was cold and hungry, and his squaw was waiting to remedy both conditions, and that Thunder and Chews Bear could stay out there all they wanted to, but he was going home. The party broke up then, but Thunder and Chews Bear assured each other that nothing was settled and they'd return to the matter at hand at a more convenient time and place.

The Indians galloped their horses down into a valley that

was protected by mountains all around. I could see fifty or more lodges clustered near a stream in the center.

They drove the stolen horses before us, cutting loose with shrieks, yells, and whoops that probably scared the people in the village half to death. They all came running out of the lodges to watch the show, and it was almost as good as an election-day parade back in Jefferson City. They rode, screeching like devils, right through the main street of the village, wheeling when they got to the end and then dashing through again, just in case anybody had missed them the first time. Jessie and I were caught up in the pandemonium, for our horses were uncontrollable and I prayed that neither of us would fall off. The squaws and children added to the celebration, some grabbing horses and joining in, and others beating on drums, tin pans, and anything else that would add to the noise and turbulence.

After things got settled down and the hunting party felt properly welcomed and acclaimed, the village went back to what I later learned was its usual quiet and even routine, which was just under that of a mule and horse auction.

Jessie and I came under close scrutiny, but nobody bothered us much. One fat squaw didn't want to let us have anything to eat, but I went to Chews Bear and said, "Eat," and he backhanded her so hard her head must have rattled for a week. After that, we had no trouble getting whatever food we wanted. I hoped Jessie had taken note of the value of making friends even under adverse conditions, but I doubted she did.

I saw Thunder and Chews Bear arguing again, but a man as old and wrinkled as the hills told them to shut up because his ears hurt from listening to them. He said that he, the great Bracelet de fer, would settle the matter. I was taken with his name and wanted to ask if he had any French kinfolks, but I didn't get a chance.

"The Boston squaw shall sleep in my lodge," he decreed. "I have only three squaws to keep me warm and one is so old that she no longer puts out enough heat. Another young one will keep my lodge warm for the winter, or until you two magpies decide who shall benefit from her trade."

That sounded reasonable to me, and I was glad Jessie would

have a warm place to sleep. I didn't think he, or any of the others, intended to marry her, since they were still talking about a trade. I had heard stories of captured white ladies being taken in marriage by Indians, but Iron Bracelet needed help getting to his feet and I didn't think he could make it down an aisle. But I resolved to move in with him, too, and keep an eye on things. I also figured that Chews Bear wouldn't appreciate any more claims being made on his property. I made a point of looking him up and telling him I'd see to it that no one took advantage while he was otherwise occupied making a name for himself as the greatest horse thief in Absaroka, which is what the Crows call their country.

He grinned and said pleasantly, "If that hermaphrodite, Thunder, tries anything, you tell me and I will make him a true woman."

I've heard some swearing and name-calling in my time, for anybody who grows up around farm animals or has the opportunity to go west in the company of mules, oxen, Missourians, and Ohians can count on hearing the pick of the crop. But those Crows beat all I'd ever heard. Some of the names they called each other rose to literary heights, and they didn't have to study on it much to let mouth-dropping, eye-popping names and insults roll off their tongues. I marveled at it.

No one paid much attention to me, so I wandered around pretty much as I pleased. The only thing they didn't like was when I got too close to the herd of horses and, as they always kept guards on them, I stayed away. It didn't take long to find plenty else to do; an Indian village is chock full of curiosities that helped pass the time. I had some worries about the younger Indians, recalling how new people were treated back home at the schoolhouse. They eyed me for a while and some ventured up close, but I just stared back as good as I got and they lost interest. It set me to thinking about how all the people my age in the wagon train had pretty much left me alone too. It was like both the boys and the girls knew something was different about me, but since they couldn't figure out what it was, they gave me a wide path. And that suited me fine and saved me, I expect, a lot of trouble.

And I think there was something different about me, because I stopped doing any more blossoming. Everything that had commenced growing and springing forth just purely dried up and stayed that way all the time I was in Absaroka. For a long time I was stuck between being Emma or Emmett, like my internals couldn't decide which they wanted to be. And I couldn't help them out, because I didn't know myself. It was a settled fact that being Emmett saved me a lot of grief from the Crows, but I wasn't sure I wanted to stay neither one nor the other. I think the blossoming must have stopped because I was so far from Mr. Garrett, even though I hadn't stopped thinking about him. I hadn't, but it was a different kind of thinking. I wasn't taken up with thoughts that stirred and roiled around inside. They were more like some kind of knowing that he could be depended on—if he only knew about our misfortunes. And in the midst of that my thoughts about Mr. Garrett moved over a notch to take on a different shade of love, one that had to do with honor and gratitude, and not so much with the carnal kind. I asked Jessie once, when I had a chance, if she had any gratitude for Mr. Garrett, and she said she would when and if he ever did anything to earn it, which didn't look very likely to her.

Another thing about an Indian village that surprised me was the number of dogs they kept for no earthly reason that I could figure out. They had packs of them and they set themselves to making my life miserable. They were a thin, whining, yapping bunch that served no useful purpose. Crows didn't eat dog like the Sioux, who relished a good puppy stew, so I guess they saw little reason to fatten them up. The dogs added to the general racket, barking every time somebody left the village and every time somebody came back, yelping and howling whenever somebody kicked them, which was twenty times a day probably. I think the Crows kept them for watchdogs, but the dogs barked so much at their own masters, nobody could tell when they were barking at strangers.

The squaws were almost as bad, talking and carrying on all the time, with the tumult broken every now and again by a shriek when one of them got whipped by her husband. The

Crows were pretty loose in their ideas of wedded life, and could certainly have used a working knowledge of the apostle Paul's teachings on the matter. The Panther, for instance, decided he'd had enough of Little Antelope's trifling ways so he divorced her, not by serving papers, but by kicking her out of his lodge and stepping on her when he brought Deer Woman home.

Little Antelope mourned and carried on enough to break your heart. She really loved her former husband, or else she was mortally afraid of spending the winter out in the cold. I saw her sitting out behind the Panther's lodge, sniffling and crying and yelling curses so that it's a wonder the new couple had any peace at all. I had a lot of sympathy for Little Antelope, feeling she'd been wronged, and when I saw her hugging and petting a puppy, my heart went out to her. I went over to offer any comfort I could, but when she blew her nose in her hand and wiped it on the puppy, I decided the Panther had sufficient hygienic reasons for replacing her.

Most of the squaws stayed busy. They were always at some chore or another, which was good for building the kind of character they were in bad need of. Jessie had brought me up on the maxim that idle hands are the devil's workshop, and the Indian ladies must have been told the same thing. I'll go so far as to say that if all the squaws came down sick, the entire village would've come to a standstill, for the men didn't turn their hands to anything but eating, smoking, gambling, or hitting somebody. Even when the squaws' work was done they'd grab one of their children, pull it down on their laps, and start picking lice out of its hair. I've never figured out if they did it to keep the children clean or for their own entertainment, for they'd search through a head like a schoolteacher, and when they found a louse, which was any time they looked, they'd pop it into their mouths for all the world like it was popcorn. It was queer doings when vermin infestation was cause for rejoicing and feasting.

Jessie was my biggest worry. On our way to the Indians' camp, she'd been too scared to open her mouth. We had both seen the end of our days staring us in the face every minute, but by now it didn't look like they intended to kill us. Jessie had figured that out, too, and was about to get her courage back, which meant trouble we didn't need.

The problem was Iron Bracelet's wives, especially the oldest one. Two younger wives weren't enough for her to boss around, she had to take Jessie in hand as well. She called Jessie Useless Slave, but she sure made use of her and just about worked her down to the bone. One day, not too long after we'd gotten there, Rivers-that-Sing started in yelling and screeching at Jessie because Jessie hadn't understood one of her orders. Rivers went out and broke off a little switch and lashed Jessie across the hands with it.

Jessie's mouth got tight and she turned on her and said, "Don't you hit me again, you old biddy."

For a minute I was so scared I couldn't move. I knew Rivers didn't understand her words, but anybody could understand her meaning. I did the first thing I could think of and ran over between them.

"I'm sick! I'm sick!" I yelled and stuck my finger down my throat and threw up all over Rivers-that-Sing.

She took herself off to the creek, swearing and calling me any number of mortifying names, and I grabbed Jessie and pulled her behind the lodge.

"Have you got a fever?" she asked, feeling my forehead. "Oh, Em, don't get sick."

"I'm not sick, but I'd rather be that than dead," I told her, "and that's just about what you were fixing to be. Jessie, you can't talk back to them like that. They'd just as soon kill us as look at us, and we've got to stay alive till somebody can get us out of here."

"Well, when is somebody coming? I want out of this awful place. Where's that Mr. Cobb of yours? He's the one that's supposed to know about Indians. Why hasn't he rescued us?"

"I think he's dead, Jessie. I think they killed him."

"Oh, Emma," she said, as the tears welled up, "I didn't know."

She put her arms around me and hugged me close. We stayed that way, just me and her, trying not to cry until we heard Rivers-that-Sing bawling again for the Useless Slave.

"Put up with it for now," I said, "and do whatever she says. I just want you to stay alive."

"We'll both stay alive," she said, squeezing me tighter. "And we'll endure whatever we have to in order to do it."

19

A violent man enticeth his neighbor, and lead-
eth him into the way that is not good.
—*Proverbs 16:29*

The braves were all resting on their laurels and lolling around camp instead of turning their hands to something useful. They had carried out a successful raid on our pitiful company, so they didn't feel they had to hit another lick at anything. It would've been better if they'd had some line of work that would've kept them out of mischief. I'd have rested easier if all the young bucks had taken themselves away from the village and gotten their meanness out by stealing, goring, scalping, and carrying out their wicked deeds in parts far away. As it was, they sat around making pests of themselves and thinking up mischief. If you want my opinion, we'd of all been better off if they'd had a few acres to lay by, since that was the season for it, or anything that would take their minds off personal griev-ances and acts of general mayhem. There's nothing that settles tempers quicker than having a job of work to do, as Papa used to say.

I'm thinking in particular about Thunder-on-the-Moun-tain and Chews Bear, for they were undoubtedly the prime troublemakers. They both went around with sullen faces and lips poked out so far you could ride to town on them and acting, all in all, like they were about three years old.

After several days of this I began to realize that the quarrel between them no longer centered in on Jessie, though they used her as their number one arguing point. I don't think they'd liked each other much before she came along, and when one thought the other was going to gain an advantage in having a captive to trade, why, it just flew all over both of them.

"How many horses will the Yellow-eyes trade for your

sister?" Chews Bear asked me one day after he'd spent three hours brooding in his lodge.

I pretended to count on my fingers while I gave it some thought. The trick was to make her seem valuable enough to keep her from harm, but not so valuable that they'd ask more than anybody would be willing to pay. And that's what stumped me, for I didn't know that anybody would be willing to put down hard cash for us. I thought Mr. Donner might put up something to get us back, but he was way off in California by this time and probably didn't even know what had happened to us. Mego was out of the picture, which I didn't even want to think about. The only other person I could think of who might be willing to pay for Jessie was Mr. Garrett, since he'd talked about doing that very thing once before. But since she'd run him off, he might not know about the calamity that had come on us. If we'd been under the care of the Mission Board back in St. Louis, like everybody but Jessie wanted us to be, they might've taken our salvation in hand. Even Dr. Whitman at Waiilatpu might've helped us, if he'd known we were on our way there. Then there was Mr. Green, and when I thought of him I figured I'd come to the end of my rope. There was no use in counting on him, for if he'd leave Indian boys to die, he'd have no qualms about our fate after what Jessie did to his only convert.

But I counted and figured and scratched my head, and finally cut loose with a big one: "My sister is of great value to the mighty hunter of Blackfeet and the true friend of the Sparrow Hawk people, Mego Cobb. He will pay well for her safe return."

"That may be so," Chews Bear replied, like he was used to bargaining tactics. "But what use is a squaw to Cut Face when he has now gone over the Spirit Trail?"

It took me a minute to figure out that Cut Face was their name for Mego and that Chews Bear was telling me that he was surely dead. A sick and lonesome feeling about got the best of me right there.

"I am not sure he has gone over the Spirit Trail," I said, trying not to give away how much I was grieving.

"Hah! Mad Wolf carried the blood of Cut Face with him from the place of battle."

"That is true," I agreed. "But Cut Face has watered the mountains with his blood many other times and lived to carry out many more trades. Besides, my sister has strong medicine with the Boston men at Waiilatpu. They will pay many fine horses for her return."

"I believe this too," he said. "The followers of the Dead-but-Living-God are extremely wealthy and can afford any demand I make."

"But they're missionaries!" I said before I could help myself, but shocked at the thought of Christians getting rich on the mission field.

"I don't care what they are," he told me. "They have amassed untold wealth in horses, cattle, and land from the foolish Cayuse. Yet and still, they will be forced to return it all before many winters come around again."

"Well, be that as it may," I said, not much believing any of it. "My sister is worth a great deal to many powerful people."

"I don't doubt this. She will make me a wealthy man if that thief, Thunder, will relinquish his false claim. But do not worry—my medicine is strong now and becoming stronger every day. I shall win this battle as I have won many others, and shitface will wear his shame forever for trying to take what is mine and failing to do so. All the Sparrow Hawk people will laugh at him until his spirit dries up and blows away, and I shall have renown and great honor for my wealth and cunning."

"Amen, and so be it," I said.

After listening to him brag on himself awhile longer, I left him still fretting over the injustice of Thunder's claim and wandered around the camp. There were times when I just had to get off by myself and away from the talking that went on and on without any letup.

Most of the time, though, I took to their easy ways and lax way of living. Idlenss suited me down the line, until I began to get tired of it, which is apt to happen when you don't have anything to look forward to when you get through doing nothing.

By this time I didn't worry so much about Jessie's temper getting the best of her. With all the work they gave her to do, she didn't have enough energy to put into getting mad. Rivers-that-Sing kept her hopping from sunup to sundown. I tried to help her with some of the chores they gave her, even though the squaws laughed at me for doing woman's work. They left me alone when I said that Chews Bear had commissioned me to watch her for him and to let him know if Thunder tried anything.

All in all, though, I thought we were fitting pretty well into the Indian way of life and learning to be content in whatsoever circumstances we found ourselves, as the Scriptures tell us to do and which Jessie started crying at when I reminded her of it in hopes of bringing her some comfort. But the Indians had got used to having us around, and I thought we were fairly safe from any sudden and awful surprises, until the morning I was down at the stream skinning a rabbit that Rivers had caught in the traps she kept set. About the time I was finishing with it, a tall, horsey-faced squaw came and hunkered down beside me.

She didn't say anything for the longest time, just kept looking and scrunching up closer.

Finally I offered her the rabbit, but she lifted her hand to her face like she couldn't bear the sight of such a naked animal. I couldn't figure out what she wanted and had about decided she was touched, but then she cocked her head to one side and commenced talking.

"You are a fine-looking young man, even if you are of the yellow-eyed people. Though not fully grown," she said, giving my arm a pinch, "even on the runty side, youth and a mighty spiritedness can make up for other defects."

"I am pleased that you are pleased," I said. I figured the more friends I made, the better, and before this none of the squaws had even tried to be neighborly.

"Yes, you are a fine one," she said, almost to herself. She peered so close at me that I wondered if her eyes were bad. "Not big, but perhaps tenderhearted and willing."

"Well now," I said, "you won't find anybody more willing

and able than me, ma'am. What do you need done? A load of wood brought to your lodge? A rabbit cleaned and gutted? You name it and I'll be more than glad to be of service to you."

She kept on staring at me, and about the time I began to get fidgety, she broke out a smile that did wonders for her long face.

"I don't want you to do anything for me," she said, running her hand down my arm, "but I want to do something for you."

Now, that was a horse of a different color, for I hadn't noticed any of the Indians going out of their way to be charitable to anybody. I thought this squaw might be good material for Jessie to practice evangelizing on.

"I'm mighty pleased to hear it, ma'am," I said. "The fact of the matter is, I could use a heavy capote. My coat is too thin for an Absaroka winter, which with its length and ferocity has bred the brave and handsome Sparrow Hawks, a superior race of people."

I was laying it on pretty thick by then, but this squaw was eating it up, squeezing my hand and looking at me like words of gold were rolling out of my mouth. I began to think I might've been suited to a political career if I'd really been born what I looked to be.

"Do you truly think we are brave and handsome?" she asked.

"None finer, ma'am."

"And I?" she asked, canting her head to one side. "What do you think of me, O Small-One-of-Strong-and-Able-Mouth?"

Chews Bear had called me Adopted-Son-of-Iron Bracelet, which wasn't a bad name, but this new title did justice to my linguistic and oratorical abilities. I liked it better.

I also decided that if she appreciated my previous oratory, I would show her what I could really do, trying, of course, to stay fairly honest, which is hard to do when a declaiming fit comes over you.

"Small-One-of-Strong-and-Able-Mouth sees in you the soft eyes of the doe, the grace of the deer, the speed of the panther, and the refreshment of a tinkling stream in a desert." I wished

Mego could hear me, for he would've been proud. Then I added the crowning touch. "Surely the braves of this village hide you from strangers so that they might keep such glory for themselves."

I declare she giggled and tittered behind her hand just like a silly girl, and she had to be well along in the fourth decade of life if she was a day. The poor soul probably hadn't had so many compliments in her life, for to tell the truth she wasn't much to look at and I prided myself on bringing a little cheer into her life.

"Now, about that capote," I reminded her, for the days were getting downright cold, and it was dropping below the freezing point at night.

"I have many things for you and a capote of the warmest fur is least among them" she said, squirming close to me.

"Well, that's just dandy," I said, though it came out a little more flowery than that in the Crow tongue.

"I have something for you now," she whispered, looking around to see if anybody else could hear.

"I would be honored to accept a present from so lovely a one as you," I said, wondering over my good fortune in having this generous lady come to my aid.

"Let me have your hand," she said, blinking her eyes several times and then closing them tight.

So I gave her my hand, and closed my eyes, too, the way we did at home when somebody had a surprise for us. I got one, all right, and it wasn't to my taste at all. That brazen woman wasn't a woman in any way, shape, nor form, for she put my hand under her skirt and on the biggest whanger in two states.

I snatched my hand away and started scrambling backward, scattering rabbit fur, entrails, and carcass as I went.

"This must be some kind of mistake, ma'am . . . sir," I said, backing away for all I was worth.

"Oh, no mistake," he crooned. "Um-m-m, my member burns for you. See how it stands and calls to you? Will you not answer, O One-with-Strong-and-Fluent-Mouth?" She,

I mean, he, grabbed my shirt and pulled me over to him.

"Not right now, if you don't mind," I said, deciding right then and there that all the ladies I'd heard talk about this were right, and there were, without doubt, some things worse than death. "Thank you anyway, but I've got to go. Thunder's waiting for me and he gets awful mad if I'm late."

"Thunder-on-the-Mountain is a handsome brave who visits me in my dreams. But for now let me see what's under your clothing. It may be small, but may do a brave's work, for all that."

"No-o-o-o!" I yelled, and crossed my legs, for he had grabbed me in a place that doesn't bear thinking about. "Get away from me! Jessie! Help, murder!"

I commenced to cry and scratch and kick, but just as quick as he had latched on to me, he turned me loose.

"A filthy female!" he spit at me, holding his hand out like it had touched something dirty. "I throw my vomit on you for such a nasty trick! You should know better than to make fun of me. I am accustomed to more respect."

"Ma'am, sir," I said, clutching my britches and feeling relieved at the turn of events. The proof was in plain sight that he was losing interest, and it was a curiosity to watch it happening.

"I wouldn't make fun of you for the world," I said. "I wasn't trying to play a trick on you, and I'm sorry you took me for something I'm not. Fact of the matter is, ma'am, I mean, sir, neither one of us is what we appear to be."

And bless my soul if he didn't start smiling. Then he reached over and patted my shoulder, which made me flinch a right smart before I could remember my manners.

"Indeed, that is so," he said. "I became a berdashe when I was about your age when my great-grandfather, the bear, came to me in a vision and told me I had received the heart of a woman. It has been a life well suited to me, but this is the first time I have made such a mistake. In fact, it has left me shaken and quite upset. I must go find my friend, Bear Claw, and let him soothe me as only he can do."

And with that he wrapped his robe across his shoulders, flipped his long hair around, and sashayed back to the camp, trying to look dignified and not mortally insulted from what, after all, was a natural mistake. I breathed a sigh of relief and some regret, because I really could've used a capote.

20

As soon as I got back to the lodge, I could tell that news of my escapade at the stream had spread around the camp. I resigned myself to being put to work full-time with the squaws, but nobody said anything to me. There was some giggling and tittering, and Iron Bracelet's youngest wife was bold enough to point at my britches and say something I won't repeat. I decided not to wait for one of them to whip me into working, so I commenced to lend a hand. But every time I started to pitch in one of them would hurry over, chattering and shaking her finger at me and telling me that my medicine would spoil if I weakened it with women's work. I soon picked up on the fact that they had a high regard for anybody's medicine, even if it led a person into strange ways. Far from going against me, my true nature, now revealed, made them like me more. They were convinced that I'd had a vision telling me that my soul was one of the masculine persuasion, so I had to come up with an account of one in a hurry. I told them I'd been kicked in the head by a horse when I was little and was asleep for four days, during which time ravens fed me, and foxes with their tails tied together circled around me, and the jawbone of an ass started speaking and told me who I was. They didn't know what an ass was, so I said more than likely it was the jawbone of a spirit animal, and they agreed.

The Crows were uncommonly easygoing that way. They didn't care a lick what you did as long as you had a vision to back it up and used your medicine as an excuse for it. I know some folks who could take a lesson from their live-and-let-live philosophy, but since Jessie didn't understand much of what was going on, I didn't mention it to her.

And speaking of Jessie, Thunder and Chews Bear gave her no trouble at all, but they evermore troubled everybody else. Those two scoundrels kept the camp in an uproar trying to best each other in every way they could think of.

One day Thunder rigged himself up in full battle regalia, complete with war bonnet, which the Crow squaws were handy at making and selling to the Sioux, and war paint smeared all over himself. He even had his horse painted up, with zigzags on its legs for speed and circles around its eyes for good vision. Thunder took up his war shield and lance, both of which were decorated with scalps taken in previous encounters with Blackfeet, trappers, and various others who had been unlucky enough to run into him when he had twenty other braves to back him up.

He started in building a huge pile of buffalo chips in the center of the village. I was amazed that he didn't make the squaws do it for him, since chip gathering was one of their main jobs. But this particular pile was for making medicine, and he couldn't allow the womenfolks to pollute it. That was one of the reasons I figured all people, red and white alike, got their start from Adam, just as the Scriptures say, for everywhere I went the men kept the ladies out of anything to do with religious ceremonials, except for covered-dish suppers.

Finally, after working all morning without saying a word, Thunder got his pile built up higher than my head. Then, with as much dramatical flair as he could muster, so as to attract the attention of everybody, he picked up his shield with one hand and his lance with the other. He stood facing the little mountain of buffalo chips and, spreading his arms out wide, reared his head back and pronounced his intentions.

"The Spirit of the Four Winds and of my father, the Sun, and of my mother, the Earth, calls the Sparrow Hawk people to shed the blood of the Gros Ventres, those with huge bellies that can never be filled. Three snows ago they insulted a band of our braves on a hunting foray for horses. That insult has never been avenged. It is now time to make the blood flow."

As it happened I was standing next to Chews Bear, who was watching the sideshow with arms folded across his chest and a smirk on his face. He came out with a running commentary under his breath to everything Thunder said.

"The insult of which you speak happened when you attempted to steal a horse from the Gros Ventres, and they stopped you with an arrow up your ass," he muttered.

"Yes, the time has come," Thunder yelled, shaking his lance, "for our hearts to sing in praise of horses taken from those who eat until they vomit, and who are not worthy to ride horses, much less own them. I, Thunder-on-the-Mountain, am the bravest, the most cunning, and the swiftest warrior of the Sparrow Hawk people. My arrows fly straight and deadly to the enemy's heart; my gun makes the most noise and causes fear among those who oppose me; my horse leaps from mountain to mountain aided by eagles' wings; my way is directed by my cousins, the elk and the antelope, who know the secret paths; my wisdom is given to me by the spirit of my grandfather, the wolf, who lies in wait for my enemies!"

"Listen to the fool brag," Chews Bear sneered. "One would think he is trying to convince himself he has nothing to fear. And, of course, he hasn't. The Gros Ventres would run at the sight of a squaw with a scraping stone in her hand."

"I challenge all those among us who have brave hearts," Thunder bawled as he began to circle the pile of chips. "I challenge each brave to follow Thunder-on-the-Mountain, who now has strong medicine against our enemies. I challenge each one to follow Thunder-on-the-Mountain into battle against the thieving, lying, murdering Gros Ventre women!"

He was getting worked up by this time, circling the mound of chips with little hops on the beat of a drum that somebody had joined in with.

"No one will follow him in battle," Chews Bear informed me and everybody else near us. "We all value our scalps too much to entrust them to a fool."

"And I challenge that one!" Thunder screamed, stopping in front of Chews Bear and shaking some dirty scalps in his face. "Let this settle the matter between us. Let us take the warpath together and in that way prove who is the bravest warrior, and the one who returns with the most coups shall own the captive outright. And who ever that is, which I already know, shall receive the honor deserved by the mightiest of the Sparrow Hawk people!"

"Don't shake your scalps taken from the heads of children at me, Short Hair," Chews Bear said to him, as cool as could be with that maniac showering him with spittle. "Show us this powerful medicine of which you speak. Then we shall see what we shall see."

Chews Bear could speak in mysterious ways when he had a mind to, and he didn't seem at all worried over the outcome.

All at once Thunder whirled himself around a few times. Then he took a bead on the pile of chips and took a running jump at it. Before I knew what he was doing he had run clear to the top of it, scattering chips as he went and yelling his lungs out. He teetered at the very top while everybody chanted some unmelodious tune and watched his every move.

"Better hurry, show-off, or the great warrior will soon be up to his neck in buffalo shit," Chews Bear called out.

Thunder shifted uneasily on the pile, each time almost losing his balance as the chips settled beneath him. Then he lifted his shield and sent it rolling down the pile to the ground, where it whirled on itself for a few turns and finally settled facedown. A low moan went through the crowd, and Thunder, with a doleful sigh, sank slowly and with great majesty up to his knees in cow manure.

It seems that the action of the shield showed that Thunder's medicine was not what he'd cracked it up to be. If the shield had landed front side up, then the Gros Ventres would've had a war on their hands. As it turned out, they were safe again, even though they probably never knew they'd been in danger.

"Come, let us go eat," Chews Bear said, loud enough for Thunder to hear. "Watching the antics of old men and squaws gives me an appetite for meat which is fit only for warriors."

I could tell that Chews Bear's remark just flew all over Thunder, but he had been publicly brought down to size by the failure of his medicine and didn't dare try anything else right away. So he tromped out of the buffalo manure and walked, stiff, proud, and noisome, out of the village to nurse his hurt feelings in solitude.

Several days later a herd of buffalo was sighted a few miles from the village, and it created the first diversion that didn't feature Thunder or Chews Bear as prime participants. It even brought Thunder out of his private sulks, which weren't so private, since he wandered around without saying a word to anybody, but making sure we all noticed that his feelings were still tender.

Every hunter that could snag a pony left the village as if that particular herd was the last thing between them and starvation. And it probably was, since they weren't given to thriftiness and thinking ahead about things. The women followed fairly sedately so as not to interfere with the stealth of the hunt. Some of them, including Jessie, had to walk, but by virtue of my position as the youngest berdashe, I was given a pony. Well, I wasn't exactly given one—I caught one and nobody took it away from me. By the time we reached the field of conquest there were three huge hairy lumps lying in the grass with a cloud of dusts hanging over them as the last evidence of a panicked herd. We could still hear and feel the rumble of their hooves as they ran from the hunters.

Since the men's jobs were done, the ladies set to work on theirs. They had it down to a proper science, working away right where the buffalo were lying. Buffalo settle down on their stomachs to die, which is a good thing, for once down there's no way to move them without a winch and a pulley, which the Indians didn't have nor know about. The squaws crawled up on top of them and split the hides down the backbone and then crosswise at the hump and again near the tail. Then they tore the hide away from the flesh and spread it out on each side in flaps. They used these flaps for tablecloths, so to speak, and laid on them the choice chunks of meat that they carved out of the carcass.

I wish I could tell more about the actual butchering procedure, but to be honest there was so much blood and gore over everybody it was hard to tell what was living and what was dead. Six or seven squaws worked, shoulder-deep, in each carcass, and within minutes they were covered with buffalo blood. They were digging and rooting and slicing around in those mountains of flesh to beat anything I've ever seen, and I've seen my share of hog-killings.

I was watching the squaws who were working in the innards of one buffalo as they scraped and cut out armloads of the tastier portions, such as the boss, the hump ribs, the fleece, liver, and two things called Rocky Mountain oysters. Two of the squaws lifted out a slimy length of intestines, with its coils slipping and sliding out of their arms. They dumped the greasy mess on the edge of the skin flaps, and Chews Bear and Thunder must have had the same thought at the same time.

They sprang into action, each scrambling for one end of the buffalo gut. They grunted and challenged and made the most outrageous claims of gustatory prowess I've ever heard tell of.

What they aimed to do was to see which one of them could eat the longest length of the intestine, with one beginning at one end and one at the other. Mind you, this contest was to be without benefit of cook fire, salt, or pepper relish. They went at it tooth and nail, poking the fat-congealed tube into their mouths with both hands, their eyes bulging out and their throats gulping with each swallow.

As the coil between them grew smaller and their bellies grew rounder, the other bucks squatted around to watch. The squaws went on with their work, but they kept an eye on the proceedings, too. For myself it was a gut-wrenching experience, and, poor Jessie, the spectacle turned hers inside out. She was over behind a bush retching like she was next in line for an alimentary contest.

For a while it looked like Chews Bear was getting the best, that is, the most, of the deal. He was fast approaching his capacity, though, for sweat was pouring from his face. But, sensing victory at any minute, he kept on pushing and shoving the slimy coils into his mouth. Neither of them did any chewing—they just swallowed whole whatever they could force in.

I finally saw how the winner would be declared. As they both swallowed they deftly squeezed the malodorous contents out of the portions going in their mouths. The one who could swallow the longest length and, at the same time, force the bulk of the unsavory contents toward the other would undoubtedly be the winner, both from a stomachtic point of view as well as a combative one.

Thunder saw the bulging contents fast approaching him, so he reached over, took hold of the gut dangling out of Chews Bear's mouth, and gave it a yank. Several feet of once-swallowed gut came lurching out of Chews Bear's mouth, giving Thunder room to squeeze the contents back toward his competitor. This made Chews Bear so mad that he lunged at Thunder with murderous intent. They rolled on the ground, gouging at each other, and wrapping themselves in lengths of intestine as it came slipping and sliding out of their mouths.

By this time, the menfolks were losing interest. They were all full, having gorged themselves with warm tongue and fresh liver flavored with gall. They stepped over and around the tangle of men and entrails and began to wander back toward the lodges so they could sit by their fires and eat some more. I straggled along behind them and overheard old Iron Bracelet say to nobody in particular, "Someone should take a large stone and crush the head of the yellow-eyed squaw. That would put an end to these conflicts that divide our young men and make dithering fools of them."

21

Verily every man at his best state is
altogether vanity.
—*Psalms 39:5*

Iron Bracelet's pronouncement dampened my spirits considerably, and for the first time the hard facts of our misfortune
began to make my stomach hurt. So many interesting and curious things had happened since we'd been in the Crow camp
that I'd hardly had time to do much more than just marvel at
them. But now I had to face the likelihood that Jessie could still
get herself killed even if she held on to her temper. I knew that
the Indians killed for sport about half the time, and the other
half was taken up with killing for profit. I thought she'd been
safe as long as they thought of her in terms of so many sacks
of flour or twists of tobacco or kegs of whiskey, but now that
the older men saw her as the cause of dissension that they'd
grown tired of, I figured her days were numbered.

What would happen to me with Jessie in her grave didn't
bear thinking about. I didn't think they would kill me, for they
seemed to accept me as some sort of good-luck charm because
of my peculiarities. But I could see years and years of Crow
companionship stretching out in front of me without the comforts of Mr. Shakespeare, or Lord Byron, or wooden walls, or
well-drawn water, or white-flour biscuits, or canned sweet peaches,
or schoolmasters. I suddenly developed a previously unsuspected
fondness for Mr. McGuffey's *Readers* and preaching on Sundays.
With a lump in my throat and an empty feeling in my insides,
I thought of all the sweet comforts of civilization and of the
people I would probably never see again.

I walked out from the camp and sat away from the wind
behind a rock and let my mind have free rein with all its morbid
thoughts. I thought of my friend Mego, lying unhealed and

feverish somewhere far to the south of us and unable to get to us before Jessie met her untimely end. The most dismal thought of all, though, was the one of Mego long dead and moldering in his lonely grave. I buried my head in my arms and snuffled and bawled at the picture of him lying stiff and white in a pine box under six feet of lava dust and rocks on the trail to Fort Hall. I about convinced myself of it and felt even worse because I hadn't been there to help lay him in the grave. I would regret that to my dying day, and I tried to ease myself by thinking up a memorial to him. I didn't have anything to write it down with, but to the best of my memory it went like this:

> *You lie so still and pale and wan*
> *Down in the cold, cold grave.*
> *We wish you would come back anon*
> *Up from the deathly cave.*
>
> *But Heaven called and took you on,*
> *They needed you, you see,*
> *And left us here and all alone,*
> *Farewell from Jess and me.*

It was too bad he'd never get to hear it declaimed. I turned my thoughts, then, to Mr. Garrett, who was the best hope we had left. The thing that got to me was knowing that if Jessie hadn't been so all-fired scandalized at his behavior, we wouldn't have been in this fix. Or if we had, he'd of gotten us out of it by now. As it was, by the time he heard of our calamity and started to look for us, the trail would be colder than a prairie winter. And that was taking into account that he even wanted to look for us, which wasn't cut and dried after the way Jessie had lit into him and sent him running.

I left that and began to think about trying to escape. I figured I could do it easy and probably not even be missed for a day or two, the way they let me ramble around on my own. I didn't think they would care enough to mount a search party, and would just think my medicine had called me to other doings.

Getting Jessie away was another kettle of fish. It wouldn't be easy to sneak her out, for she was under the eyes of the squaws every living minute. And even if we could both get away, they'd come after her and stay on our trail until they caught us.

With the most unlikely luck, we might could get away from them, but I couldn't see us surviving the winter in unknown country. The nearest civilization lay at least a week's ride on the best Indian ponies to the southwest at Fort Hall. The thought of going that distance with no roads or signposts to guide us, no weapons to protect us, and no food to keep us going made me see the pure foolishness of trying.

Still and all, it might be better that both of us died together, trying to get back, than waiting for a terrible end for Jessie and a Crow life for me. So I determined to start hiding traveling food and watching the horse guards. Our best chance lay in getting horses right after sundown and having a night's head start before we were missed. Getting Jessie out of Iron Bracelet's lodge without waking Rivers was going to be the first part of the plan to worry with. Well, the very first thing was to let Jessie in on the whole matter. I didn't figure her to put up a squawk, no matter how unlikely it was, once she knew what Iron Bracelet had in mind for bringing the local feud to an end.

I found her working under the squinty-eyed gaze of Rivers-that-Sing, who had gained a new lease on life when Jessie joined her household. Making my sister miserable gave her something to look forward to every day. Jessie was working with the hides of the buffalo that had been killed the day before. The flesh side of the hides had to be scraped clean before they were stretched and left to dry. It was a tedious and unsavory job, and Jessie wasn't helped by the switch that Rivers applied generously to her hands.

"I will watch this poor worker, O Aged-Beauty-of-the-Sparrow Hawks," I announced, to see how good my medicine was.

Rivers-that-Sing turned her black gaze on me and for a minute I thought she was going to use the switch to run me off.

"I wish only to relieve you of this thankless task, Rivers-that-Make-My-Heart-Sing," I said, reaching for her hand with a soulful look on my face.

She jumped back from me like she had the knees of a young girl and, with a shocked look on her face, walked off muttering to herself about my unseemly behavior.

"Slack off, Jessie," I said, squatting down beside her. "The old bat's gone."

She leaned back from her crouched position over the hide and brushed the hair from her face.

"Oh, Em, I am so tired. That old woman is after me every minute of the day."

Jessie looked tired. She had her hair in plaits, Indian fashion, for the squaws had taken all her hairpins. Her dress was torn and none too clean, and she wore a poorly tanned cape that barely slowed down the wind whipping off the mountains. Yet in spite of all that, my sister still looked beautiful. I felt a peculiar knot down in the area of my heart, or possibly my stomach, since I hadn't eaten for several hours.

"Jessie," I said, glancing around to be sure no one had noticed that she had stopped scraping. "We've got to get out of here, because Iron Bracelet's tired of all the commotion that's going on over you. But I have to tell you that we don't have much of a chance even if we get away."

"You don't think anyone's coming for us, do you?" she asked. There was a clear, hard look on her face, for she knew the answer as well as I did.

"Hardly a chance of it, or they'd of been here before now. Besides, with Mego dead, God rest his soul, who is there to come?"

"There's Mr. Garrett," she said, with a faraway look in her eyes.

"He's our only hope," I agreed, "but, Jessie, you didn't exactly give him any encouragement for giving us another thought, and he might not even know what's happened to us. It comes down to this. We stay here and hope for the best or we get away and hope for the best."

"God will not fail us," she said, returning to her work. "Surely He will raise up someone to come for us."

"But Jessie, if we wait too long and the snows come, we won't have a choice at all."

"I am convinced we are in His care. He has provided for us this far and He won't let us down now."

"Hell's bells, Jessie, I ain't arguing a theological problem right now. All I'm asking is should we try to escape or should we not."

"Emma Louise, your faith is weak and you lean toward blasphemy and bad grammar. Take no thought of the morrow, for sufficient unto the day is the evil thereof."

"Well, the evil is pretty nigh sufficient around here for a whole year," I told her, and right smartly too. "You think about it. We've got a choice of dying here in the presence of and at the hands of these heathens or dying in the mountains by ourselves. I, for one, would like a little peace and quiet when I meet my Maker. Think about it."

I whispered that last bit, for I saw two squaws coming to check Jessie's work and find fault with it. I gave her a tap with the switch and launched into a Crow tirade against laziness. They walked on by, but sat down too near for us to keep on talking.

That afternoon the feud came to a head, or, in more exact language, to a point. I was bundled up in a buffalo robe, since the temperature had taken a quick plunge and I could smell snow in every breath I took. I'd decided to make friends with Iron Bracelet if I could, so I was sitting with him outside his lodge. He was older than anybody I'd ever known, with a face as lined and wrinkled as Papa's old work shoes. He was smoking his pipe and taking great pleasure in watching the squaws apply themselves to the business of making his life comfortable.

We sat in easy silence as one wife stirred the stewpot and another stitched away at some piece of clothing for her lord and master. Old Rivers-that-Sing had herded Jessie to the creek for water. It was a peaceful winter afternoon in a Crow homestead.

Iron Bracelet's shoulders started shaking and a deep "Huh,

huh, huh" came from his chest. I thought he was coming down with something bad, but he was only laughing.

"What amusing thought lightens the heart of my respected father?" I asked.

"Iron Bracelet, the scourge of the mountains in his younger days, is reminded of the time when that squaw over there wished to return home not long after she was brought as a wife to this lodge," he said, pointing with his pipe toward his youngest wife, who had at least forty winters behind her.

"How could any squaw wish to leave the lodge of so brave and handsome a warrior as the renowned Bracelet de fer?" I asked, laying it on with a trowel.

"I will tell you of things which you do not know, O Squaw-with-Manly-Dreams. That young one there, Running Hare, was highly esteemed among the Piegans when I chose her for my wife. She knew the honor that was bestowed upon her, though, and she was eager to lie in my robes," he said, without a trace of humility or common decency. I'd never in my life seen anyone who thought so much of himself.

"I brought her to my own people," he went on, after drawing again from his pipe. "The first night she was my wife I had intercourse with her six times, and as I arranged myself for the seventh penetration she announced her decision to return home, where, she said, she could sleep without interruption."

I was hot with embarrassment by this time, but I'd learned that Indians think nothing of discussing out loud all those things that Christian folk never mention and probably don't do. But Iron Bracelet liked to tell tales of the old days, and I figured to gain his friendship by being a good listener. So I swallowed hard and plowed ahead.

"And what was the response from the One-with-the-Vigilant-Lance?" I asked, just like I was accustomed to that kind of talk.

A beam of pure appreciation spread over his face at my description of his virile powers.

"I hit her head against the lodgepole and she gladly spread her legs to me once again," he said, with unseemly pride. "Later in the day, however, she slipped away and, as difficult as it was for her to straddle a horse, she left to return to her own people."

"It befuddles the mind to consider how some people do not appreciate their good fortune," I said, with as much sympathy as I could pretend to.

"Ah, you are right," he nodded, feeling again the sting of ingratitude. "But, of course, I went after her, taking with me two more of my fine horses for her father. She had already cost me half of everything I owned, but I knew her father's greedy and ungenerous heart. I tied her across my pony's back and we returned to the accompaniment of her wails and moans. She provided much merriment to my people, for they were well aware of my strength and stamina under the robes."

"And did she stay that time?"

His shoulders shook and quaked again, and then he answered, "She cost me four more horses before she became accustomed to my proclivities. After that," he said with smug satisfaction, "she would give me no peace. It was then that I longed to return to my father's lodge, where I could sleep without interruption."

His youngest wife, the one we'd been discussing, bit off a piece of string she'd been sewing with and cut her eyes over to us.

"One must never start something that one cannot finish, O Industrious-Robe-Flailer," she said, and started unlacing her bodice.

Iron Bracelet snorted, coughed, and cackled at her remark.

"Come into the lodge with me," she challenged him. "Your talk of other times has made me remember with fondness that great thing that fills me with joy."

I thought he was going to die laughing before he could haul himself upright, but he made it and they disappeared inside the lodge. I got up and left them to their memories.

That very same afternoon the feud between Chews Bear and Thunder took off beyond all bounds of human decency. Just as I was leaving Iron Bracelet's fire I heard a commotion a few lodges away. Squaws were leaving their cooking and running and pushing each other aside as they bunched together around some spectacle. They were pointing and jabbering away in tones of respect and awe.

I wedged myself between two of them to see what was going on, and to tell the truth I could've saved myself the trouble, for it was a sight I hope to never see again. There was Thunder parading around with his face and torso painted up fit to kill, but he was as buck, stark naked as the day he was born. The icy wind whipped his long hair around his body, but no amount of hair could cover the huge, red member standing at full attention before him. My eyes nearly popped out of my head. As amazed as I was at the sight, I couldn't help wondering how in the world he'd kept all that inside his britches without anyone having an inkling that it was there.

"Look upon the sign of my manhood," Thunder demanded, his head thrown back in the wind, "and tell me I am not greater than the treacherous and lying thief who wishes to deprive me of what is rightfully mine!"

Well, the squaws just went crazy agreeing that he had a right to anything he wanted.

"Call him out!" Thunder yelled. "Call out the foolish one who would challenge Thunder-on-the-Mountain! Let the people decide which of us is the man who deserves the spoils of battle."

The squaws clapped and yelled, eager for more. Some of the men had joined them, and they were just as eager for an evening's entertainment. Calls for Chews Bear went out while Thunder stood alone in the midst of an admiring circle without a hint of backing down.

"He comes!" somebody yelled, and the crowd stirred with anticipation.

"Man-who-Chews-Bear takes up the challenge!" the squaw next to me cried, jumping up and down in her eagerness to see.

Chews Bear pushed through the circle, arms crossed on his chest. He strutted around so everybody could get a good view, and I thought I had already seen just about everything, but in all his naked and shining glory Chews Bear displayed something beyond the mind of man to imagine.

He had the same big, red growth coming out of the lower part of his belly that Thunder had. But Chews Bear's protuberance took on a different slant, and the sight of it sent a wondering murmur through the crowd. Instead of pointing straight up toward the sky like Thunder's did, Chews Bear's organ started out in the same direction, but took a sharp downward turn right at the end of it. It looked just like an upside-down pipe.

"Look at it!" Thunder crowed, pointing at Chews Bear's deformity. "It's as crooked as his crooked heart!"

Well, I thought that would surely settle it, but neither I nor Thunder had counted on the perverse nature of squaws. They all crowded around Chews Bear, oohing and aahing, and making indecent remarks about how it would feel, and asking if he needed a running start or would he like some help in putting it to work.

Poor Thunder looked strickened and sick to his soul as he learned, to his sorrow, how much ladies like new and unusual pretties. He turned on his heel, his glory now beginning to wane, and strode away from the fickle crowd. I felt sorry for him, for he had Chews Bear beat by a mile on any fair and accurate scale of measurement. But by a quirk of fate and flesh, his plans had misfired again.

22

Weeping may endure for a night, but joy cometh in the morning.
—*Psalms 30:5*

I stayed close to Jessie for the rest of the day, and scrunched up
close to her in Iron Bracelet's lodge that night. There was no
telling what Thunder might do to get back at Chews Bear, and
anybody who didn't mind showing off in the all-together wouldn't
hold back from anything that came into his mind. I didn't trust
him as far as I could throw him. Chews Bear, either, for that
matter. I was more and more fearful for Jessie, afraid I'd come
back to the lodge one day and find a hatchet buried in her head
while the cooking and the talking went on as usual. I don't
think she knew how bad things were getting, since she was kept
away from the village activities. She just went on with her work,
saying her prayers and reciting Bible verses to herself, like they
were keeping the awful thoughts away.

We were lying that night stacked together with Iron Bracelet and his wives on the floor of his lodge. I was having trouble
getting to sleep, being so worried and all. Then I remembered
something that had happened back in Caleb's Corner a few
years back when a traveling preacher had come through putting
on concerts. Now, Papa had had a good toe and ear for music,
so we went to the show. It turned out to be not a concert of
music at all, but a concert of prayers, where everybody was
supposed to put their prayers into one concerted effort to storm
the Gates of Heaven. I can't tell you how disappointed Papa
was and what he had to say about deceitful preachers. So, when
I remembered that, I turned over in the warm robes and whispered up close to Jessie's ear.

"Hey, Jessie, how are you at coming down with a sudden
attack of glossolalia from the Holy Ghost?"

"What?" Then she mumbled something about drawing water. There's one thing heavy work will do for you and that's not give you nights of worry, because she fell asleep every night wherever she happened to drop.

"Wake up just enough to think about this," I whispered, giving her a little shake. "Indians get along real well with crazy people 'cause they're half crazy themselves. Most of the time, they just leave them alone. Why don't you get taken with a fit of ecstasy, like the Widow Logan did back home? You could thrash around and speak in unknown tongues, even though the apostle Paul didn't put too much stock in them. That way we might have a chance of fooling these Indians and getting away."

"Em," she sighed tiredly, "that's just about the most foolish thing I've ever heard of. Put your trust in the Lord and go to sleep."

Well, hell fire, I thought, like Papa used to say. Jessie didn't know that I'd been watching her put her trust in the Lord, and that I'd also taken notice of where we'd ended up. I also remembered a few passages of Holy Writ that said Christians are supposed to be happy in whatsoever conditions they find themselves, but our conditions weren't giving me, or her, too much pleasure.

Right before sunrise the next morning I was lying scrooched up close to Jessie in the warm furs and wondering why I was awake so early. I lay there a few minutes to get my bearings, smelling the warm robes that reeked of woodsmoke and sweat, and listening to the snores and rumbles of our bedfellows. Then I heard Iron Bracelet's knees creak as he got up and disentangled himself from the two wives whose duty it was to keep him warm at night. I heard him shuffle to the flap of the lodge and go outside. I eased myself out and crawled to the opening to find out what was going on.

When I peeked out I saw a layer of snow on the ground, whitening and cleansing the pestilential pile that the Indians lived in. They hardly ever cleaned up after themselves, because when a place got too filthy even for them, they just picked up and moved to another spot. I could see the smoke from the lodges spread out over the camp, which meant there was more falling weather on the way.

Two of the horse guards were talking to Iron Bracelet and several other braves. In the early morning dark I could hardly make them out, but I could hear them plain enough.

"How many?" one of the early risers asked.

"Only one, but with two pack horses, loaded down."

"Kill him, and bring in the horses," a younger voice said.

"No," an older one said. "We must carefully consider this. If there is only one rider, he is either a fool to enter Absaroka alone or he is known to us and sure of his welcome. If that is the case, we must remember that the snows stretch long ahead of us and we will need the supplies he could bring on other journeys. It will be many moons before the grass brings the buffalo back again."

"Well said."

"Does the rider approach our village?"

"No," the horse guard answered. "If he continues in the direction he is going, he will miss us and go to the camp of the Mal Ventres."

"Then he is not looking for the yellow-eyed squaw?"

"No, he's just a trader looking for business."

"Here is what must be done," Iron Bracelet said. "Show yourselves to him from a distance and indicate our desire to trade. If he turns in this direction, well and good. We will watch closely as he approaches. But if he ignores you and continues toward the camp of the Mal Ventres, kill him and bring in the horses."

Grunts and murmurs of approval greeted this, and after a little more discussion, the group separated. The horse guards remounted and left on their errand. The others went toward their lodges, and I ducked back under my robe before Iron Bracelet saw me.

I lay there listening to my heart thud with excitement. The trader had to be a white man, our first contact with civilization. The aching hope that it might be Mr. Garrett overwhelmed me, but I knew I couldn't count on it. I had a picture in my mind of him coming with a whole cavyard of mountain men to wipe out this motley crew and rescue us in the midst of a wholesale slaughter. It just didn't make sense that he would come wandering in with trade goods. I comforted myself by thinking that whoever it was would surely help us or, at the least, take a message back to somebody who would.

I wanted to poke Jessie and tell her the news, but Iron Bracelet was lying awake two bodies away, and I dared not let on to him what I knew.

Later, when we were all up and the day's work had begun for Jessie, I looked for a chance to tell her that a white man was coming. But the cold morning kept everybody close, and every time I sidled up to her Rivers put her to doing something else. Not long after the sun began to filter through the cloud cover, one of the horse guards rode back in.

"What news? Does he come this way?"

"He comes," the horse guard said with a wide grin. "He's not far from us now, and there is no concern. He is known to us, the one called Shiam Shaspusia."

"That one!" one of the older men laughed. "Tie up the women and bury your valuables! That's a wily one and no mistake."

"The coming of Shiam Shaspusia pleases me," Iron Bracelet said. "I've had enough of jabbering squaw talk. Now we will drink his whiskey and smoke his tobacco and listen as he tells humorous lies of his great deeds against the Blackfeet. I look forward to the entertainment that will warm my lodge, even though his tales exceed the bounds of truth and reason."

They turned away and started bawling at their women to fill the cooking pot. I could feel the excitement spread through the camp. A visitor was coming with whiskey, cloth, tobacco, and blue beads. And, I hoped and prayed, with a helping hand.

I wandered out of the way of the preparations to ponder what I had heard. Shiam Shaspusia wasn't a name I knew, and it took me a while to make out what it meant. My feelings were not much improved when I finally figured out that it meant One-Who-Has-Outdistanced-the-Crows-in-Telling-Lies. Mego had told me that the Indians had names for all the mountain men, who were either friends or enemies according to which side of the bed the Indians happened to get out of on any particular morning. The names were made up to memorialize some daring deed or personal mark. Mr. Bridger was known as the Blanket Chief, but Mego wouldn't tell me if that was because he had sold blankets to the Indians or if he had been unusually active under them. Mr. Fitzpatrick was called Broken Hand for a wound he had suffered in some long-ago fray, and General Clark had been known as the Red-Headed Chief because that's what he was. As I've already said, Mego was called Cut Face, an honorary title bestowed on him by the Blackfeet, who had also bestowed the scar. This Shiam Shaspusia, whoever he was, must have really made the Crows sit up and take notice somewhere in his career. The Crows, themselves, had top billing among Indians in general, not only for being the cleverest horse thieves, but for their whoppers and practical jokes. The more these jokes took in lying, cheating, mean and underhanded tricks, and a generalized obscene embarrassment for the victim, the more they liked them. So if this Shiam Shaspusia had, at one time, gottten the best of the Crows, he must have a heart black with wickedness and a mind as twisted as a prairie waterspout. The more I thought about it, the better I liked it. He sounded like just the man we needed.

Not quite before the middle of the morning, the village stirred with excitement, for the trader came into sight. He was escorted by several of the guards and some of the Wolves, who were the scouts.

I craned my neck to see his face, but he was too bundled up for me to get a good look at him. He was riding a long-haired pony and leading two pack horses on a tight rope. His hat was pulled low over his face, and a wool capote covered him against the windless cold that steamed his breath and crusted his beard with ice.

He rode easily into the middle of the camp, nodding and waving to acquaintances as he passed. He pulled up in front of Iron Bracelet's lodge, and as he swung from his pony a flash of joy tingled my toes. Shiam Shaspusia, the biggest liar in the Rocky Mountains, was none other than our Mr. Garrett.

His beard was black and thick, and his hair was long, but

there was no mistaking him. His level gaze, the same one that had fluttered my insides months ago, swept around the jostling crowd. He looked right at me and didn't know me. He just kept on speaking to Indians he knew, shaking hands, and greeting them Indian fashion. I felt sick that he didn't recognize me, and I pushed forward to get his attention.

Just as I got close enough to give his capote a jerk, he said to the braves who were feeling his packs, "Get these squaws and children out from under foot. I have come a long way to trade with my friends, the Crows, and to tell stories around the warmth of their fires."

Then he looked dead at me and lowered one eyelid in a wink. I moved back into the crowd, sick this time with relief. He had come for us and knew what he was doing. I could quit worrying and just let it happen. I ran to Iron Bracelet's lodge to tell Jessie that Jehovah had answered her prayers since help had just arrived.

I only had time to scamble inside the lodge, where she was building up the fire. I whispered to her that Mr. Garrett was here. "Don't let on, Jessie, whatever you do, that we know him."

Her eyes lit up as bright as the fire, and a smile wiped out the tiredness and the fear that had lined themselves on her face.

"Mr. Garrett's really here?"

"Sh-h-h," I whispered. "Don't take any notice of him or we'll all be up a creek. Make like you don't even know him."

Rivers kicked Jessie and said, "Stop talking in the heathen tongue and get on with your work."

"My apologies, Ancient-and-Esteemed-One," I said, or something like that, in Crow. "I was only telling the worthless one to build up the fire, because your respected husband comes with many guests."

"Build up the fire!" Rivers cried to Jessie, and kicked her again in the rib cage.

I crawled over into a dark corner of the lodge, out of the way, but close enough to see what Mr. Garrett was up to.

The flap swung open and six braves ducked in along with Iron Bracelet and Mr. Garrett, who was carrying one of the packs. They settled themselves around the fire and proceeded to light a pipe. This was passed from hand to hand, or rather from mouth to mouth, in the proper drawn-out ceremony for welcoming a guest and opening a pack.

The Indians made out like they didn't even see the pack, which Mr. Garrett opened partway to whet their appetite for what was in it. They pretended to give their attention to the guest of honor, but they'd cut their eyes over to the pack every now and again and lick their lips like they were bad thirsty. Mr. Garrett was plied with food, lighted pipes, and welcoming speeches. Each of the braves brought up some daring exploit that would have put Childe Harold's world adventures to shame. But Lord Byron didn't have to worry about having any competition in the literary department, for not a one of them could tell his letters, much less a subject from a predicate.

There were some rousing tales told, half of which I couldn't swear to in a court of law, and they got even better when Mr. Garrett opened his pack. He pulled out cloth and trinkets and handed them around to the squaws and, all the while, took not one notice of me or Jessie. The coffee and tobacco that he gave to the men were accepted with solemn thanks, but you could tell they were waiting for a different kind of gift.

Finally Mr. Garrett pulled out a huge jug wrapped in cloth. The faces of the Indians went slack at the sight, and a few hands twitched to grab it. But they controlled themselves, since they'd been brought up to act right at home. The jug began to make its rounds, as each imbiber threw his head back as far as it would go, upended the jug, and let the fiery contents gurgle straight down to the stomach, with hardly a twitch of the Adam's apple.

Jessie was trying her best to keep her eyes off Mr. Garrett, but from the look on her face I knew she was expecting some sign from him as to our immediate prospect of deliverance. She kept on with her work of chopping up meat over in a corner where Rivers had shoved her. But from the look of her I was afraid she might fall down on her knees in front of Mr. Garrett or raise her voice in "Behold, My Redeemer Cometh," or some such thing.

I tried to catch her eye to caution her, for if the squaws

suspected anything, they'd tie her up somewhere so Mr. Garrett couldn't find her. But she had eyes only for him, and all I could do was hope she wouldn't let the cat out of the bag.

As the jug of pepper-laced whiskey went around again, the talk got down to the worst I'd ever heard and then some. Jessie didn't know what she was missing, but even if they'd spoken in good, normal American, she probably wouldn't have known what they were talking about. And I wouldn't of either just a few months ago, but it's downright amazing how your education can be improved by staying out of school and wandering around wagon trains and Indian camps.

It wasn't long before Mr. Garrett had to bring in another pack, which meant another jug of whiskey. By this time the Indians had had a hefty bait of one-hundred proof Taos Lightning, and the party was getting rowdy. Gray Wolf laughed so hard at one of his own stories that he fell in the fire and singed his hair. Everybody else thought that was the funniest thing that had happened so far.

All this while the squaws and Jessie were cooking and serving up the food, but hardly anybody was eating it. Rivers-that-Sing took charge of the presents Mr. Garrett had brought for the ladies, but she doled them out, to my mind, in something less than equal shares. I reminded myself to point out to Jessie, if we ever got out of this mess, what would happen to her if she didn't mend her bossy ways. Bossiness is bad enough in a young woman, but it's just plain cussedness in an old one.

About then Bull-that-Runs stood up on wobbly limbs and began a long, involved tale about how brave he was and how all his enemies died of fright as soon as he mounted a horse.

Everybody listened with their best company manners until he got through, and then almost had a fight to decide who was going to soliloquize next.

Standing Bear won, and he went on for an uncommonly long time. He recited all his exploits from the first time he'd picked up a bow in his boyhood and shot, by accident, his best friend, down to last week when he'd brought down a buffalo all by himself. If only half of what he said was true, the village wouldn't have needed any other warrior around but him. To hear him tell it, he alone had been responsible for all the enemies slain, all the game brought in, and each and every child born in the camp.

I declare those Indians just didn't know the meaning of the word humility. On and on they went, each one making himself out to be the greatest thing that ever walked. It came to me how close this meeting was to a testimonial service at church. The only difference that I could see was that the Indians tried to top each other in how good they were and the Christians back home tried to top each other in how bad they were. As a spectator at both kinds of meetings, I was hard put to decide which was the better entertainment.

23

. . . and as thy soul liveth, there is but a step
between me and death.
—I Samuel 20:3

The air was getting pretty thick, since the fire had been
scattered several times. Through the smoke I could see Mr.
Garrett get to his feet and sway against the lodge wall. Papa
had gotten himself in that same condition a few times, and I
can't tell you what it takes out of a strong man, which is probably
why the Scriptures are dead set against it, to say nothing of
Jessie. If strong drink was going to do to Mr. Garrett what it
had done to Papa, then our salvation wasn't as nigh as it had
seemed. Jessie was watching him, too, and she looked as sick
about it all as I was feeling.

When he finally got his balance the Indians took on like
he had performed an amazing feat, and from the looks of him,
he had.

"Speak, Shiam Shaspusia. Tell of all the Blackfeet women
you have slain!"

"We await your words, brave one. Tell us of your daring."

There was a gabble of good-natured insults flung at him,
but no more than had been aimed at their own orators.

"I have learned all I know from my brothers, the Sparrow
Hawk people," he began, and almost fell from the effort. The
Indians nodded at each other, like he'd said something they
already knew.

"I know the way of the wolf in the snows; I know the
hiding place of the grizzly in the deep winter; I know the rivers
that teem with beaver in the spring, and I know the route of
the buffalo when the cows are fat and tasty. All of this knowledge, which has preserved my life many times, has come from
this wise and mighty nation.

"I have counted more coup among their enemies than I can number; I have slain more Blackfeet and Sioux than can be buried on the plains, for their bones lie glistening in the nights to make a path for me through the wilderness. The buffalo I have slain for food, if laid on top of each other, would form a mountain that would shadow the sun. The beaver plews I have taken from the mountain rivers would warm ten thousand lodges. All of this would not have been possible without the wisdom that has come from the Sparrow Hawk people."

He had their full attention, for, like everybody else, they loved to hear themselves made over. From the way he was laying it on and from the way they were lapping it up, Mr. Garrett could have had a promising future as a politician or a preacher of the Gospel. But I didn't think he was interested in either profession.

"I have taken many wives into my lodge," Mr. Garrett went on, and with that revelation he perked my interest to a considerable extent. "I have spent the long winters with a Shoshoni woman who made the finest clothing I've ever worn; I have slept with a Sioux woman who shook my lodge from morning till night with her dancing. To my shame I have even had a woman of the Blackfeet, who later had her nose cut off for adulterous behavior. And I have had a Nez Percé woman who talked so much that my ears buzzed for weeks after I sent her back to her father. But none of these can compare in virtue, in industry, and in beauty to the women of the Sparrow Hawks."

This peroration was received with universal approval. The Crows nodded and passed the whiskey jug again.

"You know that my heart is clean and pure and that my tongue never lies," Mr. Garret went on, pretending not to notice the excessive mirth that statement brought forth. The Indians pounded and fell all over each other at his claim.

"So with a clean heart and a straight tongue, I can swear by the Mother Earth, the Father Sky, and by the Sun that travels from the east to the west," he said, making what looked to be a cross in the air.

I saw Jessie frown and pinch up her mouth. She was about ready to take him to task over the Papish sign, which the preachers back home had warned us about. She opened her mouth to say something to him, and I knew she had in mind the true way of John Calvin, who had already fought that battle. I reached over and gave her skirt a jerk to remind her that this was no time for spiritual instruction.

"I swear," Mr. Garrett said, warming up again, "that no such beauty walks the earth than that which walks in the camps of the Crow people. Take the ugliest woman you have and she will shine in loveliness beside the most beautiful of any other people. My heart grows large when I consider the women who match in beauty the bravery of their brothers, the Crow warriors.

"In this very lodge, the lodge of my friend Bracelet de fer," he said, bowing to the old man and almost losing his balance, "there grow three flowers of the prairie." Iron Bracelet beamed as Mr. Garrett heaped praise on his wives, who were giggling and pretending to be embarrassed. "It is easy to see that the Sparrow Hawk people are blessed above all other peoples with the finest of women. Just as an example, I notice a yellow-eyed slave among you."

At this all eyes swung toward Jessie, who, not knowing what had been said, looked scared by the sudden attention. The Indians grew quiet, not knowing what Mr. Garret was leading up to and being in no mood to discuss such an unimportant thing as a captive.

"If you need proof, there is your proof," Mr. Garrett declared, uncorking a fresh jug and starting it on its rounds. "Notice how poorly she stands in comparison to your own women, and, I tell you the truth, this captive would be considered a great beauty among her own people. But can she cook?"

"No," the Indians answered him.

"Can she tan leather and build a lodge that will withstand the winter snow?"

"No!" they answered, getting back into the spirit of things.

"Can she snare and kill game to assuage the warrior's hunger?"

"No!" they said in one accord, with big smiles now that they understood the game.

"And can she close out the long nights with stories of the Ancient People and their wondrous deeds?"

"No!"

"And can she warm a man's heart and fill his robes with the summer dew of her body?"

"No!" they shouted with glee, as Standing Bear made a peculiar gesture with both hands right in front of Jessie's face.

She flushed red and her mouth grew tighter, and I figured she was just about to do something to get herself killed. All the Indians, including the squaws, were laughing to beat the band and some of them were pointing at her. She knew that the joke was on her, but she didn't know the joke and wouldn't have liked it any better if she had. She picked up the pot of stew that she'd just taken off the fire and started toward the door. Just as she got to her feet she cast a pleading look at Mr. Garrett as he collapsed on the ground.

He propped himself against Standing Bear and looked up at her with a grin on his face. "My friends," he said in Crow, "this woman is so cold and dry inside that a man would strip his member to the bone if he tried to enter her."

I couldn't believe my ears, and if Jessie had understood him, she might've died right then and there from mortal embarrassment. But she didn't have to understand the words, for when she saw the gestures and heard the noise from the Indians and looked into Mr. Garrett's laughing face, she could pretty well guess the nature of what he'd said.

A look flitted across her face that I'd seen on a few other occasions I don't care to recall, and I scrambled to my feet to forestall whatever she had in mind. But, of a sudden, she lifted the pot of stew and with one sweeping motion dumped the whole hot, greasy mess over Mr. Garrett's head. Then she threw the pot with a wicked swing slapdab into his lap and stalked out of the lodge.

There was a minute of absolute silence, a minute when Jessie's life lasted only as long as it would've taken a hatchet to flip lazily through the air into her back, a minute when the Indians could've transformed the lodge into a bloody rendition of hell. Instead, the minute passed with only a few startled blinks of half-closed eyes and a further gaping of mouths already loosened by alcoholic ingestion.

The minute passed, and Jessie's life took hold of itself again as the Indians fell all over themselves laughing fit to kill. They pointed at Mr. Garrett, dripping with rabbit stew, pieces of meat sliding through his hair, and greasy streams running down his face and through his beard. They rolled on the ground; they choked and sputtered; they laughed and took on until they were blue in the face. Old Iron Bracelet fell backward, coughing and gasping for breath; Running Elk laughed so hard he was crying, and Standing Bear lay back on the ground in a laughing fit. In the doing he spilled some of the whiskey and turned on his stomach to put his face in the puddle and lap it up like a dog.

Mr. Garrett began wiping the stew from his hair and face, picking out lumps of meat with great delicacy and offering them around to the boisterous Indians. This set off another whoop of laughter, and I'll have to say, after I got my breath back at Jessie's audacity, I had to laugh at the picture he made. His white teeth grinned through his black beard, which glistened with streamers of stew, while he held the pot in his lap. He would've made even a pious parson crack open with a smile at the very least. The whole lodge was in an uproar, for of course their favorite kind of joke was one that had a victim. And to their way of thinking, the perfect joke made a fool out of somebody they had some awe of. For the lowest kind of squaw to take Shiam Shaspusia down a peg or two couldn't have suited them better if they'd planned it themselves.

Mr. Garrett slowly uncurled his legs and stood up, tossing the pot into a corner. The Indians were trying to get their breath back by this time, but when they saw the big wet spot on Mr. Garrett's trousers, they went off into new spasms. Finally he raised his hands to quiet them.

"Friends and brothers," he began, as solemn as a judge, "the yellow-eyed woman has provided great merriment and pleasure for you, but at my expense. It is a poor thing for a guest to be so treated in the lodge of one whom he calls friend."

The Indians sobered somewhat at this, but not a whole lot. They straightened themselves as well as they could and tried to focus bleary eyes on Mr. Garrett.

"I will admit that if a pot of rabbit stew had descended upon the head of someone else, I would've found it reason for hilarity. However, it is not quite so funny when it happens to me, since I am the one who is burned and wet and humiliated. I am the one whose hair is pasted together with rabbit grease; I am the one whose beard will be sprouting rabbit fur for months to come, and I am the one whose trousers resemble those of an old man who cannot hold his water."

Mr. Garrett was as serious as he could be as he said this, and he had worked his voice up into a tremble of outrage. Which just suited the Indians to a tee, for they don't like good sports or good losers. They doubled up again, pounding each other and just about raising the roof with all their carryings-on.

"No man who calls himself a man will stand for such treatment!" Mr. Garrett bellowed, his eyes flashing like a preacher's. "The woman needs to be taught respect. She needs to be instructed in seemly behavior. Has her husband no authority over her? What man would allow such conduct from a woman? Who is the husband that has not beaten this woman into submission?"

"No husband. That is the trouble," Standing Bear said as he rubbed the tears of laughter from his face, smearing his paint as he did.

"What! No husband?" Mr. Garrett cried. "No wonder the woman turns her hand against a guest. She has not been properly treated by the Sparrow Hawk people."

"How say you?" Iron Bracelet demanded. "The woman is only a slave and proper ownership has not been established. How do you question the Crows' treatment of a slave?"

Mr. Garrett grinned with a devil's gleam in his eye and addressed Iron Bracelet directly. "Honored friend, it little becomes such a one as I to instruct the man who wears so many hash marks for the number of women who have come under his tutelage. I dare not instruct such a one as you in the management of women. All I know I have learned from the Master-of-Many-Wives, the artful Iron Bracelet himself."

"Tell us what you have learned from the one who is indeed a master in the art of wifely management," Iron Bracelet urged with modest pride.

"There are two things I have learned from the great Iron Bracelet, supreme instructor in husbandry," Mr. Garrett declaimed, bowing slightly to acknowledge his debt. "I have learned that a woman needs two things regularly—a long, thick lodgepole across her back and something equally long and thick inside her!"

It took me a while to translate that in my mind, and when I did my mouth flew open and I was stunned that he could stand up there and talk out loud about things that I'd only heard married ladies whisper about. The Crows didn't mind a bit, though, and every one of them agreed with him.

"Now, as the guest and protégé of the masterful Iron Bracelet," Mr. Garrett went on, "and one, I remind you, who has suffered grievous harm, I demand the right to teach this squaw a lesson. I trust you will allow me to buy her from you in order to restore my honor and redeem myself in your eyes."

"It is rightly said and justice demands it be so," Iron Bracelet declared, for all the world like a judge passing sentence. "Besides, this will solve the trouble between the two hot-tempered ones who have disrupted my days for too long."

The other Crows eagerly agreed, especially since Mr. Garrett had uncorked the jug and sent it around again.

"Bring in her owners," Mr. Garrett said. "Let us settle the matter while my heart is hot and the fine edge of my anger is still sharp."

Running Elk kicked a squaw toward the door with the command to bring in Thunder and Chews Bear.

"How does Shiam Shaspusia plan to purchase the woman?" Iron Bracelet asked with a sly look. "His packs are empty and only a small amount remains of the whiskey."

"Shiam Shaspusia is a man of wealth," Mr. Garrett said, with a wave of his hand. "Do not trouble yourselves over such a small matter when my honor is at stake."

Thunder and Chews Bear ducked through the door and glared at the social they'd not been invited to. They stood apart, pretending not to see each other, but suspicious of signs of trickery from the other.

"Ah, the two great warriors of the Crows!" Mr. Garrett called in welcome. "Your names are spoken with reverence and fear around the fires of the Sioux. And I, Shiam Shaspusia, travel the land of the Blackfeet without fear, for they know I am the friend of Thunder-on-the-Mountain and Man-who-Chews-Bear."

Thunder relaxed somewhat at this acknowledgment of his fame, and Chews Bear grinned with gap-toothed pride.

"You have undoubtedly heard of my recent and burning humiliation at the hands of the slave who is the property of the two greatest of warriors. I wish to buy her from you in order to soothe my soul and to repay, most generously, the hospitality of the noble Crows," Mr. Garrett said, placing his case before them with proper humility.

"Shiam Shaspusia must deal with me, for I took the slave," Chews Bear said, not giving an inch.

"That will be the day," Thunder said, or something like that. "It was I who took first coup and it is I who own the slave!"

"Wait," Mr. Garrett said, "hold on a minute. I do not wish to cause friction among the peace-loving Crows, but I must have this woman at all costs. My wealth is yours, to be divided three ways."

"Three ways!" Chews Bear spewed spit in every direction. "There is no third claimant. This matter is between the dog, Thunder, and myself."

"Not so, my friend," Mr. Garrett said, as patient as Solomon. "Iron Bracelet has spoken of the trouble and disruption that has come to the whole camp because of the disagreement between the two of you. Therefore, I propose to pay one third of my wealth to you, Chews Bear, for the woman, one third to Thunder for his claim to her, and one third to the camp for the discord she has caused."

If Chews Bear and Thunder had further negotiations in

mind, they didn't get a chance to bring them up, for Mr. Garrett's proposal met with riotous approval from everybody else.

"It is settled. We accept," Iron Bracelet ruled.

"Shiam Shaspusia exhibits wisdom beyond his years," Running Elk said.

"Yes! The trade is made!"

"Where is it? Where is this wealth of which you speak?"

Mr. Garrett again raised his hands for quiet. "My pack animals were tired and I did not know whose village I approached. They are tied under a ledge some fifteen miles from here. Follow the stream south until you see where I forded last night. Cross there and continue southwest toward the mountain black with cedars. Under a rock ledge, protected by trees and near a stream, six horses with double packs are tied. Two will belong to Chews Bear, two are for Thunder, and two for the rest of my friends."

"I know the place!" Thunder yelled, and turned toward the door just in time to see Chews Bear's back end going out ahead of him.

There was a stampede of Indians as they scrambled out the door, none too steady on their feet, pushing and shoving each other out of the way. I could hear them yelling and running for horses as the whole village learned of the treasure that was waiting for them.

"Let's go, Em," Mr. Garrett called to me, without a trace of alcoholic spirits in his voice. "Let's find that sister of yours and hightail it out of here!"

24

Draw me after thee. We will run.
—*Song of Solomon 1:4*

Mr. Garrett pushed me out of the lodge in time to see the last of what looked like a free-for-all. The Indians who had been sober enough to catch horses were already galloping out of the village. Others were swarming after them, grabbing and clawing and trying to unseat riders or just holding on to a horse's tail to be pulled along behind. The women and children were running after them, and the village was just about deserted except for one or two lying dead to the world in the snow. Jessie picked herself up off the ground, where she'd been knocked over by the exodus.

Mr. Garrett's two horses had been left, which was a wonder to me, but I expect the Crows had decided not to do any stealing until all their trading was done.

"Here you go, Em," Mr. Garrett said, and swung me up behind the saddle on his horse. "Now, Miss Jessie, climb up here and let's get going."

Jessie just stood there looking at him like we had all the time in the world.

"Mr. Garrett," she said, in the same tone that she says Emma Louise to me. "You have spirits on your breath."

"I expect I do," he said without a lick of shame. "Are you going to get on this horse?"

"I don't know whether I am or not," she told him. "I certainly don't want to stay here, but I don't want to go anywhere in inebriated company either!"

"Get on the horse," he said, but she just stood there defying both him and me.

"Lord, Jessie, he's got stomach trouble just like Timothy," I about wailed at her. "Now please come on."

This was no time for her to be stubborn as a mule with salvation waiting for us in one direction and the Devil's legions apt to change their minds in another.

"Well, all right then," she said, like she was doing us a favor. "Move back and give me room to get on."

She settled herself in the saddle in front of me, carrying on under her breath about wickedness in high places while Mr. Garrett went back into the lodge and brought out a large fur robe. He draped it around our shoulders and then commenced to tuck it around our lower limbs.

"What are you doing!" Jessie jerked herself back against me. He had taken her foot out of the stirrup and was holding it by the ankle, which was a pretty daring thing for him to do.

He looked up at her with something close to a smile and said, "Preventing frostbite. Now hold still."

He wrapped the ends of the robe around both of her feet and then mine, and when he finished we were inside something like a tent, with only our heads sticking out.

He mounted the other horse and gave ours a slap on the rump, and we were on our way to freedom. I put my arms around Jessie so as to hold on, and got scared all over again when I felt how little she was. There was hardly anything left of her, and so just as I got shed of one set of worries, a whole new set cropped up. From Mego's tales of hardships in the mountains I knew that hard cold could melt layers of flesh from a person, and Jessie didn't hardly have any to start with. I hoped Mr. Garrett knew he had to make haste and get Jessie where she could be looked after.

We followed Mr. Garrett out of the camp at a good clip, going in a northwesterly direction, as near as I could make out. We were leaving a clear trail in the snow, but from the looks of the clouds overhead, another layer would soon cover them. That is if the Indians stayed in their present condition long enough. I knew, and I expect Mr. Garrett did, too, that they would reconsider the trade they had made as soon as they could reconsider anything.

I began to feel better after we crossed the meadow and plunged into the stand of trees in the foothills of the mountains that ringed the village. The snow was deeper there, and the higher we went the colder it got. Mr. Garrett didn't slow the pace except in places where the horses had trouble breaking through. Every now and again I looked back to be sure nobody was following us.

After an hour or two on an incline that had the horses panting, we stopped to rest them by a mountain stream crusted over with ice. Mr. Garrett broke the ice so the horses could drink, then he looked over our robe again to be sure we were still tucked in.

He found it necessary to take hold of Jessie's ankles again, and it was all she could do to bear up under the familiarity.

Without looking at her, he said, "You can ride with me if you want to. I can keep you warmer than Em can."

"I am perfectly all right, right here," she snapped at him. "Now, unhand my foot!"

I thought he was about to laugh, but he said in all seriousness, "I guess you don't know that I bought you in a fair trade. So behave yourself around your lord and master."

Jessie was so shocked at this that she couldn't think of a thing to say back to him, which was just as well because he'd already climbed back on his horse. He led us down into another meadow and headed for a gap in the next chain of mountains. By the time we were well into them, night fell along with the snow that had threatened us all day.

I was about to cave in with hunger, and I knew Jessie was suffering too. She had been quiet for a long time, and whenever I'd tried to talk to her she'd not said much. I wanted to know if she thought Mr. Garrett was serious about her being his bought-and-paid-for property and all, but I couldn't get much out of her. Mountain people did things different from the usual run of people and, for all I knew, Jessie might have to go to a court of law to get herself unbought. Not that I wanted her to, but you could never tell what she was liable to do.

"Are we far enough away to stop and eat something?" I called to Mr. Garrett.

"Just a little further," he said. "We've got a rendezvous up ahead. Stay close and don't get lost."

I kicked our horse up so close that his head was practically on the other one's back. I had no intention of getting lost just after being rescued.

He guided us through thick undergrowth and turned toward the sound of water. We crossed a stream that was too swift to freeze in the middle and pulled up in a curve of it. Except for the blowing and panting of the horses, the silence fell around us as it can only on a cold night in the dead of winter. I jerked my head up as the branches of a tree rustled above and snow cascaded around us.

"I see ye got back yer plunder," a familiar voice said from the darkness above us.

"Mr. Garrett!" I said, catching my breath. "Is that God or is that Mego Cobb?"

"Tarnation, young'un," Mego said, dropping to the ground. "That's the first time this coon's been mistook fer the Almighty. But it war a nat'ral mistake, if I do say so myself. How ye be, little'un?"

I slid off the horse and flung myself at him, hugging him around the waist.

"I thought you were dead."

"Now, now," he said, patting me with his big hand. "Hit'll take more'n a passel of measly Crows to put this chile under. But I'll admit to it, I had some fears fer ye an' yer sister too. They treat you'ns all right?"

I nodded against his capote, taking in the warm smell of grease, tobacco, and long living that seemed like home to me. "Where've you been? Why didn't you come to get us too?"

"Chile, them devils knowed I was with ye when they jumped us on the trail. If I'd agone ridin' in thar with Garrett, their suspicions would've riz quicker'n beaver to bait. 'Twas better thisaway, fer if Garrett's foolery hadn't of worked, I could've come in ablazin' fer ye all."

"Where're you cached, Mego?" Mr. Garrett asked.

"Up the creek aways. Found us a good spot not fer from hyar."

We moved quickly to a small clearing sheltered by the side of a mountain and near the stream. Mr. Garrett helped Jessie dismount and made her sit down against a tree. He wrapped her again with the robe and told her to stay there while they got some food ready. Mego went and hunkered down beside her for a while, asking how she was and telling her they were taking us to Waiilatpu. She smiled and talked to him and, all in all, treated him a whole lot better than she'd treated Mr. Garrett. But Mego didn't have spirits on his breath.

We brushed aside enough snow to start a fire, and Mr. Garrett started to roast two rabbits that Mego had caught while he waited for us. They put me to work gathering pine branches to build a lean-to for shelter during the night.

After the meager supper, which plain wasn't enough for anybody, we doused the fire in case anybody was close enough to see it. Then they made sleeping arrangements the likes of which would've brought us up before the Mission Board if they'd known about it. They put me and Jessie in the middle on top of a buffalo robe, then Mego stretched out beside me and Mr. Garrett beside Jessie. Then they layered the other robes on top, making sure the edges were tucked in all around. It was about the warmest bed I've ever been in, but Jessie didn't think much of it. She lay there as stiff as a board and wouldn't turn over to let me scrooch up to her back.

I felt Mr. Garrett move around on the other side of her trying to get comfortable and, like me, having a hard time of it because she wouldn't give.

"Mr. Garrett," she finally said, "I don't like this any more than you do, but would you please get fixed?"

"Who says I don't like it," he said, and Mego started laughing while Jessie stiffened up some more. "Besides, we've all got to work together to keep each other from freezing. Now just turn over and get close to my back, and let Em do the same for yours. Mego'll take care of the far end."

"I got it kivered," Mego said, still laughing under his

breath. "But if he bothers you any, Miss Jessie, you can change places with Em hyar and bundle down next to me."

Jessie said she'd let him know, and after a while I felt her inch onto her side, which put her smack up against Mr. Garrett. It wasn't long until I felt her loosen up in the warm bed, and the next thing I knew Mr. Garrett was telling us to rise and shine.

Two days later, when we'd crossed the Big Horn and the Yellowstone and were well into the old Blackfoot country, we stopped worrying about the Crows. We'd seen no sign of human life and very little of the animal variety. Twisting north, northwest, we crossed rivers, valleys, and mountains, one after the other until I began to think that we would ride clear into China by way of the Sandwich Islands. We finally gained a high, lonesome, snow-covered country after traversing Deer Lodge Plains along Clark's Fork. Mego said we were headed for Hell Gate Pass on the Buffalo Road that the Nez Percé used to take when they moved east to take on the Blackfeet. It was far off the beaten track of the emigrant trains and was used only by Indians and trappers. Blackfoot country, from all I'd heard of it, was giving me the heebie-jeebies, but Mego said that smallpox had calmed them to a considerable degree. Besides, he went on, the weather would keep any self-respecting Indian at home close to his lodge fire.

When we scraped the last of the corn meal from the seams of the pouch and chewed the last of the pemmican they had brought, I forgot to worry about the Blackfeet and started worrying about starving to death. The snow and the wind had hampered our travel so much that we'd run out of provisions before we ran out of miles to travel. We holed up for two days in a shallow cave so Mr. Garrett and Mego could look for game. They came back with three scrawny rabbits and two worried looks. Mego grumbled about the trapped-out streams and the shot-out countryside, blaming the paucity of food on old man Astor's fur company.

"We're just about in a bad way, aren't we?" I asked Mego, but doing it when Jessie couldn't hear me. She was looking whiter and sicker, and wasn't doing much talking at all.

"I'll acknowledge hit," he said, "and hit flat galls me to have ye both feelin' so wolfish without me adoin' something about it. Howsomever, we'uns is fer from starvin' times. Don't worry yore mind none. Garrett an' me've come through a heap worse'n this, aye grannies."

I couldn't help but worry, though, it being my nature in the first place, and, in the second place, the hollow growls issuing forth from my midsection kept it on my mind. After discovering the lack of game we pushed on as fast as the horses, who were suffering, too, could carry us. It became a race to get out of the mountains before starvation caught up with us. And all the while the snow kept falling and the drifts kept rising.

Finally one day, after an hour's rest, one of the horses settled down in the snow and wouldn't get up.

"Thar's meat fer the hongry," Mego said, and helped it on to greener pastures.

I didn't much like the idea of eating something I'd been riding, but my finickiness left me when I smelled the meat roasting over the fire. We tore into the horsemeat and stuffed ourselves with no thought of taste or where it had come from or anything else, just evermore thankful to have something to fill up the scary emptiness inside us. We packed as much of the meat as we could on the two remaining horses and hoped it would last longer than it turned out to do. Mego and Mr. Garrett made snowshoes from saplings and, with Jessie and me on the horses, we pushed on.

The mountain passes were getting harder to cross, what with the deeper snow and icier wind. We traveled all the time now, taking no thought of whether it was day or night, just stopping to sleep whenever we had to. At night the wind would ease off some, and then the stars would seem close enough to touch. I had never been in such cold country. Mego and Mr. Garrett kept checking our toes and fingers for signs of freezing.

We lost another horse a few days later and fared sumptuous again. Mr. Garrett made another set of snowshoes and, after that, Jessie and I took turns walking, though she was hardly able to do it.

"How much further?" I asked Mego once when we stopped

to rest. I was so tired I wasn't sure I had said the words or just thought them.

"Not too fer now," he said, pulling the end of the robe around my head. "Don't ye fret none. I'll be flyblown iffen I don't git ye out of this, an' hit's me as says so."

The snow finally stopped falling, although the Lord's plenty was already on the ground. The wind died down except on the exposed places in the high passes, where it blew great scarfs of snow against the sky. In the valleys trees snapped in the deadly cold, sounding like gunshots echoing through the icy air. We slogged through deep drifts, our limbs aching from lifting the snowshoes. By this time Crows, Blackfeet, or any other variety of Indian didn't matter anymore. I figured that if any Indian was able to be out in this cold, then he deserved to get us. Mr. Garrett and Mego didn't go out looking for game anymore, either. They needed every ounce of strength to get us across the mountains and couldn't afford to waste what they had on side trips that were as barren as the one we were on. Jessie was riding the horse most of the time, for she was failing almost in front of our eyes. The Crows had pretty near worked her to death. When I'd begin to fall every few steps, though, she'd slide off the horse and make me ride for a while. It wouldn't be long before Mr. Garrett would be carrying her on his back.

"Ort to be a good place to cache up ahead thar," Mego called.

Mr. Garrett agreed and we stopped in an open place that was in the lee of a stand of evergreens. They hollowed out a hole deep and wide enough for the four of us to sit in and not see over the edge. They lined the sides and floor of the hole with the robes, leaving a small clear space in the middle for a fire. Mego gathered wood and piled it up close to keep the fire going. We huddled around it while Mr. Garrett filled a pot with snow to melt down over the flames.

Without saying a word to each other, they both began to empty their shot pouches. Then they took off their moccasins, recovering their feet with strips cut from a robe and lacing them on with rawhide.

"This hyar's what's known as parfleche stew," Mego announced. "Hit's saved many a life in these mountains and hit's good fer ye too."

As the snow melted in the pot they cut the pouches and moccasins into slivers and dropped them into the water.

"That don't look like anything but moccasin stew to me," I said, "but if it's food, I'll eat it."

"What about the horse?" Jessie asked, her eyes large and deep-set in her face.

"We need the horse as long as it can walk," Mr. Garrett said, speaking real soft and low to her.

"It's for me, isn't it?" she asked. "If I could keep up on foot, we could eat it now."

"No," he said, brushing her hair from her face. "We don't kill the horse on account of a few skimpy days. As long as it's walking, we've still got food ahead of us."

Jessie's eyes filled with tears, so Mr. Garrett pulled her close and put his arms around her, and she didn't even snap at him. That was so out of keeping for her that I was afraid she'd get it in her head to do something else she didn't generally do. She might remember there were martyrs in the Bible and think she ought to be one too. Not that that would help any of us, including her, but it was plain that something had to be done and I didn't know what it could be.

"Wal, that done it," Mego announced as he shook his possible bag. "I'm flat outter 'baccy an' I'm atakin' it into my head to push for'ard on my lonesome. Jes' can't stand to be without my 'baccy."

"I'm as low as you are," Mr. Garrett said. "I'll go."

"Nope, an' that's my last word," Mego said. "Soon's this hyar leather's biled soft enough to chew, I'll jes' mosey on and 'plenish my makin's. While I'm adoin' it I'll pick up supplies an' head back thisaway. Won't be no trouble atall."

"All right," Mr. Garrett said. "Much obliged."

"Don't mention it."

Well, they didn't fool me with their talk, all unconcerned like. As deathly tired as I was, and feeling the energy of life drain away while I rested, I understood that Mego and Mr.

Garrett were almighty worried about the fix we were in. Mego had told me one time that a firm rule of the mountains was never to split up from your pards unless there was no help for it.

I wrestled with that worry for about a half of a minute, but couldn't seem to get a close grip on it. My mind seemed to be slipping and listing like an unbolted wagon bed and everything I put on it kept falling away. Mr. Garrett pulled me over beside Jessie and told us to huddle close together. I was used to scrooching up to her, and it wasn't long before that wagon bed in my mind just tilted all the way off.

I woke up sometime later, parched dry in the mouth and dizzy in the head. Mr. Garrett was carefully feeding the fire with ice-coated twigs that sizzled and smoked but managed to burn.

"Is your sister warm?" he asked as I sat up.

I felt around under the robe and said, "All except her hands, but they're not bad. She's still asleep though."

He handed me a tin cup of parfleche stew and slid over to feel Jessie's hands for himself. He put each of her hands inside her clothes, and then tucked the robe around her again so no air could get in.

The tin cup was too hot to drink from, but my stomach paid no attention to that problem. I skimmed the pieces of leather out with my fingers and chewed the gummy wads until I could swallow them. They hit my insides like marble agates dropping into a pouch. I drained the cup of the thin broth and was thankful for every drop.

"How long has Mego been gone?" I asked as the warmth of the stew spread from the inside outward.

"Not long," he answered, his breath steaming in the air. "Now don't start counting the hours. I don't look for him back for two, maybe three, days."

I looked into the half-empty pot and gazed level-eyed at him.

"That won't be quick enough, will it?"

"Yes, it will. We eat horse tomorrow."

His ice-caked beard cracked into a grin and he looked for all the world like a big black bear. Friendly, though, if there is such a thing.

"You don't think I'd let Miss Jessie starve to death just when I've laid out all my worldly goods for her, do you?"

I grinned weakly back at him and decided right then and there that there were worse ways of dying than in the company of Jessie and a man like Mr. Garrett. In fact, I thought of several of those ways right off the top of my head, and the present prospects didn't seem half so bad. But, since I was tired unto death, I crawled in again next to Jessie and thanked the Almighty that we had at least escaped from the Crows.

25

Who is this who cometh up from the wilderness, leaning upon her beloved?
—*Song of Solomon 8:5*

The next morning broke gray and overcast with more snow clouds. Mr. Garrett climbed out of the hole and slaughtered the last horse. I tried to wake up enough to crawl out and help him, but the spirit was more willing than the body. I couldn't make my arms and legs move like they ought to, which should've scared me but didn't. Nothing much seemed to matter anymore. Jessie was even worse off than I was, for even though Mr. Garrett had fed her some of the parfleche broth off and on during the night, it hadn't done her much good. She didn't even wake up when Mr. Garrett got inside the robe with her and rubbed her hands and feet.

Even he was getting heavy and clumsy and I knew, somewhere in the back of my mind, that we were all in the grips of starvation. I heard the shot that committed our last means of travel to the stewpot, but all I could think of was how much I craved eating it.

It seemed an uncommonly long time before Mr. Garrett slid back into the hole with chunks of fresh meat dripping in his arms. I roused up at the sight, but Jessie moaned in her sleep and stayed where she was.

"Sorry it took so long," he said as he fed the small fire with twigs. "I hung as much of it as I could in a tree to keep it safe from other animals."

"Nothing's going to get it," I answered, "for we haven't seen hide nor hair of anything living for days."

"That's the pure truth," he said with a weak smile. "But fresh-killed meat will draw them if they're anywhere around. Now come on over here and put your breakfast on the fire."

231

He skewered a chunk of meat on a green twig for me and fixed another one for himself. We sat in silence watching the meat drip and sizzle over the flame. The aroma near about drove me wild, and we ended up eating it before it was half cooked. While our portions were roasting Mr. Garrett had slivered small pieces into the melted snow in the pot, and after he'd eaten enough to get back some of his own strength, he lifted Jessie to his lap and fed her with the broth. For the first time I saw some life come back in her face and it wasn't long before she could feed herself.

We all ate until we could eat no more, which wasn't a whole lot since our stomachs had shrunk and wouldn't hold what our appetites clamored for. Even so, I could feel the strength flowing back through my limbs and, what was not so good, through my mind as well. I could think straight again, but it didn't give me much comfort. The only good thing you can say about starving is that it takes a heap of fretting and worrying off your mind.

Mr. Garrett went out again to gather firewood, for if we'd lost the fire we'd have been in even worse shape. When he came back we ate again and felt better for it.

"Are we going to move on now?" Jessie asked, sounding well and fit again.

"We're going to stay right here until Mego gets back," he told her. "If we go wandering off, we might miss him. We've got fire and food here, and he knows where we are."

"But what if he can't get back?" she asked, putting into words my own worst fear.

I knew Mego would get back if he could, but he had left half-starved and as weak as we had been. He could even now be frozen stiff in a snowdrift not fifty yards from where we were.

"Don't worry about Mego Cobb," Mr. Garrett said. "He once walked more than a hundred and fifty miles without a gun or a knife, or a stitch of clothes."

"Why?" I asked.

"He was running from the Assiniboins, who had about done him in. When he got into Fort Union he was as pitiful a sight as you're ever likely to see. But he made it then, and he'll make it now."

Mr. Garrett had a sight more confidence than I had at the time. So to be safe I began to compose myself to meet my Maker, reciting all the Bible verses I knew by heart, and recounting and repenting of my sins. I made a bargain with the Almighty that He would not call me to my reward until I'd made a full and complete confession of my shortcomings, which I estimated would take another day or so at the least. While I was doing that I was also earnestly praying that Mego would get back before I had to stand naked and unadorned before the Throne of Grace.

The hours, daylight and dark, passed like a dream, with Mr. Garrett doling out just enough meat to keep us above the starvation level. I can't say how much time passed, for I was busy with the uncommonly heavy task of calling up all my failings, whether intentional or otherwise, and taking time out every now and then to pray for Mego and for Jessie and Mr. Garrett too.

Just as I had gotten up to the point of mentioning to the Lord that I took more pleasure in reading the Song of Solomon on my own than I took from listening to Pastor Clemmons preach on the valley of dry bones, a booming sound echoed around us. At first I thought it was another tree succumbing to the cold, but Mr. Garrett knew what it was right off. He fumbled out of the robe that covered the three of us, primed his rifle with awkward fingers, and fired an answering shot in the air.

"Hear that, Em? Help is on the way!" he announced, smiling broad enough to shatter the shards of ice in his beard.

"Oh, ye of little faith," I muttered to myself as my heart pounded with joy.

I saw Jessie twist around until she was kneeling. Then she clasped her hands in front of her and said, "Thanks be to God, who has not left His people to perish in the wilderness. Em, thank our merciful Lord, who has saved us from an untimely death."

I got my knees under me with no hesitation, for I was

truly grateful to the Almighty, as well as to Mego Cobb, who had done all the hard work.

"Praise God from whom all blessings flow," I called out loud and clear. "Thank You for Mego Cobb, who has walked out of this hellhole and back. And thank you for Mr. Garrett, who has kept us from starvation. May we not forget our debt to Thy servants who have preserved Jessie for her mission to the heathen and who have kept me from facing judgment before I was ready. In Jesus' name, Amen."

Mr. Garrett started laughing like a crazy man, and Jessie tightened her mouth while she glared at me with something close to her old wrath at my failings. She'd never much liked the way I prayed, but I'd always figured if you couldn't be honest with God, who could you be honest with? It had never been my calling to pray in public anyhow, and whenever Jessie would shame me into it, why, I just cut loose with whatever was on my mind.

She didn't stay mad very long this time, though, and ended up hugging me and giving thanks to God for preserving me along with us all. By the time we'd finished our thanksgiving, Mego had gotten to us. He stuck his head over the edge of the pit and looked down at us.

"Wal, now," he said, like he was surprised to see us. "Jes' lookee hyar at what I found. One polecat and two cubs. Ain't ye a sight, though!"

"About time you got here," Mr. Garrett said, looking fierce and angry. "While you've been lolling around in some fancy-house we've been freezing to death. Get down here and give an account of yourself."

Mego slid down into the hole and he and Mr. Garrett pounded each other the way grown men do when they're glad to see each other. Though, for the life of me, I wouldn't of known that from what they'd said. Two strange Indian faces edged over our hole and stared down at us.

"This hyar's a couple of Siwash, Stomach Hurts and Fish-eater, near as I can make out," Mego said, waving his hand toward them.

They grinned at us and dropped down a sack of food. The fire was soon built up into the best blaze we'd had, thanks to the Indians, who had plenty of strength to cut and bring in wood. We all gathered around the fire, eating meal cakes, fried meat with lots of fat, and sopping up the grease. I might as well say, in case the information is useful, that it's the fat, and the grease that comes from it, that a starving person needs to get built up to walking strength. I recollected the days when I would cut the fat off a piece of meat and give it to the hogs, but after our starving time it was the fat I most craved.

As soon as we could eat no more, we climbed out, packed what food was left, and began our trek out of the mountains. Fisheater carried me on his back part of the way, but Mr. Garrett wouldn't let anybody help him with Jessie.

We camped three or four nights in the open, each time finding less snow and easier walking. I was still afraid we'd run out of provisions again, but Mego said we weren't far from the camp of the Siwash and that they had plenty of winter stores.

We finally forded a broad river and came up on their lodges near it. We stayed with Stomach Hurts and Fisheater for almost a week, resting in warmth and eating a gracious plenty. Their wives and kinfolk took on over us in the kindest way and did everything they could to take care of us. While we were there Mego and Mr. Garrett went off for several days, much to Jessie's distress. She didn't at all like being left with Indians again, no matter how nice and friendly they were. Mr. Garrett told her that it was only mountain courtesy to replace the food the Indians had shared with us. Since the snow wasn't as deep where we now were, game was available and they went to get it.

They more than replaced what we'd eaten and the Siwash were beside themselves at their good fortune in rescuing such able hunters. It was a clear demonstration of casting bread upon the waters and having it come back tenfold. I thought Jessie would surely take advantage of a ripe opportunity to missionize right then and there, but she never said a word. When she sets her heart on something it never wavers, and her heart was set on the Flatheads, for which our present Indian friends didn't qualify worth a lick, seeing as how their heads were as round as melons.

We had almost another week's journey before us, so we said our farewells to the Siwash and took to the trail again. We were still on foot, for the Siwash, neighborly though they were, drew the line at loaning out their horses. As we had nothing to trade with, we hoofed it on our own. The going was not as hard as it had been, for it was coming on to springtime along the Snake River and in the Blues. Even though the terrain was rough, the weather was mild, and we soon walked out of the snow. We continued to follow the Nez Percé trails, avoiding in that way the worst of the undergrowth and steep cliffs. Mr. Garrett told us we were in the heart of Oregon and Jessie's spirits were uplifted, since that was where she most wanted to be. She continued in good health, as Mr. Garrett made her eat a lot and stop to rest before she tired herself out completely. We no longer worried about running out of food, or about falling weather, or about enraged Crows, either. It was a good time to be alive and I was more than thankful to be there.

"We'll strike the Wally Wally soon," Mego announced. "An' I tellee, it don't set right to be awalkin' on my own two feet all over God's airth, an' 'sides that, this hoss is half-froze fer some pleasantries an' state fixin's amongst white folks agin. Suck eggs, if I ain't. How's that sound to ye, little'un?"

"It sounds better every time I think of it," I said. "I am just about tired of eating dried fish and dried leather, and I need me some greens and garden stuff."

"Wal, that too," he said, "but this chile has missionary cakes and pies in mind, more'n sech truck as greens."

"I'd pure forgot about things like that," I said, but talking about them brought them all back again.

By the time we got down the Grande Ronde to the Walla Walla and disembarked from a borrowed canoe at the Whitman mission at Waiilatpu, I figured we had Mr. Garrett for good. Even Mego remarked on the taming nature of womenfolks. Neither Jessie nor Mr. Garrett had announced anything, but it was plain to see how much pleasure they took in each other. I

began to have new hopes that Jessie would veer off the mission
trail and start thinking about a homestead somewhere. Knowing
her as well as I did, I didn't expect her to take to anything
halfway, with any part of her holding back. And that's the way
she looked to be taking to Mr. Garrett. She forgot all about his
shameful behavior back on the trail and she forgot all about the
impure thoughts that he'd stirred up at the same time. Rescuing
us from death or worse had changed Mr. Garrett in her eyes,
and she even laughed when he teased her about being his boughten
wife already. I don't know what they figured to do with her
call to the heathen, and when I asked Jessie if Mr. Garrett had
received a call, too, she'd just smiled and said all things would
work together for good.

The Whitmans, both doctor and wife, took us all right in
and made us feel more than welcome. They already knew Mego
and Mr. Garrett, as they did everybody in those parts. They
were used to receiving worn and frazzled emigrants, for Waiilatpu was right at the western end of the emigrants' trail.
Toward the end of every summer strings of emigrant wagons
rested there, bought supplies from them, and often wintered
over with the missionaries before fanning out toward the settlements in and around the Willamette Valley farther down the
Columbia.

Far from being an outpost in the wilderness, I was surprised
to find that Waiilatpu had almost all the comforts of home. The
Whitmans had been there some ten years or so, and with the
help of other missionaries who had joined them over the years,
the station had gardens, milk cows, hogs, chickens, a sawmill,
a blacksmith shop, and a number of other outbuildings. I'll have
to admit that in some ways they lived a lot better than we had
back in Missouri. The mission house, according to one emigrant
who was biting the hands that fed him, qualified for palatial
designation. It was made out of adobe and was a story and a
half high. It had a library, a sitting room, an Indian room, a
kitchen, several bedrooms, and a schoolroom in the beginning
stages of construction on the back. A nice-sized creek flowed
on one side of the clearing and an irrigation ditch for the garden
was on the other side. Willow and birch trees fringed the stream,

and apple trees grew along the meadow in front of the house. The whole settlement was a long shot better than I'd expected, but Jessie seemed put out at the discovery, for she was all prepared to suffer for the sake of Jesus. I thought she would've been pleased to find she wasn't as needed as she thought she'd be. Since the Whitmans had the missionizing well in hand, they wouldn't miss her if she married Mr. Garrett and went to farming.

We hadn't been there long before I learned she didn't see it that way. Mr. Garrett had become used to the easy ways she'd picked up while we'd been traveling together. Being back in the company of Christian folk made her more mindful of proper deportment, and she wouldn't laugh and tease with him anymore. He didn't much like it either, and liked it even less when she started in on him to answer the call to the heathen with her.

"There's only two calls I hear," he told her in my hearing. "One is to do as I please without having to answer to anybody but myself, and the other is to have you with me. I've listened as hard as I can, but there's nothing else coming through." Then he grinned at her like he knew nothing else ever would.

Later that same day Mr. Garrett explained his plans to me. "Your sister will soon get this mission fever out of her system. And when she's tired enough and out of patience enough, that's when she'll want me."

And that night, when Jessie and I were in bed, she said, "All I have to do is work here as God has called me to do and wait for that stubborn mule to see the right of it. It won't be long before he'll see the virtue of being in the Lord's will and then he'll come around."

I didn't feel good about any of it, for I could see they weren't pulling together at all, and somebody was going to be mighty disappointed. I had a notion it was going to be me.

A Journal
Concerning Matters Both Personal and Spiritual
Inscribed at Waiilatpu, Territory of Oregon

BY

Jessie Elizabeth Heath

March 1847: We have been at Waiilatpu nigh onto a fortnight, & I find myself strangely disquieted. The rigors of travel have ended, yet the travail of my soul continues unceasingly. The Ever-Guiding Hand of the Lord has led me to this place, yet nothing is as I had envisioned.

The station here has attained a level of comfort that amazes me, having prepared myself for a life of sacrifice. The Indians who are the objects of our evangelizing endeavors are of the Cayuse strain, & not of the Flat Head genus, to whom I thought I was being led. Once, upon expressing my bewilderment, Mr. Cobb offered to rearrange the head of a Cayuse to meet my spiritual requirements. His sally was received with liberal, though good-natured, mirth, even by Mrs. Whitman.

In spite of Mr. Cobb's crude humour, Emma Louise & I owe our lives & safety to him & to Mr. Garrett, of whom I shall later have more to pen.

I have not yet recovered my equilibrium so disrupted by the horrors of captivity. Perhaps I never shall. Through & because of our sufferings, I have discovered the fragility of human life, but also the Ever-Present Mercy that extends from on high.

I must record here the method of our deliverance, for it clearly shows that our God will move both men and mountains to accomplish His purposes. When Emma Louise & I were captured by those most vile and miserable beings, we left behind a scene of confusion & horror, with many members of our company sweltering in their life's blood. Mr. Cobb, who fought with the bravery of an ancient Roman, was cruelly cut down even as he sped to our aid.

The wound he suffered is still being attended by Dr. Whit-man, who has remarked that it is a miracle that Mr. Cobb retains his arm, so fiercely was it mangled. To which, Mr. Cobb assured him, perhaps untruthfully, that "meat don't spile in the mountains." Nevertheless, even as Emma & I were being carried increasingly far from our friends & all that we treasure, Mr. Cobb was staunching his wound & preparing to effect our recovery.

The company we left behind was in a state of turmoil & utter disarray. Horses had been stolen, livestock scattered, two men killed, & many others so wounded or frightened that they were unable to assist him. That is the kindest light in which I can place their refusal to aid Mr. Cobb in any way. Having lost his own horse to the Crows, Mr. Cobb asked for a replacement so he could mount an immediate pursuit. He was adamantly refused. When, in his anxiety for our welfare, he attempted to commandeer one of the few remaining horses, our erstwhile friends & companions on the Trail held their guns on him & ordered his immediate departure from their company. I can hardly warrant their behaviour, notwithstanding their urgency to reach Fort Hall after the depredations they had suffered.

Mr. Cobb, realizing the lack of Christian Charity from those more anxious to preserve worldly goods than to come to our aid, says that he left them to their own devices &, taking paths known only to those intrepid men of the mountains, he went on foot cross-country to cut back on the Emigrant Trail further to the East, on which he hoped to find friends & provisions for his foray into Absaroka. I cannot imagine the tribulations he must have suffered as he hurried across the lonely mountain stretches, without food, means of transport, or the use of his arm. Yet his valorous conduct was well-rewarded & divinely guided, for he happened upon Mr. Garrett. This man's kind heart was wrung with pity for the defenceless captives, & he immediately volunteered his services. And to think I once thought him an instrument of Satan.

Since Mr. Cobb was known by the Crows to have been traveling with us, they determined not to raise suspicions by coming into their camp together. Mr. Garrett, therefore, traveled openly, while Mr. Cobb paralleled his trail under cover from peering Indian eyes. Unaware of the careful preparations & deceptive wiles needed to allay the suspicions of the natives, Emma Louise & I could not understand Mr. Garrett's seeming disregard for our perilous circumstances when he first entered the Indian village. I fear that I almost upset his well-laid plans by a most distressful display of ill-temper.

On our flight across the snow-covered mountains, however, I tried again & again to redeem myself in his eyes, for though we suffered near-death in the frigid atmosphere, my heart did ever melt in his presence.

I must try with greater effort to understand him, for I am uncontrollably drawn to him, notwithstanding the call to mission which I have received. My serious turn of mind does not conjoin with his humour, which occasionally borders upon foolery. He seems to think that he has actually purchased me! And constantly reminds me that the Indian way of marriage (an exchange of goods & animals for a bride) is not without Scriptural precedent. His presumptuousness astonishes me, yet leaves me strangely unsettled.

O there are times when, confined by man-made walls & rules, the high, wild country calls to me! Something deep inside urges me toward the strength & safety of his arms. Something wild & free sings its plaintive note within my breast & I long to lose myself in him. Help me, Father, to follow no leading that is not your own.

Even Mrs. Whitman, who I thought would counsel me to deny those refractory & obstinate offences to my peace of mind, & to give myself over to the work of God here in this wilderness outpost, urges me toward him. She said, in fact, that Mr. Garrett offers a broader field of mission than Waiilatpu ever could. Dr. Whitman has concurred. I cannot consult Dr. Green, or rather Mr. Green, as I have now learned him to be, for he refuses to renew our acquaintance begun on the Trail. He frankly disapproves of the warmth of my regard for the Whitmans, & his spirit of dissent within this Christian community constantly dismays me. That oneness of heart & purpose which I had expected to find is sorely lacking & desperately needed in this wilderness outpost.

Emma Louise, my dear sister, who was so courageous throughout our ordeals, expresses much discontent here & has attached herself more firmly, if that is possible, to Mr. Cobb. As for Mr. Garrett, he has her complete loyalty & affection &, whether he knows it or not, a most persuasive advocate in her.

My own course of action remains unclear. O why does the Mighty God, who can melt the stoniest of hearts, not call him to mission? We could then join together, one in heart & mind. But I must not question the purposes of the Almighty for, even now, my own calling, once so clear & unswerving, seems to be abating in its fervor, leaving me more & more at the mercy of my tumultous heart. Speak clearly, O Gracious Lord.

26

A word fitly spoken is like apples of gold in
pictures of silver.
—*Proverbs 25:11*

It took some little while for me and Jessie to get months of
captivity and weeks of starvation out of our systems. For the
longest time I'd go to the table with a great fear of finding it
bare, but as it never was I came to depend on daily rations
again.

Mr. Garrett and Mego stayed around, helping at the sawmill and such like, but more to pay for their keep than as a
regular job of work. When it was clear that Jessie was on her
way to full recovery, they began going back into the mountains
to hunt and to scout beaver streams for the winter trapping and
to do whatever else they usually did. I sorely missed them when
they took off, especially since I wasn't used to staying in one
place anymore, and in a place I didn't particularly like. Waiilatpu
was fine and all that, but I still wasn't suited for mission work.
Neither was Mr. Garrett, but he kept showing back up with
Mego every now and then. Jessie kept trying to convert him to
her way of thinking, but she didn't have much success. It seemed
to me, in fact, that he was doing more to her than she was to
him.

To keep my mind off their cross-purposes, I took to studying the mission station and the people therein. Everything and
everybody centered on Dr. and Mrs. Whitman. I do believe that
the whole enterprise would've folded up without them, and that
was contrary to everything Mr. Green had said back on the
trail. Both of them were a marvel to me, since they weren't like
the general run of missionaries I'd known. They were educated
people, for one thing, and they'd both been brought up with
proper manners and deportment for another.

After Jessie got over her surprise at the state of comfort we found at the station, she said it was no more than she'd expected of the Lord. She found a real friend in Mrs. Whitman, or Narcissa, as she told Jessie to call her. And that was another thing that was different about the Whitmans. They called each other by their Christian names, Narcissa and Marcus, which I noticed didn't sit too well with the other missionaries. Those wedded couples called each other Mr. and Mrs. Whatever, just like normal married folks do, and it always shocked me, and them, to hear the Whitmans be so familiar with each other right out in public.

By the time we met Mrs. Whitman she was well into a matronly age, being close to thirty-five or maybe forty years old. Mr. Garrett, who had told us all about them in those last days of our journey from Absaroka, had what he called an unrestrained admiration for her. He said that when she first came across the Rocky Mountains, she purely stunned the mountain men. They had never seen anything like her, even back in the States. Mr. Bridger and Mr. Meek had been especially smitten and, on that honeymoon journey to her new home, they had put themselves out to bring her choice game and tell her stories and show her the sights and, I expect, to win her away from her husband if they could've. She had taken to trail life and her new country, Mr. Garrett had said, and never regretted leaving civilization for it.

But I got the feeling that something had changed with her, and with many of them at Waiilatpu. It wasn't just that she had grown older or that her thick reddish-gold hair was turning white or that her hands were rough and cracked from the hard work of civilizing heathens. There was something behind her eyes and something in Dr. Whitman's slumping shoulders that made me think that the Oregon Paradise wasn't all it was cracked up to be. I couldn't exactly put my finger on what was wrong, but by this time I had lived with fear and death for so long that I could smell it in the air.

In Jessie's company, though, Mrs. Whitman's eyes lit up, and even though it had taken a while for her to loosen up and get down to woman talk, when she finally did it was like a flood turned loose. She wanted to hear all the news from the States, like the doings in Washington City, and Colonel Kearney's progress into Mexico, and what the ladies were wearing now. Mrs. Whitman's last letter from her folks was two years old, and even though Jessie had been out of circulation for some time, she was able to fill her in on a few things.

Dr. Whitman had assigned me to work in the garden out to the side of the visitors' house, which suited me fine and kept me away from the ironing board. One day he came by to see how our crops were making and took the time to ask how I was getting along. He went on to say that our coming had been a blessing to his wife.

"She's been very tired and discouraged of late, as we've all been," he said, "but your sister has given Narcissa a new interest, and I'm grateful for it. I didn't realize how lonely she's been without a woman friend."

"I don't see how anybody could be lonely here," I said, looking around at all the people engaged in various activities on the place. Here, in the spring of the year, there were missionary ladies and preachers, teachers, mechanics and hired men, children, and Indians going about putting in crops, mending fences, hanging out wash, drawing water, and doing the general work of any farm anywhere.

"Ah, Em," he said, "it's a matter of being of like mind. Narcissa has been surrounded by people for a long time now, in contrast to the early years when it was just the two of us. Back then, when I was called to tend the sick she had to carry on alone. I shudder now to think of how often I had to leave her, sometimes for weeks at a time. Think what it must have been like, knowing that hers was the only lamp burning in miles upon miles of black wilderness."

I shook my head with the awfulness of the thought, and Dr. Whitman had the look of a beaten man on his face.

"When you grow up, young man," he went on, "you will certainly want to heed the Lord's calling, but, oh, count the cost. Count the cost not only to yourself, but to those you love. I sometimes wonder how often we frail humans confuse a call from the Lord with our own selfish desires, and then sacrifice everything good He has given to follow a false light."

I stood leaning against the fence listening to him put into words some of my secret thoughts, and wondered if he talked as plain as this to everybody. Then it came to me that he probably didn't, but figured I was too young to catch on to how dispirited he was. But as I had had the same affliction on several occasions, I knew it when I heard it.

"Well, we can't stand here all day with work awaiting, can we?" He smiled and gave me a pat on the back. "You like working in the garden, do you? We try to put our people at tasks they like and are good at, so let me know if you want another line of work."

I told him I was satisfied with the kitchen garden, having farmed all my life, and he left me to it.

That same night after supper and prayer meeting, Mrs. Whitman and Jessie started making plans for several days of sewing. Mrs. Whitman was going to help Jessie stitch up some new frocks, since we'd come to them with only what was on our backs. Everything we'd owned had either been lost in the Indian raid or been claimed by the emigrants who'd survived it. Which could make me mad if I lingered on the thought, but there wasn't much we could do about it. But the thought of new clothes and sewing in company with Jessie put a sparkle in Mrs. Whitman's eyes. They began talking about waistlines and hem lines and figure lines, and I saw Dr. Whitman watching his wife with a pleased smile. It must have been a long time since she'd been excited about anything.

One afternoon a few days later Jessie called me into Mrs. Whitman's bedroom, where they'd been working in secret. From the look on Jessie's face I figured what was waiting for me, and I wasn't wrong. Both of them stood there smiling and waiting for me to be overcome with joy at the sight of a gingham frock in my size. Instead, it was the dolefullest sight I'd ever seen. They even had a matching blue ribbon for my hair, which had grown to a considerable length by this time. I looked at the get-up and saw all my days of freedom going out the window. And

I saw embroidery hoops, dishcloths, and penmanship exercises come rushing in.

"Don't you think it's a little early for this?" I asked Jessie.

"Not a bit of it. In fact, it's much too late. We've got a tub here, so get out of that unnatural garb and get yourself clean. Wash your hair too."

I went behind the screen while Mrs. Whitman laughed and said, "I've never been so surprised in my life when Jessie told me about you. I think it was very clever of you both, and only wish I'd had the chance to do the same thing when I was your age. Oh, but aren't we going to create a sensation at the table tonight?"

I moaned as I lowered myself in the tub, for Mego and Mr. Garrett had just come back from the mountains. "I can't do it, Jessie," I said. "They're all going to laugh at me, and I can't just spring a frock on them like that."

"Give me that soap," she said. "Now duck your head under and get that hair wet."

"Jessie, listen to me," I pleaded when she let me back up, "why don't we do this gradual like? Let's drop some hints first so it won't come as a surprise."

"Put your hands over your eyes," she said, and lathered up my hair.

Mrs. Whitman sat in her rocking chair, laughing and enjoying it all. "Nobody's going to laugh at you, Em. I mean, Emma. Everybody will be delighted at the transformation."

"I don't know about that, Mrs. Whitman," I said from behind my hands. "Mego, for one, is bad to get shocked at things. Why, Jessie, he might even have a stroke. Have you thought about that?"

"Oh, hush. It's not going to bother him at all, " she said, and poured a pitcher of water over my head. "Just think what Mr. Garrett's going to say."

"I am thinking of it, " I wailed, "and that's why I don't want to do it."

At one time I had wondered what Mr. Garrett would think if he saw me in a frock, but I was nowhere near wanting to find out now. What with fear for life and limb in Absaroka, I had about overcome the curiosity that would lead me into some knowledge of the carnal kind, but a female garment was likely to set it off again. I knew everybody would look at me in a different way, especially Mr. Garrett, and they might be able to tell what impure thoughts my wayward flesh had once filled my mind with. Mr. Garrett was forever closed to me. I knew that and had known it all along, but he'd made me feel glad every now and then that I'd be a grown lady someday. Otherwise, I might've relished and hung on to the freedom and independence that the Constitution guaranteed every red-blooded male citizen. But because of Mr. Garrett I didn't want to stay Emmett for the rest of my life and have to walk hunched over with arms across my chest to hide the female evidence. At the same time, though, I didn't want the evidence to come out in a sudden fashion without any warning whatsoever. It stood a good chance of mortifying everybody to death, especially me.

But there was nothing I could say that was going to put Jessie and Mrs. Whitman off from turning me back into a girl. They even had underclothing, bloomers and bodice, ready for me, and if I could've done it all at my own pace, I might've taken some pleasure in the pretty things. As it was, all I could think about was having come through the door as Emmett and having to go out of it as Emma, bedecked with ribbons and all. I thought about crying, but couldn't work up to it. So I settled for sulking.

"There now, Emma," Jessie said, standing back to view the remains of Emmett, "now you are a little maid."

I flopped down on a stool with my limbs aspraddle, like I'd gotten used to doing, and wondered if prayer would do any good.

They waited until everybody was at the table and Dr. Whitman was calling us to come eat. I could hear them talking, the Walkers and the Eellses, Mr. Green and two hired men, several children, Mego and Mr. Garrett, and Dr. Whitman. Icringed in my soul to think of walking out there in front of them all.

Mrs. Whitman went out first and announced that she and

Jessie had a surprise for them. Jessie took me by the arm and marched me into the kitchen.

"I want everybody to meet my sister," she said, pulling me forward and smiling with a lot more pleasure than I was feeling. "Here is Emma Louise Heath."

It was as bad as I figured it would be. No, it was worse. It got dead quiet around the table and everybody just stared and gawked at me without saying a word.

Mr. Garrett, who was shaking his head in wonderment, finally said, "Two of them. I don't believe it."

Dr. Whitman got to his feet, but just as he started to make a courtly bow in my direction, Mego commenced strangling. Everybody turned toward him and saw that he was as white as a sheet. He jumped up and knocked his chair over. He held on to the table with both hands and stood there with this strained look on his face trying to say something.

"I'm a goner, Garrett!" he finally managed. "Oh, lordy, lordy, what've I gone and done?" Then he made a beeline for the door with his face in his hands.

"See that, Jessie?" I said. "He's having a stroke, like I told you he would!" And I lit out after him. I heard them all start talking as I left, but I didn't care about them anymore.

It was still in the twilight of the day and, as I ran out in the yard and turned the corner of the Indian room, I could see Mego heading for the river. He was moving in a hurry and slapping his limbs with his hat at every stride. I could hear him talking to himself and calling on the Lord as I ran after him.

"Wait, Mego! Wait for me!" I called.

"Don't, chile," he said as I came up to him. "I dassn't ever look ye in the eyeball agin!"

"I'm sorry, Mego," I said, just about to cry at the thought of losing the best friend I'd ever had. "I'm sorry I'm really a girl, but I can't help it. Don't hate me, Mego, please don't hate me!"

"Hate ye?" He stopped then, and he did look at me again. "Why, little'un, they ain't nuthin' that'd make me hate ye. Hit's me, chile, that's done in, and not you atall. Oh, me, I ain't never gonna git over this."

He turned and went on to the riverbank, sitting down under a tree and reaching for his tobacco.

"Go on back in, chile, an' eat yore vittles," he said."Ole Mego'll jes' set out hyar in the dark whar he b'longs."

I hunkered down beside him, belatedly remembering to pull my skirt over my knees.

"You don't belong in the dark, Mego. What's wrong with you, anyhow? Don't you know I'm the same on the inside no matter what's on the outside?"

"Lad, lad," he said with a mournful sigh. Then he covered his face again. "Now see thar, I don't even know what on airth to call ye now!"

"Folks've been calling me Em all my life," I said. "And I don't care what you call me, if you'll just not carry on so."

"Ye don't onderstand, chile." He stopped and took a deep breath. "Hit's the shame of it, that's whut it is. Ever' time I try to disremember all the loose talk I spouted in front of ye, hit all comes agushin' back in agin. They ain't no excuse fer sech talk to a female girl chile, an' I ain't never gonna git over it. Nossir, hit'll haint me with a blanket of shame to my dyin' day!"

"What loose talk?"

"Why, I done run my mouth 'bout wivin' an' 'bout personal enjoyments an' all sech manly doin's, till hit plum torments me to thank on it. I ain't never gonna git over the shame of makin' so free with ye. 'Tain't right fer a man to say sech thangs in front of wimmenfolk."

"I don't remember anything like that."

"Why, chile, thank back on it. Don't ye recollect when I tole ye 'bout the time I went fer Bridger's woman an' . . . Now see thar, I almost went and done it agin!"

"I'll tell you the truth, Mego," I said. "You've just touched on the most worrisome thing in my life. You see, I've got this terrible memory. Time and time again Jessie has to tell me the same thing over and over, 'cause I can't hold anything in my head for longer than a minute. It's something I was born with and can't help myself. Things just come in one ear and go right out the other, with hardly a rest in between. It's a failing, I know, but that's the way of it."

He cut his eyes over at me, and I kept as straight a face as I could. I stared back at him, trying to look regretful and sad for having a deformity of the brain.

"Air ye ajestin' me or air ye atellin' the Gospel truth?"

"On a stack of Bibles, Mego," I said, hoping I wouldn't be put to the test, but figuring it was in a worthwhile cause. "I've got a grievous case of disremembering. Now if you'd of put it in writing, I'd have it all by heart. But the spoken word is just like the wind to me, here one minute and gone the next. I try to look on the bright side, but I stay in hot water with Jessie all the time because of it."

"Do ye now?" he said, and we sat there eye-to-eye, trying to look sad and sober. I got tickled first and couldn't keep a straight face. Then he broke, too, and we commenced laughing and carrying on like demented folk.

"Whut am I gonna do with ye, chile?" he sputtered. "I sware, ye be a wonder an' no mistake."

"I don't care what you do with me," I said, wiping my eyes, which for some reason had quit laughing and started crying. "Just so long as you don't change anything. I couldn't stand it if you turned away from me because I'm different from what you thought."

"Ah, lass, ain't nobody aturnin' away from ye. Now, now, don't ye be doing no cryin'. 'Tain't no cause fer it," he said, patting my back.

"I told Jessie this would happen," I said, in the grip of a full-fledged crying spell. "Nobody's going to like me anymore, that's what's going to happen."

"How ye figger on that?" he asked, and got me settled next to him with his arm around me. "Like ye jes' said, thar ain't been no change underneath them ribbons and furbelows. Ye be the same as ye ever was."

"Well, but what's Mr. Garrett going to think?"

"Garrett," he said, shaking his head and laughing a little under his breath. "Pore ole Garrett, he's had his hands full with one female named Heath. Now he's got two outter the same pod. I feel sorty sorry fer him, don't you?"

"I reckon he won't have a chance with two of us," I said, and started laughing again.

"Not agin two purty leetle gals like you an' Miss Jessie, he won't."

"Now, Mego," I said, sitting up straight. "I don't want to hear you saying things like that about me. There's no call for coming out with what's plain not true, just because I'm a girl."

"What ye talkin' 'bout?"

"You saying I'm pretty like Jessie."

"Wal, so ye be, chile, so ye be."

"No, and I don't want to hear it anymore either."

"Can't he'p that. Hit's the Gospel truth."

I let it go then, knowing he had the same gift for stretching the truth in a worthwhile cause that I had.

27

Thou feedest them with the bread of tears, and
givest them tears to drink in great measure.
—*Psalms 80:5*

My transformation brought on a lot of head shaking whenever
some of the missionaries saw me, but since Dr. and Mrs.
Whitman thought it was all a good jest and clever besides, they
restrained from condemning me to perdition. Mr. Green, though,
was another matter. He never aimed anything right at me or
Jessie, but he had a way of hitting sideways at us, dropping
little sermons into the general table talk about modest apparel
and unnatural conduct and the wages of deceit. Most everybody
made out like they didn't hear him, but I did, and even though
it came from Mr. Green, it made me feel bad. He generally
made himself scarce whenever Mr. Garrett was around, and of
course he didn't like him being there at all. There wasn't much
he could do about it, though, since Dr. Whitman told him that
Mr. Garrett was welcome at any time and for as long as he
wanted to stay. As for Mr. Garrett, himself, he had finished his
business with Mr. Green and didn't take much notice of him.
But even if he hadn't been finished, he wouldn't have done him
any injury under Dr. Whitman's roof. I think Mr. Green finally
figured that out, for he got bolder and bolder in his admonitions
and complaints and fault-findings.

One evening at the table, when Dr. Whitman was gone
on a doctoring errand, Mr. Green took off on the first letter
that the apostle Paul wrote to Timothy, which has a good bit
to say about the manner and method of ladies' attirement. When
he finished with that he summed it up with the apostle Peter's
words on the same subject, to the effect that all a holy woman
needs for adornment is a meek and quiet spirit. I pictured that

253

in my mind and knew it would be a scandal if any woman acted on it, holy or not.

He went on about it at some length, cutting off anything anybody else tried to say. Then Mr. Garrett, without even looking around, reached down and slid his hunting knife out of his belt. He laid it on the table and kept on eating. At the sight of it Mr. Green got uncommonly agitated to have the mashed potatoes passed up to him and, when they got there, he found he had a lot of business with them.

I finished supper as quick as I could, not having much of an appetite anyway, and went down to my favorite place in the tall grass near the river. It tore me up that Mr. Green, who was neither deacon nor preacher, could correct and reprove me and Jessie about something that hadn't hurt anybody and had helped us out time and time again. I had had about as much of it as I could stand, for not only did I have to hear his ravings at the table, I had to listen to him all day long in the garden. The garden was his special fancy, and he had declared himself the supervisor of it and of everybody who worked in it, which was me and however many Cayuse he could round up. None of the missionaries would work with him or for him, so they were glad to give him a free hand there.

To give him credit, he put in a good garden, and if he had been able to work without exhorting, lecturing, and finding fault with everything and everybody, he'd of come pretty close to being in Papa's class as a farmer.

Before long I heard somebody coming through the grass and I scrunched up, not having a mind for visiting.

"I'm looking for you, Em. Where are you?"

My mind changed and I said, "Over here, Mr. Garrett."

He came up and asked if he could sit with me for a while. I nodded, glad it was almost dark enough to hide what felt like a sudden suffusion to my face.

He sat down Indian fashion and took out his makings. "Old man Green's through sermonizing on that subject," he said. "I don't believe you'll hear any more about it. Want a smoke?"

I giggled and shook my head.

"You sure had me fooled, and that's a fact," he went on. "Though I'll admit I thought you were about the finest-looking young man I'd ever come across."

"No, you didn't."

"Yes, I did. And here you are about to be a young woman on us, and even better-looking."

"No, I'm not." I put my face against my knees in shame that he had noticed what I'd been trying to hide.

"It won't be long before you'll be giving your sister a run for her money."

"Mr. Garrett, you and Mego Cobb are the worst cases for stretching the truth I've ever seen."

"Have you ever known me to lie?"

"Only about a hundred times in a certain Crow lodge I could mention." And we both got tickled over that.

Then we sat together without saying anything while the shadows crept in and overtook the light of day. I didn't feel as easy with him as I did with Mego, but it probably wasn't something he could help, since he made Jessie uneasy too.

"Tell me how you came to change yourself like you did and fool everybody witless," he said, taking out another Mexican smoke.

"Well, it happened like this. One day back in Missouri I got myself all twisted around and couldn't get out of it. Papa said I might as well go ahead and kiss my elbow while I had the chance, so I just reached down and gave it a good one and, just like that, I turned into a boy."

He had just taken a big draw and got choked up on the smoke when he tried to get it out. I had to pound him on the back to help him get his breath back.

"It's all right, Mr. Garrett," I said, "it didn't happen that way at all. It was all Jessie's idea from start to finish." Then I told him all about our adventures and brought him up to the time he knew about. He kept shaking his head in wonderment, and it all sounded pretty good to me too. In hindsight.

"I didn't know your sister had it in her to do all that."

"You'd be surprised at what Jessie can do when she puts her mind to it."

"Maybe so, but it looks like she's set on this mission work for good."

"Don't give up on her, Mr. Garrett," I said. "I declare I can't take much more of it. I was hoping you'd make her change her mind."

"I've sure been trying. But, to tell the truth, no white woman's cut out for my way of living. Not as a regular thing, anyway. Part-time, maybe, but . . ." He stopped in midstream, then took it up again. "Well, I forgot myself there, didn't I? Guess I'm not used to talking to a young lady."

"See, and that's the worst thing about it," I said. "Everybody watches what they say to me now, and everybody puts on a different kind of face. I even do it myself. I know for a fact that if I had my britches back on, I'd take Mr. Green down a notch or two. But this frock just has a stifling nature to it and neither I nor anybody else can come right out and speak their minds around it!"

"You think that's it?"

"I know it is, and it's my fate to be stuck in one the rest of my life."

"I expect one of these days you're going to be mighty glad of it. You'll find that frocks lose their stifling nature when the young men start coming around."

"There's no call to say things like that, Mr. Garrett, 'cause I don't ever aim to marry."

"Oh, you'll change your mind. Just wait and see."

"No," I said, and I meant it too. "I don't aim to marry or have any truck with menfolks except Mego and, well, and you. And maybe Dr. Whitman. But that's it, and I have my reasons for it." Which I wasn't about to tell to him.

He started to answer, but we heard Mego out in the yard calling him to come to the house. "Garrett," he bawled, "better come on up hyar fer some news. Iffen Miss Emma's with ye, brang her on too."

"If that don't beat all," I said, just about disgusted with his "Miss Emma." "Just listen to him."

Mr. Garrett laughed and put his arm around my shoulders as we walked toward the house. "I see what you mean. I guess

I'd better just call you sweetheart, so I won't make the same mistake."

I stumbled and almost fell, blaming it on a tree root, but it was my own two feet that failed me.

When we got to the house Mego told Mr. Garrett that Dr. Whitman had just come in and had some bad news for the menfolks. They went on in, and I sat on the stoop wondering if it was worth trying to listen by the window. I liked to keep up with the news, but I'd about had my fill of the bad kind.

Before I could make up my mind Jessie came tearing out of the house and ran out in the yard. It was getting on toward dark, but I could see she was tormented about something. I ran after her and caught up with her when she crumpled up by a tree. She was crying something awful and it scared me, since even Papa's passing hadn't brought that much on.

"What is it, Jessie? What's the matter?"

"Oh, Em, I can't believe it! It can't be. It just can't be. This terrible country! Oh, Emma!" She turned around, still sobbing, and hugged me close.

"What is it, Jess? Come on now. It can't be that bad. Why, look at all we've survived and lived to tell about."

That didn't help a bit, and she cried even harder. Finally, though, she began to wipe her eyes and told me to sit down with her.

"I wish I didn't have to tell you this, but you're bound to hear it sooner or later. The Indians told Dr. Whitman about it, so he went to Fort Walla Walla to see if it's true and, more's the pity, it is." She took a deep breath and pulled my head to her shoulder. I could feel her tears running down on my face. "It's about Mr. and Mrs. Donner, they . . . they didn't survive, Em. They never got to California."

I lay still, trying to take it in. I remembered how I'd pictured them warm and happy in California while we were cold and scared and hungry in Absaroka.

"What happened to them?"

"The Indians say they were caught in the winter snows down in the Sierras, wherever that is. But even by the time they got that far, their party had broken up and scattered, and their provisions were about gone. Dr. Whitman said the Indians told him that only crazy people would've taken that route in the first place."

"The Hastings' Cutoff," I said, recalling what Mego and Mr. Clyman and countless others had said about it.

"I guess so. I remember how Mrs. Donner feared it, but, Em, Mr. Hastings' book said it was an easy way. I don't understand it, but something slowed them so much that they couldn't get through before winter set in."

She was still crying, and I thought to comfort her and save my grieving for later on. "Don't cry, Jessie. If somebody's got to go, freezing and starving's not a bad way to do it. Remember how it was with us when we were that way? After you get over the first bad hunger, you just get real tired and sleepy. And then you just pass on off in your sleep, I expect."

That set off a fresh round and I couldn't do anything but put my arms around her and pat her a little.

"That's not the way it was," she finally got out. "They . . . they, oh my Lord Jesus, Em. They fed on each other."

"Fed on each other?" I asked, not being able to figure out what she meant. "How'd they do that?"

"Oh, Emma, honey, they ate the people who died. And then, then they started killing each other for food. And the Indians say"—she stopped and took another deep breath—"the Indians say Tamsen Donner was killed and eaten only a few days before a rescue party got there."

I lay there with my head on her shoulder, trying to decide if I'd heard it right. When I knew I had I felt my supper begin to move around inside. I jumped up and ran for the high grass just as Mr. Garrett and Mego came looking for us.

"See to Miss Jessie," I heard Mego say to Mr. Garrett as he came running after me.

I ran for a long time through the tall rye grass that gave Waiilatpu its name, letting it scratch and pull and claw at me as I went. I finally stumbled and fell at the edge of it, and just lay there not caring if I never got up again. Mego picked me up and carried me to a tree that had been split by lightning and settled me down between the roots next to him.

He didn't say anything for the longest time, and I sat there feeling this awful sickness roil around in the bottom of my stomach and gradually move up to the inside of my chest. It got to hurting so bad I could hardly get my breath. All I wanted to do was curl up somewhere in the dark and shut out of my mind all the horrible events it was picturing. I'd heard people talk about hurting for somebody, and I guess that's what I was doing. The thought of Lizzie and her baby sisters, and Mr. George and Mr. Jacob Donner, made me hurt so bad that I thought something inside of me was tearing in two. But every time I tried to think of Mrs. Donner, that sweet Christian lady, my mind veered off into the emptiest place it'd ever been. I thought it might not ever come back from there, which, at the time, would've suited me fine. But all the time Mego kept talking to me and calling me back, sometimes in an Indian tongue that I couldn't make head nor tails of. He told me later that I went so blankety-eyed that I looked like a Crow taken up in a vision, and that he was flat-out worried about it.

After a while the hurting in my chest settled down to a dull ache in my soul. I felt as limp as a dishrag by that time, and was glad to lie down on the ground when Mego said I ought to rest awhile. It was good and dark by then and a little breeze made me feel some better.

I lay there wondering why such things had to happen. What had the Donners ever done to bring such a thing on themselves? Whatever it was sure hadn't been out in the open for everybody to see, for they were about the kindest bunch of people I'd ever run into, like I've already said. The worse thought of all was what if they hadn't done one blessed thing to deserve such an end. And if that was the case, it didn't much matter how anybody conducted their lives, which was contrary to all the preaching I'd ever heard. Thinking about what Mrs. Donner must've gone through in her last days on this earth gave me a terrible lonesome feeling, and I felt so sorry for her and all of them that I could hardly stand it.

"I don't know how anybody could do such a thing to another human being," I finally was able to say. I lay there looking up at the stars and wondered if they'd shone down on

Mrs. Donner and her little girls with the same cold eyes. The Indians thought the stars were holes in the heavens for spirits to look through, but I didn't think anybody could just sit up there and watch that pitiful scene and not do something about it.

"Why didn't God put a stop to it, Mego?"

"I rekkin He did, chile. Some of 'em come out of it still alivin'. Not many, I warrant ye, but some."

"But we know how they managed it, don't we? I'd rather die than live that way. Poor Mrs. Donner and her babies. And Mr. Donner, too, and I don't know who all. How could anybody do that?"

"Folks've been known to do some of the orfulest thangs a body ever heerd of. 'Specially when hit's starvin' times."

"But we starved and nobody even thought about such a thing."

"No, chile, warn't no need fer it. We'uns could git out, leastways one of us could. But when folks git holed up fer months on end and they ain't et nuthin' fer some long while and can't go nowheres and can't find no vittles anywhere and can't see no end to it, hit sorty sloshes up ever'thang in their minds."

"I don't care how bad it got, I wouldn't ever eat Jessie, or you either."

"Naw, ye couldn't git yore chompers in this ole hide. But, lass, I know this hyar news be gallin' to ye, and hit's turrible bad doin's, but hit's been done afore in these parts. Ye do what ye have to do to keep on alivin', an' don't ye fergit it. I'll acknowledge, though, that some folks is quicker on the draw than need be sometimes. Why, I recollect that there warn't a man in the mountains what would walk in front of ole Bill Bennett. Atter one of his starvin' times, he hankered fer it most all the time."

"I don't care a flip about that."

"I don't blame ye. I jes' got to runnin' my flappy mouth agin. Don't ye fret now. Put yore leetle noggin right hyar in ole Mego's lap an' let them bad thangs mosey on off."

I woke up the next morning wrapped in a blanket and

lying on the ground. Mego was propped up against a tree smoking his pipe.

"How'd ye like to take a ride up to the Clearwater an' back?" he asked. "We'uns could do a leetle huntin' an' alookin' around an' some visitin' too."

"Who would we visit?"

"I got this feelin' hit's time to call in at the Spaulding place up at Lapwaii, an' I thought I'd do it this hyar very day. I'd be obleeged to ye if ye'd keep me comp'ny an', 'sides that, ye'll take to Miz Spaulding. She's a fine lady, though leaning to the bossy side. Go tell Miss Jessie if ye're agoin'.'"

I did, and we left before the sun was high. We didn't talk about the Donners anymore, being busy with trail talk and camping and exploring side trails and visiting with Indians we came upon. It took us more than a fortnight to get to Lapwaii, and by the time we made it the Donner family was buried in the back of my mind and hardly ever bothered me in the daytime again.

28

Whoso findeth a wife findeth a good thing.
—*Proverbs 18:22*

The Lapwaii mission was some hundred and twenty-odd
miles away from Waiilatpu, so the Spauldings and the Whitmans weren't exactly neighbors. Even though they had planned
to work together when they first came to Oregon, they pretty
well knew by the time they crossed the continent in each other's
company that they'd had enough of joint enterprises. Dr. Whitman was supposed to've taken on the Nez Percé tribe, since
they had sent a delegation to St. Louis in the early thirties just
to get themselves a missionary. Mego told me that what they'd
really had in mind was latching on to a slice of the spirit power
that had given white men such things as steel knives and repeating rifles and blue beads and other like spiritual gifts. What
they got was Mr. Spaulding and his lady wife.

That might sound like the short end of the stick, but the
fact of the matter was, Mrs. Spaulding was better than any of
those things. She didn't look anything at all like Mrs. Whitman,
being too much on the plain side, and she didn't act like Mrs.
Whitman, either. Mrs. Whitman spent her time supervising her
household, mostly teaching and looking after the children of
the other missionaries, the Indian children that the Cayuse had
thrown out, and several others that looked to me like the half-
breed sort. She didn't have much to do with the Indians that
lived round about the mission, and I didn't blame her. The
Cayuse were as shiftless as they come, and she generally just
made out like they weren't swarming underfoot all the time
and stealing everything in sight. She even barred her doors and
windows at night, and she made Dr. Whitman tell them they

couldn't come in without knocking. The Cayuse said she was haughty and that she thought she was better than they were. I expect she did, because almost anybody you could name thought they were better than that bunch. I don't know what Dr. Whitman was thinking of when he picked them over the Nez Percé, unless he saw right off that the Cayuse needed a bigger dose of missionizing than anybody in the whole Oregon territory.

Mrs. Spaulding, now, put her oar in the Nez Percé tribe right from the start and never took it out. She was the only one of any of the missionaries who could speak the Indian tongue, and was such a good hand at it that she'd made them a hymnal and a partial New Testament. And, on top of that, she taught the Nez Percé to read out of them. It was a wonder to me that she could get the braves to sit still for such a thing and be taught right along with the little children, but she did. Mr. Spaulding had built her a schoolroom, and the Nez Percé, young and old, came trooping in there every day to lick their fingers and turn the pages. It was easy to see how much they liked her, for they looked after her all the time and called her Woman-Who-Touches-the-Heart.

Mr. Spaulding had put a number of the Nez Percé on the church rolls, some twenty-odd, I think, but Dr. Whitman hadn't converted any of the Cayuse. I asked Mrs. Spaulding while we were up there how they had come to be so much better at civilizing the heathen, and she said it was because Dr. Whitman was a healer of the physical parts and Mr. Spaulding was a healer of the spiritual parts, being an ordained minister of the Gospel. For myself, I think it was because he had Mrs. Spaulding helping him, and because there wasn't a single Cayuse worth the trouble of baptizing.

They treated us fine at Lapwaii, making us feel right at home. Since they lived so far from the emigrants' trails, they didn't get much drop-in company, so they made over us the whole time we were there. Mego helped Mr. Spaulding repair the corncrib for the fall harvest, and I tried to make myself generally useful, like company that wants to be invited back ought to do. We didn't stay long enough to wear out our welcome, but when the weather turned nippy I began to miss Jessie. She had already sent word by the Indians that it was time I got myself back to Waiilatpu.

We took a straighter route back and made it in about a week. I had pretty much put my worries out of mind while we'd been gone, but on the way back I started thinking all over again about what Jessie had got us into. Every day that we'd spent on the Overland Trail had been new and interesting, and we were always on our way to somewhere. But now we'd gotten there, and I didn't like anything about it. Mego and Mr. Garrett kept taking off for parts unknown, which didn't help me any, and I just didn't feel at home anywhere.

Another thing I didn't like was not having our own place. The table was crowded and the beds were crowded, and there was always somebody telling me what to do or, more likely, what not to do. There were too many bosses there and, since I had been raised to respect my elders, they about ran me ragged. And I couldn't do anything about it because I was eating their food and sleeping under their roof.

I nudged my horse up alongside Mego's. "What do you really think about Mr. Garrett?" I asked.

"Ain't nobody I'd druther have at my back in fightin' times."

"No, I mean him and Jessie. What do you think he's got in mind?"

"Why, young'un, I wouldn't 'tempt to answer that'un with a ten-foot pole. That ain't somethin' you orta be studyin' on, neither."

"I'm not studying on that. I'm studying on what's going to happen to us. I just don't think I can stand hanging around all my life while Jessie gets to be a missionary, and I don't want to leave her either. Even if I had a place to go to."

"Looks like ye're betwixt a rock and a hard place, don't it?"

"That's where I am, all right. It seems to me that if Jessie would give up missionizing, and if you and Mr. Garrett would give up running all over the mountains, we could settle down somewhere and clear some land and put in some crops and get back to decent living again."

"Chile, chile," Mego said, laughing and shaking his head. "Hit's shore been a spell since this ole coon's plowed a furry. An' I don't 'spect Garrett's ever done it. I don't know as ye'll ever git him to, seein' that he ain't the settlin' sort."

"Well, it wouldn't hurt him to try," I said. "If they'd both give up a little something, Oregon wouldn't be a bad place to live."

"I'd sooner specalate on a Blackfoot's next move as try to perdict a female woman's. But hit looks to me like Miss Jessie's bound an' determined to try her hand at them savages."

"You'd think Mr. Garrett would be enough for her, wouldn't you?"

"That be the God's truth. I don't know, lass. Ye ort not to git yore hopes up too high 'long them lines. I don't know as Garrett'll ever put down roots."

"What about you? Could you and me do it?"

"Law, chile, that's somethin'll take a heap of ponderin' over and cogitatin' on. 'Sides, Miss Jessie ain't gonna let you go runnin' off by yore lonesome, even with me."

"Well, I don't know what to do. I've prayed about it till I'm blue in the face, and it hasn't done any good. I just can't live all hemmed in like this."

"Listen to ole Mego, now. Since the weather's gittin' a mite airish, hit be about time fer me an' Garrett to head fer the beaver streams."

"Ah, no! You're not going to go off and leave me here all winter, are you?"

"Have to. Cain't make no cash money without workin' at it ever' day. Now, jes' listen hyar to me. Come the sprang of the year, Miss Jessie'll likely have her fill of missionizing attar bein' cooped up with 'em all winter. Leastways, that's what I thank Garrett's acountin' on. Though he did mention needin' some blanket warmin' fer the cold season. Which I didn't aim to mention to ye. But hit don't do no harm, fer Miss Jessie ain't gonna go fer that kind of doin's, I don't 'spect." He hooked his leg over the front of his saddle and rode that way for a while, looking like he'd forgotten what he'd started to say. "Anyways, give it till then, an' mebbe she'll be ready to move on down to the Willamette whar they's more civilized folks. Kin ye stand it that long?"

"I guess I'll have to, won't I?" I said, none too happy with the prospect. "I'll tell you the truth, Mego, we had to spend last winter with the Crows and now we have to spend this winter with the missionaries and the Cayuse. And I'm hard put to tell which is worse."

We heard Waiilatpu before we saw it. Just as we came out of the trees to the edge of the first tilled field the commotion hit us. It wasn't any one different noise, but more like the everyday level had been raised a notch or two while we'd been gone.

"What in the world's going on around here? Sounds like everybody and his brother's got a hammer in his hand."

"Lookee yander in the front yard," Mego said, pointing his pipe toward a cluster of Conestogas. "Hit be the fall of the yare, an' the emigratin' trail ends smack up on Dr. Whitman's doorstep ever' time. Looks like 'bout half the United States be parked over thar, don't it?"

And it did. Eighteen and forty-seven was a bad year for emigrants. They clamored over the Blues and swarmed through the mission station from August on till the snows cut off the trails. Some of them stopped for water and supplies and a day or so of rest before pushing on to the Willamette settlements. Others stayed several weeks, too tired or too fearful to face the last of the wilds. They spent the time repairing wagons, nursing their sick, and eating off the mission stores. Some broke down trying to cross the Blues, and Dr. Whitman and the others would have to go bring them in, half-starved and worn to the bone. A few decided to sit out the winter in the front yard, swearing they couldn't take another step for love nor money.

It got so that Dr. Whitman had to put a limit on the supplies he sold to them so that the station would have enough for itself through the winter. The emigrants didn't like that at all. The corncribs, barns, and smokehouses were crammed full of more food than they'd seen in months, or even years in some cases. A lot of them had the notion that the missionaries had been set there for their relief and benefit, and were supposed to give them whatever they wanted, and do it free and clear too. It purely galled them to pay for supplies from missionaries, who, as I heard one emigrant say, "ort not to be makin' no cash money outta the Lord's work."

A few of the emigrants felt obliged to help out around the station, especially if they didn't have any other way to pay for their keep. In that way Dr. Whitman got more land cleared so he could raise more crops for the next year's batch of travelers. It looked like Waiilatpu was heading up to be a prime way station on the Overland Trail.

The influx of emigrants gave me something else to worry about on top of the load I was already carrying. There were so many of them that I was afraid they'd stake out the best land in Oregon and, even if Jessie changed her mind, we still wouldn't be able to farm. And I found out that the Cayuse were worried about the same thing. Not that they were looking to farm, but they didn't want anybody else breaking up land that belonged to them. I can't say I blamed them for that, but the fact of the matter was, not one emigrant aimed to stay around Waiilatpu. It was too far from civilization for them. Still and all, the Indians feared they would, and a delegation went to Dr. Whitman and told him that he could count on every emigrant crop put in at Waiilatpu being watered with blood. And furthermore, Split-Lip told him, they were about fed up with missionary crops too. Dr. Whitman talked to them for the longest time, telling them that the emigrants didn't even want to stay and that he knew Waiilatpu belonged to them, and that the missionaries would pack up and leave anytime a majority of the Cayuse wanted them to. The Indians left with somewhat easier minds, knowing the Doctor was a man of his word. He really knew how to handle Indians and keep them on an even keel. I've never known a man to have so much patience and forbearance in the face of never-ending aggravation from them.

Day work, Indian troubles, and a spate of complaints weren't the only things the emigrants gave us. They brought in and left with us a strain of measles that found a natural breeding ground in the Cayuse tribe. By the time Mego and I got settled back in it was plain to see that the disease was intent on strewing death and destruction everywhere. Dr. Whitman had lost some of the heft he usually carried, and he looked drawn and strained from fighting the sickness every day and night. Mrs. Whitman and Jessie had set up sickbeds all over the house so they could tend the little children who were struck down. Everybody was short and snappy, especially Mr. Green, who didn't like children even when they were well, and who didn't like selling or giving supplies to anybody who hadn't worked for them and who especially didn't like thieving Indians.

I found out that the Cayuse had deviled him for weeks by plundering his garden, and he had taken steps to put a stop to it. The first thing he'd done, after dressing-downs and fulminations hadn't worked, was to put up a scarecrow, as like unto himself as it could be. It worked for a while, since it was the first of its kind the Cayuse had ever seen. They thought it had some kind of magic medicine that put their own out of kilter. But as soon as they saw birds roosting on it, they knew its power was gone.

All in all, there were a lot of sulled-up faces around Waiilatpu. The emigrants were broke and mad; the missionaries were tired and mad, and the Indians were sick and mad. I had a mind to light out for Lapwaii again, but Jessie told me to settle myself down and find something to do.

The best thing I could find to do after my chores were done was to go off by myself down by the river and get away from the strife and contention. It was worse than a Crow camp. That's where I was one forenoon, sitting there in a spot of sun, minding my own business and brooding over Mego and Mr. Garrett fixing to leave us for so long.

I heard Jessie and Mr. Garrett talking, and pretty soon they came in sight. Jessie was giving him a piece of her mind, like she usually did when he was being fractious. Which she said was his general and natural state.

"I declare, Mr. Garrett," she said, "it seems to me that you and Mr. Cobb could find enough to do around here. You're badly needed, you know, what with everybody so sick and busy. Why do you want to go off, anyway? I can't understand traipsing all over creation when you could stay here and live like decent folks."

"Maybe that's just it," he told her. "Maybe they're too decent for me. Besides, you're the only reason I've been here this long."

"Now, Mr. Garrett, I've told you and told you this, and I'm not going to tell you again." She shook her finger right up under his nose, which was a pretty brave thing to do to a man like Mr. Garrett. Then she remembered herself and took a different tack. "I'm truly thankful to you for rescuing us from the Indians, especially since there wasn't another man in the country with enough gumption to do it. I'll never be able to repay you for that. The only thing I can do for you is to lead you onto the path of righteousness for His name's sake, if you'd just be heedful of the great need you're in."

"I'm heedful of it," he said, with a peculiar twitch to his mouth that would've warned me off but didn't bother Jessie at all.

"I've just never seen anybody so stubborn in my life," she went on. "I wish Brother Akins from back home was here. If anybody could get you to the door of salvation, it would be him. The Lord knows I can't seem to do it, no matter how hard I try. And I really do care for your soul, Mr. Garrett, as any Christian would."

"I appreciate that, Miss Jessie, but it's not my soul that's giving me trouble."

"Well, it should be. But if it's not, what is?"

"Don't you know?" he said, and he just sort of folded her up in his arms and buried his face in her neck.

And the surprising thing about it was that Jessie let him do it, pretty much like she had when she'd tried to bring him to salvation once before. She should've known not to start up on that subject again, for it sure gave him notions that didn't have anything to do with church matters, as far as I could see.

He moved his face all around hers, and finally ended up kissing her good and proper, and this was in broad daylight

too. Jessie acted like she didn't care who saw them, but she
probably had her mind on something else.

"Oh, John Calvin," she said, and turned her face up toward
his again.

John Calvin, I thought, so that's his given name. It was no
wonder he didn't take to missionizing after living with that all
his life. I started easing myself back through the grass and away
from them, being shamed by this time at what was going on.

"Come with me to the mountains," I heard him say to her.
I had to stop then to hear her answer, since it had to do with
me as well as her.

I heard her say something about having to marry before
anything else could be done, and he said he wasn't going to live
with a bunch of missionaries and that was his final word. Then
he started telling her about mountain weddings, which weren't
the long-lasting kind, and he should've known better than that.

"There's just one thing on your mind, John Calvin Garrett," she snapped, and tried to pull away from him.

"Yes, one thing, but not just one time. And I'll take you
any way I can get you. You can ride out of here with me
tomorrow and stay till you want to come back, or we'll have a
preacher say the words and make it binding on both of us. But
I'm not a missionary and won't ever be, so make up your mind."

"I can't just go off with you," she said, like she'd like to
but couldn't bring herself to it. "And even if I could, that'd be
the end of my mission work. They wouldn't ever let me take
up the cross again. Then where would I be?"

"With me," he said, "with me, for as long as you want to
be. Wouldn't you like that?"

"Oh, John Calvin," she said, so limp and lazy-like that I
had to peep through the grass to see what was wrong with her.

I wish I hadn't done it, for Mr. Garrett was taking liberties
around her bosom, and she was letting him, with the most
scandalous display of amiability that I've ever witnessed. Mr.
Garrett had as strong a desire for carnal knowledge as anybody
I'd ever heard of. It was so strong that it put Jessie in the same
frame of mind in spite of the Ephesian armor that Mr. Green
said all the missionary ladies ought to wear. Which just shows

what love can do even to somebody like Jessie, who didn't ordinarily hold with base behavior and familiar conduct of any sort.

There was no question about it now. They would have to stand up to a marriage service or burn in hell fire like the apostle Paul said, which I knew Jessie wouldn't stand for. So I left with a considerably lighter heart than I'd started out with.

29

As coals are to burning coals, and wood to fire,
so is a contentious man to kindle strife.
—*Proverbs 26:21*

Jessie came to the supper table that night looking like a lamp with a fresh supply of oil, and Mr. Garrett looked pretty pleased with himself too. I figured they'd make some kind of announcement of their forthcoming nuptial plans and could hardly wait to hear them. To tell the truth, everybody could've used some cheerful news, for all the missionaries were solemn and tired and not half eating.

"How many today, Marcus?" Mrs. Whitman asked, pushing strands of hair from her face.

"Two more infants and an old man," Dr. Whitman answered. "We'll bury them tomorrow, but they'll probably have companions before the night is out."

"When will it all end?" somebody asked.

"Soon," Mrs. Whitman answered. "This disease will run its course before long. We just have to bear up under it till then."

Dr. Whitman looked down the table at her and smiled his tired smile. He thanked her for the encouragement and said they all needed her strength of mind. But it looked to me like it was Mrs. Whitman who needed encouragement worse than any of them.

"What about the children here at the station, Narcissa?" Dr. Whitman asked. "Any more of them come down while I was gone?"

"Two are recovering, and the fever may break tonight on some of the others."

"I'll have a look at them after supper. What about the rest

of you? Is anybody sick or have any symptoms I should know about?"

"We're all well, praise God," Mr. Green said, speaking for the internal goings-on of us all. "But there is one thing I must speak to you about, and that is the perfidious thievery that's going on in the garden. I've got melons, winter squash, and cabbages still growing and, I remind you, they will be the last before winter sets in. We need those vegetables for our own table, yet every morning I find that the Indians have been at them again. They even leave the melon rinds right there in deliberate defiance of my orders. I tell you, Dr. Whitman, something has to be done, or I won't answer for the consequences!"

"Calm yourself, Mr. Green," the Doctor said. "It's not that serious a matter. The Cayuse know that I don't want them to be hungry, so they feel free to eat whatever they want."

"Hungry!" Mr. Green said, banging his fork on the table. "They aren't hungry! We already supply them with every mouthful they eat. There's absolutely no reason for them to raid the garden. You've said yourself that they can come to the kitchen and have whatever they want. But no, they have to steal from the garden as well. I'll tell you, Doctor, there's something more important here than a few melons and squash. What's at stake is the whole matter of authority. Do the Cayuse run this station or do we? And there's more to it than that. The Almighty has instituted a chain of command that's being dismantled here, and if we don't get them back in line, our whole enterprise will come to naught."

"Now, Mr. Green," one of the missionaries said, "let's not create any more trouble for the Indians. They've got enough on their plate as it is with this epidemic."

"I don't aim to create trouble," Mr. Green said, working up a full head of thunder. "I'm aiming to create decency and orderliness, or is that something none of you know anything about?"

It got real quiet around the table, and the women lowered their eyes while the men pretended they hadn't heard anything out of the way. But Mr. Green wasn't through.

"It's time we got this out in the open," he said, directly to Dr. Whitman. "The Lord has been laying this on my heart for a long time now. I don't say it's all your fault, Doctor, but you're so busy ministering to the sick that you've let the business of the mission suffer from pure neglect. Something had to be done, and I've done it. I've posted a letter to the Mission Board outlining our problems and suggesting they appoint someone else in your place. In that way you'll be freed from administrative duties and able to devote your time to the ill."

"Oh, Thomas, Thomas," Dr. Whitman said, looking like he'd been slapped. "What have you done?"

Mrs. Whitman made to speak, but one of the other missionaries beat her to it.

"Of all the underhanded tricks I've ever heard of, Green, this beats all. How could you undermine us this way? You're not an ordained minister and you're not entitled to speak for us. Nor are you equipped to pass judgment on Dr. Whitman or this station."

"Somebody had to do it," he said, not backing down an inch. "None of you have the courage to see what is as plain as the nose on your face. Dr. Whitman has allowed the Cayuse to use this mission for their own benefit. He has allowed the emigrants to beggar us into poverty, and he has allowed the moral temper of this establishment to sink to unjustifiable depths."

"What do you mean by that, Mr. Green?" Mrs. Whitman asked, thereby doing one of the things that Mr. Green was on record as opposing. He didn't think the ladies ought to speak out in public, and would always cut in with a prayer of his own when any of them wanted to take part in the prayer meetings.

"You know what I mean, Mrs. Whitman, and so does everybody else. Especially since you've had a hand in it."

Mego laid down the knife he'd been eating with, and Mr. Garrett pushed his chair back. They didn't generally pay much attention to the missionaries' business, but they wouldn't stand for anybody hurting Mrs. Whitman's feelings.

"Explain yourself," Dr. Whitman said.

"Not in this company," Mr. Green said, "but I'm more than willing to discuss it in private."

"That won't do," Dr. Whitman told him. "You've made a public accusation and you can make a public explanation."

"So be it then," Mr. Green said, like he was being forced into something he didn't want to do. But I didn't think he was. "You're all witnesses to the truth of what I say. Is there not, even at this moment, in the room above us a child of mixed parentage?"

Mr. Garrett commenced to rise out of his chair, but Mego shook his head at him.

"Has there not been a child of unholy and unsanctified union received gladly, and without foresight as to the harm it does her witness, by Mrs. Whitman? Is not the child's presence among us enough to taint the testimony of each one of us, since we're forced to take to our bosoms the fruit of all we labor so diligently to stamp out?" Mr. Green sounded like he'd been holding all that inside of him for months and was glad for the chance to finally get it out.

I knew he was talking about Janie Songbird, a little child about two years old, who had had an Indian mother. I'd heard that one of the trappers had brought her to Mrs. Whitman to raise when her mother got killed right after she was born. She was just about Mrs. Whitman's favorite, and Jessie had taken to her too. Sweet Janie was everybody's pet, since she was as close to being an orphan as you can be without being one.

"Can any of you deny this?" Mr. Green asked. "No, not a one of you. You go about preaching the sanctity of marriage and the blessedness of children of the covenant, yet, by your actions with that illegitimate half-breed upstairs, you cancel out your own words. Little wonder that the Cayuse are confused and disrespectful. They can see no relation between your words and your deeds. Do I make myself clear or shall I go on?"

"What would you have us do, Thomas? Throw the child out?" Dr. Whitman asked, but everybody else was so discomposed that they just sat there and stared at Mr. Green. Mrs. Whitman looked about ready to cry.

"And while we're clearing the air," Mr. Green went on, without answering the Doctor's question, "there's another matter you ought to do something about. Not only do you nurture an unnatural child as one of your own, you receive and welcome to your hearth and table the very perpetrator of the evil deed!"

He swung around then, and pointed his finger at Mr. Garrett. "You! You come among us out of your filthy union with an Indian squaw, bearing the result of it for us to raise. You come among us without shame for your evil lusts, without even the decency to hang your head before godly women. You flaunt youself among us without a smidgen of remorse!"

Jessie sat as still as stone, staring at Mr. Garrett as the words slammed around the room. It took a minute before I could get a handle on what he'd said, but when I did I knew Mr. Garrett was Janie's father.

Mr. Garrett stood up then, but Mego tipped his chair back so he couldn't get by.

"Do you want to go outside or do you want your throat cut right here?" Mr. Garrett asked, and the hair on my arm started rising up of its own accord.

"You see!" Mr. Green said, with a spray of spittle. "Do all of you see his true colors? Not only is he a squaw-man, he also threatens murder, which I have no doubt already stains his soul many times over."

I'll say for a fact that either Mr. Green didn't believe in living a long life or else he didn't have a lick of sense.

"Marcus," Mr. Garrett said, without taking his eyes off Mr. Green, "I aim to kill this man."

"This chile'll be helpin' him too," Mego said. "But we'uns won't do it hyar at the table, will we, Garrett? Name yore buryin' place, Green, fer we'uns aim to have yore hair an' no mistake."

"Now, Mr. Cobb, Garrett," Dr. Whitman said. "Let's not get carried away. Thomas is not well. I think it would be more suitable to send him home on sabbatical."

"You'll not be sending me home!" Mr. Green yelled. "You call me sick, when all I do is speak the truth? None of you can stand on the side of what is right and just and pure! This man, Garrett, as well as Cobb here, is widely known for the Indian women he's taken and abandoned. Not once has he been united in holy matrimony, as if any minister of the Gospel would be a party to such licentious behavior. And now he comes from their filthy lodges to stain the purity of a young white woman, and not a one of you has the courage to say him nay!"

Jessie looked sick to her soul, and I wasn't feeling too good myself. She got to her feet, stumbling against the chair, and without looking at anyone made her way out of the room. Mr. Garrett watched her go, but didn't try to stop her.

"Garrett, I beg of you," Dr. Whitman said. "Display forbearance, in the name of God."

"I'll shed no blood in front of Mrs. Whitman," he said, "but my word is good. Green, you're a dead man."

Having said that, he followed Jessie out of the room. Mego nodded as if the deed was as good as done.

"You will notice," Mr. Green said, like he'd come out on top of an argument, "that he could not deny the truth and had to resort to empty threats, which is no more than I expected."

"Shet yore trap," Mego said to him. "Ye've already dug yore grave deep enough an' I, fer one, has heerd all I want to hear fer one day."

"I agree," Dr. Whitman said, "enough is enough. Let us go to the library for evening prayers. We're certainly in need of them this night."

And that was the first night I stayed awake all through the praying, for I had a lot to study on and a lot to lay before the Lord. But in the light of what happened later on, the Lord must've dozed off as it had been my former custom to do.

The next morning I found Mego sitting in the sun oiling his guns, so I hunkered down beside him to watch. The sun felt good on my shoulders, since the day had begun with a nip in the air. My mind was still on the events of the night before. It was whirling with Mr. Green's charges of fornication, murder, and bastardy. I'd heard such things before, of course, being a churchgoer of long standing, but never aimed directly at somebody I knew and over a supper table at that.

"Mego, what do you think about what happened last night?" I ventured as a starting point.

"I don't misdoubt that the way of a man with a maid is beyan' scientifiky calkilations," he said, rubbing a long barrel with oil-soaked wool. "But I wouldn't worry none about it. Garrett ain't never let too much stand in his way when he sot his eye on a woman afore."

"Well, he may just have a problem on his hands this time. Jessie, she don't take kindly to playing second fiddle, especially to a bunch of squaws."

"Wal now," he said, with a peculiar glint in his eyes, "squaws ain't so bad. They's warm and good comp'ny when the snow's deep. Yore sister wouldn't do half-bad to foller 'em into Garrett's lodge. To my knowledge, he treats his women first-rate. Never heerd tell of him doin' no nose-cuttin' nor lodgepolin'. So ye kin go tell that leetle gal that she won't find a man as good as J. C. Garrett anywhars in the mountains. She won't never go hongry, nor lack fer cunnubial enjoyments, neither. You tell 'er that, and to let go of bygones, and quit fulminatin' on sech thangs what ain't got nothin' to do with her."

"But what about little Janie?" I asked. "What's Jessie supposed to do about her? I mean, Janie's the evidence of Mr. Garrett's sinning ways."

"Sin? Sin, ye say?" He looked at me so hard that I felt cold and peaked. "How many times war yore own pap married, littl'un?"

"Three, to my count."

"Carry any young'uns over to the next wife?"

"Reckon he did."

"Thar ye be, then," he said. "Now I'll jes' tellee 'bout the rules of the mountains. Menfolks don't tote their squaws up in front of preachers nor jedges, 'cause in the first place, thar ain't none. An' in the second place, the Injuns wouldn't stand fer it. Nossir, they has their own ways, an' Garrett war married all nice an' legal 'cordin' to Injun ways. Ain't much difference betwixt a few coins fer a marriage paper an' three hosses to a squaw's pap, air thar?"

"Put that way, I guess there's not."

"Yore dang tootin' thar ain't. Now hyar's the way I figger it. Miss Jessie'll dangle him a leetle while jes' to sorty save face, then she'll want him back. But I'm atellin' ye, littl'un, don't let 'er dingle-dangle too long. Garrett ain't a man to fool with fer too long. An' thar ain't a squaw in the Snake nation what wouldn't walk two hunderd mile to lay in his lodge."

"You mean he might give up on her?" I asked, my heart failing at the thought.

"I mean he ain't knowed fer bein' patient when hit comes to connubials. About which," he said, blowing his nose with the oily rag, "I dassn't say another thang. So don't try an' git me to prospect that vein no further."

So I prospected on my own for a while, then ambled on down to the riverbank. Mr. Green's revelations had set me back to being all winter at Waiilatpu, and probably the rest of my life as well.

I hadn't exactly been expecting them, but since they seemed to like the same places I did, Jessie and Mr. Garrett showed up before long. Jessie looked like she'd been crying, and I knew for a fact she had. She'd been shut up with Mrs. Whitman all morning, not being in a fit state to even come to breakfast. Mr. Garrett looked about half mad, which was some improvement over the night before.

"I just don't understand you, Mr. Garrett," Jessie was saying, and I noticed a return to formal address. "What do you expect me to do in the face of your unseemly behavior?"

He laughed a little in a way that didn't sound too funny. "You can do whatever you want to do," he said.

"But, those Indian women!" she said, clouding up to cry again. "Oh, Mr. Garrett, how could you?"

"It was easy," he said, hooking his thumbs in his belt and looking down at her.

"Easy!" she snapped, firing up to her usual head of steam. "I should say it was easy! Just pick up a squaw any time and any place and take off with her!"

"That's about it. And none of them gave me half as much trouble as you."

"Well! You don't know what trouble is if you think you can just stroll in here and treat me like one of your loose squaws, you debauched barbarian, you!"

I'd never heard Jessie swear that way before, and hadn't

thought she had it in her to do, but she was always surprising me. I think she must've been reading one of Miss Porter's novels that Mrs. Whitman ordered from the United States and hid under the bed from the other missionary ladies.

"I don't want to see you again! I want you gone and out of my life, you, you squaw-man, you!"

Mr. Garrett's mouth went tight and thin at that, and I didn't know whether he was going to whip her or walk off and leave her. Instead, he laughed and grabbed her up close to him and started whispering something real important in her ear. At first Jessie stayed still to hear what it was, but when she got the full import she commenced squirming and screeching and crying and promising to cut his vulgar tongue out for him.

He just laughed again, but finally had to kiss her to shut her up. Then he turned her loose and walked off. Jessie let him go, because she was too busy crying to do anything else. She cried awhile and then she prayed awhile and then she fell to lambasting Mr. Garrett for a fickle, heartless, sporting man who wasn't fit husband material in the first place. She got pretty worked up over that, which put her in enough fettle to march back to the house and give him another piece of her mind.

I caught up with her about the time she flounced into the backyard. She had her teeth clenched together so hard it's a wonder she didn't grind them loose. She stopped short when she saw Mr. Garrett swing up on his horse, which was packed with blankets and saddlebags. Mego was tightening the cinch on his horse.

"Just where do you think you're going?" Jessie demanded, stalking right up beside Mr. Garrett's horse.

"I told you," he said, pulling the brim of his hat down low. "I'm giving you time to make up your mind. I'll be back in the spring. Once. You be ready then."

"Well, I never!" Jessie was so mad she could hardly get her breath. "Who do you think you are to give me an ultimatum like that?"

I sidled over to Mego and just shook my head at the spectacle. He winked at me and made like he was busy with his horse.

"I'll tell you who I am," Mr. Garrett said, leaning down from his saddle and running his finger down the side of her face and across her mouth. "I'm the man who's going to bed you one way or another before another robe season passes."

Well! Jessie couldn't stand that, so she opened her mouth and clamped down on that finger and bit the living daylights out of it. And Mr. Garrett laughed like it was the best thing that'd happened all day.

"Want one more kiss to keep you warm through the winter?" he asked, lunging down at her.

She dodged out of the way, sputtering and fuming at something she called his audacity, and then danged if she didn't haul off and kick his horse.

The horse danced and sidestepped out of her way while Mr. Garrett lifted his hat to her. "Save it up for next spring, Miss Jessie. I'll take care of it for you then."

"Get off this place and don't come back!" she yelled. "I don't need you to take care of anything, and I'd rather be a veiled nun than married to a heathen like you!"

He put his hat back on and firmed it down. Then he pushed his horse into a slow canter out of the yard. Jessie, who lately had not been known for moderation and civility, started running after him.

"John Calvin Garrett! You come back here! I'm not through with you yet!"

He laughed and waved his hand, but didn't turn back. The Cayuse who were wandering around in the yard had been taking all this in and I wondered what they made of it. The missionaries who had seen Jessie's display of fractiousness looked pained and tired to pretend they hadn't noticed anything out of the way.

"Listen hyar, littl'un," Mego said, checking the gear behind his saddle. "Don't ye fret none 'bout yore sister's heartable concarns. They'uns'll work it out betwixt 'em. But, heed me now, thar's thangs hyar which this chile don't like the smell of. These hyar Cayuse," he said, spitting out their taste, "be asettin' up fer mischief or my name ain't Meshach Abednego Cobb."

"It is? I mean, they are?" I looked around and couldn't

see any signs of mischief, just the laziest Indians God ever made.

"Hit'll take some time fer thar medicine to git worked up, else we'uns wouldn't leave ye. I figger springtime, after they've been cooped up all winter nursin' thar grievances. Me'n an' Garrett'll be back afore then. But if thar's any leetle thang you don't like, hightail it outta hyar, either to the Spauldings, but preferable to Pambrun at Fort Wally Wally. Ye hyar me, now?"

"Yessir, I do. But I wish you wouldn't go."

"Have to, little'un," he said, swinging into the saddle. "Can't eat offen these folks ferever. Take keer now. An' iffen ye need me, send word by any trapper what comes through, or by most any Nez Percé."

"You'll come back, won't you?" I asked, holding on to his stirrup.

He patted my head and said, "Make wager on it. I'll be smashed to flinders and throwed in hell if this chile ain't back afore the snow melts."

I stepped back, trying to swallow something achey in my throat, and he loped off after Mr. Garrett. When he was out of the clearing I knew I couldn't bear the thought of any company for a good long while. I went off by myself, out of sight of Mr. Green especially, who was the particular cause of my present misery. A funny kind of sick feeling had spread all through me when Mr. Green had been talking about Mr. Garrett and his squaws, and about Mr. Garrett and Jessie. I had to think out why that'd happened, since I'd never had it before even when I'd thought in a good bit of detail about connubial pleasures. Then it came to me that my sicky feeling probably didn't have anything to do with such pleasures, but had a lot to do with the very way that Mr. Green had talked about them. He'd made those pleasures sound like some dark and noxious secret that nobody would ever know about if they didn't cause babies to be born and be the visible evidence that they'd gone on. Mr. Green didn't have any babies himself, so he couldn't be accused of doing what Mr. Garrett had plainly done. But the Bible said that the marriage bed is undefiled, and if Mr. Garrett had married his squaws like Mego said, then why was Mr. Green so exercised about what was done in it? I couldn't figure it out, but I know Jessie was offended by it, too, though from the way she'd let Mr. Garrett hold her so close, it didn't look like she particularly dreaded the thought of being in a marriage bed with him.

30

Now a thing was secretly brought to me, and
mine ear received a little of it.
—*Job 4:12*

With Mego gone I felt the same way I had when Papa died and went on to Glory. Only I didn't even have the comfort of that where Mego was concerned. He was off somewhere with Mr. Garrett on the Popo Agie or in the Marias facing who knows what kind of dangers, not the least being cold mountain streams that would aggravate his rheumatism, to say nothing of a Crow arrow in his back. I worried and fretted, and grew more melancholy by the day.

Jessie didn't help matters, either. She got over being mad about the time Mr. Garrett was out of sight and took to repairing and replenishing her missionary demeanor. She told me that wrath was just as impure as some other thoughts she'd had, and that she'd now overcome it with an humble and meek spirit.

But to tell the truth I think she was barking up the wrong tree. If a vote had been taken to admit her to the full-fledged missionary fold, she would've lost it. Dr. and Mrs. Whitman were about the only ones who thought there was any hope for her. The rest of them gave her a wide berth. But we didn't have anywhere else to go, having sent off the only likely prospects for a way out of the mission field. Or rather, she had, and I was feeling like the last rose of summer about it too.

Even the garden, which had occupied a lot of my time, was on its last legs. We'd had frost for several mornings in a row and the cabbages smelled to high heaven. But Mr. Green hadn't let down his vigilance one whit. What was left of the scarecrow had become a joke to the Indians, and I heard some of them saying it looked an awful lot like Mr. Green himself. One morning he went out and discovered the scarecrow's hat was gone. That was enough to start him on a rampage, but when he saw it on the head of a Cayuse squaw, he just had a conniption right then and there. He wanted the miscreant punished, but was afraid to do it himself. So, since Dr. Whitman was off seeing to more measles cases, Mr. Green went running up to the squaw, coattails flapping, and snatched the hat off her head. He tore into her about thievery, sneakiness, and all manner of general devilment, and she didn't like it a bit. Not that she understood all the references to her moral character, but she got his drift. Three Cayuse braves who'd been working in the barn came over with scowling faces and crowded around Mr. Green. One of them pulled his nose, which is pretty close to being a mortal insult, and the other two pushed him around a little. Mr. Green got away from them and hightailed it to the house, calling down retribution on them as he went.

Mr. Eells and Mr. Rodgers tried to settle things down, but didn't make too much headway. The Indians grumbled and muttered and gestured toward the house all day long. Hardly any work got done, and the little that was might as well not've been from the looks of it.

Mr. Green stayed in the house for the rest of the day. He holed up in Dr. Whitman's study preparing another manifesto detailing all his grievances, and it took him till nightfall to list them all.

Dr. Whitman rode in just as we were finishing supper. He looked like death warmed over, for every time he thought he'd gained the upper hand on the measles, they popped out somewhere else.

"I hate to tell you this, Marcus," Mrs. Whitman said, helping him off with his coat, "but more of the children have come down with it today."

"Who is it now?" he groaned as he sank down in a chair.

"The McKenzie child, one of the Indian babies, and little Janie."

"I'll just rest a minute, then go up and see to them," Dr. Whitman said, with his eyes closed.

"Drink this while you rest," Mrs. Whitman said, handing him a mug of soup. "You probably haven't eaten all day."

"Ah, Narcissa," he said, leaning his head back against the chair, "it's getting worse. I've lost count of how many we've buried. Now my calomel supply is running low, and I don't know how long we'll be able to fight this thing."

"I know, dear," she said, rubbing his forehead. "Surely the Lord will allow us to overcome. Oh, Marcus, I almost forgot. A note from Mr. Pambrun came today by messenger."

Mr. Pambrun was the British factor for the Hudson's Bay Company at Fort Walla Walla, which was down the river some twenty-five miles or so from us. He lived there with his Indian wife, who, Mrs. Whitman had told us, owned a set of real bone china that had come all the way from London, England.

Mrs. Whitman called me from the front room, where I'd been reading, and asked me to bring the message from her bedroom. I did, and when Dr. Whitman read it he folded it up and laid it aside.

"Call the others in, Narcissa."

When we'd all gathered in the study he said, "Mr. Pambrun advises us to abandon the station. He says that the Cayuse are embittered and resentful, which we all already know. And, of course, they have every right to be, with children and old people dying in every lodge. And now the young men and women are beginning to sicken. The question is, do we take Mr. Pambrun's advice and abandon them when they most need us or do we stay?"

Mr. Rodgers, who was studying how to be a missionary and a minister of the Gospel, nodded and then said, "That's what it's come down to, all right, and maybe we'd better take into account an incident that happened today while you were away. It involved Thomas Green, and almost turned ugly."

"When is there not an incident involving Thomas?" Dr. Whitman sighed. "I'm sure the Indians know him by now, so it probably meant nothing."

"I had resolved not to burden you with this, Marcus," Mrs. Whitman said. "But in the face of Mr. Pambrun's warning, perhaps I should tell you. Two or three of the Cayuse broke into my bedchamber last night while you were gone. I asked everyone not to mention it to you, but it's better that you know."

"What!" Dr. Whitman jumped up and put his arms around his wife. "Were you hurt? What happened?"

"They did no harm," she said, "only frightened me. I held the Bible up to them, and they left."

The other missionaries began to get these scared looks on their faces, and the ladies reached for their husbands' hands.

"I don't like that at all, Narcissa," Dr. Whitman said. "That was very bold of them, and I thought they had more respect for your person than that. Furthermore, the fact that the Bible could make them withdraw means they are falling back into their old superstitions, and we've made little headway against them. They think our Book is magic, and the Romans, with their black robes and crosses and signs and symbols, haven't helped either. It seems that everything I've worked for these twelve years is suddenly being destroyed by illness and Papists."

Nobody said anything, but there was a lot of thinking going on. It wasn't like Dr. Whitman to sound so dispirited, for he was the one who generally bucked up everybody else. Then, one by one, the others began telling of little things that had happened to them over the past several days. Mr. Walker had been struck across the face just last week by a Cayuse he'd corrected. The doors of the corncrib had been broken down a few nights before by braves on a thieving run, and a fire had been set over at the grain mill.

Dr. Whitman listened, his head bowing lower at each account. Finally he straightened up and looked around at us all.

"We all knew it wouldn't be easy when we first accepted the call," he said, clasping his hands together in front of him. "The Cayuse are heartsick and frightened at the deaths among them. But it is our task to help them and to comfort them, even to extremities. I admit, though, that they are less malleable than ever, so if any of you want to take Mr. Pambrun's advice and remove to the fort, nothing will be held against you. For myself, I must remain, not because I'm brave, but because I don't think we're in any real danger. They are like children, and children strike out against their parents when they're confused and frightened. But also like children, the Cayuse know we mean them no harm and that we're here to help them. They may take out their anger on us in childish ways, but I feel that we, as Christians, are strong enough not to retaliate or hold it against them or to run from them. But, as I've said, each of you will have to make that decision for himself. Narcissa?"

"My place is with you, as always," she said, and somehow or another she brought to my mind Mrs. Donner on that last morning before they took the Hastings' Cutoff.

The other missionaries talked it over and agreed that their place was also at Waiilatpu. Mr. Green, though, hadn't had a chance to express himself on the subject, for he'd made himself scarce all evening. I didn't doubt he'd have something to add when he showed up again.

I slid over by Jessie, who hadn't said anything. She was looking pretty tired, because she'd been up with the sick children half the night and all the day.

"Jessie," I whispered, under cover of the general talk, "let's us go pay the Hudson's Bay Company a visit for a while."

"We can't do that, Em," she said. "There's too much to do here. I'm not scared of a few childish pranks. Besides, the children are too sick to be moved, and I'm needed here."

"I just thought you might need a little rest. You sure have been working hard ever since Mr. Garrett left."

"Don't," she said, looking down at her hands. "Don't remind me. Em, little Janie, his . . . his daughter, is very sick. I couldn't leave her, don't you see?"

I put my arm around her and leaned my head against her shoulder. "I'm not afraid and I do see, Jess," I said, probably seeing more than she did. If she cared so much for the daughter, then some of it might rub off on the father.

After prayers and the reading of the Scriptures, Dr. Whitman dismissed us. I pondered in my heart the Ninety-first Psalm, which I'd just heard, thinking it was an apt selection for our present situation, especially the part about pestilence, terrors by night, and arrows that flieth by day. As we left the room for our beds I heard Dr. Whitman tell his wife that he was sending Ups, one of the trusted Walla Walla Indians, to Lapwaii in the morning.

"Even though we're not going to accept Pambrun's kind offer," he told her, "I would be remiss in not sending his warning on to Mr. Spaulding. They're much more isolated than we are, and perhaps they should consider moving closer in."

Mrs. Whitman nodded, but didn't say anything, and I started up the stairs behind Jessie. I couldn't get the words of the psalmist out of my mind. King David wrote like he had a firsthand knowledge of Indian tactics, having been in a number of tight spots with unfriendlies himself. I figured he'd had a few run-ins with Cayuse ancestors, seeing as how the Indians descended from the Ten Lost Tribes of Israel. I resolved to study how King David had dealt with them from his war record in the Chronicles, for he always came out on top, getting crowned and becoming king and all. Of course he did have a speaking acquaintance with the Lord Jehovah, which I couldn't count on, but I figured to learn something useful from his adventures if I applied myself to them. I also resolved to ask Ups to get word to the Nez Percé when he went to Lapwaii the next day and have a message sent to Mego, like he'd told me to do. There was getting to be a number of things I didn't like the feel nor the smell of and I figured it was time to let somebody know about it.

As we reached the top landing I heard firm footsteps in the hall below and, looking over the railing, I saw Mr. Green cramming on his hat and moving toward the door. He was carrying his doctor's satchel that he'd had back on the trail and which Dr. Whitman had told him to get shut of. He slammed the door behind him, and I wondered if he was on his way to doctor on some ailing Cayuse who didn't know any better than to let him do it.

"I think I'd better go to the outhouse before I go to bed," I said to Jessie, thinking up an excuse to follow him. The last thing we needed now was for Mr. Green to bring us more trouble, as he had a way of doing.

"Why can't you use the slop jar?" she asked. "I don't like you going out at night."

"I'm not scared," I told her, on my way back down the

stairs. "Besides, the moon is full and it's bright as day outside and, besides that, I've got more business than the slop jar calls for."

"Well, all right," she said. "Just be quick about it and come right back inside."

"Yes'm, I will," I said, closing the door behind me and easing into the shadow of the house.

I waited until I could see, like Mego had told me how to do. Sure enough, the moon was bright enough to throw shadows, while the middle of the yard was light and clear. I stood still a while longer to see if anything was moving out there. I could hear people moving around inside the house, some getting ready for bed and others looking after the sick. But not a soul moved in the yard.

I edged around the house, intending to make a circuit to see if I could spot Mr. Green and at the same time not get too far from safety myself. I'd told Jessie a story when I said I wasn't scared.

From the back of the house I could hear the horses in the barn shuffling and snorting, but not enough to mean somebody was saddling up to ride out. So Mr. Green was on foot, and he couldn't have got very far.

I decided to dig down for some backbone and cross the clearing to the barn. From there I would be able to see across the back lot down toward some of the Indian lodges. I made it there with nothing untoward happening to unnerve me. I squatted down to rest awhile, for sneaking around is a tiresome business. I leaned back against the barn to think what to do next and remembered something Mego had once told me in one of his stories. He'd been hunting some Piegans and came up on them before they got to him. The way he'd done it was not by hearing them, but by not hearing them. He said you'd better look out when there's no noise and nothing's going on. And that's just what was happening at Waiilatpu. There were no campfires burning over on the edge of the clearing, no Cayuse telling war stories, no squaws arguing and quarreling in the night. It was eerie and real lonesome.

Then I caught a movement out of the corner of my eye.

I held real still so I wouldn't lose it, and so whatever it was wouldn't see me. Then I centered in on a hunched-over shadow in the garden. It moved slowly down a row and then back up through another one.

When it straightened up I saw it was Mr. Green and couldn't figure out what he was up to, trying to tend the garden in the middle of the night. I scrunched back against the barn as he came by swinging his satchel on his way back to the house. When I heard the door close I sneaked over to the garden and went down the rows he'd been in. I found a few late melons that the frost had already got to and some dried stalks that rustled as I went by, but nothing else. I felt around the stems of the melons to see if he'd tied them to the vine to keep the Indians from stealing them, but they were the same as they ever were.

Then I smiled to myself, for I'd figured out what he'd been doing. He'd been counting every little nubbin, every head of cabbage, and every one of the squash in the garden. I expect he intended to read them off the next morning, alongside another list he would make of what was left after the Cayuse hit the garden again. That way he could prove his charges against them in writing. He could niggle something to death, and I knew there'd be another uproar when he commenced on this.

I took myself on to the outhouse then, since I don't generally pass up an opportunity to relieve myslf in comfort and since the rim of the slop jar is cold as ice, and also so I could tell Jessie that I'd done what I'd intended to do.

31

Fearfulness and trembling are come upon me,
and horror hath overwhelmed me.
—*Psalms 55:5*

Mr. Green must have decided to hold off on opening his case against the Cayuse, for we didn't hear a peep out of him the next day nor the next. He pretty much stayed to himself, biding his time, I expect.

As for myself, I was glad I'd gone ahead and sent a message to Mego. I had had some fears of crying wolf and taking him and Mr. Garrett away from their traps for nothing. Even though the Cayuse hadn't done anything to make matters worse for us, they hadn't done anything to make us feel any better, either. But something was going on that Mrs. Eells called a sense of doubt and foreboding, which was as good a name as any. Everybody was infected with it, jumping at the least little noise, and not sleeping too good, and looking back over their shoulders, and talking in quiet voices. It about scared me just to watch them, and then I found myself doing the same things.

I think it was all the sickness that was doing it. Most of the little children were down with it, and just about all the Cayuse. And instead of running its course and dying out, it was picking up steam. Dr. Whitman said it was the most virulent strain of measles he'd ever seen. The ones who didn't get it, mostly the missionaries, were almost as bad off as the sick folks from the work of taking care of them.

Little Janie had about the worse case, and Jessie was worn to a frazzle sitting up with her. It got so that she wouldn't let even Mrs. Whitman help out and give her a rest. I did what I could, like bringing water and broth up the stairs for her and holding the covers over Janie when she thrashed around with chills and fever. Dr. Whitman said that the fever would cool down once the variolous matter erupted, but it just wouldn't do it. We kept the windows closed, the fire burning, and quilts and wool blankets piled high, but the measles just wouldn't pop out. It was a stubborn case and no doubt about it. She got weaker and weaker, what with throwing back most of the little nourishment we could get down her. It was a good thing that Jessie was able to get her to keep down the calomel that Dr. Whitman dosed her with, for there's no telling what would've happened without it.

The Cayuse, on the other hand, had their own ways of treating the measles, which was the same way they treated everything else from a cut finger to pneumonia. They were too ignorant to heed Dr. Whitman and take the standard remedies, but resorted instead to magic and superstition. Which would've been all right if they'd worked, but they didn't. Dr. Whitman would go see their sick and leave doses of calomel for them, and as soon as he got out of sight they'd give it to their dogs. I don't guess I have to say what calomel-treated dogs can add to an already fairly noisome Indian camp.

The Indians looked on bodily sickness as spirit infection, and they were bound and determined to rid themselves of it in the only way they knew how. The way they did it was like this. First they roasted themselves in a steam lodge until they were about parched, and then they'd run buck-naked down to the river and jump in. As it was already November, the water was nigh on to freezing, so most of them moved from there right on into the burial grounds.

It was a curiosity to me to find out that the very sickest Indians were the ones most likely to get well and go back to stealing and pestering and their general run of shiftless living. The real sick ones were too weak and frail to get down to the river by themselves to take the cure, and it was a settled fact that no other Cayuse was going to help them. So they had to lie there begging to be thrown in the river, and nobody paying the least mind to them. It was pretty pitiful, since they believed in their medicine men and yearned to take the treatment even if it killed them, which, as I've said, it generally did.

But my time was pretty well taken up with helping out

in the nursery upstairs at the mission house, and I didn't get
over to the Cayuse lodges very much. We had what Mrs. Whitman called a veritable sanatorium up there, what with little
children coughing, moaning, vomiting, and crying from one end
to the other. Like I said, Jessie had pretty much taken on Janie
as her special sufferer. She stayed by her cot and rocked her
when she couldn't sleep and nursed her like she'd done for me
when I had scarlet fever one time. By this time I don't even
think Jessie saw that Janie wasn't as fair as the missionary
children, and might not of cared even if she had.

She was rocking Janie one night when I brought a supper
plate up to her. "Emma, look here," she said, "don't you think
she's beautiful?"

"Who?" I asked, being too tired to notice much of anything.

"Why, Janie, of course." Jessie smiled and pushed back the
soft black hair from Janie's flushed face. "I see a lot of John
Calvin in her, don't you?"

I moved a lamp nearer and studied the tiny brown face,
but couldn't see that she looked like anybody but Janie, which
was good enough for me.

"Well," I said, "I do believe I see the resemblance. And
it'll probably get stronger as she grows up."

"Do you really think so?"

"It's a recorded fact that strong qualities outweigh weak
ones, and nobody can deny that Mr. Garrett has pretty strong
qualities. So I don't think you have anything to worry about."

"I don't think so either. But, oh Emma, I've done and said
so many wicked things that I look on Janie's illness as my
punishment."

She began to cry, but not like she usually did, which was
like an overflow of wrath and general frustration. This time
she was crying like she was hurting somewhere down inside,
and it hurt me to see her do it.

"It's not your fault, Jessie, so don't take on so. Come on
now, you know it's not your fault that Janie's sick."

Then I opened my mouth to tell her there was no way in
the world that she could be blamed, for it was the sins of the
fathers that are visited upon the children unto the third and

fourth generations, and certainly not the sins of second wives, or whatever number Jessie would be if she did get in the line. I held my peace, though, for I didn't think she'd find any comfort there, even if it was from the Bible. Besides, I didn't much believe it myself, having seen too many children prosper from their fathers' wrongdoings.

So I cast about in my mind for some other words of comfort from the Scriptures, which are the best kind of quotations if you can pick up on the right one for the occasion, and they have brought solace to countless numbers.

"Do you remember how it says in the Book of the apostle Luke to let the little children come unto me?" I asked, not especially taken with the aptness of it, but it was the best I could come up with, being taken unprepared for quoting from memory. The only verse I could call to mind at any time without any worry of getting it wrong was the first one I ever learned in Sabbath School, since it's the shortest one in the whole Bible. The apostle John wrote it, and I'll ever be grateful to him for helping me out whenever I'm called on to recite a verse of Scripture. It hasn't stood me in much stead, though, for any other occasion, since "Jesus wept" doesn't fit too many problems I've had to face.

"I love you so much, Em," Jessie said, and hugged me. "Thank you for reminding me that our Lord cares for the little children. I'm ashamed of myself for losing heart. I'm just so tired. And lonely, somehow. Missionary work is not what I thought it would be."

"Mr. Garrett'll be back," I said. "He said he would and he will. But you better treat him better next time."

She smiled amongst all the tears, and almost managed a laugh. "I'll tell you the truth, Em, I expect I'd have him now if he came up with a hundred Indian babies."

"Hold on, there," I said, "don't get carried away. That may be a little more than we can manage. And besides, you'll probably want to have a few of his babies yourself."

"Emma Louise!" she said, pretending to be shocked, and pretty nearly was. "You mustn't talk about things like that. It's not decent."

That was a pure shame, because I would've liked to have
talked about things like that to somebody. But now that I was
back in a frock, the best I could manage was to try to listen in
when married ladies got together to sew or string beans. Jessie
kept telling me that I'd know everything when I met the man
who would be one in spirit and in flesh with me. "Two become
one," she'd said, "and that'll make three, just like the mystery
of the Holy Trinity," which didn't do much to enlighten me.
But I'd already figured out, from watching her and Mr. Garrett,
that love went hand in glove with carnal knowledge, which
together could bring on babies. The only thing I couldn't figure
out was that I'd seen a lot of marriages that didn't look to have
a smidgen of love in them, or either the two people in them
hid it real well, yet babies kept cropping up year after year
without fail.

I'd heard one of the missionary ladies talking to another
one the other day when they didn't know I was around. She
was crying and lamenting the trouble in the flesh she was having,
which was exactly what the apostle Paul had warned would
come to any virgin who married. "I render unto my husband
his due every time he wants it," she'd said, "but, I declare, I
would rather space it out a little more." The other lady had
agreed and told her that all her husband had to do was put his
britches on the bed and she found herself in the family way
again. That was pretty much of a surprise to me, but it was all
a mystery, like Jessie said it was.

"Well, Jessie, if you really are more amiable in your thinking about Mr. Garrett," I said, after studying on it awhile, "I
guess that means you're going to give up on mission work,
because I don't think he's ever going to come around to that."

"I don't think so either," she said, wiping away the last of
the tears. "I worried about it for the longest time, but I must
have misread my calling, as unlikely as that sounds. But, oh
Emma, I do so long for marriage, and the Scriptures bid us to
submit to our husbands, so there you are."

"That's a fact," I said, a little stunned to hear her admit
right out that she'd been wrong about something. And as far
as submissive wives go, she was about as far from my notion

of what that meant as I was. I decided not to bring that up, though, and let Mr. Garrett worry with it, since I had something else on my mind.

"Now, Jessie, if you've a mind to marry, and I hope you have, have you given any thought to what's going to happen to me? I just don't think I've got it in me to stay on here, not ever having a call for missionizing in the first place, as you'll recall."

"Now how could you even ask such a thing? Your home is always with me, wherever I am and whatever I do. Always and ever, until you want your own."

I figured as much, but it felt good to be sure about it.

"And besides," she went on, "before that last awful night when I learned about Janie . . . and . . . and other things, Mr. Garrett and I had talked about that very thing. And he wants you, too, Em. He said, if nothing else, you might keep Mr. Cobb in one spot for a while. And I'll tell you something else he said. He told me that he wouldn't have me unless you were included in the package."

I don't know what happened to me then. Something strange and along the lines of an unexplained feverish feeling welled up in me. I had half a notion to cry, too, but was trying to get over doing that so much.

"Is that a fact?" I was grinning so hard my jaws ached.

"He certainly did. You weren't worried about it, were you?"

"No, I wasn't worried, it's just that I've known some new husbands who wouldn't take on a wedded wife and her family too."

"Well, John Calvin will," she said, then she started laughing. "Tit for tat, Em. He brings Janie and I bring you. How about that?"

That sounded fine to me, so we kissed each other good night, and I went to bed and slept better than I'd lately been accustomed to doing.

We woke up to a gray morning, the rain having fallen most of the night and leaving an overcast sky and a yard full of mud behind. At first light I went to see how Janie was, and to see if Jessie'd had any rest at all. She hadn't, but she was in high spirits. Janie's fever had broken during the night, and the malignant illness was well on its way out. As she was still sleeping, Jessie decided to go down to the table for the morning meal.

Lamps and candles were lit in the kitchen, for the morning was dim from the off-and-on drizzle outside. The men were already eating, so they could start the butchering they had planned for the day. There was some talk of freezing rain, but most felt it would hold off until they'd done the outside work.

The ladies lingered around the table after the men left. Since a goodly number of them had been up during the night, they were slower to start the day's work. They talked about how to rearrange the sick children upstairs, putting the Indian children who were almost well apart from the sicker ones. The Sager children were so close to full recovery that they were getting rambunctious, so they needed to be separate from the others too. After comparing degrees of fever and numbers of measle eruptions, they decided that Janie was probably the sickest one of all and that Jessie was to move her into the smallest back bedroom up over the kitchen.

"Where is Mrs. Whitman? Has she already eaten?" Jessie asked, looking around like she'd just missed her.

The ladies all started talking in these low voices, and I couldn't hear everything, but they were saying things like Mrs. Whitman wasn't feeling good, and that she hadn't been able to come to the table, and that somebody had taken a tray into her, and that she was just sitting in a rocking chair, crying and not eating a thing.

"She's probably getting sick herself," Jessie said. "I'll look in on her."

"No," one of the ladies told her. "She said she just needed some time to herself. She's just dispirited, I expect."

"Despairing's more like it," another lady said, none too pleased about it. "She ought to find something to do and not give in to it."

Jessie looked like she wanted to say something to that, but the other ladies nodded in agreement and she saw she was outnumbered. So she said she would go up and move Janie and then get some rest herself.

"That is," she said, on her way out, "if going to bed in the daytime after being up for three solid nights in a row is not giving in to it."

I grinned into my oatmeal and listened to the ladies whisper behind her back. Jessie's days as a missionary were surely numbered.

She slept all morning and missed a lot that happened but not all of it, and even that was too much. I left the kitchen not long after she did and went down toward the barn to watch the butchering, which wasn't my favorite pastime, but listening to the ladies whisper about my sister wasn't either. There were a number of the Cayuse helping Mr. Rodgers and the others butcher an ox. Some of the squaws were there, too, and they were doing most of the work.

Hog-killing time back in Missouri is something like a social, for neighbors get together to help and there's a lot of jokes and pranks and admonitions on the right way to do things. It wasn't that way at Waiilatpu. The Cayuse were all sulled up, and got worse about it when somebody told them to do something. The missionaries didn't take any pleasure in the work either. They were quiet and busy, and worked like they just wanted to be done with it. Two of the squaws keep pushing and shoving the missionary men out of the way and giving them these glaring kind of looks. It wasn't anything like the hog-killings I'd been to before, but maybe it was because it was an ox and not a hog.

Toward noontime Dr. Whitman rode in, so tired that his knees almost gave way when he dismounted. Mrs. Whitman met him at the door and led him into his study, which was the only quiet room in the house. I wandered back in and found a bench in the front room to rest myself on. I didn't want to exactly listen in, being a private person myself, but still and all I didn't like the way Mrs. Whitman was acting. It wasn't like her to outright despair, and if she was doing it, then I wanted to know why. The missionaries had made a decision to stay at

Waiilatpu come hell or high water, but I hadn't. And now that Janie was getting well, Jessie had nothing to hold her there either. Besides, Dr. Whitman hadn't closed his door.

"Narcissa," I heard him say, in a voice that sounded like an old man's. "This disease, whatever it is, is about to get the better of me. It's something new, not measles at all now. In the last three days twelve of the Indians have died and more than half the tribe is ill beyond describing. Whatever it is, it's becoming more virulent every day, and if I don't find some way to stop it, there won't be an Indian left in the territory. I buried three children just this morning."

"There's something else you ought to know, Marcus," Mrs. Whitman said. "I hate to tell you, since you have enough to contend with, but the Cayuse women are speaking openly of *tamanowas*."

"The evil eye?" he said with a little laugh. "I don't doubt it. It's just one more instance of their superstition. I, myself, have been accused of sorcery, and all this week they've refused my medicine for fear that I'm poisoning them. It's only to be expected that they'd blame us for all their misfortunes. Father De Smet and the rest of those black-robed idolators aren't the least to blame for encouraging and abetting this kind of thing. Did you know that the Cayuse have been negotiating with the Papists to give them our mission?"

"Oh, Marcus, has it gone that far?"

"Now, don't worry. Not even the Romans would agree to that. No one in the territory would stand for it."

I lay on the bench thinking of what I was hearing. It was a settled fact that Dr. Whitman flat had no use for Popish priests, long gowns, crosses, beads, or anything else that smacked of Romanism. Mr. Spaulding held the same views, and so did Mr. Green, although he thought the Britishers over at the Hudson's Bay Company had even the priests beat for perfidy and underhanded tricks.

"I don't like it, Marcus," Mrs. Whitman was saying. "Too many are dying, and if the Cayuse blame us, we could be in real danger."

"Nonsense, my dear. We've lived here for twelve years without trouble. They like us, but naturally they blame us too. As soon as the epidemic abates they'll be just as quick to credit us with stopping it. We're all tired now, but we must be strong and of good courage. With the Lord's help, we will prevail."

Before Mrs. Whitman could say anything back, there was a loud pounding at the outside door of the study. I heard Mrs. Whitman go over and open it, and then I heard the sound of moccasins shuffle into the room.

"Want medicine," an Indian voice demanded. I knew it was Split Lip, who was the worst of the Indians for telling the missionaries what they were doing wrong. Nobody could ever please him with anything.

"Who's sick in your family, Split Lip?" Dr. Whitman asked as I heard him rummaging in the cabinet where he kept his medicine.

"All sick. Cayuse die all day. Want medicine."

"Take this to them, and see that they take it," Dr. Whitman said. "I'll be along directly and see to them."

I didn't hear anything else for the longest time, and I stretched out on the bench to rest my eyes for a while. I heard Dr. Whitman sit back down in his chair, but the Cayuse still hadn't left.

"Is there anything else you want?" Dr. Whitman asked.

"One thing only," Split Lip said in a funny kind of way, and I heard an awful crunching sound that was drowned out when Mrs. Whitman started screaming.

Without even thinking I rolled off the bench and scrambled under it, wanting only to shrivel up and hide somewhere far away from the sounds coming out of the next room. I crouched under there, trembling so hard that I could hardly hold myself together, and listened to Mrs. Whitman's screams and the Indians' curses and the blows of whips and hatchets. I didn't hear anything from Dr. Whitman.

It went on for about a hundred years, and I finally got the courage to peek around the edge of the door. Dr. Whitman was lying on the floor with a tomahawk sticking out of the back of his head. Blood was splattered on the floor and the walls, and three or four Indians were standing around Mrs. Whitman. I can't even say what they were doing to her.

The same awful sounds, mixed with gunfire, started out in the yard, and I could hear running feet pounding through the house. All I could think of then was getting to Jessie, and I took to the stairs knowing I wouldn't have to die to find out what hell looked or sounded like.

32

For death is come up into our windows, and is
entered into our palaces.
—Jeremiah 9:21

I ran through the front bedroom past the ladies, with faces gone
gray and suddenly old as they stood there listening to the
unbearable noises coming up from below.

"They're killing Mrs. Whitman!" I yelled on my way
through. One lady fell across the bed and gathered up a child,
and another one sank down on her knees in prayer.

"Jessie! Jessie, get up! For the Lord's sake, get up, Jessie!"
I cried as I threw open the door to the little room where she
and Janie were sleeping.

"What is it?" she asked, still half asleep. But then, as she
heard the commotion in the yard and underneath us, she sprang
out of bed, wide awake.

"My Lord, what is it?" She ran to the window and looked
out.

"C-C-Cayuse," I stuttered, shaking and trembling worse
than I'd ever done with the Crows. "I think Dr. Whitman is
dead, and maybe Mrs. Whitman too."

"Oh, no! Oh, Lord Jesus, protect us in our hour of need!"
Jessie ran for the door, but I grabbed her and held on.

"Don't go down there, Jessie! There's nothing you can do,
and we've got to save ourselves and Janie."

"Janie," she said, and turned back to the bed. "What can
we do, Em? Oh, my Lord, listen to them!"

We stood looking at each other for a minute, not knowing
which way to turn. We were in an upstairs room with one door
and one window, which looked out over the backyard. I knew
what was happening downstairs, and I caught a glimpse of even
more of it through the window. Indians were running all over

303

the place hacking and slashing at the people I'd had breakfast with only that morning.

"What'll we do, Jessie? There's no way out. And they'll be up here in a minute, I know they will."

Then we heard moccasined feet pound up the stairs, and an unholy shriek bounced and echoed all through the house. The hair on the back of my neck rippled along with it. The little children in the front room started screaming and crying, and I knew the heathen savages were doing to them what they'd been doing to Mrs. Whitman.

"If there's no way out," Jessie whispered, white-faced and determined, "we'll stay right here. Get Janie out of bed and smooth it over like no one's been there. Hurry!"

I did what she told me to do, asking no questions and glad somebody had a plan. I wrapped Janie in a blanket and grabbed a bottle of milk. Jessie was pushing a settle back against the fireplace wall as quietly as she could. She stood on the seat of the settle and then climbed up on the back of it. She reached high over her head and unlatched the cupboard built on the side of the fireplace up near the ceiling.

"Quick, Em, scoot up in here and let me hand Janie to you."

I've never climbed anything as fast in my life, for there was no letup in the hellish din outside the door. I pulled myself up into the cupboard, which was about as big as a trunk. Then I reached down for Janie. Mercifully, she was light as a feather and still half asleep.

"It'll be snug up here, Jessie," I whispered, "but it'll do. Hurry on up."

We had a time getting her in, for she had to boost off from the top of the settle without turning it over. We wanted to leave the room looking like nobody had been in it. After a mighty struggle, in which Jessie came close to damning skirts and petticoats and women's attire in general, we got her up and in. The three of us were folded up as tight as sausages in a crock. She finally got the door closed, making sure that none of her skirts were hanging through the edge. We settled down then, and tried our best to breathe without gasping too loud.

The din and commotion outside were muffled now, but we could hear enough not to complain about our cramped quarters, even though one limb was fast going to sleep on me. It was dark as pitch inside the cabinet and hot as an oven, which, come to think of it, it was. It must have been built to match up with the drying or curing oven on the side of the fireplace down in the kitchen.

"Jessie," I whispered, "we might suffocate in here. Have you thought about that?"

"Be quiet," she said, right up in my ear. "Don't say another word. Can you find Janie's mouth?"

I felt around and nodded.

"Good. Keep the bottle right next to it, and if she moves, cram it in. Our very lives depend on no sound at all."

I nodded again and gritted my teeth, determined that if they found us, it wouldn't be on my account or Janie's.

Finally we heard what we'd been waiting for and dreading. The door to the room slammed open, and I think the whole Cayuse nation must've crowded into the room. They were jabbering and grunting and breathing hard with excitement, and they sounded like they were having the time of their lives. We heard the chest fall over with a crash, then the sound of sheets and quilts being ripped. Hatchets splintered the walls and furniture, sounding dreadfully like the bone in Dr. Whitman's head.

When they'd done as much damage as they could there, they left the room and ran in an almighty hurry down the stairs. I guess they didn't want to miss out on any of the ravages still going on in the yard.

I can't tell you how long we stayed cramped up in that little cabinet. It was so long that I couldn't feel anything below my waist, and the heat was stifling us so bad we could hardly breathe. If I hadn't felt so sorry for myself, I would've worried about Jessie, for she was on the bottom and had more to cram into the tiny space than I did. Janie slept on, moaning every now and then, which got her a mouthful of milk every time.

Things began to quieten down on the second floor. I thought I heard Mrs. Whitman and Mr. Rodgers talking one time, but

I must've been dreaming. A baby cried once, I'm pretty sure, and then I know I heard some of the missionaries talking in one of the front rooms downstairs. I thought maybe they'd turned on the Indians and put a stop to their depredations. If they had, we could climb down and help bar doors and windows until help could get to us.

"Jess?" I whispered, fixing to suggest we go and see what was happening.

She clamped her hand over my mouth, getting my nose in the process. I was glad she did, though, for the next sound we heard was a door being smashed in downstairs. My heart just about failed me again, knowing that bars weren't going to keep them out, and knowing also there wasn't a gun on the place. Well, there was one that Dr. Whitman kept for killing stock he wanted butchered for the table. And it must've been down at the barn for that very purpose this morning. There was another one, too, if you could count it. It was only a barrel that had been kept under a bed in the front bedroom, waiting for repairs that nobody ever got around to doing. Dr. Whitman didn't believe in keeping the mission armed, saying that they had come to save the Indians, not to kill them. I wished now that he'd had a different view.

Even though it was so dark I couldn't see Jessie's face in front of me, I began to be able to picture just where the Indians were and what they were doing from the sounds we heard. They had gone through every room of the house already, but it sounded like they were going back through to make sure they hadn't missed a chance to render even more death and destruction. I heard them congregate in the kitchen right below us, heard doors being hacked open and havoc made of the pantry.

They must have found more missionary children hiding somewhere, for I heard crying and pleading for a little while. It stopped after a while, and I guess I was glad it did. I recognized the Bulee girl's voice, and after that my mind just closed up shop and I sat and stared into the dark without thinking of much of anything.

Some time later, and I have no notion how long it was,

Jessie moved under me and whispered, "Em, it's been quiet in the house for a long time now. Do you think we could chance getting out of here?"

"No!" I whispered back, wanting to stay where we were for the rest of my days.

"We've got to sometime," she said, "or we're going to be crippled for life."

"Better crippled than dead," I said, and meant it. I wasn't ready to take any chances, and would as lief stay where we were until help could get to us.

"Stop it, Em, and help me. We've got to get away from the mission, and you've got to help. It must be dark outside by now, and it's the best time to risk it. Now, help me think what we can do."

I thought about it and then said, "Mego told me if there was any trouble to head either for Fort Walla Walla or for Lapwaii. Lapwaii's the furthermost, but I know how to get there."

"All right. The first thing to do is get out of this cupboard and find out if our limbs still work. But be careful and be quiet. I'm not dead sure the Cayuse are gone yet, and the least noise will bring them back up here."

"Hold on a minute," I said, not especially eager to go down into the house again. "Let me feel around here a bit."

I shifted Janie to one side, trying not to squash her or bury her face in anything. She whimpered a little, but didn't cry, thank the Lord.

I reached up and began to feel around the side of the chimney where it curved up into the ceiling.

"There's a hole up here, Jessie! It's not very big, but it's sure a hole of some kind."

"Can you tell where it leads to?"

"The attic, I guess. I think I can feel a rafter. If we had a candle, I could tell you."

"If we had a candle," she said, giving me a little pinch, "I wouldn't have to ask."

I let that go and eased myself upright, sticking my head

through the hole in the ceiling. Lord, my limbs commenced to quiver and give so bad that I had to lean against the chimney to stand up.

"Be careful," Jessie whispered. "It's me you're standing on."

"Sorry, but I can't feel a thing. I'm just going to have to stay here a minute till I get some feeling back. Don't get put out with me."

"That's all right," she said. I felt her pat my foot, so I knew it was still living. "Can you see anything up there?"

"Not a thing. If anything, it's darker up here. I think I'll give it a try, though. Don't worry if I'm not back for a while, for I'll be going real slow and quiet."

I hooked my arms up through the opening and pulled my whole self into the attic. I found out the hard way that it was too low to stand up in, so I lay full length between the rafters, savoring the relief of being unfolded at last. Then, using knees and elbows, I squirmed the width of the house, detouring around another chimney, and saw a dim glow of light. When I reached the far eave I looked through some ventilating chinks and got a view of the side yard and a curve of the river. I could've gone all my life without it too.

There were several campfires blazing on that side of the house, reflecting off the water and lighting up more of the yard than I wanted to see. People's bodies were lying crumpled up everywhere, and there was even one on a bed. I couldn't figure out what a bed was doing out in the yard, but didn't worry too much with it. I tried to count the dark lumps that looked like piles of old clothes thrown out in the mud, but I soon lost the heart to do it. The Cayuse were still around, though I didn't see any right up near the house. I could see their shadows against the fires, and I heard them singing and laughing, and probably bragging about how brave they'd been during the day.

All at once a Cayuse boy younger than me streaked out of the barn waving a tomahawk that was almost as long as he was. He ran over to one of the lumps lying in the yard. I was pretty sure that whoever it was had already passed away, from the looks of it, but that didn't matter to the little hellion. He started in hacking away at it, yelling like a banshee while he was doing it. A squaw, his mother I guess, came over and snatched the tomahawk away from him, and I was glad she made him stop. She threw the hatchet aside and pulled a knife from her belt, and before I knew it she was holding up a handful of long hair. She held the scalp in front of the boy, like she was giving him a lesson in the family business. I was glad I couldn't see the color of the hair, because then I'd have known whose crowning glory it had been. I bowed my head against a rafter and begged the Almighty to have mercy on those of us who were left.

After a while I turned around and started back across to the other side of the attic, making myself think of Mego and what he would tell me to do. "Don't never let yoreself git panicky." I'd heard him say that a million times, and it was a whole lot easier to say than to do. "Always thank ahead and be adoin' it all the time, fer Injuns ain't got a powerful tolerance fer doin' neither one, an' ye kin outsmart 'em most ever' time," had been another piece of advice. I didn't know about outsmarting them. All I wanted to do was outrun them. I did resolve, though, to shut my mind off from what had already happened out in the yard and in the house and set it on things I might could do something about.

I felt around the wall when I got to the other side of the house, for there was no light there at all. I hoped that meant that all the Cayuse were down by the river, since that's where their fires were. I prayed they'd stay busy with whatever they were doing and not be wandering around in the dark on this side.

"Glory!" I whispered, for I found a small door in the wall. It was no bigger than a cupboard door, but one of those had already preserved our lives and I praised God for letting me find another one.

I eased it open and saw that it led out onto the roof of a one-story room. The room had been added on for the unwedded emigrants, who stayed for months sometimes helping out on the place. But I couldn't figure out why a door had been built so high up on the outside of the house. Then I recollected hearing somebody talk about rechinking the chimneys in the attic. The little door must've been the way they got into the attic, but for all I know it could've been put there just for us, seeing as how I'd been doing a sight of praying, to say nothing of Jessie.

I scooted back to the hole in the attic floor and stuck my head down through it.

"Come on up, Jessie. I've found a way out."

She handed Janie up to me and, I'll have to say here, that was the best baby in the whole wide world, for she hadn't made one noise throughout our imprisonment, or entombment, or whatever you want to call it.

Things got tight when Jessie started to pull herself up into the attic, and it was a fair struggle to get it done.

"Em, I'm stuck. I can't get through."

"Let me help. Where're you stuck?"

"In my . . . never mind. You may have to go on without me."

"Lord, Jessie," I said, struck with fear at the very thought. "I can't do that. Try harder."

"Give me your hand," she panted, "and help me wiggle through."

I felt around her, and she had gotten her head and one arm through the hole, but the rest of her was stuck tight.

"Take a deep breath," I said. "No, don't do that! Let all your breath out! That's it. Now pull up."

She popped through the hole like a prairie dog springing out of his little hill. Then she lay full length on the attic floor, breathing hard.

"I may never be the same again," she said, half laughing and half crying, which scared me all over again.

"What kind of damage did you do?" I asked, wondering if Mr. Garrett would throw her over if he came back and found she was different from what she'd been when he left.

"It's all right. At least I don't think it's permanent," she said, to my relief.

Then we settled down to let Jessie's limbs get their feeling back and to listen for any sound that would mean we'd been discovered.

"They're still here, aren't they?" she whispered.

"I think they're all down by the river. At least that's where their fires are. They're celebrating or something."

I felt her shiver and I did likewise. She gathered up Janie and said, "Let's go."

"Keep low, then, and crawl along behind me," I said, and we commenced moving toward our only door of hope.

33

And I said, Oh, that I had wings like a dove!
For then would I fly away, and be at rest.
—Psalms 55:6

We made a perilous descent through the door and down
onto the roof of the men's dormitory room. I went first,
dangling on the side of the house for the longest time before
getting the nerve to turn loose and drop down. Jessie didn't
have as far to fall, being taller than me, so she had an easier
time of it. We finally crouched together on the roof in the
shadow of the house, feeling like every Cayuse eye in the territory could see us. It was chilly out there, but I had shivered
just as much in the cupboard as I was doing outside, so I couldn't
tell whether it was coming from cold or fear.

"We've got to cross the yard and get over in the woods,"
I whispered to Jessie. "If we can make it there, we ought to be
fairly safe for a while."

"Oh, Em, I don't think I can do it. Maybe we ought to
stay up in the attic until John Calvin can get here."

There wasn't anything I'd rather have done than crawl
back and stay under cover, but I knew we'd be trapped there.
Janie would come full awake sometime, and then they'd find
us. If they didn't fire the house first.

"It's going to take him a while to get here, so we'd better
wait for him somewhere else."

We sat there some little time, fearing to move out of the
shadow and venture to the ground. Once there, we'd be in the
greatest danger we'd yet faced, and we'd already faced a mortal
plenty. I put my mind to the lay of the land. The yard on our
side of the house ran right up to a grain field, which didn't
have a lick of cover, having been cut and harvested. The barn,
corncrib, and smokehouse were clustered down toward the back

and far side of the house, which was where the Indians were enjoying the fruits of their labor.

All at once we heard loud yells and screeching, and the yard lit up with an orange glow.

"Is it the house?" Jessie cried, clutching at me. "Is the house on fire?"

"I think it's the barn. Look where the light's coming from. But I don't think we're going to get across that yard now, Jessie."

"Oh my goodness," she whimpered, and started to cry. "Em, let's go together, if we have to."

"We will, Jess. One way or the other, we'll go together," I said. Then I thought about those ways, and knew I'd rather die trying than die doing nothing. And if we didn't do something pretty soon, we'd still be hunched up on the roof at daybreak.

"Listen," I said, "those Indians're going to be so taken with the fire that they won't be looking for anything else. This is the best time for us to try it."

"Do you think so?" I felt her trembling against me, but it could've been me that was making her shake so hard.

About that time we heard a lady's voice screaming, and a little child crying over and over for its mother. I knew then that not all the mission people were dead, and I purely wished they were. After that night I never had another hard thought for the Crows. Barring a few slaps and kicks that Jessie'd had to endure, they had treated us almost like human beings, or People, as they called themselves. At least they hadn't shed a drop of our blood, which would be the prime thing the Cayuse would do if they found us. I recalled Mego talking about Indians getting up a bloodlust, which they were likely to do whenever they saw any. He said that once they got caught up at the sight, they'd keep on spilling it until they plain wore themselves out with the effort.

"Here's what we can do, Jessie," I whispered. "We can drop down on the front side of the house, and as soon as we hit the ground we'll scrooch right there until we're sure nobody's seen us."

I felt her nod, and I went on. "Before we move one inch after that we'll cover ourselves all over with mud. You understand, Jess? Not a smidgen of white or anything light-colored can be left showing. Hands, face, clothes, even Janie and her blanket. Then we're going to crawl through the mud and cross the yard."

"I don't think I can do it," she said.

"Well, you're going to. Look here, if we're covered with mud and stretched out on the muddy ground, and if we move only a few inches at a time and stop dead still in between, there's not a Cayuse living that can pick us out. Considering how they're occupied right now, anyway."

"All right, then," she said, setting her mind to it. "Let's do it. It'll be better than letting them find us squatting up here."

"Amen," I said, and thought a good deal better of my plan since she liked it too. It might even work.

We slid down the sloping roof of the dormitory room until we got to the edge. I didn't see anything moving in the front yard, so before I had time to think about it I let myself over the edge and dropped to the ground. I clung to the shadow of the house, with my heart thudding worse than the Cayuse drums. After I got my breath back I reached up for Janie, and then Jessie fell in a heap beside me.

I put my mouth beside Jessie's ear and said, "Cover everything without stint, and no more talking."

She nodded, and we set to work smearing ourselves all over with mud. We worked on each other's backs and looked ourselves over good to be sure nothing that could catch an eye was showing. The mud was awful. It was wet and cold, and my teeth began to chatter so much, I was afraid they might give us away. I took Janie's blanket and sopped it around in the mud until it was layered pretty good, then wrapped her back in it. Jessie patted mud over her face, and she struggled a little when she felt it, but settled back down when Jessie held her close.

It was about time to venture away from the house, so I gave Jessie and Janie a last good look, and they just about blended right into the shadows. I tapped Jessie's shoulder so she would follow me and, lying facedown on the ground, began crawling away from the house out into the yard.

I could feel Jessie right at my feet, starting and stopping

whenever I did. I couldn't ever decide which was the best to do. I wanted to get up and run as fast as I could across the yard, but every time I stopped I didn't ever want to move again. We crawled on that way for the longest time, and the only untoward thing that happened was when we were some ways from the house. I came right up on somebody's body. I hadn't been looking where I was going, having aimed myself in the direction of the grain field and keeping my eyes down on the ground before me. I stopped and drew back when I felt what it was. I made myself reach out and feel for signs of life, but I didn't find any. I squirmed around it, not letting myself think who it could be. I don't think Jessie came up on it, for she followed my detour.

I don't know how long it took us to get to the grain field. It could've been a few minutes or it could've been half my life. We progressed in a crawl-and-stop fashion, faces down in the mud, until we reached the stubble left in the field. The ground had served us so well that I didn't even think of standing up. We kept on crawling through the field, getting scratched and jabbed by the dry stalks as we went.

I didn't worry about that, though, for it was a sight less than what we were running away from. About the time I began to think we'd be crawling all the way to Lapwaii, I skinned my nose on the root of a tree and took heart at once. Reaching and feeling in front of me, I kept on crawling through the under-brush and around the trees. We finally came up on a clump of bushes some ways from the clearing and we squirmed inside of them to rest. We didn't need to say anything, for we were still alive and entirely taken up with being thankful for it.

We didn't linger there for long, though, but set out again as soon as we'd caught our breaths. I wasn't even thinking about which direction we were going in, since all I wanted to do was to put as much distance between us and the mission as it was humanly possible to do before daylight. I stopped every now and again to get my bearings, having heard how easy it is to go in circles when you don't have a mark to aim at.

When the sky began to get light and we could pick out tree trunks before running into them, we cast about for a place to wait out the day. There was an Indian trail over to our left, which I'd been staying as far away from as I could. Still and all, it was the only guide we had, for we had left the mission in the direction of Lapwaii and not in the one toward Mr. Pambrun.

"Jessie," I whispered, once we'd snuggled up in a thicket for the day, "I hate to tell you, but we're headed for Lapwaii and not the fort."

"Well, can't we circle around and get to the fort? Lapwaii's too far."

"I don't see how we can. We'd have to either go through the Indians or cross the river and skirt them that way. One way or the other, we'd have to backtrack, and I don't think I have the heart to turn back toward them now."

"No, let's don't do that," she said.

We sat there without talking for a long time and thinking, or at least I was, about what it would take to get to the Spauldings. It would be just about as perilous as facing the Indians again, but I'd pick a long, hungry journey over the Cayuse any day.

Now, I could give a day-by-day account of that journey, but if it's all the same, I'd as soon not do it. Not that I've forgotten any of it, because I haven't and never will. It was the worse time we ever had, and we'd already had the Lord's plenty of bad ones.

Let it be enough to say that we followed the trail to Lapwaii, the one I'd gone on with Mego and the one the Indians used every living day we were out there. So we followed it, but we stayed way over to the side of it. After several days of trying to keep it on our left, without getting too close, I began to wonder if the effort was worth it. The hardest thing to do was to stay as close to the trail as we had to, so as not to get lost, while wanting to flee from it as fast as we could.

Some of the traffic we heard on the trail might have been friendly to us and helped us, but neither of us wanted to take the chance of hailing them. Several times I was sure I heard some Walla Walla Indians, who were generally taken as friend- lies, but they were in an all-fired hurry and probably wouldn't of taken kindly to being interrupted. One thing I was eternally thankful for, we neither saw nor heard any Cayuse. They were either still busy with the work of Satan or, if they had begun to come to their senses, they'd scattered for parts unknown. They'd know, as soon as they could know anything, that the Hudson's Bay Company and the trappers, who'd kept the peace in these parts for an untold number of years, wouldn't sit still for a massacre. What I kept listening for was the sound of shod hooves and American or British talk on the trail, but there was nothing but the slither of moccasined feet, and we took pains not to hinder them.

Maybe it was because I was listening so hard for sounds of a rescue party that I kept hearing a horse running along beside us on the trail. The first time it happened I stopped Jessie and we crouched in some bushes to wait for whoever it was to come in sight.

"What is it?" Jessie whispered.

"A horse is coming this way. Sounds like just one, but I've been hearing it for a good while. Maybe somebody's riding up and down the trail looking for survivors."

"Em," she said, looking at me in a peculiar way, "I don't hear a thing. There's no horse out there, honey."

"Listen, can't you hear that?"

"No, there's nothing out there. Come on, now. Let's gather these hickory nuts and push on."

And that's the way it went for ever so long. I'd hear that horse pounding alongside, and just be sure that somebody was looking for us, but Jessie'd shake her head and we'd keep on. Pretty soon I knew, too, that I wasn't hearing a real horse, but the main reason for knowing it was that it never got any closer, which is the way of phantom horses. It never passed us, never got any closer, and it never went away. It was like a horse that was always running but never getting anywhere. I lived with that sound all the way to Lapwaii and, at odd and unexpected times afterward, I could still hear it running beside me.

We didn't eat too well on our journey. In fact, we just about starved. There was plenty of water, for we crossed several streams and a good stretch of river at one point. Jessie said she'd heard that the Digger Indians to the south of us subsisted on roots and nuts, and beetles and ants, and that we could, too, if we had to. We found plenty of nuts on the ground and a lot of wild and bitter berries, so we made do with that without having to turn over any logs.

It was Janie, though, who suffered the most. The fever overtook her again, and she didn't like what we were eating. It was a worry to us the whole time, but we crushed nut meats and the sweetest berries with water and forced that down her. Even though she weighed hardly anything, it got so that our arms gave out carrying her. That was when we thought to take one of Jessie's petticoats and strap Janie up Indian fashion. We took turns carrying her on our backs in that way.

We stumbled into the Lapwaii clearing some three or four weeks later, more dead than alive. Janie had stopped whimpering and crying some days before, and we were too near our last legs to try to rouse her. Our only thought by then was to push on for the Spauldings without stopping.

It came to me later on to wonder why neither of us even thought about the same thing having happened to the Spauldings. If we'd walked into that clearing and found Lapwaii burned and the Nez Percé splattered with blood, I guess our spirits would've gone from us right there. We were so sure that safety lay in that direction that we never once thought of anything else. I guess it was because the Nez Percé weren't Cayuse, being several cuts above them in every way you could think of.

The Spauldings received us with an outpouring of kindness, for we were the only ones from Waiilatpu to make it there. They were still shocked and overcome with grief at what had happened, having heard about it from their Indians. So there was more than the general amount of thanksgiving and praise for our safety, which I was just about too give out to join in with. Mrs. Spaulding set to work getting us clean and preparing hot broth and putting us to bed.

While all this was going on we told of what we'd seen and heard, though it was hard to tell about, and they told us that all the Indians in Oregon were overcome with fear of reprisals. Mrs. Spaulding said that parties were already forming down at the Willamette settlement and the Hudson's Bay Company with the express purpose of wreaking vengeance on all and sundry. The Indians knew that most of those men would shoot first and then ask what tribe they belonged to, so they were all fearful and agitated. There was even talk of a general and full-scale uprising of all the tribes in Oregon, but nothing ever came of it.

"What about the Nez Percé?" I asked, realizing then that we were even farther from civilization at Lapwaii than we'd been at Waiilatpu.

"Why, bless your heart!" Mrs. Spaulding said as she spread another quilt over me. "Don't fret yourself about the Nez Percé. As soon as they heard about the tragedy at Waiilatpu they came and settled right around the house to demonstrate their protection over us. Have no fear of the Nez Percé, for they'll have no truck with the likes of the Cayuse! Fact of the matter is, some of our men are leaving to join up with Mr. Pambrun to help hunt the devils down. Now go to sleep. You're as safe here as you were back in the States."

Being about worn to the bone, I decided to chance it and slept through a whole day and night of my life and have no regrets for anything I might've missed.

34

Then a spirit passed before my face; the hair
of my flesh stood up.
            —*Job 4:15*

My strength came back to me in full force after a few days
of extra sleep and Mrs. Spaulding's cooking. Jessie didn't
snap back like I did, for she still had Janie to tend to and
wouldn't take much help from anybody in doing it. Mr. Garrett's
Indian baby was at the door of death, in spite of all the medical
and spiritual remedies Mrs. Spaulding could think of. If will-
power and plain determination could've cured little Janie, then
she'd have been well in no time. But good intentions don't go
very far down that road, for Oregon and its inhabitants still
suffer all manner of fevers, colics, agues, and malignant diseases.

Mr. Spaulding got a message from the Hudson's Bay Company telling him that he ought to pull his family out of Lapwaii
and come in closer to the settlements. Mrs. Spaulding was dead
set against it, and reminded him that she'd stayed right by herself
with the Nez Percé while he'd gone to see what the damage
was at the Whitman mission. The fact of the matter is, she'd
been alone with them while the massacre was going on, though
none of them knew it at the time. Mr. Spaulding had been away
from home down around Waiilatpu, and almost got caught in
the general slaughter himself. But she wouldn't hear to moving
anywhere until the baby got well enough to travel, and besides,
she told him, it would look like they didn't trust the Nez Percé
and she said she certainly did.

It didn't matter to me what we did, just as long as we
stayed clear of Waiilatpu. With Jessie and the whole household
taken up with nursing Janie and talking about what we ought
to do, I wandered around outside most of the time. For some
reason I couldn't abide long spells inside the house and would

have to get away from the walls every now and again. On the other hand, I couldn't let myself get too far from the house either, so that kept me pretty much in the yard within earshot if Jessie happened to need me.

The Nez Percé around the mission were real jumpy, and I didn't blame them. The whole territory was in ferment by this time, with outlying settlers riding into the forts to join the hunt for the Cayuse murderers. Men everywhere were up in arms and threatening to inflict punishment on any Indian they found. The Nez Percé were sending their families deeper into the Blues for safekeeping, and it was beginning to look like nobody was safe from anybody else.

I learned most of this from The Hailstorm, who was an old man of the Nez Percé tribe who liked to have somebody to talk to. Everybody was too busy to sit around and talk except me, so he would come up to wherever I was and start in. He let me know right off that he was bad worried.

"My dreams see blood everywhere," he told me one morning while he split kindling and I stacked it.

"I don't have to dream to see it," I said. "It's behind my eyelids every time I close them." And that was a fact, for I was having trouble with my sleeping. Every least noise jounced me awake, and every time I let down my guard I saw Mrs. Whitman's blood splattering all over again in my mind.

"It is not good," The Hailstorm declared, as if I didn't know it.

"No."

"Many were slain at the Place of the Rye Grass," he said, as if I'd not been there to see it.

"Yes."

"Many are held to this day as hostages against the heathen Cayuse's safe conduct."

"Captives?" He had my full attention then, for he was finally telling me something I didn't already know. "Some of the Waiilatpu missionaries are still alive?"

"Ah, yes," he said. "Not many and not well cared for, but some. I know this for a fact. The Cayuse cowards enjoy the women and the children, even though some are so young that the knife has to be used first. Yet, even now, the great Hudson's Bay Company offers ransom for them. But the Cayuse will certainly not escape their just retribution. I, myself, shall join in that slaughter."

I shivered at the thought of another slaughter, even though the Cayuse clearly deserved one.

"Do you know Mr. Mego Cobb, the great fighter against the Blackfeet, and the eminent trapper, formerly of the Rocky Mountain Fur Company?" I asked.

"I know him well, if he is the one also called Cut Face. He has slain almost as many Blackfeet as I, myself, have. He has often fought our enemies and, sometimes, he has fought against us as well. He never wins then."

I let that pass and said, "He is my friend. I don't doubt that even at this moment he is hurrying to our defense. Do you also know Mr. J. C. Garrett?"

He laughed, nearly cutting his thumb off with the ax. "Who doesn't know the one who can outlie the Crows, a feat unsurpassed by any other warrior? I have ridden with that one. He is a terror to enemy and squaw alike. Every man watches his squaw when that one appears."

"Well, he's spoken for by my sister now," I told him. "His wandering ways are over, if I'm not mistaken. He comes with Mego Cobb to claim her for his wife."

"I'll believe it when I see the sun rise at midnight," The Hailstorm said, and about made me mad. "I have no doubt that he comes to claim the beautiful sister, but it is too much to expect that such a man will be satisfied with only one woman. It's against his medicine."

"I'll put my money on Jessie making him change his medicine. She'll keep him in line, if that's what she's put her mind to."

"It is my experience," he informed me, "that a woman's mind is a fitful thing, and not a primary attraction to a warrior."

He had me there, for I'd observed the same thing in countless cases. We stacked kindling for a while, which calls for the least amount of effort and can even be done sitting down. We'd probably have made it last all day if a racket at the edge of the clearing hadn't interrupted us.

I'll admit to a gripping seizure that came near to paralyzing me when people started calling out and running from the house. The Hailstorm had a sick look on his face too. I figured then that I had a *compañero* that would as soon run from blood and gore as I would, despite his brave talk.

We peeked around the shed and saw Mr. Spaulding run from the house toward a group of Nez Percé who were holding up and half carrying what looked like a bundle of rags.

"Godamighty!" I said, before I could help it. "That's Mr. Green, alive and staggering."

I never thought I'd ever be happy to see Mr. Green, but I was, for he'd survived the same perils we'd been through. I ran to the house and watched while the Spauldings set him close to the fire and plied him with food. I'll have to say that he was a pitiful sight, and just looking at him started up my shivering. He brought it all back again. There was no telling what he'd endured, for it had taken him almost a week longer to get to safety than it had taken us.

He sat there by the fire, dirty and lean with hunger, and talked without letup. I could hardly make out a word he was saying, and I don't think anybody else could either. Mrs. Spaulding said something about raving to beat the band, and I guess that's what he was doing.

"Poor soul," she said, putting his blue feet in a basin of warm water. "His mind is still roaming, and no wonder. Only the Lord knows what horrors he's seen, and all that he's been through."

"What's that he's saying, Mother?" Mr. Spaulding asked her. "Can you make it out?"

"Nare a word," she said, with the best good humor, "but don't trouble with it, Mr. Spaulding. When he eats and sleeps for a few days, he'll be his old self again. I have no doubt of it."

"I wonder if he escaped as early as the Heath girls did, or

if he's been held captive. He may be able to tell us the condition of the others if he's been with them."

"That's so," she said, scrubbing away at Mr. Green's feet. "We'd better send one of the runners to Mr. Pambrun and let him know we have another survivor with us."

"Yes, I'll do that right away. Let us hope that Brother Thomas can tell us more in a few days."

Mr. Green was put to bed and tended with the same care we had received. Since the weather had turned bitter, I had to stay indoors a good bit of the time. I didn't like doing it, for reasons I've already given, but I also didn't like hearing Janie cry. She wasn't able to come out with a hearty and healthy cry, which doesn't bother me at all. What she was doing was too thin and fretful and hurtful to make it easy to listen to.

Mrs. Spaulding put me to sitting by Mr. Green's bedside, as he remained puny in spite of her ministrations. She was pretty exercised over having two in her household that wouldn't get well no matter what she did.

Sitting by a sickbed is not a thing I'd elect to do if I have a choice, but not many people can turn Mrs. Spaulding down when she tells them to do something. It wasn't so bad, though, because Mr. Green was as witless as ever, as Mrs. Spaulding said, and paid no mind to me. I took the opportunity to try to get back to reading, but it was hardly worth the effort. I read all the tracts in the house, but they all said pretty much the same thing, although from the way each of them started out, you'd think they were going to say something different. The only other reading material was the Holy Bible, and so I resolved to read it straight through, like I was always promising the Lord to do and had never done. I didn't do it that time either, for just like always, I got bogged down on the begats and gave it up.

There was soon nothing else to do but listen to Mr. Green's ravings. After a while it got interesting, for he'd lie real still and quiet, and I'd almost doze off, and then he'd wake with a start, his eyes bulging out of his head and his limbs shaking with ague. Then he'd light into an oration the likes of which would make my skin crawl.

More than once he held forth to Dr. Whitman, who, it appeared, was visible to him and in the very room listening to him.

"I told you, Dr. Whitman," Mr. Green said in great agitation. "Listen to me now. I've told you for months on end that something had to be done. But you did nothing, nothing, not a thing would you do."

And here he would shake his long finger in such a way that I'd turn around to be sure Dr. Whitman's spirit wasn't standing behind me.

"It devolved on me!" he cried out on one occasion. Beads of sweat stood on his face, and he was bound and determined to make Dr. Whitman understand. "None of you would see it . . . and the cold, and hungry, so hungry . . . my God, my God, why hast thou forsaken me? Send thy angels to relieve me. You lacked leadership, Whitman . . . we all knew it . . . no one left but me . . . but I am vindicated. Don't let me die in this wilderness . . . thine angels to keep charge over me . . . in the garden . . . contaminated with filth . . . defiance rampant everywhere . . . typical, typical of the whole expedition from start to finish. Finish it, should have finished it!"

He reached out one time and grabbed me by the shoulder, scaring me half to death. "Listen!" he whispered, then his eyes ran back and forth in his head. "Listen to me. It was a mistake. I let hesitancy guide my hand! Faint-hearted! Unable to keep my hand to the plow. I, who have never before faltered in my duty! When the moment came I hesitated!"

He turned me loose and fell back on the bed in a fit of crying. "God forgive me! If I had not faltered at the last moment, they'd still be alive."

He settled down after a little and went on off to sleep, for which I was thankful. I couldn't make head nor tail of what he'd said, but whatever it was, he was mortally suffering with it. The longer I stayed in that room with him, the less I liked it. His ravings brought to mind all the people at Waiilatpu, who

were no more, and I started to feel that maybe Dr. Whitman
and the others were still roaming around and might even be in
the room with us. Mr. Green sure acted like he could see something, and I didn't like it a bit.

I decided I could safely leave him, especially since I felt
the need for some spiritual guidance. I tiptoed out and went in
search of Reverend Spaulding.

I found him in his little back study, bowed over his
desk either in prayer or in despair at the ledger open before
him.

"Come in, Emma," he said when I tapped at the door.
"What can I do for you?"

"Mr. Green keeps seeing ghosts, Mr. Spaulding, and I know
there's no such thing, but still and all . . ."

"You must put it behind you, child," he said, removing
his spectacles and rubbing the bridge of his nose. "It's best not
to dwell on it too much. Mr. Green is very ill, and it's his
sickness that makes him talk that way."

"But it's not just ghosts that worry me, it's, well, Mr. Green
is plagued about the massacre, and he said they would all still
be alive if he hadn't stopped doing something. But he didn't
tell that part."

"Indeed?" Mr. Spaudling's eyebrows went up at that. "What
else did he say?"

"Not much, just that over and over. He kept saying he
shouldn't of hesitated, for then everybody would be alive now.
Do you reckon he had a gun and couldn't bring himself to use
it on the Indians?"

"I don't know, child." Mr. Spaulding sighed and put his
spectacles back on. "I'd best examine him and prepare a doc-
ument to present to the court. I don't know if evidence from a
sick man is admissible, but there are plans for a trial and they'll
want to consider anything having to do with the tragedy. It's
late now, Emma. Why don't we give Brother Thomas a little
more time to recuperate? I'll question him tomorrow, and don't
you worry about ghosts. Just say your prayers, and the Lord
will look after you."

"Yessir," I said. "Good night, sir."

I got in bed to say my prayers, feeling safer under the covers than kneeling on the floor. I prayed some, but mostly wondered when I'd ever be able to sleep like decent folks again, and then wondered how close Mego and Mr. Garrett were, and wondered after that if they even knew of our recent time of troubles.

35

There is none that doeth good, no, not one.
—*Psalms 14:3*

I didn't hear any more of Mr. Spaulding's plans to question Mr. Green, not being called on to view the proceedings or to witness a deposition. I do know that Mr. Spaulding and another missionary closeted themselves in Mr. Green's bedchamber for the great part of a morning a few days later. I was curious to know what they'd found out, for I'd been more and more troubled, like Mr. Green was, in thinking up ways that the whole awful scene could've been forestalled.

The morning that the investigation was taking place I looked in on Jessie to see how Janie was and to keep my mind off the speculations that were running through it. She was kneeling by Janie's crib in a posture of prayer, but on closer inspection I found she was sound asleep. Janie lay dead to the world, her little arm next to Jessie's face. I didn't disturb them, having enough disturbance in my heart to send me outside by myself.

I took to sitting on a knoll not far from the clearing, but still in sight of the mission house. My perch overlooked the trail from the south, and I sat up there hoping one day soon to see Mego and Mr. Garrett riding toward us.

Every time I went out there I made myself think only of the birds and the small animals scurrying around in the bush. I tried to set my mind on watching the clouds or on listening to the wind or on anything except what was inside it. But it was hard work, for I was still hearing the running, thrashing, screaming, crunching, and maiming that made up my lasting mementos of Waiilatpu. I guess, though, it was the voices of the little children calling for their mamas that plagued me most.

I probably won't ever be able to be shut of those memories. They haunt me to this day, and I might as well tell the worst of it while I'm at it. It wasn't her husband that Mrs. Whitman called upon in her last extremity, nor her Lord. From behind her bloodied arm held up against the blows, she had cried over and over, "Oh Mother, Mother, help me!"

I sat there on the knoll, wrapped in a blanket against the December wind, and watched the trail. All I wanted to see was two riders on it. It seemed to me that if Mego and Mr. Garrett would ever get there, things would be better and I could start sleeping again. The sun was low in the west when I heard moccasined feet plodding up behind me.

"I hope they don't set you to trailing the Cayuse, Hailstorm," I said before he showed himself. "They'd hear you a mile off."

He pushed through the branches and squatted down beside me.

"I made myself heard so as not to frighten a young squaw," he said, sounding like his feelings were hurt, but not much.

"I'm obliged to you, but what brings you this far from the supper fires?"

"I come to watch with you in your Place of Sorrows," he said with so much kindness that I near about cried and felt purely sorry for deviling him.

"My heart thanks you," I told him, looking away so he wouldn't see my watery eyes.

"It is always the way of the People to grieve when Death comes," he said. "That one is not a respecter of persons. He comes to the missionaries as well as to the People, to the young as well as to the old. No one can stay his hand, although bravery helps."

I nodded out of my deep misery.

"All at Waiilatpu are now on the Spirit Trail and none can bring them back."

"I know, Hailstorm, but it's so hard."

"One thing makes it easier," he said, "and that is to smear the blood of the perpetrators from the mountains to the sea. Once you have seen the arms and legs of the shit-eaters hacked from their bodies, your heart will find peace and sleep will return as you once knew. Revenge turns the Place of Sorrows into the Place of Joy."

The Hailstorm was one of Mr. Spaulding's prime converts, but I declare I think he missed a sermon or two somewhere along the line. I knew he meant well, though, so I nodded and thanked him for the comfort.

"Now," he said, rising creakily to his feet, "the Most Reverend Spaulding wishes to have words with you."

I followed him back to the house and went to the little study. Mr. Spaulding was sitting alone in the near darkness, it being that gloomy time of day when sparing people wait before lighting a lamp.

"Come in, Emma," he said, his hands templed in front of him. "Come in, child, and take a chair."

I did, and waited to see what he wanted with me.

"On the table there," he said, pointing across the room, "is something one of the Nez Percé found and brought in today. See if you recognize it, please."

I walked over to the table and saw the medical satchel, plainly emblazoned with the initials T. H. G. It was the one I'd seen back on the trail and at Waiilatpu, and always in Mr. Green's hands.

"Yessir, it's Mr. Green's doctor's satchel."

"Is that the one Dr. Whitman forbade him to use?"

"Yessir. I heard him myself tell Mr. Green to desist from practicing medical skills, which he didn't have any of, and to refrain from having on his person any accouterments of the profession for which he was not suitably trained."

"Very good, Emma," he said, looking at me in some surprise, for I have a knack for recalling somebody else's exact words, and when I use it, it often makes folks sit up and take notice.

"Would you look inside the bag, please, and see if its contents are familiar to you?"

I unhinged it and rummaged around inside, drawing out several strange and wondrous instruments. There were two sharp lancets, a long-handled medicine dosing spoon, a set of amputating tools, several folded linen pads, and a leather pouch full of pocket instruments that looked for all the world like a lady's etui.

I dredged out a venesection apparatus, which I recognized as such from the one Dr. Vansant had used on Papa in his last days, in spite of what Papa kept telling him. He'd said over and over again that he didn't trust anybody who practiced king-craft, priest-craft, lawyer-craft, or doctor-craft, and he was right not to, as it turned out for him.

As that was the first opportunity I'd had to handle the implements of the Aesculapian art, I foraged around in the bag seeking what I could find. I held up for Mr. Spaulding's view a wicked-looking device made up of a hollow tube with a trocar inside. It had a bulb on one end and also a tourniquet contraption, which was a long leather strap affixed to a vise and turn-screw. I'd seen one used the time Mr. Sawyer got his limb crushed when a log fell on it back home. The bottom of the satchel, when I finally got to it, was filled with flasks and vials, most of which were empty.

"Do you recognize any of those things?" Mr. Spaulding asked.

"Yessir. Some of like sort were used, without success, on my papa in his mortal illness, and some of it looks like what I've seen used on horses when suffering internal blockage after feeding on wet fodder. Their bellies swell up so bad that they have to have them punctured with this to let out the noxious gases."

"Ah, well, yes," he said. "Emma, I have had a most distressing day, having questioned Brother Green extensively and being unable to get a coherent sequence of events from him. The recovery of this satchel, which he must have carried with him from Waiilatpu, and its contents, coupled with the fragments of his dementia, make me shudder at the conclusion before me. I hesitate to verify what seems to be the truth in this matter, but in fairness and for the sake of justice, I must pursue it.

"The bag, which without doubt is Brother Green's, contains the implement capable of injecting internal medications

into animals, as you've pointed out, but also into human beings
as well. The flask you hold in your hand contains, or did contain,
emetic of tartar, a most vicious purgative of the upper and lower
digestive tracts. Now, if Mr. Green's ravings can be given cre-
dence, and I have never heard him utter an untruth and doubt
that he could even under the most severe circumstances, he, in
some way, injected the Cayuse with this medication. If he did,
it would've had the most serious consequences on a people
already debilitated by disease."

"Well, I don't see how he could've done that, Mr. Spaulding," I said. "I know for a fact that Mr. Green wouldn't go near
the Cayuse lodges. He told everybody who would listen that it
was his duty to stay clear of ill humors, for his continued good
health was too vital to the mision for him to risk infection. For
myself, I think his feelings were hurt because Dr. Whitman
never would ask for his assistance."

He looked at me right sharply and said, "Perhaps so. I
suppose, then, that none of this means anything and I can, in
good conscience, put his claims of responsibility down to the
disorder of a fevered mind. I am relieved to do so, for, frankly,
Mr. Green expresses no such remorse that would ordinarily
accompany such a deed, if it had been done. Rather it is his
anguished regret, if his words can be accepted, that he did not
use enough of the emetic to weaken the whole Cayuse tribe to
the point of annihilation."

"Maybe he just wished he could do it," I said, "for there's
just no way that any Cayuse, measled or not, would hold still
and let him jab this thing into them." I held up the trocar, four
inches long, and knew I'd have to be chased all the way to
Missouri if it came at me.

"Good, I feel easier in my mind now," Mr. Spaulding said.
"Brother Thomas just needs something to occupy his mind, now
that he's safe from physical harm. Concentration on something
he enjoys would help suppress the dementia. It's too bad the
winter season is upon us, for gardening is his chief delight and
would be a restorative for him."

A chill started up somewhere behind my eyes and traveled

all the way down my back. I put the trocar down and looked Mr. Spaulding square in the face.

"Sir, there may be something else."

"Yes?"

"The garden. At Waiilatpu, Mr. Green was hopping mad at the Cayuse for stealing from it all summer long. Even when there was hardly anything left worth harvesting, he was still railing at Dr. Whitman for not putting a stop to it. I heard him say that if nobody else would do it, he would."

"And did he?"

"Not to my sure knowledge. But I did see him crawling up and down the rows of melons and squash in the dead of night one time when I had to go to the, uh, when I had to answer the call of nature. Begging your pardon, sir, but that's why I was out there and why I happened to see him. I couldn't see exactly what he was doing, but he had this very satchel with him, for I saw it plain as day. And something else. After that night he never said another word about what the Indians stole."

"And did they continue to take from the garden?"

"Cleaned it out in a matter of days, for Mr. Green gave up on guarding it. Just left it to them."

"Were there . . . that is, can you recall any increase of illness among the Indians after that night?"

"Yessir, I think I do," I said, for I remembered hearing Dr. Whitman talk about a new illness, unlike the measles, that was striking the Indians left and right. "Dr. Whitman said that, all of a sudden, they'd commenced convulsing and dying like flies and he couldn't understand what was causing it, for he'd almost brought the measles to its knees."

"So," Mr. Spaulding said, leaning his head on his hand, "that must've been how he did it."

"How, sir?" I asked, not following his meaning.

"Everything fits together now," Mr. Spaulding said, running his hand over his face and sighing from somewhere deep down inside. "It's not dementia that's causing his raving. It's demon possession, I'm convinced. There's no other explanation for such a deed."

"A demon?" I asked, looking around into the dark corners of the room. "What did it make Mr. Green do?"

"It appears that Mr. Green injected the vegetables in the garden with a purgative. It all fits with what he's been saying, and that must be the way it happened. He has caused untold suffering and death to the Cayuse, all for the sake of a few vegetables given to us from the bounty of God. Ah, my child, can He ever forgive us for what we've done?"

I let that pass, not seeing how either him or me could be taken as part and parcel of Mr. Green's perfidy, or of a demon's either. In fact, Mr. Spaulding hadn't been within a hundred miles of that garden, and even though I was, I didn't have a thing to do with it and didn't even know what was going on.

Mr. Spaulding sat with his head bowed, and the silence stretched out in the darkening room until I began to get restless.

"Sir, if it's all the same to you, I believe I'll look in on supper."

"Yes. Yes, that's fine," he said, sounding so sad that I wondered if grown men ever wanted to cry. "I'll just linger awhile longer. Tell Mother Spaulding I have no appetite to-night."

As I closed the door I saw him slip down and kneel on the floor, his head bowed over like he had a load he could hardly stand up under.

I went up the stairs to find Jessie and tell her of what Mr. Spaulding had uncovered. I was full of the import of it, for even though Mr. Green's deed was awful and about the most un-Christian act I'd ever heard of, there was now a reason at least for the Indians to've wanted to rise up and destroy the missionaries. That didn't excuse them in my mind, nor did having a demon inside of him excuse Mr. Green, but at least I could understand what had stirred them up. I probably would've been stirred myself if somebody had set out to poison me and Jessie. Now I knew there were sometimes reasons for terrible happenings, and that they didn't just strike us out of the blue, without any rhyme or reason to account for them. There were still a number of things, like Crow captivity and the general cussedness of some folks, that I couldn't come right up with reasons that would account for them, but now I felt sure that I could when I had the time for it.

I wanted to tell Jessie about Mr. Green and his demon, and sit and talk to her for a while. I hadn't seen much of her since we'd been at Lapwaii because she'd been busy with Janie and I hadn't felt much like talking anyway.

I looked into the room upstairs and saw her sitting in Mrs. Spaulding's rocking chair. The room was lit only by the fireplace, and it was warm and quiet in there. Jessie was holding Janie and rocking back and forth real slow. The light from the fireplace had turned her face a beautiful golden color.

"Jessie?" I whispered, for even though the chair was moving, she looked asleep.

She opened her eyes and smiled. "Come on in, Em. Janie's fever is gone at last. I've been rocking her, and now she's resting. Come see how sweet she looks."

Something about the way she was holding the baby, and something about the way she smiled, made me go over and lift the blanket. I felt Janie's face and then her hands.

"Jessie," I said, "Jessie, Janie's passed."

She looked up at me with such a piteous look that it near broke my heart. Tears were running down her face, and she reached out for my hand.

"I know," she whispered.

36

Mrs. Spaulding washed Janie and laid her little body out for burial. She wrapped it all around with a blanket and left it on the bed while she took the measurements out to the men. Jessie borrowed one of Mrs. Spaulding's frocks and got herself ready for the services. Then she sat by the bed to wait for the men to finish building the coffin. We could hear the sawing and hammering out at the woodshed as they put the boards together.

I waited with her, not knowing what else to do, and fell to thinking about all the dead and dying we'd seen since leaving Missouri. It was a settled fact that I'd had enough of it and longed for a place of our own away from places of sudden destruction, like Rocky Mountain trails and mission fields and the whole blamed Western territories. Everybody I'd known out here, whether California or Oregon emigrants, had come with hopes of a new and better life of some kind or another, but mostly they'd ended up tired and sick and grieving. And that was just the ones who'd made it through still living.

"Jessie," I said, "what're we going to do now? Looks like mission work's all washed up for us in Oregon. Where are we going and what's going to happen to us next?"

"I don't know, Em. I declare I don't. Everything I've turned my hand to has fallen apart, and even though I thought mission work was my calling, it's plain to me that the Lord is leading in other directions now."

"It is to me too. I just want to know where the other directions lead to. We've spent or lost all our money. We can't get back to Missouri, even if we wanted to, and we can't live

336

off these mission folks forever. What's going to become of us?"

"There's only one thing open to us, and that's for me to marry." The set of her mind was plain to hear, and to see on her face. All the time she'd spent tending to Janie must've brought her all the way back to the very place we'd been in back home.

"I've given it a lot of thought," she went on, "and it's the only thing left for us. We'll go on down to Oregon City when the Spauldings pull out, throwing ourselves on their mercy for a little while longer. When we get there I'll find a settled gentleman that wants a wife. There's a dearth of womenfolk in Oregon, so it shouldn't be too hard to do. And don't worry, Em, you'll be part of the contract, and so will repaying the Spauldings for our upkeep right up to the wedding rites. I'll make that clear from the start."

"Well, blame it all, Jessie, that don't sound right. Can't we do any better than that? What about Mr. Garrett, if you're going on the market?"

Her eyes filled up then, and she reached out and smoothed Janie's blanket. "I have to put that behind me," she said. "He's not the marrying kind. I thought it was just mission work he was opposed to, but it's the whole settled, decent way of life. But he stirred me, Em, and I'll never forget him. You know, I hated him because of Janie. Purely hated him, which, if anything else hadn't, proved I wasn't cut out to be a missionary."

I knew hating hadn't stopped a lot of other folks from being missionaries, but didn't bring it to her attention. I was just glad that her mind was set against it now.

"How long do you think it'll take to find a settled gentleman?" I asked.

"I hope not long. I'm ready to put all this behind me, if I ever can. And I'll make whoever it is a good wife, Emma, I'll promise him that, for I know now that that's what the Lord intends for me."

"Well, it does look like the only door open. But I think you ought to give Mr. Garrett a chance. Wait till he gets back, anyway, 'cause you don't have to take the first offer that's made."

She nodded but didn't say anything. I could see that she

was grieving over Janie, and a lot of other things as well, so I left her to it and went off to ponder what she'd told me. I went downstairs and out the front door. Sitting down on the rock that was the doorstep, I thought about Jessie's plan. It smacked of market trade and commerce but, when you come down to it, just about every marriage contract did. You give something to get something back, and even the Mission Board knew how it worked. The ladies who wanted to go to the mission field had to help their wedded husbands contain themselves in exchange for getting to go.

That's the way everybody did it, all right, even in Missouri, which didn't even have a mission field, and it seemed to work out in the long run. Except for ladies like Mrs. Donner and Mrs. Whitman, who, having once made the deal, had to stick with it to the end in spite of maybe having some second thoughts.

I reached down for a stick and started scratching in the dirt. I recalled Mr. Spaulding's lesson from the night before and wrote out the warning that had come unto Belshazzar when he was feasting with this wives and concubines. *Mene, mene, tekel, upharsin,* which is biblical for the handwriting on the wall. Numbered, numbered, weighed, divided, Mr. Spaulding had said it meant, and clearly foretold destruction and death, like Daniel had warned about over a dozen times. The same warning should've been given to Oregon, it seemed to me, what with massacres, uprisings, raiding parties, threats, divisions, and general meanness on every hand, but the Lord didn't give out warnings anymore. It looked like He'd just left us with it and we had to look out for ourselves.

"Ho-o-o, the mission!" I heard the voice I'd been waiting for echo up from the trail.

"Lord God Almighty! They've come back!" I jumped up and ran toward the trail as hard as I could go. "Mego! We're here! Oh, Lordy, Mego, I'm coming!"

I rounded a curve in the path and saw the two riders coming fast, but I didn't slow down to wait for them. I flung myself at Mego's stirrup, crying and laughing and pulling on him.

"Come on up hyar, young'un," he said, and swung me up

behind him, where I laid my head against his back and bawled like a baby.

Mr. Garrett reined in close and patted me on the head. Mego kept saying, "Now, now," and blowing his nose.

"Where's Miss Jessie?" Mr. Garrett asked. "Is she here too?"

"She's here," I said, crying and snuffling and clinging to Mego. "And she's all right, but Janie's passed over, and most everybody's lost or killed and Jessie's fixing to find herself a settled gentleman in Oregon City and get us out of the mission field and I wish you'd do something about it. If you've a mind to. And where've you been all this time?"

"On the way, littl'un, we been on the way, ever since we heerd," Mego said, but Mr. Garrett had already spurred his horse toward the house.

Their coming put the whole place in an uproar. Mr. and Mrs. Spaulding welcomed them and wanted all the news before they even got inside, and Jessie came running down the stairs like she'd heard the trump of the Second Coming. Mr. Green, who'd regained about half his senses, put his head out the door to see what was going on and when he saw Mr. Garrett he had a relapse. He took to his bed and stayed there. It was some little while before everybody could tell everything, and while we were doing it Mr. Garrett and Jessie went upstairs together, raising my hopes for a bid in the commerce that Jessie intended to set herself up in.

We buried Janie that raw and bitter afternoon right next to another tiny grave that belonged to a missionary baby. Jessie leaned against Mr. Garrett throughout the services around the grave. A few of the Nez Percé came, listening with long, sad faces to Mr. Spaulding's eulogizing. He did a praiseworthy job of it, too, taking as his text the story of King David's baby boy who died because of the mess that the King got into with Bathsheba after he saw her bathing right out on an open roof, which meant trouble to anybody with a lick of sense.

To Mr. Spaulding's credit, though, he didn't linger on the sinful circumstances that brought on the baby's demise. Instead, he made his three points on how King David accepted God's will in the matter. First off, the King did all his grieving and praying and fasting while the baby was sick, taking on enough about it to break your heart. Second, when the baby went ahead and died in spite of his lamentations, King David laid aside his grief, washed and dressed himself, and said there was no use for any more carrying on, which amazed his councillors, who'd expected him to purely lose his wits when he found out that the baby had passed. And third, King David was able to pick right up on his royal duties afterward, because he said the child would never come back to him but he would surely go to be with it on a later day.

It was the most comforting interment I'd ever attended, for after his three points were made Mr. Spaulding tied it all up with a poem about little children and angels playing on the clouds, with God's smile making the sun shine all around them. I cried at the picture it made, but the best thing about it was the promise that there wouldn't be any more death or dying up there.

After the last amen the Indians filed by the grave and dropped in stick dolls, tops, and rattles to be buried with the baby. It was a most moving example of heathenish practice and belief, and probably was acceptable to the Lord since Mr. Spaulding let them do it.

Mego took a shovel from The Hailstorm and began to fill the grave with dirt. I stood and watched him while the others went back to the house. Mr. Garrett and Jessie walked off together toward my Place of Sorrows, and I hoped they'd find something there better than I had.

Mego tamped the dirt down around the little mound so it wouldn't settle and cave in at the first rain. Then he pounded in a wooden marker with Janie's name and date of death on it. They hadn't been able to put her birth date on it, for Mr. Garrett had been off at rendezvous or somewhere when she was born and hadn't an idea of the exact day she'd entered the world.

Mego wiped his hands and allowed that was all the damage he could do, and we walked back toward the house.

"Mr. Cobb! Oh, Mr. Cobb!" Mrs. Spaulding was standing in the door beckoning us to hurry on.

"Le's us hump it, littl'un." And we did.

"What's the trouble hyar?" he asked as we gained the door.

"It's Thomas Green again," she said, wringing her hands in her apron. "We can't find hide nor hair of him. Said he was too weak to attend services, and now he's up and gone."

"Wal, now, don't ye fret," Mego said. "He can't of got too fer, an' I'll jes' go fetch him fer ye."

"Now, Mr. Cobb, that's just it," she said, and I thought she might tear that apron right in two the way she was wringing it. "Mr. Spaulding and I wonder if that's the thing to do. Tell him, Mr. Spaulding."

She turned to her husband, who'd just come outside. He took off his spectacles and studied them for a spell, then he said, "We're thinking it might be for the best to leave it this way, but would like to have your opinion on it. The Territory is torn up enough already, and I fear we don't have enough to convict him and settle the matter. Now that he's recovered from dementia, he denies everything that he was so free with during it. To have this story brought out at a trial, which I would have to do under oath, and then fail to convict for lack of hard evidence would inflame every breast in Oregon. I'm thinking it's best to leave it in God's hands."

Mrs. Spaulding nodded, and Mego did a little spitting and clearing of his throat, but finally said he'd abide by their recommendations.

It seemed to me that there was an awful lot being left in the hands of the Lord lately, where it was laying around without being attended to. So I went to the woodshed and sat down by a cord of wood. After a while Mego came and sat beside me. I guess he knew me well enough by then not to open his mouth and start talking. He took his fixings out and filled his pipe. After he got it lit I watched the smoke curl up and roll around us like a soft cloud that angels and babies might could've played on. I leaned my head on his shoulder and went to sleep.

Later, when I stirred awake, it was nigh on to dark and cold besides. Mego had wrapped us both in his capote, and he was still puffing on his pipe.

"Let ole Mego put yore mind to rest now," he said from

around the stem of his pipe. "Me'n and Garrett made a stopover at Waiilatpu afore acomin' hyar, fer we didn't know whar you an' Miss Jessie'd got to. I tellee when we learnt about them depredations thar, we war fair tore asunder with grief an' torment. Wal, from thar we lit out fer Fort Wally Wally, hopin' to find ye safe an' sound, but they told us ye war hyar, so now we found you'ns, an' hyar's what we specalate to do. First off, we got this hyar friend, name of McLoughlin, down at Oregon City, an' he'll take keer of ye an' treat ye right. He's a English feller, but they don't come no finer. The both of ye'll be all right till me an' Garrett git this business finished an' done with."

"What're you aiming to do about this business?"

"We aim to settle some hash, but that ain't fer ye to worry on. Jes' ye leave it to us, fer we mean to take a hand in it."

With all apologies to the Lord Jehovah, I felt considerably better to learn that retribution wasn't all going to be left in His hands.

"And what about Mr. Green?" I asked. "There's no telling where he'll get to if you wait too long. Why don't you go out there and find him right now?" The way I was feeling brought The Hailstorm's recipe for comforting the sorrowful to my mind.

"I misdoubt he'll git fer. Too many men, red an' white, that'd like nothin' better'n to slit his gullet. The Nez Percé done already spread his story roun' to ever' lodge in the Territory, an' the Injuns don't like what happened any more'n you nor me. Ever' hand be turned agin the Cayuse an' ole man Green, an' will be till hell freezes over."

So that was the plan. They were going to let Mr. Green run wherever he wanted to go, because nobody would take him in. He'd have to hide from everybody, because everybody would want to kill him. And he didn't have the Lord's mark of mercy on him, like Cain had, to save him from it. Justice is served, I thought, and felt a whole lot better.

"Le's us go to the house now, fer I'm nigh famished an' you need a bite too," Mego said, setting me on my feet.

I'd better tell here something I heard later in the evening, for I might forget about it, which is another of those things that

I aim to do as soon as I can make myself do it. Mr. Garrett was talking to Mr. Spaulding in the front room, telling him about what they'd found at Waiilatpu. They'd got there some twenty suns, he said, after the massacre and a rescue party had been there before them. The Cayuse had long since pulled out and scattered, but not till they'd got themselves a hefty ransom for the ladies and little children they'd kept alive but who probably wished they hadn't. The rescue party had been hell bent to ride down the Cayuse, so they'd buried what was left at Waiilatpu as quick as they could.

"They were in too much of a hurry," Mr. Garrett told him, "for they didn't dig the graves deep enough. Wolves had been there, mostly at Narcissa."

Mr. Spaulding groaned like his soul was hurting, and Mr. Garrett helped him to a chair.

"We fixed it," he said. "It won't happen again."

"I . . . when I was young," Mr. Spaulding said, "before we all married, I once loved Narcissa."

"We all loved Narcissa at one time or another," Mr. Garrett said, hurting just about as bad as Mr. Spaulding.

"I expect you're right. I . . . forgive me, Mr. Garrett. Too much has happened lately. I think I shall retire to my study, if you'll excuse me."

And Mr. Spaulding, looking about a hundred years old, walked to his study, and you can see why I want to forget it as soon as I can.

After supper we all went to our beds, but even after the house quietened down I was still lying wide awake beside Jessie. I crept out of bed and went to sit on the stairs, thinking about Mr. Green and Mrs. Whitman and Oregon City and what kind of hand Mego and Mr. Garrett planned to take in all of it.

The next thing I knew, Mr. Garrett eased onto the stairs beside me.

"Can't sleep?" he asked.

"Nossir."

"Have to put it behind you, Em, and go on doing the best you can."

"I keep trying to do that very thing," I said, trying to keep from crying again. "But every time I about get it done, something just as bad or worse hops up to take its place. The plain fact is, every time you go off and leave us, we get into trouble with Indians. I purely hate to see you go again, for there's no telling what'll happen next."

"Nothing's going to happen next, except getting you two to the Willamette settlement," he said. "You'll like it down there. There's lots of people and stores and river commerce. And schools and community socials. It's got everything Missouri has and maybe more."

"Mrs. Spaulding said it was near civilized, since they've got a Temperance Society going full force now."

I saw his teeth shining in the dark as he said, "I wouldn't worry about that. Most folks don't pay it much attention."

And, doing something I'd thought I might never do again, I laughed with him.

"Mr. Garrett," I said after a while, "how many settled gentlemen has Oregon City got for Jessie to choose from?"

"None," he said. "I've made her choice for her. It's time I came out of the mountains, anyway, before I'm stove up with an arrow in my back. It's like this, Emma. Miss Jessie's promised to give up mission work for good, so I guess I can give up something too. Might as well try the settled life. See how it goes, anyway. Besides, you two do seem to get into all kinds of trouble when I'm not around. It's probably my Christian duty to look after you, don't you think?"

I had to put my hand over my mouth to keep from laughing and waking the whole household. I felt downright light-headed, and got even worse off when he put his arm around me and hugged me tight. For the life of me I couldn't figure how Jessie'd ever thought missionizing could be better than that.

The next morning everybody was stirring around, getting ready to pack up and leave for Oregon City. Even Mrs. Spaulding had come to see the need for it, since instead of calming down by now, the Territory was fermenting worse than ever. Some Indians who'd had nothing to do with the massacre had already been killed, and some of the settlers had killed themselves out of being in too much of a hurry to kill Indians. Mr.

McLoughlin had sent word for the Spauldings to close up shop and he didn't mean maybe, because he had enough on his plate with one massacre and didn't want to hear of another one.

So they were getting ready to move out, too, but Mrs. Spaulding was taking her time doing it. They planned to leave later in the week, after she'd given her Nez Percé everything she couldn't move and some that she could, and after she'd given them all the spiritual instruction they'd stand still for. Mr. Garrett and Mego, though, wanted Jessie and me safe in Oregon City and intended to get us there as quick as they could so they could join the law and hunt down the Cayuse.

"Now, that might suit Mr. Cobb and Emma and Miss Heath," Mrs. Spaulding said to Mr. Garrett, shaking her finger at him. "And I don't doubt that it suits you as well. But the idea! The very idea of this young woman going off cross-country and rafting down the Columbia in the company of her intended is more than I can sanction!"

"Why, Miz Spaulding," Mego said as he sopped up gravy with a biscuit, "this hyar chile an' me'll be with 'em ever' step of the way, an' ye know I won't stand fer no unwedded doin's an sech."

"Mr. Cobb," she said, turning on him then. "You know very well it just won't look right, regardless. Now you men have your own ways in the mountains, and I know that. I won't speak against it here, but I haven't noticed heretofore you setting up to be a guardian of manners and morals. No offense intended."

"None taken," he said. "An' steal my mule if ye ain't got me thar. Now, what's to be done to remedy the foregoin'?"

"It's plain as day what's to be done," she said, throwing open the oven door for another pan of biscuits. "They'll just be united in holy matrimony right here and now, or I'll not countenance their leaving together. Mr. Spaulding, get your Bible."

"But nothing's been decided," Jessie said, her face having a time between turning pink and draining out. "Besides, Emma and I are looking for a settled man, not one that takes off at the drop of a hat or every time the weather changes."

"Speak for yourself, Jessie," I said. "I say we take Mr. Garrett while we can get him, and worry about settling him later on."

"That sounds fair to me," Mr. Garrett said. He got up from the table and went over to where Jessie was standing by the stove. "Are you willing to take on a wandering man, Miss Jessie, or am I going to have to scandalize these good folks by carrying you off unwed?"

"Just you try carrying me off if I don't want to go!" Jessie propped her hands on her waist section and looked almost like her old stubborn self again. "If you think that I'm going to go into the married state with somebody as footloose and unsettled as you, you've got another think coming!"

"Jessie, please," I said, "don't mess it up again. He'll settle down, won't you, Mr. Garrett?"

"I expect I could try, if your sister'll ask nice enough," he said, and before I knew it, he'd put his arms around her and was kissing her right there in the middle of the kitchen.

"Mr. Spaulding, get your Bible!" Mrs. Spaulding cried, flinging her hands in the air and fluttering around like the perilous temptations of unwedded travel were coming up on us fast. "Put your hand to the plow, Miss Heath, it's too late to draw back now!"

Mr. Spaulding did another bang-up job, proving he could marry as well as bury, and while he was doing it I thought to myself that we might've been saved a lot of trouble if Mrs. Spaulding had been around long before this. She would've laid the law down to them about scandal and other impure goings-on, and probably would've shook her finger at Mr. Garrett and made Jessie do the right thing without us having to go through all our suffering.

But she'd gotten after them now, and it was done before either one of them could back out. I've never seen a bride go into her nuptials about half mad, but that's what Jessie did, and Mr. Garrett didn't mind a bit. In fact, from the way he kept laughing at her, I think he liked it.

When the rites were over, and Mr. Garrett had shut Jessie up again in the only way that would serve, Mego announced that he intended to gift them with a prime buffalo robe, well-cured and vermin-free. He allowed that it'd take some time to get it that way, and he might be persuaded to come calling on us, and might even see if he recollected how to push a plow.

So there you are, Emma Jane. That's every bit of it and then some. Probably more than you needed to know, too, but I got carried away with the telling. But that's what happened before you were born, and how you came to be born in the first place. If your mama hadn't got it in her head to be a missionary, she wouldn't ever have met your papa, and where would you be then? Well, it's not given to us to speculate on such things, and I won't. And don't you, either.

But you're here, so I guess the Lord had His hand in it all along. Though I'm hard pressed to account for the rest of it.

Listen to that rain, and here we've idled away the whole afternoon, sitting here talking and talking like there's not a million things to be done. Run on down to the shed now and see if you can wash bottles for Mego. But don't you linger out there too long. Your mama'll be home directly, and suppertime's staring us in the face with not one bite on the table.

Well, Lord, talking about it after all these years brings it all back again. Maybe I should've left it alone and told the child some made-up story like the church ladies do when they tell Bible stories. They take out all the interesting parts and make you think the patriarchs were Christian gentlemen of the first order. But it's done now and the truth never hurt anybody. Or so they say.

I ought to be up from here and doing, but I declare it's a time for reverie. I'll just sit a while longer. That child'll be out there with Mego till Doomsday if I let her. It won't hurt to rest my eyes for a while before Jessie gets back. . . .

When we left Lapwaii for the Willamette Valley settlements, I hoped we'd seen the last of our misfortunes in the mission field. I was ready for the peace and safety of farmland. There's one thing you can say about farming—harvesttime comes around just as regular as the sun rises and sets. You can count on it and, if you've done your work, it won't let you down. But harvesting souls is a risky business, and I don't hold with gambling.

We built our cabin on two quarter sections some several miles from the settlement, near a stream that feeds into the Willamette. I staked out the 320 acres that in Oregon a woman can hold in her own name, but some fool said I wasn't eligible on account of the rule being for married ladies only, or at least for females old enough to be married whether they were or not, and he wasn't even sure about that. I just about turned around and went back to Missouri or Absaroka, it didn't matter which. Mego fixed it for me, though, by filing on it and having the judge draw up a will right then and there that will pass it on to me. I hope it won't ever come that way, but he says it's as good as mine now and I can do whatever I want to with it.

Papa would've liked it here, but nobody else yearned for agronomical pursuits like I did. Mr. Garrett took no pleasure in it at all, though he bent his back to a kitchen garden out of need. I'll say this for him, though, he soon had Jessie thinking that connubial bliss was far and away better than any other kind of living. She entered wholeheartedly into the marital state and, after their baby girl was born, she convinced herself that marriage was not only the Lord's will for her but for every other woman besides. I had hardly passed what we figured to be my seventeenth birthday when she commenced talking to me about my unnatural condition. She was after me morning, noon, and night, and brought home and fed every single gentleman between here and California, I do believe. But not a one suited me, and I'm not that hard to please.

I don't know how she can take such pleasure in it, though,

for Mr. Garrett never has been able to settle down. He says he's
seen the far side of the mountain and it keeps calling him back.
He just can't stay still. Like all his kind, he was born footloose
and lives footloose. I see him get that trapped look in his eyes
after he's been home awhile, and I know it won't be long till
he's saddling up again. But at least he kept starvation from the
door in the early years, what with herding horses between here
and the California settlements and guiding the odd emigrant
train or so up from Fort Laramie.

I don't know how Jessie stands it. I know she misses him
when he's gone, but she keeps herself busy with her church
doings and her good works. She never has stopped fretting over
the plight of the Indians, and I guess somebody needs to. What's
left of them around here, now that civilization's taken root,
aren't worth the powder it'd take to shoot them. They've lost
all sense of themselves, poor, bedraggled creatures. Nothing but
thieves and beggars left around the settlements, and they need
Jessie's good works if anybody ever did. I'd worry about her
getting her hair raised if they had the gumption they used to
have. Not that it's all gone, though. The ones with fire in their
blood have gone back into the mountains, and they're still there,
hating us and plotting revenge, most likely. We've killed a many
a one just to be able to plant a crop, or plant the Gospel, as the
case may be. Wouldn't surprise me if they came thundering
down here one day and massacred us all. Still, there're enough
outrages committed round and about, especially against women,
for Mr. Garrett to tell Jessie not to go traipsing all over creation
without somebody with her. And she minds him, too, even if
she has to drag me along.

Mego and Mr. Garrett scarcely got us settled in here when
they lit out, along with every able-bodied man around, to find
the perpetrators of the Whitman massacre. It got so that nobody
was safe anywhere but under their own bed, and not even then,
sometimes. Every man and boy in the Territory was out looking
for Indians, and it didn't much matter whether the Indians they
found had ever even been near Waiilatpu. Mr. Garrett got right
heartsick over it, and Mego got so mad at Mr. Andrews, lately
from Philadelphia, for shooting a Siwash that he almost cut him

up for firewood. The upshot of it was that five Cayuse finally surrendered, and we had ourselves a court trial. I had to testify, and so did Jessie, and every last one of them was condemned to die. Now I know that Tamahas was guilty as sin, for I saw him with my own eyes in the act of murder. All of them, except Kiamasumpkin, confessed, and I can't say to this day whether he'd had a part in it or not. I told the court I hadn't seen him there, but it didn't help him any. Bloodlust was running high among the spectators, and the sentence was to be hung by the neck, and they were.

I never have found out what happened to Mr. Green, not being able to get a word out of either Mego or Mr. Garrett. Some say he still wanders in the wilderness, abandoned and shunned by red and white alike, with his mind still fixed on the horrors of that day, now some ten years past. Others think he's long since been dead, but nobody ventures to speculate on how he met his end.

I wonder what Sheriff Matthew McHenry Stone would do if we had an all-out Indian war, like some think we will sooner or later. He wouldn't have time to be after me all the time then. I don't know what he wants with me. Lord knows it's not like I had Jessie's looks, but he says he likes my looks as well as any he's ever seen. He says he likes my spirit, and the soul that goes with it too. I don't know what he means by that. All I know about souls is that they exercise preachers and missionaries beyond all human understanding. According to them, souls are just something to be lost or saved, and don't have much to do with anything else, especially courting. But Mr. Stone says mine is right for him, and doesn't need a thing done to it. He's a strange man and no two ways about it. At least, strange in comparison. Take, for instance, how he calls me Sweet Emma. Not Miss Heath or Miss Emma, mind you, like a gentleman caller ought to do, and never Em, or Miss Em, like Mego does. Every time he says it in their hearing, Jessie and Mr. Garrett act like they've never heard of such a person, and Mego tells me I ort to thank twicet about taking on a feebleminded man. He may be right. Sweet I'm not, and never have been, and anybody who thinks so needs tending to real bad. Foolishness is what I call it.

I don't know what to make of him. I've told him a million times that I don't aim to marry—at least I don't aim to marry the kind of man that comes to Oregon. There's something about this place that draws the restless and the unsettled and the hard-headed one-track kind. And that's not for me. I'd rope and tie Mr. Garrett to a plow if it was up to me, but that's Jessie's business and not mine. I want a steady man if I have to have one. One that'll be here when the crops need him and not off gallivanting here, there, and yonder.

I declare, I used to think Mr. Garrett was the finest man on two feet, and in some ways he is. I guess I said too much to the child, with all that talking. Should've known better than to get started, but maybe it went over her head as young as she is. We all have to go through it, though, learning what it is to be female, and that means learning to cipher the male species and what they do to you and how they make you feel. The Lord made both kinds—male and female created He them. Eve was made meet for Adam, suited to him in every way. I wonder if I was made to suit a particular man? But the better question is, was a man made to suit me?

If there was, he'd be something like Mr. Garrett, but a sight steadier than he is. He'd have some of Mego's good sense and the comfort he gives just from having him on the place.

And what else? The decency of Mr. Donner and Dr. Whitman, who were as fine as they come except for one thing— neither of them paid enough attention to their wives. I still remember Mrs. Donner's melancholy when she realized that her husband was bound and determined to go against all advice and take the trail that killed them. And Narcissa, overcome with dread, took to her room the morning of the massacre, as if she knew what was about to happen. Both their husbands had set their courses and would not be deterred by womanly fears.

One thing's for sure and certain, I want a man who'll listen to me and take into account what I think and feel and say. I guess that's what I want most of all—somebody who won't expect me to turn deaf, blind, ignorant, and witless just because vows have been said. Mr. Stone says he won't ever make the mistake of counting me short, since I've got more sense than any two men in the valley. Which I already knew and told him so. But he said I needed him to keep me in line and within the law. And he wouldn't explain himself, just stood there as close as my own garment and had the audaciousness to wink at me and say, "I'd hate to have to lock you up, Sweet Little Emma, even if the church folks would give me a medal for it."

He might suspect, but he doesn't know a thing. When Mego first had the notion of bottling the waters from the Popo Agie, I didn't think much of it. He claimed they were good for the rheumatism either taken inside for the internals or applied on the outside for the externals. I didn't see any reason to doubt him since he was going as strong as ever on liberal doses of it. I tried to talk to Jessie about what we ought to do, but she was still relying on the Lord to feed us and letting her husband run loose everywhere, with nobody to put in the crops, or see to the cattle, or anything else. Mego tried his best to help me farm since that's what I wanted to do, but his heart wasn't in it. He's seen the far side of the mountain too. He said following a mule wasn't in his constitution, but at least he knew we had to do something. Lord knows Indians aren't worth two cents in the fields. You can't count on them to be there when something needs hoeing or harvesting. You can tell them a million times that something has to be done at a certain time, but if their medicine tells them to stay in bed all day or to pick up and go hunting, then it's like talking to the wind.

I do the best I can with Indian help, and none from anybody else, because even if farming's not in their constitutions, it is in mine. Mr. Stone's not a farmer either, it's plain to see. I told him I aimed to farm and if he was of a mind to help me, I'd consider letting him. And he told me that if working these fields went along with bedding the owner, then he thought he could manage it. I said the owner would likely oblige him, and showed him the deed with Mego's name on it. Mr. Stone never has got over it.

When Mego's water from that mountain river began to sell a little, I changed my mind about it. And it's been our salvation ever since, to use a preaching word. We've got a regular trade now, and customers who depend on it day in and day out. Our biggest problem is bottles. We can sell only one to a customer and they have to bring them back to get their refills. Another problem is keeping certain customers from mingling with certain other customers, so I serve the ladies and the finer element here at the house and Mego takes care of the other commerce down at the shed.

I don't know what Mr. Stone means about church folks giving him a medal to lock me up and put me out of business. They're our best customers, and that includes the Methodist preacher's wife and the Presbyterian preacher's wife, and the Roman blackrobes, as the Indians call them, who send for a jug of it every week that rolls around. There'd be a lot of people in real misery if they couldn't get our Medicinal Waters from the Popo Agie, Famous Indian Cure-All for Emigrants and Settlers, Miraculous Panacea for Rheumatism, Lumbago, Ague, and Fevers of All Kinds, Especially Efficacious in the Cure and Treatment of Melancholy, Bile, Indigestion, and Female Disorders. For Ringworm, Flea and Spider Bites, Take Externally.

We had pretty slow going at first. We sold hardly enough for Mego's trips to the river to be worth the making. I put my mind to it and decided we needed to flavor it up some. We knew it had good properties just as it was, but most folks couldn't tell the difference between Popo Agie water and Willamette water. What we needed was a difference they could taste. So I told Mego to study on it, and he did, and we've sold untold gallons of it ever since. And Mr. Stone is welcome in my house anytime, but nowhere else on the place. Mego and I have a business venture that's keeping this farm going. He makes the product, and it's his business how he does it, and I market and sell it and don't ask questions.

Well, just listen to me. I'm as bad as a missionary claiming it's the Lord's will that he save souls and get rich at the same time. What really makes me mad as thunder are all the rules and regulations that the church folks have come up with. Oregon's not a state yet, even if it's about to be one. Just because a few busybodies in the Temperance Society have announced that making liquorous spirits is illegal in the Territory doesn't make it so. And I know what Mego's doing. I put him up to it, so I ought to. Besides, I thought we all came out here to get away from the way they do things back home—every man for himself is what I've heard a million times. There's no pleasing some people.

Well, let the churches make their laws and let the churches abide by them before they order anybody else to. None of them've been elected or appointed lawmakers. Just took it on themselves, and the day the last church member stops doing business with me will be the day I shut down. I don't hold with making laws you don't intend to follow yourself. Besides, we don't sell to Indians because I know, and Mego knows, that they can't handle it. If they want to purchase a bottle, they get the pure, unadulterated water straight from the river, and do just as well on that as Elder Cox does on his daily intake of the adulterated kind.

Now, if Mr. Stone took it in his mind to farm and quit hiring himself out to church boards and self-appointed town councils, I might change my mind about a number of things. Jessie says I could do a lot worse, even though he's not a church-goer. That means she likes him, in spite of herself. Mego does, too, for I heard him tell Mr. Stone that a woman ort not to stay a spinster too long in case she spiled. And I'm the only spinster around here.

I've told Mr. Stone no and no again, I don't know how many times. And he just tells me to take all the time I want to make up my mind, and that, besides, he needs time to get himself in form to be a match for me. That beats all I've ever heard. You'd think the marital state was nothing but a round of battles. Which it will be if he expects me to be as submissive as Tamsen Donner and Narcissa Whitman, or as easy to please as Jessie. I'm not like any of them, and he better know it now or regret it for the rest of his days. He may come home singing from the wedding but he'll go to bed weeping if he tries to change me in any way, shape, or form. I won't have it, and I won't have a man that won't take me the way I am. I may just put it to him that way and see what he says. Or does. It's up to you, Mr. Stone, is what I'll say.

Jessie gets on to both of us about not going to church, saying it's our Christian duty, and that staying away from services is a poor testimony to the community, which needs all the testimony it can get. I don't doubt that for a minute, but I'm no hypocrite. She's done everything she can think of to get Mr. Garrett in the bosom of the church, and nothing's worked with him either. Once, she clapped his hat back on his head before he was hardly in the door and marched him off to services for a good dose of spiritual instruction. It didn't take, though, because he said he never had liked four walls or three-point sermons. The last time I went to services with Jessie, there was a jackass in the pulpit. He kept talking about how the Israelites wouldn't listen to the Lord Jehovah and how the Lord put up with them as long as He could, and how He finally had to put His blessing hand on the New Israelites which happened to be us Americans. But he warned us that He'd take that hand away if we didn't stay on the straight and narrow, because the Lord didn't like stiff-neckedness and wouldn't put up with it all. Well, I couldn't help myself and almost strangled trying to stop laughing. Jessie said it was past time for me to grow up and learn to behave myself in church, but I figured I'd better stay home from here on out and not embarrass her anymore. My sister never has had much success with missionizing, which is a pure shame as hard as she works at it.

Well, we've come a long way from Missouri and what's the difference between here and there? Jessie's still keeping house and going to church like she did back then, and I'm still trying to farm, same as always. But we have Mego and Emma Jane and Mr. Garrett, and they're worth what we had to put up with to get them. I wouldn't change anything except all the dying that went on around us, but dying goes on in Missouri too. Just look at Papa. Mr. Stone says it's given unto every man to die, and the only thing we can do about it is make sure we live with people we love before it's given to us. And he says too that as long as he's around, I won't have to worry about it being given to me by shot, knife, arrow, or tomahawk. And now that I think on it, that would give me a lot less to worry about.

There's another thing I wouldn't have to worry about too. I told Emma Jane how I came to learn what it means to be a woman, but I still haven't penetrated the final mystery of a man's ways with a maid. Jessie says if I'm so all-fired curious, why don't I let Mr. Stone teach me since he seems willing enough. That means I'll have to darken the church door again, and stand there and promise to do something I have no intention of doing. I wonder if the rest of the service would take if I cross my fingers when the obedient part comes up? Maybe the thing to do is ask Mr. Stone.

F
Ross, Ann B.
The pilgrimage.